"Mark Harrell has fired these weapons, jumped these 'chutes, and led these troops. Nobody writing today knows the reality of present-day Special Ops like Captain Harrell."
—Jim Morris, author of
WAR STORY and FIGHTING MEN

PENETRATORS

MacIntyre's senses suddenly sharpened. He became alert and wary of every noise in the suite. He was alone. Checking the safety of the Browning, he reached for the doorknob. The door suddenly banged open, barking his hand away.

An Asian woman before him leveled a suppressed pistol from where she stood in the hallway. MacIntyre still clenched the Browning. The first round plowed through MacIntyre's upper left arm. The second punched through his right shoulder, as if his assailant were crippling him on purpose.

As MacIntyre crabbed away, his assailant began to rapid fire . . .

* * *

This volume also includes an exciting
excerpt from *Operators*, Mark D. Harrell's
next adventure featuring Captain Matt MacIntyre.

Also by Mark D. Harrell from Jove

INFILTRATORS

Penetrators

MARK D. HARRELL

JOVE BOOKS, NEW YORK

This novel is a work of fiction. Names, characters, places and incidents are either the product of the author's imagination or are used fictitiously. Any resemblance to actual events, locales, organizations or persons, living or dead, is entirely coincidental and beyond the intent of either the author or publisher.

PENETRATORS

A Jove Book / published by arrangement with
the author

PRINTING HISTORY
Jove edition / February 1992

ISBN: 0-515-10788-3

Jove Books are published by The Berkley Publishing Group,
200 Madison Avenue, New York, New York 10016.
The name "JOVE" and the "J" logo
are trademarks belonging to Jove Publications, Inc.

PRINTED IN THE UNITED STATES OF AMERICA

10 9 8 7 6 5 4 3 2 1

For the covert warriors who protect and defend the Constitution of the United States of America against all enemies, foreign and domestic. May God guide your hand always, and keep your integrity and your perspective intact.

ACKNOWLEDGMENTS

Words will never describe the respect, admiration, and thanks I have for all those "old soldiers" influential in my career who had something *important* to say: Colonel Vladimir Sobichevsky, Lieutenant Colonel Hermann Adler, Colonel Jim Humphries, Colonel John Gritz, and Lieutentant Colonel Pete Armstrong. Now for the future "old soldiers": Major George Lanigan, Major Mike Murley, and my old pal and Ranger buddy, Captain Rudy Valrey. *De Oppresso Liber!*

PROLOGUE

Kaiserslautern, Germany

As their backup man donned the dead MP's clothes and took his position in the now-silent guard shack just outside the compound's main entrance gate, two people—a man in the dress blues of an Army officer and carrying a heavy briefcase, and a tall slender blonde dressed to the nines in high heels and a teal blue cocktail dress—walked the last hundred feet to the officers' club, their heels clicking on the cobblestones so prevalent in West German kasernes. A cold, biting wind seared their faces into expressionless masks of death.

The man, Simon, was a Uruguayan who really worked for the Russians, but he never told that to the woman he was evaluating; it would have compromised his position as the GRU's network liaison for Germany's Red Army Faction. He had to see her in action up close, accompany her even. As far as Monika Stern was concerned, her "escort" for the evening's events was just another temporary, unwanted comrade assigned, for reasons she did not have a need to know, by her case officer to participate in her cell's current operation.

Already, the cold had numbed Simon's exposed fingers clutching the briefcase. Switching it to the other hand, he stole a quick glance at the woman walking beside him. He saw no traces of anxiety on her carefully made-up face as they approached two spit-shined American MPs guarding the officers' club entrance. She was not an unattractive woman, Monika Stern. She had turned thirty just the day before, but the past eight years as one of Germany's most elusive terrorists had failed to dim her cold, ascetic beauty. Simon wondered briefly what it would be like with her . . . then snapped his mind back to their mission, in concert with the MP sergeant's salute as they reached the club's entrance.

"Good evening, sir," the sergeant said tersely, bringing his loaded M16 back to port arms. "ID card and guest pass, please."

Simon smiled broadly and carefully set the briefcase down as he fumbled for his wallet, allowing enough time for Stern to open her purse and drop her billfold to the ground. She and the younger MP bent over at the same time to retrieve it, allowing the nineteen-year-old soldier-cop an unobstructed view of her cleavage. The kid stared, transfixed. Smiling, Stern straightened up and pulled out a small atomizer of perfume from her purse. Simon's left hand slipped inside his trousers pocket for the cyanide spray disguised as breath freshener.

Stern smiled sweetly at the boy, and as he stood up to return her billfold, sprayed him full in the face with the bottle of perfume. Whipping out his breath freshener, Simon gassed the distracted older sergeant. Both soldiers crumpled, instantly dead, their M16s clattering noisily to the ground with them.

On cue, two of the cell's men, disguised as MPs, sprinted to the club entrance from the guard shack and dragged the dead guards into the bushes surrounding the area. They moved quickly into position and cracked back to parade rest with their newly acquired M16s. Simon and his lady entered the club, the briefcase heavy in his hand.

A maitre d' materialized from the shadows of the hallway leading to the ballroom and met them in the foyer. He was a nervous old man, beads of sweat forming a wet crescent on his high forehead. Simon could almost feel the fear knotting this tall, thin man's gut into coils of dread.

"Is it veal cordon bleu or prime rib tonight?" Stern asked politely.

"The cordon bleu has been prepared just for you, sir," the maitre d' answered, correctly. Had he answered the bonafides otherwise, he would have sealed his granddaughter's fate and met a premature death from Stern's silenced Makarov hidden inside her purse.

Simon handed the old man his briefcase, looking him hard in

the eye. He barely suppressed an inward laugh as the maitre d' almost dropped it from the unexpected weight.

"Follow me . . . please." The maitre d' led them down the hallway and turned left around the first corner to the double doors that opened into the ballroom. He then departed, holding the briefcase tightly underneath his arm.

Simon and Stern entered the ballroom and caught several dozen reproachful stares, as if they had just arrived at church late and conspicuous. Their places at the first table by the door were right where the maitre d' had left them. Servers pushed carts loaded with entrees of veal and prime rib through the aisles. They were served within minutes of seating.

"I told you we were late," Stern snarled under her breath, glaring at Simon.

"But the receiving line wasn't supposed to start until 1930," Simon sputtered. "I swear, it's what the CO put out."

"You can be so scatterbrained sometimes, Raymond. It's enough that you make me go to these things."

"C'mon, Jeri," Simon whined at his nagging "wife." "People are watching." Several nearby couples had turned to eye the noisy newcomers. They were obviously new to the command, and the post veterans would have been more than happy to ignore them if only they would keep quiet. No one bothered trying to initiate small talk with "Raymond and Jeri" as the servers passed out the evening meal.

A half hour later, Stern looked up for the first time at the head table, which formed the center of a giant horseshoe encompassing three ranks of ten-person tables throughout the officers' club ballroom. There, the Commanding General of the 41st Infantry Division (Mechanized), the Commanding General U.S. Forces Europe, and the guest speaker—Senator Howard Torne from Kansas, the chairman of the Senate Armed Services Committee—along with their wives, all sat, finishing their meals.

Stern let her hand rest on Simon's thigh, hidden underneath the table. She squeezed his flesh seductively, plying her fingers toward his groin. "Want dessert?" she said, smiling at him.

Taken aback, Simon turned around and caught the movement of the kitchen doors as they suddenly flew open, the dessert server rolling a huge metal cart of cheesecake and apple pie à la mode out toward the VIP table. He turned back toward Stern and grinned.

"Of course I want dessert," he answered her, feeling a growing warmth. *She really wouldn't be too bad.* . . . He slipped his hand onto *her* thigh. High up. As expected, her eyes flew open, her nostrils flaring as she inhaled.

"*Here?*" she snapped. "Get your hands off me!" Heads turned. Table neighbors scowled. Out of the corner of his eye, Simon saw other servers exiting the kitchen.

Slap! His cheek burned where Stern had hit him. *Bitch.*

"Jeri!"

Monika Stern leaped up from the table and stormed away, heading for the lobby. Simon followed, as though angry and intending to have it out once and for all with his pretty, but obnoxious and petulant, wife. As he passed through the door, he glanced back in time to see that the dessert cart was parked immediately in front of the VIP table, centered in front of the senator.

The hallway was empty. They sauntered to the main entrance, back to the safety of their two "MPs," then to the guard shack. The Volvo was waiting for them, in the hands of a very capable driver.

The maitre d' ran out of the club.

"*Please!* I did as you said; *now give her back to me!*"

"Follow me," Stern hissed at him. Meekly, the old man followed her, his head bowed in shame, his frail knees trembling with every step as he forced his pace to match theirs.

They reached the guard shack. The two "MPs" at the lobby entrance dashed back toward them. Kneeling behind the shack, Stern retrieved two items from her purse: a digital transmitter, not unlike a television remote, and a tiny syringe.

Strong hands gripped the maitre d' from behind, clamped his mouth shut, and crushed his larynx. Stern jabbed the old man in the thigh with the syringe. The maitre d' lost consciousness and convulsed on the ground, his bleeding tongue caught between his front teeth. Stern pried the dying man's fingers open and pressed the transmitter inside his shaking, impotent fist. After punching the sequence code into the transmitter, she dropped the maitre d's hand and straightened up.

The Volvo pulled quietly up beside them, and they climbed inside. Moments later, Stern and the rest of her cell were doing a cool hundred kilometers an hour down the highway accessing the autobahn.

Inside the maitre d's cold, white-knuckled fist, the sterilized remote detonator ticked away the final seconds until the officers' club exploded, tongues of flame spurting out the windows into the drizzling German night.

PART I

"We must above all keep our hatred alive and fan it to paroxysm, hate as a factor of struggle, intransigent hate of the enemy, hate that can push a human being beyond his natural limits and make him a cold, violent, selective, and effective killing machine."

—**Ernesto "Che" Guevara**

"To choose the victim, to prepare the strike with circumspection, to satisfy one's implacable revenge, and then go to bed—there's nothing sweeter in this world."

—**Joseph Stalin**

CHAPTER ONE

Being awake at four o'clock on a frozen Moscow morning in January did not appeal to Simon, especially when approaching the old Khodinka Airfield strapped inside a Sukhoi Su-24 with G-forces pushing his cheeks back into a grotesque smile. He still could not believe he had been ordered back to see Ishutin so soon, so abruptly. But then again, power in the Kremlin was volatile these days; change was everywhere, dissent growing. Anything was possible.

An incredibly brief period of time had passed since he had found the Lufthansa tickets twelve hours earlier at his Nuremberg dead-letter drop, with orders to fly to Athens. No, it wasn't an "immediate" recall. This one was a "flash." Four hours later he had found reservations for a flight to Belgrade waiting for him at another drop. Then, the Su-24. He had filled no less than three plastic bags with his stomach's contents during the two-hour flight in the Su-24.

Throughout the entire trip, he had carefully rehearsed in his mind what he knew would happen, inside the Aquarium.

Like an astronomer's black hole amidst the glum Moscow night lights, the Khodinka runway loomed into view. Simon could make out the buildings surrounding GRU headquarters—the aviation buildings, the rocket construction complex, the aviation institute and aviation academy—he remembered the layout so well. It had once been his campus, but he had attended the college *inside* the complex of buildings, headquartered in the long, rectangular building next to the airfield with the immense courtyard in the center. No windows on the outside. They faced only in. The Aquarium, all nine stories of it, was a black monolith housing the most secretive and powerful intelligence organization on Earth.

There were only two ways to get inside the Aquarium, and this time, for once, Simon would not have to pass through countless guards who pocketed his money, took his watch, and even his belt buckle. No, this time he arrived by air.

Simon's stomach clenched as the pilot rolled off the throttle. He wished he *could* have gone in the other way.

Looking down, Simon saw the runway lights along the tarmac blur together like parallel neon highways. Swirling snow devils danced before steady blasts of arctic winds, chasing after infinity, feeding the chill that had crept into Simon's gut an hour before, as he instinctively knew he was back inside, deep inside, the Soviet Union, the *Rodina*, the Motherland.

Ishutin!

Simon pictured the short, squat man who had personally guided him through his entire career. He had not seen him in quite some time now; what was it? Two years? Simon wished he could have remained in Paris to service his auxiliary net monitoring the RAF cells in the recently reunified Deutschland, being productive, anything but coming back to this godforsaken—

The wheels of the Su-24 screeched against the tarmac and cold, wet saliva flew from Simon's lips as he tried to restrain his tender stomach once again.

Simon, aka Vladimir Bolivar Marighella Rozo, strode quickly through a narrow corridor hidden by thirty-five-foot high walls that led inside the main GRU headquarters building. He was flanked on both sides by burly security men.

Simon had been given his names as the result of an enthusiastically paternal Communist commitment befitting his father's style of politics and an undying identification with the Bolivian national hero of the nineteenth century: Simon Bolivar, the original South American revolutionary; Vladimir Ilyich Lenin, founder of the Soviet Union; and Carlos Marighella, the Brazilian revolutionary, author of the infamous *Minimanual of the Urban Guerrilla* and peer of Che Guevara and Fidel Castro.

They were the examples to follow, according to Simon's father. But to a now older and wiser Uruguayan, growing up in

Communist idealism and education was simply fact and a way of life; that Simon secretly preferred a mercenary's philosophy was what mattered more. The years had hardened him, money and position were worth far more than idealism and concepts. Those were things better left to college students—like he had once been in his naive youth—and lying politicians. Now, walking through this corridor, Simon thought not of these things, but instead focused on containing his single most abhorred phobia: fear of enclosed spaces—spaces where he could be cornered, spaces where he could be trapped.

He remembered the last time he had walked through this corridor. It had been almost twenty years since he had "graduated" from the Patrice Lumumba University in Moscow. Simon had studied Subversion 101 inside the GRU Training Center of Illegals, far away from the campus of his alma mater. A master operator's protégé, he had attended all five years of that international college, even if the professors who had once kicked him out of Patrice Lumumba had never known it. The Uruguayan playboy completed his studies within a select body trained by the Illegals Section of the Glavnoye Razvedyvatelnoye Upravleniya, the Chief Intelligence Directorate of the General Staff. It was a long title, better known by three simple letters—GRU.

The GRU was for external security: to ensure no external forces could destroy the Soviet Union. The KGB was for internal security: not to let the Soviet Union fall from within. But duplication within the troika—the Party, the Army, the KGB—ensured that no one part of the triangle seized total power. And the Army's GRU and the KGB each canceled out the power aspirations of the other, while keeping check on the Party. But to some within the troika, visions of power beckoned like a narcotic, in these days of *perestroika* and *glasnost*. . . .

Change was everywhere. The ruble was worthless. And the trolls inside the Kremlin were grumbling.

Simon was tired. All those years had only produced long queues and a thriving black market. What was it he had been working for? Was he first and foremost just a mercenary?

They all became mercenaries after a fashion.

After his graduation from the Training Center of Illegals, Simon's entire life had comprised a lie, a cover story, a chameleon-like series of identities—identities he built up as a carefully groomed and rich lawyer's son from Uruguay.

After passing through the corridor and walking inside the Aquarium, Simon and his guards entered the lobby's elevators. One of the guards, a humorless fat-faced man with a hairless skull, unlocked a compartment beneath the elevator's control panel and deftly punched a series of coded buttons. The elevator descended into a subterranean office located far below the basement. There, they stepped out, where Simon was escorted to a lavatory to freshen up prior to seeing the Directorate Chief. Once inside, he turned the wash basin's tap on full blast.

Ishutin!

Simon plunged his face into the frigid water inside the wash basin and held it there, leting it numb. Simon welcomed Moscow's ice-melt tap greeting his face with its frozen Party smile.

Simon was not to report to a Directorate Chief from one of the six Directorates, each one a colonel-general in the Army; he was to report to the *head* Directorate Chief, a full-fledged Army general, a man possessing immense power with his very own private Illegals Section no one else knew about, *plus* power over the six Directorates, each responsible for a continent.

The general also privately controlled four Directions, each one a separate GRU intelligence agency unto itself, each possessing enough intelligence tradecraft to match or exceed any of the Western European countries. Of the four, Moscow constituted the First Direction, Berlin the Second, Cuba the Fourth. And then there was Simon's home Direction—the Third Direction of the GRU: Liberation Movements.

Simon pulled his face out of the water and studied its sopping, haggard reflection in the dirty mirror, gasping for breath. The lines marking his cheeks had deepened into the face of a man closer to sixty, instead of one only forty-two. His generous mouth melted into a double chin matching the gut that had crept up on him during the past two years of savoring the pleasures of the West after the Wall came down and Berlin became fair game. Worry lines creased his forehead, and his thinning black hair, usually kept long and wavy and swept toward the back of his head, now visibly showed the white of his scalp. Never athletic, his frame, just under six feet, was soft and unimposing. Yes, it had been Paris; Rome; the operations in Vienna; and the Arabs who guaranteed ulcers with their Muslim irrationality.

It had also been too many meals eaten in a hurry, on the run, under pressure. The pallor of his skin told of too much time spent indoors, waiting for the next phone call, setting up the radio, expecting the right bonafides from an unknown telephone repairman, decoding messages collected at easily compromised dead-letter drops in parks, cafes, nightclubs, and smoky *gasthauses* . . . and waiting for fate at any moment to come swooping down on his head like a sledgehammer, introducing him to his demise in the form of the British M-5, the German *Bundesnachrichtendienst,* the American FBI.

Simon was out of shape, and the day-old grizzle of his beard from his twelve-hour pilgrimage back to *Rodina* made him look even older. Hopefully, the old master would understand. Simon inhaled four deep breaths and rubbed his face forcefully with the rough Soviet-made paper towels. Definitely not the quality he had become used to in Germany.

Another man pushed the washroom door open, startling his escorts. A minute's walk down the dark, unlit hallway, and they stood by Ishutin's door. It was a plain entrance, one easily confused for a part-time janitor's closet.

Three sharp raps, and an unsmiling, sexless secretary let them in. She guided them to the Directorate Chief's office. The escorts disappeared, melting away from the door as if it were the gate to Hell. Simon entered the dark room, lit only by the banker's lamp on the mahogany desk.

A short, athletic man wearing bifocals sat behind that mahogany desk which had borne testament to thousands of confessions and debriefings. The man's thick luxurious mustache flecked with gray, his high cheekbones framing a cherubic grin, and his swept-back iron-gray hair often earned him his look-alike's nickname: Father Joe. That Comrade Directorate Chief of the Intelligence Directorate of the General Staff Ivan Mikhailovich Ishutin resembled Joseph Stalin stroked his Georgian ego down to his bone marrow. Ishutin had often bragged to his grinning deputies about being Stalin's personal student back in the old days before the Kremlin had gone soft. But Simon could not allow the luxury of being cowed by Ishutin's persona and power. His career had always depended on his bold delivery and straightforward opinion, which, in the Soviet Union, was a rare commodity among workers of the State.

"You, Comrade General," Simon began bravely, "if anyone, knew I should not have—"

An upraised hand. Simon fell silent. Ishutin cast aside the report he had been reading, removing his bifocals. "Vladimir, it has been too long. There is much for you to tell me. Those words I must hear from your lips alone, my young friend, not from the countless vassals swarming my desk every morning, reporting glowing renditions of our accomplishments in the Liberation Movements Directorate. *You!* Tell me everything, Comrade European Network Chief." Ishutin settled back into his chair and folded his hands over his thick torso. "First, your analysis of the operation. Then I want your appraisal and recommendation."

Simon knew as much. Maybe his cover *was* blown, coming in from the cold like this. Then again, maybe it wasn't. It was time for real communication to the top. After all, his chief sat on the Politburo, whether most of the Politburo members knew it or not.

From the top. Simon sighed inwardly. "Monika Stern, Comrade Chairman, Germany's most wanted, yet elusive and incognito terrorist. She is audacious, and ruthless when careful timing is of the utmost. She is a cold, calculating woman, but one who can easily be as charming and sensual toward her target as a snow leopard toward her mate. She is a carnivore, Comrade General, a cunning, brutal cat of prey."

"Yes, Vladimir. I know these things already." Ishutin leaned forward in his chair and stared hard at Simon, his fingers propped under his chin, his brown, pouchy eyes glinting. *"Vladimir!"*

Simon clicked his heels.

"What is her weakness?"

"Yes, Comrade General!" Simon's back stiffened in an almost masochistic pleasure, having never forgotten the old man's discipline and his characteristic habit of cutting to the quick for information; getting to what the Americans called the "bottom line." "Comrade General, she is resourceful, audacious, utterly ruthless. But that, Comrade General, that ruthlessness and cruelty of her character are also the sword upon which someday she shall impale herself. My evaluation: She is useful—brilliant even—but she will eventually compromise herself and her cell because of her own intense, nihilistic rage."

The old Communist let his hands drop in an open-palmed slap on the desk, and nodded his head. "Good." He nodded once again, sharply. The corners of his mouth slowly upturned. "Now you know why I sent you to evaluate this—what did you call her?—this *snow leopard*." Ishutin relaxed and leaned back in his chair again. "I respect your abilities, Vladimir." He gestured to the chair by his deskside, not the one at its front. *That* chair was for vassals only. "Sit down, my son, and tell me more."

Simon hesitated, then took the seat. "She is cold, absolutely unforgiving," he continued. "The briefcase bomb her team designed was more than adequate for its purpose. It blasted lead pellets in all directions like an anti-personnel mine. She included napalm in the core of the briefcase. Those who survived the blast were pathetically burned."

Ishutin picked up from his desk a miniaturized bayonet, his letter opener. "My young comrade." Ishutin chuckled lowly, tapping the letter opener against the front edge of the desk, staring at the minute nicks forming underneath the blade. "Have you grown a conscience with your stomach?"

Simon's cheeks glowed as if he had been slapped, yet he refused to show anger at the remark. It was another of the old man's ways in extracting the "belly answer" as he would call it. "My point, Comrade General: She will sometimes do more than is necessary to accomplish the mission. It is always the overkill, when overkill is neither desired nor needed. The briefcase bomb killed everyone at the head table. The American senator and generals, all their wives—they were vaporized. That part accomplished the mission. But sixty to seventy percent of those attending the function were either killed outright or died shortly afterwards in the base hospital's burn ward. The bomb was simply larger than it needed to be. To the Americans—what is a general here, a diplomat there? But destroy many, too many of their citizens abroad, and they will awaken with resolve. They depend on a crusade to win wars, not what their military leaders call *low intensity conflict*."

"Go on."

"The night before the operation, she tracked home the maitre d' from the officers' club, an elderly German national. Posing as a representative from the Red Cross, she entered his house. She discovered that the German was the sole surviving relative of his granddaughter who lived with him, whose parents were killed in a car accident the preceding year. Hours later, in the early morning, Stern's gang silently kidnapped the girl from her bedroom. The old man woke up to find Stern perched on his bedside with her Makarov against his temple, instructing him what to do in order to keep from seeing pieces of his granddaughter delivered to him through the Bundespost. He complied with her instructions.

"When we arrived at the officers' club the following night, she personally dispatched one MP with a perfume atomizer loaded with cyanide."

"An ugly death," Ishutin grunted.

"What of the little girl?"

"Stern's garrote."

A moment's silence. Simon had never before seen his mentor at a loss for words. But even GRU chieftains had grandchildren.

"Sadistic, is she not?" Ishutin offered. It was an unusual comment for the old murderer, grandchildren or not.

"That is my point, Comrade. There was too much blood on this operation."

"But it was successful!" The hard glint had returned to Ishutin's eyes.

"Yes, Comrade. It was successful."

"Then we must have her! Tell me why we shouldn't!"

Simon wondered if he shouldn't spare his second thoughts about Stern. Ruthlessness a weakness? Yes. Always, if not moderated and used under the right circumstances. She could get sloppy with her narcissistic, murderous passion. But then again, that was exactly what the soft American denizens of a decadent country needed—a series of violent shocks to confuse and overwhelm them. They had once been a different people, toughened and hardened by their Depression years. Those qualities had enabled them to defeat the Nazis and the Japanese imperialists. Now, crusades and the will to fight no longer mattered in their country. Simon mentally retracted his earlier statement about an American galvanization, an American crusade. The years during the Second World War were long past. Americans had forgotten what it meant to want. And they had no more honor, only greed.

Ishutin made a fist around his bayonet letter opener's handle and pounded it into his desk top. "Stern could be the catalyst to throw the Americans off balance," he said.

Simon nodded. Ishutin had read his thoughts, though they were best left unspoken. Change in the Kremlin these days was fluid, whirling. The machinations of power between the right and the left were steadily laying a deadly foundation for possible civil war. And where a vacuum of power existed, opportunity beckoned. Stern could shock the Americans easily enough.

Ishutin leaned toward Simon and slapped him paternally on the leg, nodding. "Simon, the Soviet Union can never engage the West in conventional warfare, as the younger generals of our magnificent Soviet Army believe. Quite simply, we are a bankrupt nation, and Europe would be turned into a vast, utter wasteland from our nerve and blister gases, tanks and multiple rocket launchers alone. And thermonuclear war would . . . no, Vladimir, the United States must fall from within. NATO will of course follow now that German reunification has degraded the very reason for NATO's existence. The Americans are soft and fat. They are spoiled with greed and wanton decadence. They are under-educated and materialistic, chained to their culture of instant gratification and sensory masturbation."

Simon said nothing; he knew when to keep silent. Ishutin had that glazed look in his eyes, a look that overcame his grizzled countenance when the old man contemplated his service on the German front during the Great Patriotic War as a young captain in the Red Army. Ishutin continued. "When kicked in their bellies, hard and sudden, they will demand their government eradicate the wave of terror sweeping their nation. Their government, like any democracy, will react slowly. More chaos, more confusion will follow. Perhaps their government will even resort to martial law, but that too shall fail to control the anarchy and the madmen running wild through their cities and villages.

"Their people will demand their freedoms. . . ." Ishutin paused and glanced upwards at the picture of his mentor on the wall. As an afterthought, the current President occupied the space next to Joseph Stalin.

"Even as they watch their children die," he concluded. Ishutin stared hard at Simon, leaning toward his protégé. "Use this woman, this Monika Stern. Supply her with only the best talent available throughout your European network and with all supplies necessary. What rubles we have left in our treasury we will spend for this woman, Comrade Network Chief, and you shall see to it that many more follow her lead."

Simon blinked. He'd heard this line before. "There are never enough rubles, Comrade General. Especially now, when . . ."

Ishutin's eyes turned opaque. He leaned over the desk and stared hard at Simon, who felt sweat suddenly dampen his armpits. "Then use your Colombian contacts to fund Stern's team," the GRU chieftain muttered.

"I serve the Soviet Union!" Simon replied promptly, snapping to attention.

Ishutin grinned and leaned back in his chair. "You are an imaginative and resourceful operator, Simon." His eyes regained their glitter. "Your results, as always, never go unnoticed."

Simon resisted swallowing. It was a neutral statement. Ishutin could coin a threat and a compliment in the same phrase.

But what, exactly, was a ruble worth these days?

CHAPTER TWO

JFK Airport, New York

Three weeks in Europe! David MacIntyre, fourteen years old, Eagle Scout (newly promoted), and on a winter semester break from the private boarding school he attended in Maryland, was in an out*standing* mood, as his big brother Matt would put it. For his birthday, his dad had given him round-trip plane tickets and a bonus allowance for the International Scouting Convention being held in Germany, near Munich.

David pushed open the door leading into the airport and held it open for his buddy, a young executive from one of his father's corporations. David tried to remember which one: Atlas Insurance, or was it that new rental-car agency his dad had bought out? He couldn't remember. There were too many. In any case, Alexander Kurakis had turned out to be a good buddy who had just missed being drafted in the NFL two years before, after graduating from the University of Oklahoma.

As the two walked inside JFK, Alex looked as if he was Big Brother taking Little Brother on his first trip abroad. In effect, that was about the way it was. It had been so much of a head rush, David thought. The flight out of Tulsa just after New Year's to La Guardia in New York, a few days in the Big Apple, and now they were at JFK, en route to Munich! It was just too cool. David was already up to a full five-feet-six, possessing a stocky wrestler's frame with dark, wavy hair cut long in back and short on the top and around the ears. Already, the girls at school this year, even the sophomores, had been a little extra nice to him.

David glanced up at Alex. Alex, like David's brother Matt,

19

was the best example a guy could have. Curly-haired, bull-necked, knuckle-dragging Alex, complete with one eyebrow, stood a full six-feet-five. He had started as nose guard on the OU defensive lineup during his last two years in school. But he also had a mind as sharp as the fountain-tip David's father had personally given him for his work within the Dustbowl Enterprises conglomerate. David's old man liked Alex. Not only for his business sense and as *the* contributing player in the Fortune 500 Club Corporate Intramurals, but because he had enough maturity and common sense to know how to take care of a fourteen-year-old on a three-week trip abroad.

"Hey, Bear!" Alex grunted, stumbling through the entrance. "Why don't you help me with these suitcases, you little moron. It'll give you something else to do with those pencil-lead arms of yours besides whackin' off."

"What'sa matter, Wimpo?" David retorted promptly. "Can't take the strain, my man?" It was their standing joke. The big guy was Wimpo and the little guy was Bear, as several stewardesses on their last flight had labeled them. It had been an interesting flight between Tulsa and New York. David took one of the suitcases, giving Alex a free hand with the door, which flew open in front of the pounds per square inch generated beneath his scarred knuckles.

"You know, Bear," Alex mock-snarled, "one of these days your alligator mouth is gonna catch up with your humming-bird ass."

"Better watch it, Wimpo, I'm the only one between us who speaks German. You want me to set you up with the fräuleins over there, you'd better kowtow like a good fella." David laughed and dragged the suitcase up the stairs into the lobby, jostling in the crush of the terminal's travelers.

They struggled up the remaining stairs and checked their baggage in at the ticket counter. Thirty minutes, two sodas, and a couple of cheeseburgers later, they waited beside a lone janitor cleaning the windows near the line forming up for the security check. They had yet to go through the ritual of emptying their pockets of change, watches, pocketknives, and other metal items.

They moved closer to the archway of the security checkpoint metal detector. David looked back to see how far they'd come, as a couple joined them at the end of the line. David turned around and looked at them out of idle curiosity. The woman wore sunglasses and seemed nervous. Her companion said something to her, and she got angry. He left, only to return moments later. More people had joined the line but he stayed at the rear. That was weird, David thought. She kept tapping her fingers to the time of a drumbeat against her purse. Her boyfriend or husband or whatever didn't talk to her. David instantly psychoanalyzed them: She was on the rag, he was an asshole, and they had just fought over things matrimonial. He realized he was staring when the woman scowled right through her Ray-Bans at him.

David redirected his attention to two old ladies of the blue-rinse set yakking over a cup of coffee while presumably monitoring the X-ray machine by the baggage check conveyor belt. Christ, he and Alex would have to go through the hassle of emptying their pockets. He didn't know why they bothered. Those old gals rarely did more than give their monitor a cursory glance anyway.

Alex glanced at his watch. "Man, it's already eleven-thirty . . . they'd better hurry this line up or else TWA's gonna have to delay their flight a few minutes. We're outta here at twelve."

"We'll make it okay," David said. He fell silent. They had some time to kill, as the line creeped ahead.

"Alex?"

The big man looked down. There was a serious note in David's voice, which meant he was going to ask another one of those questions few kids his age had the brains to ask.

"Yeah?"

"You don't mind this, do you? I mean, Dad is basically paying you to be my baby-sitter for the next couple of weeks."

Alex paused before answering, and they moved up a couple of steps, out of the janitor's way, as the line crawled closer toward the security archway. Then: "Yeah, I know what you mean. I thought about it as baby-sitting at first, but your dad made himself pretty clear. You know the way he is—always up front with you. He wanted you to have a bodyguard. But not just anyone, you know? Shoot. I can't remember his exact words, I laughed so hard when he said them . . . something like, 'I know you don't look it with that Alley Oop face of yours, Kurakis, but you do have at least a peanut-sized brain underneath that cleat-sheared scalp of yours.' Almost died."

David laughed. "Yeah, that's my old man. I think he could charm the bra off Queen Elizabeth."

Kurakis turned serious again. "You know, he gave me one hell of a break after I found out I wouldn't be playing pro ball. I mean, he didn't automatically assume I was just some dumb jock who made it through school because I was on the team. So I busted my ass for him. Hell, I'm pretty proud of what I've done in the company. He told me that if it made me feel any better, to just consider this trip as this year's bonus. And besides, he said I was the right man for the job, so I was going whether I wanted to or not. So to answer your question, I don't mind this one danged bit."

David nodded his head. "For a rich ol' SOB, he don't exactly put on airs, does he?" David decided to do something unorthodox. If anything inwardly pleased him more, it was the word unorthodox. Unconventional. Different. All of the above. He wasn't afraid to try something new, like rock-climbing on his Boy Scout camp-outs or parachuting (if he'd ever get *that* chance). He decided then that not only would he keep his pocketful of change, but also his Swiss Army knife (complete with all sixteen tools) in his right pocket and see how loud the metal detector in the archway would beep. What would happen? Like his big brother Matt would say, "What are they gonna do? Bend my dogtags and send me back to Ranger School?" David knew Matt would try it. Donny would never have done it, but Matt would. Matt was Special Forces, a Green Beret. Matt was awesome.

Behind them, the woman's mind whirled. *An opportunity postponed is one lost forever. Seize the opportunity and never lose the initiative*. She remembered the words of the East German instructor years back who had trained her and other members of the Weather Underground in the camp located on the southern tip of the Arabian Peninsula in South Yemen: *Listen to what your victims are saying before you strike. You will always be in a tight spot in a skyjack. It is wise to single out special passengers for their use as hostages, to find the wealthiest passengers*.

The woman eyed the boy and his escort closely. The boy was evidently the scion of one rich enough to employ the brute guarding him, and from the way they were talking, Daddy was worth mega-bucks. The woman's black eyes twinkled behind her sunglasses. She glanced at her partner, who had repositioned himself seven people back. He'd been watching too. They nodded.

Geraldine Donner, now in her forties and showing it with her thickening middle and graying hair, had worked herself into exhaustion after finally being contacted last year by Havana, after having spent the past fifteen years of her life on the run. She had dedicated, used, and thrown away her youth in an organization that had just reached the brink of success before the FBI had finally cracked their key nets in the mid-seventies. The Symbionese Liberation Army, the Weather Underground, the Puerto Rican FALN—even the Black Panthers—were all gone, save for a few old cadre still in hiding.

But then a miracle had happened. Havana, the DGI, their Colombian proxies. She never actually saw him—it would have been a breach of security—but a European Network chief, code-named "Simon," and operating on a scale only Carlos the Jackal had once achieved, now rivaled the dreaded Abu Nidal group in funds, training, equipment . . . and action. No, she never saw him; only the cutouts and unwitting accomplices who passed along his messages; only the banker subsidizing her cell's account in Panama City. It was rumored that a Colombian drug lord was bankrolling this particular operation, but what did that matter? Terror was terror, and anarchy paved the way for martial law, which paved the way for revolution. And when revolution came . . .

Donner's thoughts returned to the boy in front of her. The jock he was with had just walked through the archway, and was putting change back into his pocket from the little basket that had been whisked along the conveyor belt through the X-ray machine.

She saw the boy walk through without emptying his pockets, while keeping his fist clenched tightly in the front pocket of his Levi's. She glanced at the two women in their sixties who were supposed to be monitoring the X-ray. They were engaged in updates on the latest episode of a soap opera one lady proudly proclaimed she was taping, even as they spoke, on her brand-new VCR.

Which was very convenient indeed. They weren't paying attention, and certainly did not seem to mind the boy as he boldly strode through the silent archway, the machine's sensitivity control turned down low to keep it from sounding off too much that busy morning.

"Hey, Wimpo, check it out, dude." David fished the Swiss Army knife out of his pocket. "That and a whole pocketful of change just made it through past the Geritol set back there and the security system."

"What?" What the—" Alex glanced back over his shoulder, then guided David firmly by the shoulder off the gateway toward the nearest men's room on their left. "Put that thing away. You want to get us in trouble?"

No alarm. She wondered what the kid was hiding in his pocket. Then she saw, as the rich man's brat proudly fished out a huge Swiss Army knife and bragged to his jock bodyguard about how he had faked out the "two ol' Geritol-setters" behind the counter.

Just as she thought, having planned to do the same thing. Craning her neck, she peered around the archway and saw only one middle-aged security guard forty feet away leaning against the hallway, sucking down Twinkies and coffee. She could barely see the .38 holstered on his hip because of his huge gut. The guard looked at his watch. Abruptly, he strode past the archway, muttering and looking at his watch. He had obviously pulled a little unwanted overtime. Soon he was out of sight, having melted into the crowd behind her. Even better.

First things first. She had purposely left her suitcase behind in the hallway. Her purse contained its normal innocuous complement of makeup, billfold, and other sundries. But it also contained two highly prized cans of aerosol hair spray. A full roll of fifty-cent pieces were deposited in her left pants pocket.

Like the boy, she slipped her hand deep inside her pocket and closed her fingers tightly around the coin roll. Glancing around to make sure her partner had seen her, she then placed her purse on the conveyer belt and strode through the arch. Again, no alarm. The sensitivity device was turned down too low to detect the boy's knife and her roll of fifty-cent pieces. That was good. Her heart picked up as the adrenaline surge relayed her final decision to go through with the mission.

The Colombian bankrolling their cell would be paid back for last summer's training in Havana after all. Had the roll of silver set off the alarm, she would have quietly exited the gateway and tossed her newspaper in a trash can, initiating the mission abort signal. Geraldine Donner would have traveled on to Munich to pick up her message from their European contact. Peter, her partner, would have met them three days later back at their safe house in Manhattan.

But it was a go. The mission would go down as planned. The archway's dulled sensitivity level would not detect their weapons.

"Oh, damn!" she exclaimed loud enough to catch the attention of the two monitors. They looked up at Donner, dismayed that their discussion about Luke and Sara or Tim and Sondra or whoever was up to no good on their soap opera had been interrupted, and they were reminded they were actually supposed to be working.

Donner breezed back through the archway (double-checking the non-existence of an alarm), the picture of harried exasperation. "I can't *believe* I forgot my overnight bag," she intoned in her best Silicon Valley accent. The two old women immediately resumed talking while Donner retrieved her overnight bag. She glanced at her partner, Peter, who walked through the archway. Inside his pocket was an asthma inhaler loaded with an emetic vomit-inducer. It was a tiny bomb that would prove its usefulness within the next hour. In his other pocket was a Beretta .22 with a seven-shot clip and an eighth round chambered. It was the same deadly effective pistol with which the Israeli Sword of Gideon vengeance team had assassinated the '72 Olympic Munich terrorists and, tragically, an innocent Turk in Sweden. It was a tiny pistol, yet accurate enough to send all eight rounds into a target's head at twenty-five feet as fast as you could pull the trigger. With a little practice, that is.

Donner joined him on the other side with her "travel kit." JFK Airport security has been penetrated.

Despite herself, Donner smiled, and then forced it away. The corner of her right eye started twitching, an impromptu muscle spasm revealing frayed nerves stretched taut since early morning. Inside her travel bag was a disassembled 9-millimeter Glock 17 semi-automatic, its minimal steel and plastic components indecipherable to the monitors who would give it nothing more than a cursory glance, or if their supervisor was around, a glance of studious ignorance if anything, to demonstrate their willingness to work hard at their boring airport security job.

The Glock had passed through the archway. So had the plastic explosive lining the suitcase. So had the additional cans of aerosol she so highly prized.

Alex pulled David inside the men's room.

"It's only a pocketknife," David protested.

"Yeah, well put it away."

They both decided a pit stop was necessary before the long trip. Moments later, they turned to go, David walking out first. Just before he reached the door, it swung open. A large man, middle-aged, blond, with a thick beard barely filtering his incredibly foul breath, brushed roughly past David, knocking him against the wall.

"Hey!" David wiped his mouth and nose in disgust from the strong smell of alcohol on the man's breath. The man paid him no attention and tried to shoulder his way past Alex.

Alex grabbed him by the shoulder. The man was over-weight, and the ex-nose guard felt flabby skin melting under his grip. "Apology accepted, *asshole*." Alex tossed the man aside as if he were a screen door and followed David out. The man stared at their departure, saying nothing. "People with no manners bug me," Alex muttered as they turned left and walked down the gateway. David said nothing. Alex turned to him. "What's with you?"

"That guy. He didn't even say anything, just kind of pushed me aside, like I wasn't even there."

"Yeah. So I shoved him back."

"But . . . ah, never mind."

Something was troubling the kid, Alex decided. "Go ahead, Big Bear. What?"

"Well, he looked at you, like . . . well, after you shoved him and then turned around to go, he gave you the weirdest look. Know what I mean?"

"Nope."

"He was smiling, man. Not busting a gut or anything, but real calm. Like he knew something you didn't."

"Forget it. He's just an asshole. This place is full of freaks."

They found their gate after a few moments of walking. Alex led the way inside the packed waiting area.

"When's the flight taking off?" David asked, trying to get

Alex's attention away from the girl next to him, who was reading *Vogue* magazine and paying them no mind. Alex finally found what he was looking for without being too obvious: a gold wedding band on her ring finger with another accompanying it fastened to a rock the size of Rhode Island. He shook his head in disgust, looked back at David, and said, "What?"

"Wimpo, my man, you're acting like a dumb jock. I said, when does our flight take off?"

Alex glanced at his watch. "In another twenty minutes. Chill." He swung back around to reevaluate his chances.

David fidgeted in his chair, unable to sit still. The fat lady with the noisy newborn who just had to sit right next to them didn't help matters much. David occupied himself by swiveling his gaze from the right to the left, watching the steady stream of passengers and stewardesses pass by.

His eyes came to rest on a bearded man with sunglasses walking slowly toward their gate; a middle-aged blond man with a gut and wearing an indistinguishable gray-black suit that looked more like it belonged to the Salvation Army.

The same man who had sent him reeling against the wall in the men's room.

"Alex."

"What?" the big guy said, feigning irritation. He had finally established eye contact with his projected love companion for the trip and didn't want to be bothered while he made his next move. David tugged at his shoulder. Alex gave his target his best smile and then turned to David, instantly changing it to a scowl. "C'mon, little man, I got better things to—"

"Check it out!" David's voice cracked, and he cleared his throat, pointing at the man. "That's the guy from the men's room. Look. He's in the back of the line at the counter."

Alex looked toward the counter and followed the line back. "Yeah," he said, spotting him. "That's him. Almost didn't recognize the bastard."

David looked up at Alex. "Not that it really matters or anything, but why did he change clothes?"

"Yeah. He was wearing something different. You know, more colorful."

David settled uncomfortably in his chair. "How do you figure it?"

"Dunno. Keep an eye on him."

• • •

It had been too long, and she'd gotten entirely too jumpy. Fifteen years ago, Geraldine Donner still had an ample supply of zealous fanaticism that could get her through the tough spots: the waiting, the countdown, the precarious balance on a razor's edge immediately before pulling a trigger or yanking an ignitor's fuse train of stolen National Guard munitions.

She found the other Skorpion in the water tank behind the toilet where her auxiliary had hidden it earlier. Once she'd made sure no one else was in the rest room with her, she entered the stall and retrieved the weapon from the water. Moments later, after wiping it down and placing it inside her purse, she had to sit down and collect herself. A sudden wave of nausea hit her with the force of Yosemite Falls. Rising, she vomited in the toilet, gagging, convulsing from her overloaded nerves. The tic in her right eye flared up violently, encompassing her entire cheek.

She had to get a grip on herself. She knew she would lose it otherwise. Geraldine drew in several deep breaths, rinsed her mouth out by the mirror, and then breezed out of the women's room, leaving behind the hydrochloric smell of the bile still assaulting her stomach.

As she strode down the gateway toward Peter, she overcompensated for her strung-out nerves. Her gait was too free, her arms swung wide. When she finally reached Peter and smelled the alcohol misting his breath she lost it.

"Idiot!" she hissed, nudging him sharply in the side. She turned her head away from her partner in disgust from the smell of alcohol and body odor. Peter Lundgrendt had already sweated through his shirt so that huge wet rings stained his armpits, visible where his jacket hung open.

"Easy, Donner. Relax." Peter tried to keep his attention on the line in front of him as it crept slowly toward the ticket counter.

"How can I relax? You're slurring your words."

"Cut the crap," he replied, glancing down at her stuffed overnight bag. "Did you get everything?"

Geraldine drew a deep breath and clutched her bag to her chest.

"C'mon, ease up," Peter breathed noisily. "We'll pull it off." His was the braggadocio of a drunk man, an ex-revolutionary whose time had passed with the sixties. A man who was washed up, Peter Lundgrendt had seen his heyday years ago as a college student at Berkeley.

Geraldine curled her nose again at his breath. "Can you still remember what to do with the aerosol cans?"

"C'mon, Bear, it's time to go." Alex got up, stretched, and yawned. David climbed out of his seat, still watching the guy who had bumped into him earlier and his nervous companion.

"They're trouble, Alex."

"Yeah, they're trouble."

"You don't sound too convinced."

"Well . . . look, Bear, you're just—"

"C'mon, man. You thought so too, earlier."

The loudspeaker above sprung to life with a bell-tone: *"Good morning ladies and gentlemen. All passengers for Flight 968 will begin boarding at Gate Twenty-six, please. Would all elderly, handicapped, and other persons requiring special assistance please begin boarding—"*

David and Alex shuffled slowly toward the jetway, where a stewardess stood ready to receive passengers. Standing beside her, a security guard had produced a hand-held metal detector and began passing it over the passengers before allowing them through the gate. The fat woman beside them, her baby still squalling, got up hurriedly, trying to pacify the infant with one hand while struggling with her carry-on suitcase with the other.

"Here you go, ma'am," Alex offered, extending a hairy arm toward her suitcase. The fat lady flashed a big, toothy smile and eagerly nodded her appreciation.

"It's so nice of you to help," she breathed, switching her grin to David.

David swallowed and half-smiled back. He wished he didn't feel so uneasy.

Something bumped hard against his hip, a hard, metallic nudge. David wheeled around and saw the nervous lady and the creep brush by him in a hurry.

"Attention, please, will all passengers with seat numbers twenty-six through fifteen please enter the aircraft. Will all—"

"Oh, Christ!"

Peter said nothing, but kept his hand closed tightly on the Beretta deep inside his pocket.

"The security guard's got a metal detector!" Donner hissed.

"Well—?"

She inhaled sharply.

"Alex!"

The big man had been talking politely to the fat lady. He almost fell over as David tugged hard on his arm. David MacIntyre, wide-eyed, pointed to his front. *"Look!"*

Alex swung back ground. He saw a woman with a tic pulling a wicked-looking metallic toy gun out of her purse. Only when she snapped out the folding wire stock and yanked back on the submachine gun's bolt did he realize it wasn't a toy.

"Freeze!" Donner's piercing scream echoed through the lobby. Like novice tourists, the passengers stared at her with their jaws on the floor, then panicked into action when they saw the Skorpion, groping for their husbands, wives, and children, all jabbering at once.

"I said freeze, goddammit!"

Peter pulled the Beretta out of his pocket and walked steadily toward the scared, trembling stewardess and an equally scared security guard. The security guard dropped the metal detector as if it were a weapon and held his hands up in the air.

Peter twisted the stewardess's head into his armpit. The girl lost control and shrieked, her blond bangs askew, her eye mascara running down her face with her sudden tears. "Let's get on with the goddam plan, Geraldine," he said calmly, hauling the stewardess into the jetway with him.

Donner pulled rear guard as they entered the mouth of the jetway. She kept her Skorpion level at the passengers behind her. A movement caught her eye, and she recognized the young boy whose daddy was into big bucks. Insurance. *"You!* Come here!"

David did not move. Donner aimed the machine pistol at his chest and thumbed the Skorpion's safety selector to the fire mode. "C'mere," she growled, like an alley cat guarding her starving litter.

David swallowed and took a step forward.

"No, David!" Alex yelled, thrusting the suitcase back to the fat lady, who let it fall to the floor.

"Shut up!" Donner screamed. "You, asshole, stay right where you are!"

David stumbled toward the terrorist, trembling in fear and mounting rage. Donner shoved his overnight bag underneath her armpit, and grabbed the boy by his arm. She snarled in his ear: "You don't make a fucking move, kid, or so help me God I'll shoot your little rich boy ass."

"Up yours, lady."

A stunned pause, then *"I mean it!"*

"Go on, then."

Donner yanked him forward as she and her partner dragged the two hostages down the jetway toward the 747. They rounded the tunnel's corner just in time to see the jet's cabin door being slammed shut by an intrepid stewardess who had more sense than the rest of the crew on board to figure out what was happening.

Geraldine Donner and Pete Lundgrendt stopped, paying no attention to their hostages. They stared at each other. The gambit had failed. Their years in hiding were over. Next stop: jail, for a very long time. The tic in Donner's cheek grew and pounded. She was ballistic. Peter was more fatalistic, numbed by several shots of Smirnoff. He clenched the stewardess tighter around the neck and wheeled her around, facing back toward the jetway entrance.

"You're hurting me!" the stewardess squawked, gagging through her compressed larynx.

"Shut up. Geraldine, we have a decision to make, babe. We can't blast through that plane door."

Donner stared at her partner, and then dropped her overnight bag. "You know what we have to do then," she muttered, unzipping it.

The terrorists dragged their hostages back toward the passenger waiting room.

"Oww!" David yelled. The bitch had dug her fingernails into his arm again, this time drawing blood.

Donner paid him no mind. The girl Peter dragged beside her wept hysterically.

David saw Alex loom into view, the first person he saw as they reentered the waiting room, the big man, the nose guard; his friend, the guardian his old man had handpicked. David watched Alex's lips move in slow motion as the big guy said:

"Lady, for the love of God, let them go!"

Pick out the biggest, toughest, the strongest—military, if they're around—and make them your first kill, Donner remembered from her training days in Aden. She pulled the trigger.

Alex flew backward, his chest caved in from the impact of the Skorpion's six-round burst of 7.65-millimeter bullets.

"Bitch!" David screamed, tearing loose from her grasp.

"Fuck you pigs!" Donner shrieked inside the waiting area. *"All you pigs!"* She sprayed the crowd with her machine pistol. Screams, explosions, and flying lead turned the crowded waiting area into a screaming frenzy.

David leaped over to Alex, whose chest was a bleeding mass of holes. His friend's bewildered death-stare confirmed the result of the burst's last round, which had centered on his forehead: Alex was dead.

David could not interpret what his senses told him. All time and space had frozen. Reality had vanished. Numb, he glanced up from Alex's still body and saw people around him jerking about like marionettes while the staccato blast of Donner's machine pistol sprayed rounds everywhere. The security guard with the metal detector was stretched out on the floor, dead. The wailing mass of people overwhelmed him. The screaming, the noise . . . and the fat lady who clenched her baby between two pendulous breasts, her eyes, her eyes so wide, so scared, her mouth a huge O, her screams interrupted by bullets ripping violently up her abdomen, her baby miraculously unhurt, but thrown upward toward the ceiling. So high. David saw it all. *The lady . . . shot . . . her—her baby!*

David dived forward and caught the infant in his arms, gunfire ricocheting off the floor next to him. He cradled the screaming baby underneath his chest, pressed to the floor; he felt lead tearing, burning, ripping his adolescent muscle and bone and tendon apart . . . his arm exploding. It was gone, wasted. He was slammed into unconsciousness.

The baby screamed into David's ear, unhurt.

Donner had already expended her first clip. Frantic, she clawed at her overnight bag. The aerosol cans! She tore open her purse and grabbed a lighter. Then, she held out her specially designed Breck's Super-hold Special, depressed the nozzle, and spun the ignitor wheel of the lighter. A ten-foot tongue of flame shot out and engulfed the first row of polyester seats.

Smoke, fire, and confusion. Burning people crawling back to the hallway, their shrieks echoing throughout the terminal. The burning smell of vinyl and cordite permeated the air. The three security guards plunged through the chaos and came face-to-face with a crazed woman who spat flames at them through a can of hairspray. A middle-aged man beside her backed into the jetway, holding s squirming stewardess hostage in a headlock, a tiny .22 pressed tightly against her temple.

It was no time for negotiation, and certainly no time for waiting. The security guard leader, a trim young man who had spent three years in the Ranger battalion at Fort Stewart, took matters into his own hands: He shot the male terrorist twice in the face with his Browning Hi-power at a range of no more than twenty feet. The stewardess crumpled to the floor, hysterical and screaming. His two partners fired instantly on the woman spraying firey aerosol at them and felled her with their combined firepower.

Geraldine Donner achieved the martyr's state of nirvana she had so desperately sought all her life. She died instantly, her bloody torso smearing skid marks against the corner of the jetway entrance as she voided her bowels and was thrown violently backward from the impact.

Inside the smoking waiting area, a fourteen-year-old boy slumped over a baby whose life he had saved. His arm had fared much worse, as a severed artery gushed blood onto the carpet.

And the man who had watched it all from the terminal corridor took notes in his mind.

Humberto Werner-Miranda had much to answer for with this fiasco, Simon thought, walking calmly away from the melee.

CHAPTER THREE

"Go!" The cameraman pointed at her. Rita Seleson, the young, attractive on-the-scene reporter for ABC News, said:

"Anxiety reigns at New York City's General Hospital tonight as survivors fight for their lives after this morning's bloody terrorist massacre at John F. Kennedy International Airport. At least sixteen men, women, and children were killed before airport security overcame the terrorists. Officials speculate the terrorists are linked with a Colombian drug lord, currently under house arrest in Madrid, while his extradition proceedings remain stalled by Spanish authorities.

"One of the survivors, fourteen-year-old David MacIntyre, remains in critical condition following the shoot-out. MacIntyre, the son of prominent Tulsa, Oklahoma, businessman Wayne MacIntyre, and his traveling companion, Alexander Kurakis, also of Tulsa, were among those shot at JFK while en route to Munich. During the attack, young MacIntyre completely disregarded his own safety as he heroically shielded a six-month-old baby in his arms after the baby's mother was brutally cut down in the cross fire."

Seleson paused as an assistant thrust a paper in her hand. At the same time, a motorcade of three limousines under escort by twelve motorcycle cops drove up the causeway to the hospital's main entrance. They pulled to a stop.

"This just in," Seleson interjected suddenly, her eyes flashing back and forth from the note she held to the motorcade. "Vice President Stuart Lawson has just arrived at the hospital, where he has come to present the condolences of the President of the United States to relatives of the victims gathering in the hospital lobby." She glanced back down at her note.

"The Vice President's visit also concerns him personally. Wayne MacIntyre and Lawson are childhood friends, and MacIntyre contributed heavily toward the Administration's campaign in the last Presidential election. MacIntyre, who arrived this afternoon in his private jet, has remained secluded behind hospital doors since five o'clock this evening, shortly after his arrival. The old friends will be reunited under tragic circumstances.

"This is but the latest of a recent string of tragedies involving the MacIntyre family, including—"

Stuart Lawson, Vice President of the United States, hanging precariously on the edge of sixty with an ever increasing gut and a network of broken capillaries around his nose to prove it, clambered heavily up the stairs to the hospital. He paused at the top amidst a phalanx of Secret Service men to ponder what kind of shape he used to be in when he was halfback and his friend inside was quarterback of the class of '50 at Talulah High. He reminded himself, as he had for the past forty years, of the importance of consistent exercise and the virtues of abstinence from things tempting, and automatically associated that feeling with a fleeting sense of envy aimed at the man he had come to see, an old friend who could still throw a ball with the same force and accuracy as he had over forty years ago. But then, he concluded, that was the way Wayne MacIntyre had always been. Unlike others. Lawson patted the expanse of his gut and inhaled deeply.

He would talk to the other families later. After leaving behind his assistants and a rear guard of Secret Service men to block the media's Medusa tentacles, he and the rest of his guard entered the hospital's main entrance, occupied two elevators, and finally reached the twelfth floor.

There, Lawson saw MacIntyre down the hallway staring out the lobby window. Three other men stood near him. Two were from MacIntyre's own security organization. The third one was MacIntyre's middle son Matt, an Army Special Forces officer from Fort Bragg.

Lawson cleared his throat and strode purposefully down the hallway, knowing MacIntyre had heard him. The Secret Service men parted as he walked, constantly scanning the hallway. It was overkill. Another two dozen men had secured not only this floor, but the ones above and below it two hours earlier. Fifty feet later, he entered the waiting area and MacIntyre turned away from the window to face him. The two men looked at each other for several long moments. Lawson had never seen MacIntyre looking so old.

"Wayne." Lawson slowly extended his hand.

"Stuart," MacIntyre's gravelly voice rasped, as he reached out for Lawson, "thanks for coming, you old . . ." He broke off and choked back a spasm deep within his throat, wiping his wet face with the sleeve of a thirteen-hundred-dollar suit. Matt MacIntyre reached forward and put his arm around his father's shoulders, which began to shake.

"I'm sorry, Wayne," Lawson said softly, stepping in close, holding his friend's hand tightly. "I'm so awfully damned sorry."

MacIntyre stood fully erect then, dropping Lawson's hand, his dark five-o'clock shadow turning his Oklahoma rough-neck's weathered, craggy features into a black mask of fury. It was the same look that had once instilled sphincter-blowing fear into the bowels of three North Korean soldiers he killed with nothing more than his M1's bayonet.

Lawson shivered. He remembered a tall, skinny kid who had once willed the Talulah Bearcats to victory in the state championship; and later, while in college, he'd read about an older, taller, skinny kid winning the Distinguished Service Cross as an Army private in Korea by taking out an enemy machine gun position on a barren, snow-covered mountain on that frozen peninsula in December 1950; the same man who had always done the right thing at the right time and place, and if it wasn't the right thing, then it was something his friend believed in, and he would always shoulder the responsibility for his actions and then some.

It was the look—that Wayne MacIntyre look that no one else in the world could possibly match—a look of determination, defiance, and the incredible will to take action, that had made MacIntyre into one of the most powerful and wealthy men in the country. One who had been this Administration's king-maker.

MacIntyre knew power. He was the manifestation of power, a power of innate integrity and strength, tempered by savvy and wisdom. And Wayne MacIntyre was mad.

"Stu," he growled, china-blue eyes sparkling against a shock of black hair, "tell me why my son nearly had his arm blown off at the airport this morning."

MacIntyre steadied his ragged emotions through the solace of a steaming cup of coffee. His son Matt and the Vice President of the United States sat with him in a doctor's lounge, guarded by a secret army outside on the floor; they had the room to themselves.

MacIntyre let out a sigh and swirled his coffee grounds in slow circles as he contemplated the bottom of his mug. Then he drained it and set the mug down with a clunk on the table.

"You know, I got hit pretty bad once in Korea. Chicom burp gun emptied a couple of rounds in my gut. Thought it was all over."

"I remember, Mac," Lawson said, nodding his head, thanking God he was able to sit *that* one out in school.

Matt MacIntyre glanced respectfully at his father. The only action he'd ever seen was the year before at a desolate ranch in southern New Mexico; a drug bust his team had participated in—at least, if you believed the unclassified version. The reality was a short, violent firefight, a Soviet tilt-rotor plane, a KGB defector and a Spetznaz major involved in the attempted theft of top-secret SDI technology. But even with all that, he knew full well he had never been through the kind of hell his old man had.

"Yeah," MacIntyre continued, his eyes finding his son's. "I really thought I was gonna die. They wheeled me into a MASH hospital in a deuce-and-a-half. Goddam, I still remember that ride, bouncing over mudholes in the road two feet deep, arty tearing the skies apart overhead. . . . Got sick every day with the fever and dysentery that set in. Docs took out at least ten feet of intestine." He paused, and his audience allowed him his time.

Matt studied his father's face, reaching out for the old man, trying to bear more of the hurt in his own heart for his little brother—his poor little brother Davie. *Goddammit, how in the hell could it have happened? Why? I promise you, little bro, I will get whoever did this to you.*

All this on top of the accident. The accident that had killed their mother in front of the entire family, the boating accident his older brother had caused, even though it hadn't really been Donny's fault . . .

"But I got over it," MacIntyre finally continued. "Healed up and all. Don't even feel any pain now. But how in Christ . . . " MacIntyre broke off again, getting up so fast that the chair he had been sitting in tipped over, and the Vice President of the United States flinched. "How in Christ's name can my little boy, my little *baby,* go through life *without his right goddam arm*? And what about all the others who are dead? *They were innocents, Stuart!*"

Lawson stood up to placate his friend, whose thundering voice had caused security men to throw open the door with guns drawn. He waved the three men out.

"It's . . . it's okay, Stu. I'm okay." MacIntyre righted his chair and sat back down, Lawson joining suit. "Stu, tell me—please—who were these people that shot David and the others? Hell, not only David but Alex Kurakis, one of my most devoted employees. My God, that young man was in his very prime. And now he's dead. My son. Alex. All those people, Stuart. *Who were they?*"

Lawson measured his response. "Terrorists," he said.

"Dammit, man, I *know* they were terrorists."

"Take it easy, Mac!" Lawson asserted, wresting control of the conversation. He did not want to risk one of Wayne MacIntyre's legendary rages, yet he did not want to hurt his friend in his time of grief. But he had to give him answers. It was the only tranquilizer Wayne MacIntyre took. Answers. With answers MacIntyre could reason things out.

Lawson got up from the table, walked across the darkened room to the blinds, and drew them open. He cracked open the window, letting the crisp January air steal through the room, ventilating it, chilling it for the hard words to come.

"Okay," he began. "I'm going to tell you a few things that you are not to pass outside of this room, Wayne." He looked at him hard, then switched his gaze over to Matt MacIntyre. "Is that clear?"

"Of course," MacIntyre replied.

Beside him, Matt MacIntyre nodded his head in solemn agreement. "Yes, sir."

Lawson leaned against the window sill and felt the cold draft bite him in the back. He folded his arms over his gut and stared at the father and son before him whose son and brother had been shot by a Czech Skorpion machine pistol only hours before. The survivors and their families needed answers. Hell, the Administration needed answers—and solutions—for the problems yet to come.

"They get attention by shocking the hell out of people," Lawson began, pausing just long enough to chew the inside of his cheek. "We, the American people, are the target audience. We think that . . . Wayne, you've heard of my special advisory committee on international terrorism."

"Right."

"It's an advisory board that keeps me posted on the flow of international terrorism, the goings-on throughout the world, what new groups have formed; more importantly, a strict accounting on who—whether private, public, or governmental—caves in to their demands or tries to appease them through non-prosecution or by averting their eyes."

"Go on."

"These people that hit JFK today—and who shot your son—we know who they are: Geraldine Donner and Peter Lundgrendt. Twenty years ago, they were both active campus radicals during some of the most violent riots and demonstrations in 1970 and '71. Up until today when they were killed, they were a couple of washed-out bums on the run. They'd been in hiding since the seventies, when they participated in a string of bombings with the Weather Underground. They may also have been involved with the Symbionese Liberation Army toward the mid-seventies."

"The people that took Patty Hearst?"

"That's right," Lawson answered, amazed at MacIntyre's memory. He hadn't thought he'd remember any of the short-lived domestic American terror groups that sprung out of the campus radicalism of the late sixties. "Like I said, they were washed up, but somehow, they'd been contacted—probably by sources in Cuba or Europe—and were subsequently retrained somewhere in the Middle East or Cuba and resupplied."

MacIntyre fumed in his seat, his face twisting into knots of rage.

"I know how you feel, Wayne, but I need your help."

MacIntyre's eyes shot up, meeting Lawson's. "Help? What kind of help?"

Lawson did now answer immediately, letting the fish taste the hook. "The reason the U.S. has felt so little impact from international terrorism is because of the FBI. It's damned good. Also, an international cell must have logistical support—you know, well-stocked safe houses networked across the target area, the right people in the right place, people sympathetic to their cause—take Northern Ireland, for example.

"Well, we've had it easy in that respect for too long. The American people would never lend popular support to terrorism here in our homeland. But we've also been pretty blind. There's every reason to believe that on a basis much more frequent than ever before, more incidents of this nature will occur within our national boundaries. On *our* soil, Mac."

Wayne MacIntyre found himself thinking about how an executive here, diplomat there, a soldier . . . overseas . . . he glanced at his son Matt. It was always so far away. Overseas. Matt was awaiting orders for Germany, and would leave in another few weeks.

MacIntyre wondered exactly what kind of "help" Lawson needed. He had a hunch. He'd formed his own security organization for the protection of his employees, especially those stationed with his South American interests and in the Middle East. To a large degree, his employees had always been safe because of his security chief's effective anti-terrorism program. But still, it was coming home. What kind of shape were his men really in? Moreover, how sincere was the Administration when push came to shove?

"Mac, I'm going to ask you to—"

"I know what you're going to ask me. Like the time you asked me to recruit a team to go into Southeast Asia, and then asked me *not* to do it after they had already crossed the Thai-Laotian border. Remember that, Stuart?"

Lawson shifted his eyes. It had been the first disgrace of the Administration. A private one, though, one that had never been leaked to the media. Lawson realized he'd lost control of the conversation.

"I know you remember, Stu," MacIntyre continued.

"It happened twelve months ago, Mac."

"I know," MacIntyre replied, not unkindly. "They're dead, of course. Or captured. No fuss, no problems. Those men never existed. It was just one of those—what do you call them, Stu—deniable operations? Yeah, that's it. Now you want me to do the same thing about these terrorists."

"Mac—"

"Save it. I already had my mind made up before you came. I'm getting even with these contemptible bastards, and whoever sponsors them."

"It's more complicated than that, Wayne."

"How?"

"Because we still don't have any details, other than the fact that the people at JFK today were a narco-terrorist faction working for the cartel in Medellín."

"Drugs," MacIntyre snorted with venom.

"We don't have any hard and fast leads yet," Lawson continued. "We've had this one incident, this enigma, if you will. But the fact that it *is* an enigma bothers me. I think something much more substantial will happen in this country in a very short time."

"What can I do, then?"

"Look at your security organization. Look at them hard. See what you've got. Recruit." Lawson winced at MacIntyre's reaction to his last word. "All right, we have the FBI, the CIA, the Special Forces." He glanced just then at Matt MacIntyre. "But Mac, what we *don't* have is flexibility."

MacIntyre's eyes narrowed. He knew now what Lawson was getting at. It was time for hard decisions. He let him continue.

"We need a deniable organization, Wayne. Private. Well funded and equipped. An organization the media cannot use to destroy the Administration with. You can make that happen."

MacIntyre thought about it. An image immediately sprang to mind of IVs and an oxygen mask clinging to a young boy's face like so many tentacles in a surgically sterile room without the warmth of a mother to hold his hand. A boy without the use of his arm.

His boy.

The image of a rattlesnake came to MacIntyre's mind then, poised and ready to strike.

The snake was pissed.

CHAPTER FOUR

Munich

A tall, blond-haired woman strutted down the park's sidewalk in the Munich Zoo. She wore an ankle-length fur, a running suit, and Adidas sneakers on her feet instead of heels. Stylish wraparound sunglasses hid her jade-green eyes from the glare of the late-morning sun as she walked past the occasional passersby to find her park bench.

Across from the lion's den, she found the bench and sat down heavily upon it, reflecting on just how stupid it was to service this dead-letter drop, so ideal in the spring and summertime, in the middle of the winter with no cover from the barren limbs. She'd have to talk this one over with her contact in Frankfurt.

Monika Stern let her arm hang lazily through the park bench's green armrest and closed her fingers around a small, metallic matchbox fastened magnetically to the metal frame underneath her seat. Removing it, she slipped it inside her purse. After a few minutes Monika stood up and walked back to the park exit.

Aden.

Stern's eyes widened at the first word, as she decoded the message in her Munich safe house. Lazy wisps of steam from the coffee cup resting on the arm of her couch wafted up to her nose as she stared at the word, a word that conjured up austere images of sand, wind, and gun oil. It was a word that, like an old familiar song, reminded her of youth.

Five minutes later, the decoding was done. The message told

her to cut off all contact with members of her existing cell, order them to hibernate in deep cover, and conduct no further activities until further notified. She was to report to the Red Army Faction's training liaison officer in Aden, Yemen, as soon as possible.

That Monika Stern did not particularly care to be uprooted like this did not matter. She had been ordered in no uncertain terms to report to Aden, a place she held in awe and contempt at the same time. Such a place. Forgotten in the world press. Unglamorous. Destitute. Sandy, windy, barren Aden, Yemen, the armpit of the Arabian Peninsula, the rocky, lizard-ridden southern coast of a brain-boiling conglomeration of sand and desolation.

But it was for those very reasons she and virtually every other Western European revolutionary trained there. Especially members of the Red Army Faction.

It had been over eleven years since she had last seen Aden. That would have been 1981; she'd had to drop out of the Free University of Berlin for two semesters to receive her initial training there, and then every summer thereafter for follow-on training in Syria or Lebanon. The sand, oh, how she despised the sand. The sharp, jagged rocks and canyons and Arabs— She suddenly halted her internal complaint: It did not matter, the sand did not matter. *Maybe only Inge back in Munich* . . . No, even Inge did not matter. It was better for Inge not to know her any further. She did not want the one person in the world Monika Stern cared anything for caught up in the heat of Stern's malcontented life and burned.

All that mattered was the mission, the violence, the message, and her making it all happen. And if the RAF leadership deemed it necessary that she go back to her old training grounds, then she'd go back.

Aden. She'd only been nineteen then. Monika Stern, at that age, had finally been given a reprieve from life.

Munich, 1981

They sat in their favorite coffee shop by the campus, comparing notes on the morning's lecture and talking. It was a very comfortable atmosphere, with heavy wooden tables and green tablecloths on the tiny hardwood floor and steins hanging on the wall, but this was no traditional German *gasthaus* cum coffee shop. It was a Bohemian place, a place that attracted the intelligentsia on campus, a place for free thought and discussion, a place where any kind of costume and personal grooming and dress would do. Communists and Green Party activists, anarchists and nihilists, peace-lovers and anti-nuclear demonstrators, they all came here; their common denominator was free thought and free association. Their common denominator was dissent.

"Did you find Professor Reidl's lecture today on the Palestinian Resistance very interesting?" Renate asked Monika. She rubbed the toe of her shoe against Monika's calf.

Monika stared at her friend. "Yes," she said. "I did."

"Why?"

"Because the Palestinians have taken matters into their own hands. They fight for what they believe in."

Renate raised her coffee mug to her lips and considered Monika's jade-green eyes. Monika returned the look. Renate's large gray eyes were really her best feature. Her pale skin and black, short-bobbed hair and thin body led her to no male companions. But her gray eyes, soft, alluring, were quite appealing.

Renate set her cup down. "I disagree with Professor Reidl. She said something about how the Israelis were justified in the assault into Lebanon last spring, how they were compelled to do it because of the terrorist attacks along the border."

Monika leaned back in her chair and crossed her legs underneath her heavy woolen skirt. She shivered slightly in her sweater, the cold October wind shooting through the coffee shop every time the entrance opened. She picked up her coffee mug and took a sip from it, letting the china's warmth heat her hands. She decided to play devil's advocate. "And why not?" she said. "Their children's schools were rocketed and bombed with Syrian artillery."

"But the Syrians did not do it."

"No, the Palestinians did from the Lebanese border."

"They were justified," Renate said coldly.

"But it did not work," Monika replied. "The Israelis moved into Lebanon and virtually destroyed the Palestine Liberation Organization. The Palestinians were inept. They made the wrong decision."

Renate was taken aback. "How do you come by this judgment? How do you know?"

"I read, my friend. I study economics, international relations, insurgencies. . . ." Monika shrugged. "Simple enough," she continued. "The world is run by money. You have no money without oil. You have no oil without land—that is, the Arabs control what they can of the world's economy with their virtual monopoly on oil. And war is fought in the name of religion and for land. And the Palestinians want a home."

"Yes!"

Monika was taken aback. Why had her friend reacted so enthusiastically to what she had just said?

"Absolutely!" Renate cried. Then, softly, she added, "You are right, Monika." She drained her coffee mug and looked intently at Monika. She set the mug down on the table. "I have a book for you to read," she told her, reaching inside the day-pack she had draped earlier on her chair. "It's written by a fellow named Che Guevara. He was a Latin American revolutionary in the fifties and sixties. He and Fidel Castro wrested Cuba away from the dictator Batista during the Cuban Revolution."

Monika eyed the book and returned it to her friend. "I've seen this. The tactics he writes about seem to make sense. His doctrine, however, is dialectic and naive."

"But—"

"I gathered that Guevara was just another chauvinist pig. He got himself killed through typical male stupidity and bravado in Bolivia. He violated his own principles of insurgent warfare."

"Yes . . ."

"Renate, have you ever seen the paintings of Salvador Dali?"

Renate was taken aback. Why the abrupt change in conversation? What did Dali have to do with Che Guevara?

Monika Stern continued. "Double images. Salvador Dali painted many hidden scenes in one picture. You see it one way; then you see it in another, entirely different way. For example, a very pretty lady sitting before her vanity mirror can be made to look like a skull. That sort of thing."

"So how does this relate to—"

"Guevara was a poet, a dreamer. He was imbued with

insecurities and had to constantly prove himself. He was his own worst enemy. Look at the cover of your book."

They both glanced down at the book Renate had tried to give her friend. A picture of the bearded Latin revolutionary was emblazoned on the cover. He wore the same scraggly beard his mentor Castro affected. The picture was vintage '59, taken as he stood by Castro on the balcony of the presidential palace, where they addressed the throngs of people before them shortly after seizing control.

"Look at his mouth," Monika said quietly. "It is an effeminate mouth. His eyes are soft. He looks like a soft, spoiled baby. He could not even grow a full beard. He knew that. That is why he died at the hands of the Bolivians; he always had to prove himself."

"Why do you say these things?" Renate asked, reaching down and brushing her hand against Monika's. "Why is it so important to see the double image of a man's face?"

Monika jerked her hand away from the skin contact and immediately transformed the movement into brushing her hair back with both hands, so as to not offend her friend. Then she leaned toward Renate. "If you trust someone enough," she told her, "to bypass the hidden message in his face, then you will open yourself up for hurt. For deception. People lie; that is a basic human trait. I've been hurt badly all my life."

"You can trust some people." Again, Renate brushed her hand against Monika's. This time, Monika did not pull away. She looked down. Renate caught Monika's eyes with her own. "You can trust some people," she repeated in a softer voice.

"Very few. People can beat you. They manipulate you. I-I had to learn how to manipulate people before they could manipulate me." Monika stared at the tablecloth before her, and held her friend's hand with a firmer grip. "I once fucked a man many times so he would provide martial-arts instruction to me when I was fourteen, just to learn how to defend myself against my father who beat me. My father . . . would also . . . would. . . ."

Renate's hands clenched Monika's tighter.

"I got an acquaintance of mine who owned a camera to take pictures of my karate instructor with me. He had a business and I was a minor. I blackmailed him to force him to continue teaching me, free, until I became an expert."

"Did your father still beat you?" Renate glanced towards

Monika's lap. "Did he continue to abuse you?" she added, a strange, hopeful note in her voice.

"Not for long," Monika replied. "Finally I was the one who beat him. Very badly." She looked up from the tablecloth. "My mother and I never heard from that pig again after their divorce. *I* was the one who beat him." Monika's voice rose, and it carried out through the cafe. "I *broke* him. I could have killed him."

Renate sat back in her seat, the candlelight from the tabletop flickering across her young friend's features, revealing a cold half smile and glittering eyes. *Yes*, she thought. *Yes*. "Perhaps the Palestinians realize this as well," Renate said carefully. "That they can beat the Israelis through cunning and their hidden strength."

"Of course."

"They have been beaten many times in the past."

"Yes."

"And now they take matters in their own hands."

Monika's eyes widened slightly, and stared at Renate as if her friend were made of glass. Then: "Yes."

Renate slipped her foot out of her shoe and played her toe against Monika's calf muscle. "There is no hidden meaning with them, Monika. There is no hidden meaning with anyone who has had enough, anyone who says, 'To hell with you and what you stand for.' People like that, who fight with deeds and action instead of hidden meanings and transparent, hypocritical messages, are direct. They are true and right." She tightened her grip on Monika's hand. "They will prevail."

Monika felt her control slipping. Her guard was down and she knew it. She looked at Renate closely. Could she trust this woman? How many friends had she ever trusted before? She knew what Renate spoke of. She knew what Renate wanted—on both counts. She thought about it. After several moments, she realized she wanted it too. At least part of it. She wanted to . . . trust. To confide. To know that there was someone there for her.

"People," Monika began, hesitant, "are up front about what they want." Her breathing picked up, and she felt a warm glow spread across her midsection. "What is it you want, Renate?"

Renate's answer was quiet and soft. "I want you."

Monika's hand relaxed. She glanced back down at the tablecloth. Then she looked back up into gray, alluring eyes.

And for the first time in her life, Monika Stern's shell was broken.

The days passed by into weeks and months and semesters. Monika discovered gentleness, caring. The touch of a hand. The closeness and heat of passion, warmth and caring, emotions far removed from hate and contempt. The steadiness and dependability of a special friend who could transcend distrust and fear. Finally.

They lived together in a tiny flat in the center of Munich by the Marienplatz, while Monika studied at the university and worked with Renate at the bookstore near their flat to supplement their income. Monika switched her major from economics to art. Always an admirer of Salvador Dali's work, she specialized in surrealism. In this medium, she was able to exploit the double meanings and the alternate dimensions she was always able to detect in other people and her surroundings. Soon, her instructors took note of her work and encouraged her developing style. By the end of her first semester, she had two canvases on display in the Art Department.

One work was an oil of Che Guevara. That painting, at first glance, showed the Latin revolutionary as he was on Renate's book cover: smiling his cherubic, effeminate smile beneath a adolescent's sparse beard. But underneath the innocence and androgyny of her subject's appearance lurked an evil undertone of malevolence and superiority, the face of her father, a face with wrinkles cobwebbed around hollow, cruel eyes, laden with contempt.

No one ever told Monika that they were her eyes.

Renate had dropped out of school altogether. Monika thought at first that she meant to work longer hours at the bookstore, but that did not happen. Instead, Renate took unannounced vacations, often for weeks at a time. Upon her return, she would only tell Monika that she was off in the countryside, hiking with other friends, but her answers were always vague and open-ended, yet tinged with an unspoken promise that they would somehow involve her lover. Monika had always prized her privacy, and so she allowed Renate hers, despite their growing and maturing passion for one another. For now, at least, it was enough that Monika had a real friend.

Monika continued with her art and her international relations classes, and was caught up in the idealism revolving around nuclear disarmament. That year, the United States, with its second-rate actor President, had introduced Pershing missiles into Germany as a backstop against paranoid delusions of Soviet invasion. That development catalyzed intense, nonstop discussion between her and her fellow students. Soon, Monika was swept into student demonstrations and sit-ins. One drizzling November afternoon, the West German Polizei scraped her and three dozen other protesters off the asphalt outside the campus administration building's executive parkway and tossed them in jail for several hours. After posting bail, Renate took her home, grinning, but saying nothing. Monika knew she approved. But where had she gotten the money?

There were other sit-ins and protest marches condemning the Pershing missiles. Once, they marched through the American military housing area outside the U.S. Army's McGraw Kaserne in Munich at seven o'clock in the morning, waking up the American dependents and chanting anti-American slogans. American GIs would walk by, some keeping to themselves and ignoring the process, others yelling obscenities in reply. Monika grew to hate Americans and all that they stood for. She despised them for their macho, uncultured Yankee pride, and she despised their overweight, loudmouthed citizen-tourists throwing their money away on stupid German wood-carvings and beer steins. She hated their snobbery and their despicable, unsophisticated ways. They would not even learn the German language! She grew to despise them and their actor President and their materialism and their Army almost as much as she had despised her father's barbarism and weak-kneed cowardice. She held the Americans in contempt. They were only a paper tiger. Some day they would pay for their superiority with the rest of the world, and for the way their Zionist-controlled government sucked up to Israel's every desire and demand. She talked constantly to Renate about these things during their suppers together, and her friend always listened, nodding, smiling her queer little half smile. Renate's opinions were few, sparse, but always supplied at the right time to open Monika up into another tirade.

Eventually, Monika's suspicions about Renate grew into confirmation. She was more than a bookseller. She was more than an avid hiker. Her library in their flat included the writings not only of Guevara, but of Marighella, Mao, Nietzsche, Sun Tzu, and Marx. Monika read them all. Some of the books—the ones by Sun Tzu and Marighella, both treatises on small-unit warfare, the guerrilla in the countryside, and the urban guerrilla in the streets—she liked. The political books by the others, she dismissed with a pragmatism born of her abused childhood and her sense of self-reliance and survival. They were nothing more than wistful philosophies written by timid men who hid behind their pens and opium habits.

One night, after she and Renate had eaten their dinner of steamed vegetables and rice, she turned on the radio and tuned it in to a local station that played music from the Classical and Romantic eras. She walked over to the easel standing in their living room and resumed work on her third painting. Renate, as usual, had opened a book, and remained at the dinner table.

"Is it good?" Monika asked her from their living room.

Renate looked up at her, the concentration and effort the book demanded still having wrought furrows in her forehead. "What?"

"The book. It is interesting?"

Renate gave her a pert grin. "Yes. Quite."

"What is it called?" Monika asked needlessly. She had already scanned its pages an hour before Renate had come home.

"*On War*. Clausewitz."

"And you agree with his principles? Surprise, economy of force, mass, and so on?"

Renate was surprised. "You've been reading my books!"

Monika smiled inwardly. Renate had not spoken vindictively, nor accusingly. She had sounded happy. Monika carefully phrased her next remark. "You are truly the scholar, *Schatz*. I admire you for it."

Renate's mind whirled. She loved it when her lover called her *Schatz* when she least expected it. She ground her buttocks against her seat and lost her place with Clausewitz. She rose from the table and walked slowly to Monika. "Thank you," she said, as she draped her arms around Monika's neck. She pulled Monika close and kissed her lightly on the mouth, and then with more passion. They drew close to one another, feeling, caressing.

Suddenly, Monika pulled away. She was not abrupt, just firm and gentle. Renate looked at her, puzzled.

"Take me with you tonight," Monika said.

"I haven't said I was—"

"You are. I know you are."

Renate tensed up inside, her desire for Monika replaced by her professional acumen. *Is she ready for this?* "Yes, tonight I meet with friends."

"Your revolutionary friends." Monika held Renate out at arm's length, studying her closely.

"Yes. My revolutionary friends." *Those eyes! Why do I let them—*

"And what do you talk about? What is it you do?"

Renate paused before answering, letting herself become mesmerized by Monika's jade-green eyes and her soft, yet controlling voice that always made her weak and submissive for sex. "I think—I think that you are not ready to meet my friends," she began.

"Then why do you do this!" Monika snapped, her fingers digging into Renate's shoulders. Renate was shocked, and winced under the pain in her shoulders from Monika's finger-nails. It was the first time she had ever heard Monika's voice carry out like this. "Why do you read all those books, talk to me about the Palestinians, why do you . . ." She broke off and looked away, and her face illuminated with sudden reality. She said, lowly, "Why do you love me, Renate?"

"I *do* love you! Oh, *Gott*, Monika, don't be angry with me!" Renate pried Monika's fingers from her shoulders and clasped her hands together. Tears burst from Renate's eye sockets. "Don't be—"

Monika put her arms around the woman five years her senior and comforted her, as Renate sobbed into her breasts. "I'm not angry, Renate," she said coolly. "I just want to know and meet your friends. You have left me out of that part of your life."

"I'll introduce them to you. It will only take a call. I will do it, Monika."

And as Renate clutched Monika tightly, feeling the comfort of her lover's breasts as she hugged her, Monika Stern came to the realization that trust indeed went only so far as you let it. Her eyes gleamed in the dark as she drew Renate down to their bed.

CHAPTER FIVE

March. The snows blowing in from Austria ceased their frozen bitterness, and the sun began to shine its warmth upon the Free University of Munich, draping the air with the promise of an early spring. It was on such a beautiful day that Monika walked home from class to find a note with Renate's handwriting on it, instructing Monika to meet her for an early supper at Oscar's, a local cafe. Monika was excited. Perhaps the time had come.

Monika had waited; she was patient. She'd made her mind up to concentrate on art and economics. During her second semester, Monika had concentrated on fine-tuning her mastery of English to complete fluency, realizing that it would indeed come in handy in the years to come. Now she walked out of the apartment with the note clenched tightly in her hand. The time had finally come for her induction into Renate's group. Within minutes, she stood outside the cafe's entrance.

She pushed open the door that led into the dark, Bohemian atmosphere that only Oscar's could create: a long bar along the side of the establishment, its beer-stained mahogany counter, the heavy green tablecloths on the tiny wooden tables, the local intelligentsia hanging out, beer steins on the wall. . . .

Monika picked out a table and consulted her watch. She was late by three minutes. Inwardly, she swore at herself; she had always prided herself in showing up on time for meetings and classes. But where was Renate? She should have been here already, but she wasn't.

The waitress appeared from behind the bar and glided to Monika's table. Silent and unsmiling, she took Monika's order.

"A cappuccino, please," Monika told her. "Have you seen

Renate?" Renate had intimated that the cafe was a conduit to her group.

The waitress studied Monika with appraising eyes. Then: "You will see her soon enough."

She returned to the bar, and three minutes later, returned to Monika with a steaming brown mug of Italian cappucino, with a thick layer of whipped cream sprinkled with cinnamon on top. She pulled out an "Oscar's" coaster from her apron and placed it on the table, followed by the cup. She retrieved a pen from her pocket and underscored the numbers she had written on the coaster from behind her. "No need to pay, *Schatz.*"

Monika saw the thinnest trace of a smile on the waitress's lips. It had no humor in it. Then the smile disappeared, replaced by the same pencil-streak of a mouth the waitress usually maintained. "Do you understand?" she said.

Monika simmered with impatience but did not show it. Yes, she understood, she told her. The waitress left. Monika glanced down at the coaster, knowing from her talks with Renate what the drill was to be followed.

Again, numbers. This time, 275, the Student Union, and a phone number.

Half an hour later, she was at a phone booth by the university Student Union. She dialed the phone number and waited for an answer.

"Heinz Wentle's Taxi." A low voice, laced with a gruff, guttural Bavarian accent. She remembered that voice.

"My name is Monika Stern. I'm at the student union and would like a taxi, please."

A pause. "Five minutes. Be at the library's entrance."

And five minutes later on the dot, Monika Stern stood by the entrance of the library. A taxi appeared in the traffic and parked in front of her with an abrupt screech of its brakes, a huge, bearded man slung over the driver's wheel. Monika climbed in the back seat, and for the next several minutes the man drove into the heart of Munich, saying nothing. Monika kept her silence as well, tense, adrenaline pumping. She was ready for anything. She enjoyed the adrenaline rush. She was fascinated by this new game she played, a game she would eventually control.

The taxi pulled into a garage near the Marienplatz district, where shoppers from all over the world came to see the baroque cathedral towers surrounding the Glockenspeil and buy cuckoo clocks and sample Bavarian wurst and beer. But the garage the taxi driver pulled inside was cold and dark. No tourists here. He parked the car next to a van.

"Get out."

Monika tensed. She did not like the way the man ordered her about, but she complied. She got out of the cab. The driver pulled away and disappeared from the garage. It was cold inside, dark and cold. And quiet. Very soon, Monika was aware of her heart beating inside her head and how her breath misted with every exhalation.

The door to the van opened and a man wearing a ski mask pointed at her. "Inside," he ordered.

A high voice, Monika thought. *Cultured. High German. Military-sounding.* Climbing inside the van, she saw two more hooded figures and a space between them on the back seat. She occupied the center place.

But only until the two men flanking her had blindfolded her eyes. Monika was then told to lay upon the floor. She played the game.

A long trip this time. For the next two hours, the van drove, curving and taking many different roads. No conversation from the others entertained her. It was a silent trip. Monika dozed, the result of a conscious effort to conserve her energy for the night's events, be what they may. It took self-discipline; it took self-reliance.

Finally, the van pulled up to a halt.

"Stay here," the same voice as before said, before everyone deserted the van. Monika waited inside for another ten minutes. The back doors to the van were opened and she was hauled out. She could tell she was outside, but only for a moment. She was in the country; the sick-sweet smell of fresh manure and hay filtered through her nostrils, and her feet stood on soft dirt, not the asphalt and cobblestones of Munich. She was guided into a house and instructed to sit upon a chair.

Someone yanked off her blindfold. There were two figures dressed in ordinary clothes, and wearing ski masks.

"You may call me Ludwig," said the high, cultured voice. "Do you know why you are here, Monika Stern?"

"Yes." Monika's voice was dry and raspy. It was the first time she had spoken all afternoon.

"Tell me."

Monika thought for a moment. "I am here to join you."

"Join us for what? What is it you think we do?"

Monika's patience snapped. "I know what you do! The oil cartel members you kidnapped in seventy-five. Hanns Schlyer, the industrialist you kidnapped in seventy-seven! The Stockholm embassy takeover! Entebbe! Mogadishu!"

One of the men laughed. "She is like an American child with a comic-book litany of our exploits."

Monika detected a French accent.

"You seem angry," Ludwig said after a moment.

"Yes, I am tired of playing games!"

Neither said anything for a moment. Monika said, "You are the Red Army Faction. I want to be a part of you."

"You are only nineteen. A young girl."

"Twenty," she corrected.

"Twenty, then. You are young."

"And I daresay you aren't much older."

The French-accented man broke out laughing. "Monika Stern, to say we are the Red Army Faction is to say that we are a tree upon which many, many limbs grow."

"Then what are you?"

"You will find out soon enough. Those events you mentioned—Schlyer, Mogadishu—they happened long ago."

"GSG9 wiped those groups out, I know."

Both exchanged glances. The *Grenzschutzgruppe* 9—GSG9—was Germany's elite counterterrorist force. They had stormed the plane where members of the RAF held several dozen hostages after hijacking it to Mogadishu, Somalia. The RAF operation had been a glaring failure.

"You've done your homework," said Ludwig, his voice very calm and even.

"Yes, I have. I make it a point to know the people I choose to associate with."

"Arrogant bitch," the Frenchman muttered.

"I read," Monika retorted. "I've studied your history. The library has plenty of books, you know."

"Ah, yes," Ludwig said. "You are a student, and a very good one. I understand you pull very high marks in art and foreign languages."

Monika said nothing.

"So tell me, Fräulein Stern, why do you want to join us?"

"Because I am tired of chauvinists telling me what to do in my society. I am tired of the American occupation forces in my country, who rape our culture and debase our politicians with their dollars. I am tired—"

"Sounds more like a Fascist than a Marxist," the Frenchman commented.

Ludwig snorted. "Our Latino friends don't care either way. But I can tell you right now they and our Muslim contacts don't like working with women. I say take her home."

Monika sat up straight in her chair and lowered her voice. "I am tired of these games you play."

"Enough," the Frenchman hissed. "Enough of this impertinent shit from this child." He glared at the German. "It was a mistake to bring her here, Ludwig!"

Monika glared defiantly at Frenchman. "So what are you going to do . . . spank me?"

Ludwig suddenly produced an automatic pistol with one hand and a tube-like object with the other. He screwed the tube onto the muzzle of the automatic. Monika knew nothing of guns, but refused to let herself be intimidated by one. She kept calm.

"Turn around," Ludwig ordered. "Stand up, and turn your chair around and face the opposite wall behind it."

Monika did as she was told. Facing her in the dim light thirty feet away was another chair with a target-practice silhouette laced on the backrest. The rest of the room was completely barren.

"You have never fired a gun before, correct?" the Frenchman asked her.

"Correct."

"Are you afraid to try?" A patronizing sneer.

"Of course not."

"Then shoot that silhouette. I want to see you do it. If you cannot hit that silhouette, then you are nothing more than a child energized with campus idealism."

The German thrust his automatic into Monika's hands.

"This is a Marakov. It is equipped with a silencer," Ludwig offered. "It will still make a loud noise for this room, but not as loud as it would make without one."

"And there is another one aimed at the back of your head, child," the Frenchman added. "Do nothing foolish."

Inhaling deeply, trying to control her fury at the French bastard behind her, Monika pointed the pistol at the silhouette. She liked the heft, the weight of the weapon in her hand.

"Pull the receiver back first to load the round," Ludwig instructed. "It is a slide mechanism in front of the hammer that loads the first round into the chamber. It will be a stiff pull."

Monika immediately grasped the receiver where he told her and pulled. Nothing happened. It indeed was a stiff pull.

The Frenchman guffawed. "I told you, Ludwig."

Monika gripped the automatic tightly and yanked the receiver back. *So that's how you do it,* she thought. *Wasn't so hard.*

The Frenchman ceased laughing.

Monika aimed at the silhouette with both hands, instinctively holding her arms out stiff to absorb the recoil in her elbow joints. She fired—and missed. The round plunked into the wooden beams behind the chair.

"Try again," said Ludwig.

She fired again. This time, she hit the shoulder of the silhouette. Most of the blast from her first two shots was indeed muffled, but it was still plenty loud enough for her in the room. The smell of cordite stung her nostrils. She liked the smell.

"Again. Keep shooting."

Monika fired the remainder of the clip. Most of the rounds punched randomly through the silhouette.

"Not too bad," Ludwig said.

"Shit," the Frenchman muttered.

Monika stared at the silhouette, a faint smile playing up the corners of her mouth. She had shown that bastard Frenchman.

Someone plucked the gun out of her hands. Both men walked to her front.

"So you want to join us then," Ludwig said more than asked.

"Yes."

"My friend here thinks you are a child."

"He has said that many times already."

"Children do not kill. Could you kill someone?"

Monika thought of her father. "Yes."

"Women and children?"

"Of course."

"That's talk," the Frenchman growled.

"Yes, Phillipe, I'm inclined to agree with you," Ludwig said, looking down at the young, pretty woman before him.

Ludwig bent down to where he could look Monika in the eyes. She looked him full in the face for the first time. He had pale blue eyes, which pierced her from behind his mask. "Are you ready to commit?" he asked her.

"Yes."

Phillipe motioned at the doorway from which they had entered ten minutes before. "Bring him in!" he snapped.

After a moment, the door banged open, and two figures with ski masks dragged in a slumped, beaten man. He was young, that much Monika could tell, but he had been horribly beaten around the face, and his short brown hair was soaked with blood from the knuckle cuts lacerating his scalp, lips, and eyebrows. Monika watched them drag him to the chair by the silhouette, where he was shoved down and handcuffed to the armrests.

"This man," Ludwig began, "belongs to the *Polizei*. He is thirty years old, but he looks young enough to pass for a man ten years younger. You may have seen him before; he was a student at the University."

Monika studied his face. *Polizei,* she thought. *An infiltrator and a liar.*

A pig.

"He is, in fact, an informer for his narcotics squad. As we have connections in that form of profit, he infiltrated one of our cells and turned them in. That cell was captured by the police, and our Latino friends promptly deserted us. Fortunately, the cell members do not know our hierarchy. We are very careful about those things. We have to be careful to survive, Monika."

Monika stared up at Ludwig. She rather liked him, certainly more so than the pig Frenchman standing next to him.

"But to keep the authorities scared of us," Ludwig continued, "and to exact retribution from those who have harmed us, and to satisfy the desires of those in our hierachy, we must execute this man, and leave his body where it can be found by his kind. In that manner, our message to the authorities is driven home."

Monika began to realize what was expected of her.

"Now, this presents us with a unique situation on your part. You shall kill this man for us. To put it bluntly, before we can fully trust you and induct you into our organization, you must first demonstrate your willingness to kill and to follow orders. It is really the only way."

"This is *shit*, Ludwig," Phillipe sputtered. "She cannot do it."

Ludwig slapped a fresh clip in the Makarov and thrust the pistol into Monika's hands. "So let's see," he said. "If you do not shoot this man, then we will let you go, and you will forget tonight's events."

Monika contemplated Ludwig's glittering blue eyes as they locked onto hers from behind the mask. She wasn't stupid. This was the ultimate test indeed. If she didn't shoot the man in front of her, she would surely be executed herself. She had already seen and heard too much.

The two who had brought in the victim retreated to the rear of the room. The beaten man in the chair looked up at Monika, too broken to say anything. Instead, he silently pleaded at her with his soft, doe-brown eyes. A helpless keening began in his throat.

Monika raised the gun, cold and numb. She conjured up the image of her father, remembering the pain, the humiliation, the shame he had caused her, and for an instant, the young face before her was transformed into a thick grizzled one with a double chin and cruel, porcine eyes squinting at her beneath bushy black eyebrows. She centered the front sight post of her pistol on her father's nose. . . .

She fired and the face exploded and the chair blew backwards, toppling over. Taking a step forward, Monika fired again into the dead man's body. And again and again and again until her clip was empty.

Then silence. A silence that grew with time and the smell of cordite and the echoes of the clanging receiver ringing in Monika Stern's ears. She remembered the recoil of the pistol in her hands as she fired the gun. She remembered the thunk of 9-millimeter lead rounds entering the Polizei pig's body that was supine and twisted before her, pools of blood staining the concrete floor and crimson rivulets running toward a crack where the floor met the wall behind him.

Monika Stern stood up and looked down at her pistol.

And then she realized that she had liked it.

June 1982

It was a circuitous route that began in Zurich and ended in Aden, South Yemen. In between were layovers in Athens, Kenya, and finally, Beirut. In Beirut, she spent a week with a weapons expert who gave her a crash course in basic demolitions, the Kalashnikov assault rifle, and a multitude of Czech submachine guns. After Beirut, she was put on a plane to Aden, the capital of South Yemen.

Located on the southern tip of the Arabian Peninsula, the People's Democratic Republic of Yemen, as it was called, was a Soviet satellite long in the service of insurgents, guerrillas, and terrorists worldwide. Their training center helped keep their poor economy afloat through Warsaw Pact trade and military support during the seventies and early eighties. Aden constituted the terrorist training headquarters for the PFLP—the Popular Front for the Liberation of Palestine. International instructors and trainers from all over the world, East Germans, Cubans, and terror cell leaders in refuge, flocked there to breed and cultivate their philosophies, tactics, and techniques.

Their students came to that barren, salt-flat desert and eroded mountain coastal land to learn as much as they could: South Moluccans from Holland, the earlier Baader-Meinhof gang members and their future generations as manifested in Germany's Red Army Faction, Italy's Red Brigades, South Americans, Canadians, Spanish Basque terrorists, Irish Provisionals—even some Americans from the Weather Underground and the Black Panthers in the early seventies—they all made their pilgrimage to Aden.

The Soviets supported the South Yemenis through this fifth-column trade; they supplied them for their continual war with tiny Oman, fighting for a sea of oil underneath the Arabian Penninsula that South Yemen—a country the size of Nevada with a population little more than two million—had not been blessed with. South Yemen did control the southern approaches to Bab el Mandeb, linking the Red Sea to the Gulf of Aden, one of the world's most active shipping lanes. The Soviets knew this, hence their support. But in return for their help, South Yemen had to provide a haven and training center for Marxist-Leninist progeny in Aden.

When Monika Stern stepped off the plane in Aden, she was greeted by her new mentor.

Siegfried.

The bright-eyed Aryan with wild blond hair and a natural grace in his stride took her to the training headquarters twenty kilometers outside the capital. Siegfried was Monika's sponsor, Siegfried was the primary martial-arts instructor, Siegfried was her guide and mentor from the new-generation Red Army Faction (RAF), whose exploits in the late seventies were virtually destroyed by Germany's GSG9 counterterrorist unit.

Siegfried gave Monika her orientation during the first few days of the camp. Airstrips, Soviet Hind-24 helicopters, firing ranges, demolitions ranges. Cubans, Russians, Libyans, North Koreans. Her training class was an international mixture of fifteen students pooled from a revolving series of European recruits. At night, there was even a separate club for Monika and other Western European terrorists, whose terrorist hierachy paid the Palestinian cadre in Aden well. Hashish and sex were basically their only form of recreation during the brutal training curriculum. But for Monika Stern, there were only long bouts of celibacy, or an infrequent partner of one gender or the other. Not even Siegfried could make love to her, so he gave up trying. Monika's relationship with him was only as mentor to student, her shell hard and unyielding.

Monika was a privileged trainee, but she underwent the same training as the rest of her compadres—demolitions and light weapons at first.

She marched many kilometers through the desert with a forty-pound rucksack on her back for the toughening drills to pass the initial physical screening. She learned a myriad of demolitions techniques, whether mixing soap flakes and gasoline together in a wine bottle for a Molotov cocktail firebomb, or rigging suitcases laden with plastic explosive and setting them off by remote radio transmissions. She learned to send and receive code, encrypt and decrypt messages, forge documents, set up clandestine communications by using dead-letter drops, mix minute secretions of chemicals in vitamins for instantaneous death, how to kill with a knife, a garrote, a pencil, a razor. . . .

When her depth of knowledge in martial arts was discovered by Siegfried, Monika gained stature as his assistant trainer. There, Monika honed her skills to adopt the killing form that another instructor in that department taught.

That instructor was a Russian, but he never talked about himself. It was rumored in the camp that he was a senior sergeant in the Soviet Spetznaz forces, elite counterparts to the American Special Forces, British Special Air Service, and German GSG9. Known simply as Viktor, he taught them how to deliver crushing blows to the larynx, how to use objects—

everyday objects such as a fountain pen, a rolled-up magazine, or a broken bottle—to deliver paralyzing, killing blows, or at least blows that could cripple and wound for the coup de grace to follow.

And there were "training aids" for the budding martial artists, prisoners from the Siberian gulags. Eastern European dissidents never lasted long in Aden.

She learned about discipline within the organization of a secret net, how an entire underground consisted of an auxiliary that supplied logistics or safe houses in support of certain personnel with the right code delivered at their message site. The action people themselves, Monika learned, were divided into four- and five-person cells, so that if one person was compromised, they could only be forced to finger a few comrades. No one knew the ultimate leader, or the hierarchy thereof; that would be disastrous upon compromise.

Always an attractive woman, Monika Stern also discovered how to make herself plain, ordinary. A chameleon's instinct was paramount in concealing her identity during an operation. That instinct, the role-playing and self-reliance she had always depended upon, was brought to the fore during the disguise phase of her training.

Monika Stern learned. She learned for over six months. She knew now how to handle a Browning Hi-Power or a Makarov with deadly accuracy, how to treat it as an extension of her index finger. She knew the techniques of assassination and interrogation. She knew everything that could possibly have been crammed inside her over a summer in the blazing hell of South Yemen. She now knew the basics.

At the end of that time, she returned to Munich, tanned, tough, hardened.

And resolute. She had found her purpose in life.

In the years that followed, Monika continued her enrollment at the Free University of Munich. She continued to work at the bookstore, a haven for messages and her contacts. The RAF's high command took note of her potential and kept her out of most operations for more important usage later on. She did, however, continue training in the summertime, returning to South Yemen the next summer for her second cycle of guerrilla warfare training. The third year, she received urban training in the streets of Beirut.

By her last year in the Free University of Munich, she was

ready. She had obtained the higher education she had always sought.

As Monika Stern's jet started its downward descent into Athens, the Lufthansa A-300 she rode was buffeted by the clouds covering the ceiling that day. It woke her up.

At thirty, she had seen much; she had traveled and killed and manipulated. And she had led. After eleven years, she was now a leader in the RAF, and she had a mission. One that brought her back to the place she had left so long ago. Like a student visiting the school of her childhood, Monika Stern came home to Aden.

Blasted Aden, its countryside denuded of anything beautiful or refined. Nothing but erosion and saltwater swamps along the coast; rocky, barren mountains inland.

But she was used to it all. The years had taught her to become used to the no-notice uprooting her life-style warranted. Inge, Ludwig, and the others in her cell back in Munich would be relieved to go into deep cover while she gathered her orders. Her new orders might not even demand their services. Who could say? Anything could happen. It suited her fine.

Half an hour later in the Athens airport, she booked a pre-paid flight to Beirut, and three hours after that she landed there.

And the following day, she flew the final leg of her journey to Aden, arriving at the weathered, untidy airport in a decrepit and barely serviceable Boeing 707.

Where she met her new team.

Chapter Six

Tulsa, Oklahoma

A late-model black Bronco glided noiselessly through the carefully landscaped gateway of the Farm Hills Cemetery in Tulsa, Oklahoma. At the wheel, behind its mirror-tinted windshield and side windows, was Wayne MacIntyre.

He had taken time off from his island thirty-five stories up at the top of the Tulsa skyline where his offices overwatched the epicenter of the Oklahoma oil industry. He had been back to work for a month now since his son David's terrorist ordeal at JFK Airport, but today he needed time. Work was good for the soul, work let one relieve one's mind of screaming, unbearable agony, and gently eased one back into the routine of life. But now, now was the time for Wayne MacIntyre to discuss things with his wife about David, how he was doing back at his boarding school in Maryland, how he was getting along in therapy.

He still talked things over with Maria. It helped him clear his head.

MacIntyre steered his Bronco slowly toward his wife's and eldest son's plot that crested a gently sloping hill at the back far reaches of Farm Hills. MacIntyre had the window down so he could breathe in the mild mid-fifties air with his left arm hanging out as he drove. It was beginner's spring, the time of year Wayne MacIntyre enjoyed the most. The bass were biting, and the rivers were up, just right for shooting rapids in that brand new kevlar canoe he and David had picked out just before Christmas. . . .

It was a separate plot; there were very few other gravestones near the MacIntyre family. It was shady and cool, at least ten degrees cooler here than anywhere else, because a huge elm with draping branches blocked the sun overhead. Now, at four o'clock in the afternoon, long shadows already crept downhill toward the rest of the cemetery. Wayne MacIntyre parked the Bronco on the gravel driveway. After a moment, he slowly got out.

He stood there, letting the late afternoon sun warm the back of his neck. The Levi's and Tony Lama boots on his feet felt one hell of a lot more comfortable than the charcoal-gray three-piece suit and starched white shirt with accompanying red tie he normally wore in the office. He removed his Stetson and placed it thoughtfully on the driver's seat of his Bronco. He approached the two marble headstones underneath the elm. He stopped. Stared at them.

Then, Wayne MacIntyre stuck his thumbs in the belt loops of his Levi's, swallowed, and the movie reels began to roll.

Tenkiller Lake, three years ago. Donny looking a little haggard and thin. Matt, a first lieutenant on leave fresh back from his first overseas tour in Korea. David, just starting junior high.

The boys were driving the boat with the twin 150-horse Mercs. Donny was at the throttle, and MacIntyre had been water-skiing in tandem with his wife. The office separations had taken their toll in the parental-supervision department. The night before he'd caught Donny with a crack pipe.

MacIntyre returned to the Bronco and swung open the tailgate. Reaching inside, he grabbed two oak saplings, still bound and potted with plastic around their roots. Someday they would rival the elm behind the headstones in height, branches, leaves . . . they would contribute to the soft gentility the place deserved.

After depositing the saplings by the tombstones, MacIntyre went back to his truck for the shovel. He felt a slight ache in his shoulder where a Chicom bullet had splintered his shoulder blade in Korea. It was always there, that slight, persistent pain.

Splash! He remembered how he'd cartwheeled into the water when his skis had crossed at the tips, and how the tow rope had wrenched his shoulder out of socket, because Donny was just going too goddam fast. The pain was unbearable, and it it hadn't been for the life preserver he wore—

Goddammit, Donny, slow the boat down!

MacIntyre cleared his eyes, shook his head, squinted through the lake water that had smashed into them from the fall. Donny had to have been going at least forty miles an hour. It was that damn dope. Not only did he have a college dropout for a son, but a whacked-out doper as well. He should have sent him to that clinic.

Where's Maria?

Maria!

There, waving! Only fifty, seventy-five feet away. You okay, sweetheart? Good. MacIntyre allowed himself the luxury of a groan, as he tried to pull his arm back into its socket. Then he heard gunning boat engines.

Donny?

There, circling back around.

Too fast! Donny! Slow Down!

He saw the other boys fighting with him at the wheel, Donny shrugging then off.

The boat was headed directly for Maria.

MacIntyre's shovel bit into the earth next to his wife's grave. He enjoyed manual labor. He liked digging and growing things, tilling the yearly garden Maria had always insisted upon . . . but no, there were no more gardens to dig. Maria had been gone for the past three years now.

MacIntyre jammed his shovel into the dirt and felt the bite of its rough, wooden handle punish his office executive palms, palms that were once roughnecker's palms, calloused and hard; he slammed his foot into action for that extra deep bite of the blade into the ground and greeted the stars shooting up his calf and shin, because he felt like he wanted a little physical pain right now.

The boat closed in.

Donny! MacIntyre screamed, waving his good arm, ignoring the pain in his other, seeing his wife waving at Donny as he sped toward them.

The glare. The water was like a mirror, the sun low, in Donny's eyes. He couldn't see! NO!

Forty feet, thirty-five. MacIntyre's arms chopped weakly at the water as he tried to swim toward his wife.

The twin 150-horse Mercs howled toward them, roaring louder, filling his senses.

Maria turned around in the water, eyes flashing wildly for her husband, eyes filled with panic.

MacIntyre remembered how she'd mouthed his name before Donny hit her.

MacIntyre planted the sapling into the hole he'd dug and then filled it up. He crossed over to Donny's grave and started digging there. Donny would have been thirty-two this year. Maybe he would have gotten over his cocaine habit somehow, if it hadn't have been for the accident, the grief that followed, that soul-crushing grief: the guilt, the tears and depression that only prescription drugs could numb.

The boat swerved wildly at the last possible moment, throwing the other boys clear, Donny somehow hanging on to the steering wheel. The sun's setting rays turned the Kingfisher's hull a bloody sunset red as Donny nearly overturned it, trying to avoid killing his mother.

Horrified, MacIntyre saw how the propellors gleamed fish-belly white, like sharks' teeth churning the water, as the twin Mercs bore down on his wife's head.

He screamed.

They found Donny a month later in his room, a crack pipe in one hand and a .357 in the other. The ceiling was a bloody mess.

MacIntyre drove the blade of his shovel deeply into the ground.

After planting the second sapling, he returned to his Bronco. The six-pack of Coor's Silver Bullets he'd brought to the cemetery was therapy too. Part of it, anyway.

MacIntyre grabbed the six-pack waiting for him and walked back to the headstones. He stared at the engraving on the marble for a moment, then sat down against the trunk of the elm shading his wife's and eldest son's graves.

He unhooked one of the tall boys from its plastic six-pack ring and popped open the top. Lifting it to his lips, he studied the cold beads of condensation dripping down the side of the can as he guzzled it. He set the beer down beside him and burped. Thoughtfully, he pulled out a can of Copenhagen from his jeans' back pocket, thumped the contents to one side, then pinched a dip from it and stuck the finely ground tobacco into his lower lip. He popped open another beer, and looked at the graves again, this time feeling a little more numb. The twin saplings looked nice, flanking them.

"Maria," he mumbled, "David's all right now. He was hurt

real bad, but I put him in a new boarding school and his arm is doing okay. . . ."

An hour later, as the sun set, a lone rifleman with sunglasses and a young, athletic frame came out of the woods and drove Wayne MacIntyre home

All that was left on the MacIntyre plot was a plastic six-pack ring holder.

A three-piece-suited Wayne MacIntyre leaned forward at his desk, depressed a button on his intercom, and said, "Sally, please send Mr. Whitehead in."

Seconds later, a tall, lanky man with black hair sweeping down his forehead walked inside the office. He was in his forties, but like his employer, had kept himself fit. His high cheekbones, dark skin, and broad nose, coupled with a sinewy, tough frame, bore testament to the Choctaw legacy his grandmother and parents had passed on to him. Charlie Whitehead was a Choctaw-Scots blend, in true Oklahoman fashion, and the best damned security man Wayne MacIntyre had working for him, because he was also an ex-Special Forces officer.

"Sir," Whitehead said, standing in front of MacIntyre's desk.

"When're you gonna quit calling me 'sir' like that, Charlie? Ain't no goddam *sir*. Used to work for a living, you know."

Charlie Whitehead grinned at his boss. He liked Wayne MacIntyre. The retired Special Forces major with over three tours in Vietnam fully appreciated and respected his employer's service with the 9th Infantry in Korea. MacIntyre must have been one hell of an NCO then.

"Habit, *sir*. Can't seem to break it, *sir*."

"Sit down, Charlie, you cocky sonofabitch. Wanna cigar?"

"Thank you." Whitehead reached out for one of the prized Havanas MacIntyre was always handing out.

"How's Janice?"

"Fine, sir, just fine."

"And those boys of yours?"

"Phillip just got that Sooner football scholarship—" Whitehead began, jubilant, until he remembered what had happened to MacIntyre's youngest son. "Why, everyone's just fine, Mr. MacIntyre," he ended, on a solemn note.

"Well, that's great!"

Whitehead looked up. *Enthusiasm,* he noted. *He's keeping up well.*

"You know, now, you'll have to keep your boss in season tickets."

"Of course."

"And that Phillip'd better get the Heisman four years from now."

Whitehead grinned slowly, compassionately. He knew the old man was in pain. *Damn those people who shot up his son.* "Sir, he's a good kid. He'll do well and I'm very proud of him."

"I know you are, Charlie," MacIntyre agreed. He gazed through the window at his side, studying the Tulsa Oilers stadium below his perch in Tulsa's stratosphere. "I know you are," he repeated, quieter. "I'm proud of my boys too." MacIntyre rose abruptly from his desk and clapped a hand on his chief of security's back. "Charlie," he began, "there's something we've got to do. It's going to take a lot of time and a lot of help and total secrecy on your part."

MacIntyre walked toward the window, studying Tulsa, Oklahoma, at his feet. It was a clean town, a new town, a town that had survived the rise and fall of the oil market over the years. He pulled a cigar out of his shirt pocket. Whitehead met him at the window, and together, they lit their cigars, smoking for a moment without saying anything. MacIntyre walked back to his desk and pulled a folder out of one of the drawers. He opened it up and spread it over top of the desk.

"Take a look at this."

Whitehead took a quick glance and saw that MacIntyre had several solicitations from private security organizations for their services. At his boss's request, he had forwarded them to the Old Man for his review. He hadn't thought MacIntyre was keeping any of them.

"Why do they send us these things when they know I already employ you and over a hundred security men throughout Dustbowl?"

Whitehead recognized several names on the letterheads from his days in the service. They were men from Special Forces, the Rangers, operators from Delta. Some were good. Some were career-minded opportunists, the way they'd been on active duty. Some talked a good line but were basically incompetent. Whitehead wasn't impressed. "These guys are offering executive protection, Boss," he answered. "Anything you want: armor-plated cars, snipers, courses in defensive driving, that sort of thing."

"But you already do that for me and all my key execs throughout Dustbowl."

"Right. Security's a big business these days. They want your business, Boss. They will try to sell you on gadgetry and training. Some of them are good, but most of them will take advantage of you."

MacIntyre knocked ashes into an overflowing ashtray filled with stubs. "Charlie, I want to run something by you. I've been given tacit approval by the Administration to run my own covert counterterrorist operations. They feel I have enough money, business contacts, and motivation to do it."

Whitehead felt his mouth hang open. *He'd said it, just like that.*

"What do *you* think?"

"Wayne, I think it's something that would ultimately burn you and anyone else involved."

"Well . . . thank you for being up front."

"Who in the government?"

"Lawson." MacIntyre held no secrets from Charlie Whitehead.

Whitehead blinked. He should have known. It made sense. The Vice President of the United States and his boss were friends from way back. "What about that mess in '87, sir, the Iran-Contra affair? It ruined a good part of that Administration's credibility. It was Watergate all over again. The same could happen to you, if you fronted their deniable operations."

"I know." MacIntyre walked over to the bar, a richly upholstered black leather bar on the far side of his executive suite. "Jim Beam or J. D. Black Label, Charlie?"

"I'll take the Black Label. On the rocks."

"Believe I'll have the same." MacIntyre poured the drinks and brought them back to the window, where they both sipped them quietly, staring out, reflecting on what was being suggested.

"You know," Whitehead said, "a small, highly compartmentalized unit—"

"Compartmentalized?"

"A five- or a six-man unit working for us with no one else knowing of their existence could conduct special operations for what you have in mind. The question is, Mr. MacIntyre, exactly what *do* you have in mind? What did you and the Vice President discuss?"

"Counterterrorism."

"The Army and FBI already have a grip on that."

"They don't," MacIntyre said flatly. "They simply fucking don't. Look at us, Charlie. America's an open society. We have laws that prohibit the military from taking action within our country's borders. That's the FBI's job. And they are too small to look after every major corporation or college or airport or whatever the target may be in this country to prevent the slaughter that crippled my son and killed Alex Kurakis at JFK last month."

"Sounds like you have your mind made up about this thing."

Returning to his desk, MacIntyre slumped back in his chair, a veil cast over his face. "Were you ever in the Boy Scouts, Charlie?"

Whitehead blinked. The Boy Scouts? Hell, no, for what it was worth. He'd grown up just pretty damned poor in Clayton, Oklahoma, down in the southeast part of the state, and he couldn't afford the uniforms and so on. "No, sir," he said.

"Neither was I. Couldn't afford the uniforms. But I believe in them. Know why?"

"Wayne, what does this have to do with counterterrorism?"

"It has to do with David making Eagle Scout last year. Just before he was promoted, he had to earn his citizenship merit badge. He'd been studying the Declaration of Independence in his eighth-grade history class, and he had read that document very carefully, and wrote an essay on what it meant. He came into my den one day back at the house, excited as hell. Told me that he'd read it word for word, and wasn't it neat . . . that . . ."

Whitehead had listened to MacIntyre's voice go from commanding and confident to subdued and broken. He averted his eyes as MacIntyre continued on with quiet tears running down his cheeks.

"He said," MacIntyre continued, drawing in his breath, "that the men who wrote the Declaration of Independence had many legitimate grievances against the King of England, and that they were willing to forfeit their lives, their properties . . . their scared honor." MacIntyre glanced up at Whitehead. "How many times have you heard anybody talk about *honor*,

Charlie? David knew what honor was. He saved a baby's life at the risk of his own in that airport. He knew! Goddammit, I'm proud of him for it!"

Whitehead felt his own eyes grown warm. The Old Man had struck home. He watched MacIntyre get out of his seat and wipe his eyes with the back of his shirt sleeve and loosen the tie from around his neck. And he saw that the Old Man's eyes were gleaming with that MacIntyre look. A look of determination and a will to make things happen.

"*Balls,* Charlie! That boy of mine has bigger balls than most of the Congressmen who run this country. Eighty-five percent of those assholes—*eighty-five percent*—never spent a moment in the military. My generation fought in Korea; yours in Vietnam. Despite the political quagmire in which those wars were fought, Charlie, we served. We still *served.*

"Our leaders are weak. They lie. They're corrupt. Not all of them, mind you. There's still some men who believe in duty to their country on Capitol Hill instead of the usual blatant, bald-faced careerism, but they're precious few and far in between. On the other hand, there are those on the right who claim a 'higher morality,' as the Iran-Contra scandal proved. Well, shit, Charlie, where do you draw the line?" MacIntyre paused and looked steadily at the chief of security of Dustbowl Enterprises.

"I believe in my country, Charlie. Everything I've worked for today I got because of my own efforts and a belief in myself. I'm tired of our people fucking themselves and drugging themselves into oblivion. I'm tired of our children growing up illiterate and abused. And I'm tired of my countrymen being murdered in the name of some goddam revolutionary cause. I want to see the day when our children can grow up in safety and not have to worry about child-molesters, rapists, thugs . . . and terrorists. They're coming, Charlie. They're coming to our neighborhoods and airports to kill. We're going to be ready for them.

"And I'll tell you something else, my friend. I will lay my sacred honor and my Fortune-Fucking-Five-Hundred business down on the line to make a reaction force happen."

MacIntyre paused and caught his breath. He swirled the ice cubes in his shot glass and drained his Black Label. Then, casting ice-cold eyes at his chief of security, he said in no uncertain terms: "I want a counterterrorist cell formed."

Charlie Whitehead blinked. He cleared his throat. Then he stood up from his seat and walked slowly over to Wayne MacIntyre. He held out his hand. "A man's honor today is something that usually stands alone, Wayne. But not this time. You can count on me."

CHAPTER SEVEN

Ft. Bragg, North Carolina

"What's it gonna be, Manny, .45-cal or 9-millimeter?" Matt MacIntyre opened up his tote bag resting on the shooter's bench and stared inside, trying to decide which pistol to shoot with today.

"Only one kind of round I prefer, *Dai-uy,* you know that."

"And the debate rages on between .45 and 9-mil. Knock-down power or more shots. What'll it be, what'll it be?"

"Way I figure it, if you know what you're doing, you ought to be able to take out your target with one, maybe two shots. Don't matter what kind of weapon you're shooting." Master Sergeant Timothy Manuel "Manny" Santo handed MacIntyre two clips. "I'll give you two seven-round clips to warm up with, *Dai-uy*; .45, of course." Then, the muscular black-haired man of medium height, wearing summer-weight BDUs, scuffed and worn jungle boots, and yellow tinted shooter's glasses on his acne-scarred face, clapped his hand on his ex-team leader's shoulder and added, "Then I'll show you how to *really* shoot."

"Bullshit," replied Matt MacIntyre, Captain, Operational Detachment A Team Commander. He stared at the silhouette posted twenty-five meters to his front. "So what do you want to put on this? I drink Coors, you know. I will send these *first* seven rounds downrange, all in the black, and all in the face." He glanced at Santo and gave him a cocky half-grin. "So what's it gonna be, my man?"

Santo snorted and pushed his beret up out of his eyes, letting it rest back on the crown of his head. Had any of Fort Bragg's post brass shown up just then, he would have received a stinging lecture about how Special Forces personnel were absolutely *not* supposed to push their headgear up on top of their heads like that.

"Case a beer, *Dai-uy*."

"You know, you wouldn't make that bet with Hanlon," MacIntyre grumbled.

"Shit," Santo replied, grinning. "Randy Hanlon may be good, but he's no match—"

MacIntyre arched an eyebrow at Santo. He'd quit talking in mid-sentence, and now the master sergeant's face was covered with a black look, his eyebrows creasing to furious, bushy points over his eyes.

"What's Sergeant Hanlon doing now?" MacIntyre relaxed his stance and kept his pistol pointed up in the air. He'd just come back from home, and the situation with his erstwhile team senior engineer sergeant had occurred while he was back in Oklahoma.

"He's pushing guns over at Jim's Pawn Shop. They've always wanted him. Thought you knew."

"No, I didn't. Just got back from leave last week." Now, a black look came over MacIntyre's face and he resumed his shooter's stance.

Santo watched MacIntyre fire in rapid succession, his Colt .45 kicking with the sharp recoil from each of his seven shots. He took off his shooter's glasses when MacIntyre was finished and squinted his eyes at the target.

"Jesus," Santo swore, taking his eyes off the silhouette and looking back at MacIntyre. "You done good there."

MacIntyre's eyes lit up. "How good?"

"You say you drink Coors?"

"That's right," MacIntyre said, his mood swinging back for the better. Maybe this would be the first time he'd outshoot Santo after all. He'd been nervous, but was damned careful not to show it.

"Let's get a closer look," Santo said.

They paused for a moment until the other shooters on line were finished. There were only two others on the range with them. Santo liked McKellar's Lodge. It was located about two miles outside the 82nd Airborne Division area on the western side of Fort Bragg. McKellar's Lodge was the post's hunting lodge and family picnic area, nestled up on top of a pine-tree-covered hill next to a small lake. You could sign out a canoe, fish, or sign up for hunting deer in designated areas on the reservation; it was great for outdoorsmen. But Santo liked the range the best. You could shoot trap or black powder if you were into that. He preferred to shoot his pistols. That was his hobby. At any rate, McKellar's Lodge was a great place to go in the late afternoon to send a few rounds downrange and throw a beer down your neck before going home.

"Okay, the line's clear," MacIntyre announced, seeing that the two muzzle-loader shooters a few benches to their left were finished.

Santo and MacIntyre walked slowly toward the second line of postholes, where they had stapled their target silhouette against a post and stuck it in the hole earlier. Upon reaching it, they counted three rounds in a tight shot group in the center of the silhouette's head, two rounds spread an inch apart in the forehead region, and one round just barely touching the black at the top of the head.

"Fuck," MacIntyre breathed.

Santo tried to keep a serious face. "Hey, you still done pretty good."

"Yeah, but I shot too high with that last round."

"Ain't over yet, *Dai-uy.*"

"I know what's coming."

After marking the bullet holes with masking tape so as not to mix Santo's rounds up with MacIntyre's when he shot next, they walked back to the firing line.

Fortunately, the other two shooters on the firing line were still fiddling around with their black-powder Hawken .50-caliber rifles. That was good, since it gave Santo time enough to plug all seven of his shots into his silhouette before they were ready to resume their firing. Within minutes of inspecting MacIntyre's shot group, they were back out looking at Santo's.

"Man," MacIntyre said softly, poking his finger all the way through the silhouette's face and wiggling it around. All seven of Santo's shots were neatly clustered in the nose region, and the resulting hole was big enough to stick his fist through.

"I'm a Bud man myself, *Dai-uy,*" Santo chuckled. "Should'a known. Should'a known."

"Get bent."

"That's no way for an officer to talk."

"Get bent."

Chuckling, they walked back to the firing line, Santo limping as they went. MacIntyre noticed the limp and quit laughing. Not abruptly, but the mood shifted toward the down side.

"How's the leg doing, Manny?" he asked, refilling his clip with more ammunition.

"Ah, Christ, it's just fine. But they still won't take me off profile."

Profile. It meant that Master Sergeant Timothy "Manny" Santo was considered undeployable because he had a permanent limp from the round he'd caught in the calf muscle of his right leg when he and his team had taken down a KGB drug operation in New Mexico the previous year. Or rather, the newspapers had called it a drug operation.

And who were the players in that particular game of secrets, drugs, and spies? Santo and MacIntyre's A team and the Spetsnaz team they combated. Elite Cold Warriors, fighting a conflict the newspapers said was over.

During the final encounter with the Soviets at their safe house, Santo had caught a round in the lower calf, which had partially severed his Achilles tendon. He hadn't walked the same since, and had been "awarded" a permanent profile to go along with his classified Silver Star.

Profile. A profile was a slip of paper signed by the Group Surgeon that said you were only allowed to run so much or do so many pushups or whatever, but in any case, it dictated exactly how much physical activity you were allowed to conduct after an injury. A *permanent* profile was a kiss of death career-wise if you were in Special Forces, where you had to be physically ready to deploy anywhere at any time.

"Why won't they take you off profile?" MacIntyre asked Santo as they reloaded their pistol clips. "I mean, you've healed up for the most part."

"You tell me, Matt," Santo replied. "I ruck every day and run. Hell, you've seen me out at the mata-mile area."

MacIntyre indeed had. When he and his team, on Tuesdays and Thursdays, shrugged on their rucksacks loaded with fifty- and sixty-pound sandbags, then proceeded to take the long route on the cross-country track post engineers had constructed in the early sixties near Fort Bragg's Smoke Bomb Hill— known as the mata-mile—they had often run across Santo, a man who was hard enough to make the kind of physical comeback most lesser men who had sustained an Achilles tendon injury would not have dared attempt. They would simply have been complacent enough to retire quietly with their leg brace and work for the Postal Service, or with Fort Bragg's civil service, handing out canteens and shelter halves and tent pegs to incoming troops at the Main Post Quartermaster building.

"What'd the Group Surgeon say?"

"That pussy," Santo snorted. "He's not like Doc Bender, the last one. This new guy says that once a P-3 profile's been put in your medical records, you can never have it removed. I think it's horseshit."

"That can't be right! Christ, look at you. You're not hurting anymore."

"And the wheels of bureaucracy grind on. Save it, *Dai-uy*. Been thinking about getting out anyway."

MacIntyre jammed a loaded .45 clip into his pistol and waited for Santo to do the same. Seconds later, they were both blazing away at the silhouette, letting the shooters' therapy do its work. Afterwards, they loaded up two more clips and repeated the process.

"Jim's Pawn Shop, huh?" MacIntyre asked Santo, thinking again about Hanlon. The old team had split up. CW3 Wintz Maslow had retired and was living out in New Mexico; Master Sergeant Manny Santo was washed up where he was at the Group S-3 shop; he himself was just biding time until reporting for an overseas assignment in Germany . . . and Sergeant First Class Randy Hanlon had just been chaptered out of the Army in disgrace.

"So Hanlon's selling guns now for a living," MacIntyre said wistfully, stating a fact rather than asking a question. Jim's was known throughout the Carolinas for its vast selection of new and second-hand guns, any kind of guns. Shotguns, assault rifles, semi-auto submachine guns and pistols; automatics and revolvers. If it was made, Jim's had it. And the local resident shooter expert, a man who had been the honor graduate of every military training course he'd attended in the Army; a man who had saved his team's lives down on that classified mission in New Mexico; a man who had blown dope and was thrown out of Group for it; that man, SFC Randy Hanlon, now worked at Jim's Pawn Shop as a civilian.

"Yeah, he's selling guns," Santo replied. "Doing a great job too. But you know and I know, and above all *Randy* knows, that he fucked up and that's why he's pushing pistols at Jim's and not here." Santo glanced at his feet. "What a goddam waste," he muttered. He tried to think of a way to change the subject. "Here, look at what I brought along," he said, pulling a kitchen timer out of the paper sack of ammo and sundries he'd brought along.

"So?" MacIntyre watched Santo wind the second timer back to five seconds and hold it there.

"Hold your weapon at the waist level. This is for quick fire." Santo held the timer up. "When I say go, immediately raise your .45 and start shooting. Don't aim, just point."

"Okay." MacIntyre grinned, warming up to the challenge. He liked challenges. *"Go!"*

Santo released the timer and five seconds later, it rang out. MacIntyre had shot all seven rounds in less than four. Moments later, they walked downrange to look at his shot group. They were all in the head.

Santo grinned at MacIntyre. "You done good."

"Couldn't have a better instructor," MacIntyre said happily. He clapped his arm around his ex-team sergeant's shoulders. "C'mon, I owe you a beer."

"You don't want to shoot anymore?"

"Nah."

They walked back to their equipment by the shooting bench and started to wipe their pistols down, anticipating the cold ones to be guzzled in McKellar's Lodge's rustic, beaten-up lounge.

"Tell you what," MacIntyre said, "I've done all the shooting I want today. I'll go back and order the burgers and fries, and then holler at you when it's ready."

"Whatever turns you on, Boss. I could send a few more rounds downrange, now that you mention it."

MacIntyre put his pistol and gear inside his camouflaged tote bag and then walked back to his car behind the range shack and put it all in the trunk. It was a charcoal-gray, brand-new RX-7. Being a single captain did have its advantages in the Special Forces. And the RX was his favorite toy next only to his collection of guns. "Be back in a few minutes," MacIntyre called out to Santo, who was about to resume firing. Santo waved back at him and MacIntyre walked off the range and across the street to the Lodge. Then Santo raised his .45 up to the silhouette at the same time a Chevy Blazer pulled up to the parking area MacIntyre had just left.

By the time Santo had finished rapid-firing another seven-shot clip, a tall, lanky black-haired man with a dark Choctaw face had climbed out of the Blazer. He was wearing dark sunglasses, and his hair was long and cut like a civilian's, brushing past the tops of his ears. The man knew his hair set him apart, and here, at Fort Bragg, he was reminded of how much a civilian he had become. Nevertheless, he felt as if he'd come home. The man was a civilian now, but once, long ago, he'd been assigned to Fort Bragg as a Green Beret, honing his shooting skills out here at McKellar's Lodge with his own ammo, his own pistol, and on his own time. Why? Because he'd been a professional, and professionals kept up on their skills. Just like the senior Special Forces NCO in front of him was doing now.

The man unlocked the back of his blazer and pulled out an ancient blue-gray parachute kit bag, warming up to the smell of gun oil and the rustle of gunmetal inside. He locked the Blazer back up and approached the firing line, nostalgia now hitting him full force as sure as the smell of cordite filtered through his nostrils. He had indeed come home.

He hoped the Beret shooting in front of him now was the man he'd flown all the way out from Tulsa, Oklahoma, to find.

Santo left the firing line to put up a fresh silhouette. When he had finished stapling it over the old one and started walking back to the firing line, he found he had a visitor at the shooter's bench next to his—a civilian, dressed in designer blue jeans, lizard-skin boots, and a brown plaid Western shirt. Tall, sunglasses, lanky black hair, Indian features—Santo was reminded of someone.

"Nice day for shooting," Santo said.

The visitor did not reply, just kind of nodded his head and went about the process of opening his pistol case and setting up ammunition boxes on his shooter's bench.

Santo arched an eyebrow his way. *I know this guy.* . . .

"Nice piece you have," he said, trying to strike up a conversation. He watched the civilian who once was not a civilian load up a Czech 9-millimeter CZ-75 automatic. It was a prized gun for those who could get them. The CZ-75 was reputed to be at least as good as a Browning Hi-Power, but could be bought for half the price—if it could be found.

The civilian said nothing, grunted noncommittally.

Santo snorted. *Dour sonofabitch,* he thought. Deciding to ignore the civilian, he reset his timer and readied his pistol with both hands for another rapid-fire sequence. He blazed away, letting the pistol kick in his hands, but controlling it, making it work for him, not fighting it, but letting it point itself and then touching off round after round with the tip of his index finger.

The receiver clicked all the way back, his rounds spent. Santo paused, holding his weapon out, in his final moment of concentration after shooting his clip before setting the .45 down on the bench.

Shots rang out! Surprised, Santo turned his head and watched the newcomer spit sixteen rounds out of his 9-millimeter. But what was he shooting at? *I'll be a sonofa-bitch! My fucking target!*

"Hey, buddy, where do you get off—"

Looking at him the man grinned hugely and pulled off his sunglasses, his own 9-millimeter's receiver locked all the way back. "Always could outshoot your ass, Manny," he said, chuckling.

Santo picked his jaw up off the ground. "You son of a—for Chrisakes! Charlie Whitehead, you old buffalo-fucker, what the hell are you doing here!"

"My, my," Whitehead clucked. "Yep. You're the same ugly ol' foul-mouthed Cuban buck sergeant I always knew." Whitehead reached out and touched the three rockers underneath the stripes pinned on Santo's collar. "Made master sergeant, huh? Fuck up and move up, you know, like they say . . ."

Santo grabbed his very first team leader around the torso and lifted the big man completely off the ground. "How ya doin', Charlie?" he cried happily.

"Set me down, you ugly little man."

Grinning, Santo heaved Whitehead up and watched him crash heavily to the ground. "Hey, Charlie, hope I didn't get your pretty boots all dirty."

Whitehead picked himself up and brushed the dust off his clothes, grinning. "Careful," he said. "You could hurt an old man like me, you know."

"Shit, Charlie," Santo replied, finally sticking out his thick, blocky hand. Whitehead took it and tried not to grimace when Santo shook it. "I couldn't hurt an old fart like you."

They stood there, looking at each other for a few moments.

"What's it been, Manny, ten years?"

"Yeah, about that." Both of them automatically began reloading their clips.

"A lot can happen in ten years, you know."

"Why'd you ever get out, Charlie?"

"Wasn't getting any younger. I was lucky to be promoted to major during my last three years in Group."

"You were a company commander," Santo countered. "You could have stayed in and commanded a battalion. Hell, maybe even the Group by now."

"I had other reasons, Manny. Personal ones. On top of the situation in Group."

"You mean the politicking around? The social things you officers had to go to? Ass-kissing with Battalion?"

"You know better than that, Manny. There's enough politicking around in the NCO corps as well. No, this was all personal. Wanted to see my kids grow up in a place other than Fayetteville, North Carolina."

Santo grinned. Fayetteville was Fort Bragg's civilian home. Most of the troops had a better name for it, Fayette 'Nam. It had an endless array of pawnshops, bars, used-car lots, restaurants, and malls. "Can't really blame you there, Charlie."

"You could do the same."

"What's the job offer, Charlie? That's what this is all about, right?"

Whitehead's demeanor turned serious. "Thought I'd talk to you about it after dinner tonight. That is, if Sally's cooking is still as good as I remember it."

Santo's face clouded. There was no way Whitehead could have known that his wife and daughter had been killed by a drunk driver two years ago. He mentioned their passing in as few words as possible and tried not to stare at the dust coating his jungle boots.

"Sorry, Manny," Whitehead said, at a loss for anything else except that tired but sincere cliche. At the same time, he selfishly was glad something like that—death or divorce—hadn't torn his own family apart. Whitehead had been one of the lucky ones. His wife, Janice, had borne him two boys, and had done most of the raising before he'd gotten out ten years ago and retired. That was his personal reason for getting out. He'd owed it to Janice and he'd be damned if he'd miss out on his kids when they were teenagers. While you still had them . . . He thought of Santo's dead wife and daughter . . . of Wayne MacIntyre's ruined family . . .

"Then dinner's on me," he told Santo, trying to brighten up

the mood. "We'll go to The Barn tonight, if it's still around; is it?"

Santo's eyes lit up. The Barn was one of Fayetteville's premier steak and lobster places. First-class eating. "You got it, Boss. What time?"

"I'll meet you at Bennigan's for beer at 1730."

"*That* place?" Santo laughed. He'd been practically living there for the past year ever since being placed on profile. "Well, sure. But wait a minute. Come inside the lodge and let me buy you a burger. Got a buddy of mine waiting for me there. I want you to meet him."

"You got it. Could use a beer too."

They packed their gun bags and stored them inside their vehicles. Minutes later, they walked inside McKellar's Lodge.

"Manny, over here!" A voice and a wave. Santo saw MacIntyre sitting at the booth on the wall opposite from the bar. He guided Whitehead toward the booth.

Joining his ex-team leader, Santo saw MacIntyre's smile replaced by a look of recognition.

"*Dai-uy,* this is my old team leader from about ten, twelve years ago," Santo began, introducing Whitehead.

"Charlie."

"Matt."

"What's this?" Santo said, "You guys know—"

"You kidding?" Whitehead said, smiling sadly and sticking out his hand. "I used to take this kid hunting when his old man was off on business trips. . . ."

"What're you talking about?"

"Manny," MacIntyre informed, "Major Charlie Whitehead here works for my father."

Santo and Whitehead took their seats. After ordering for Whitehead, he said, "Your dad? What kind of work?"

"Security work, Manny," Charlie Whitehead answered, combing his lanky black hair toward the back of his head. "Damned important security work. I came to Bragg to do a little recruiting."

"So he's really going to do it," Matt MacIntyre said in a low voice. "I'm glad."

"Do what? What're you guys talking about?"

"Did he tell you?" Whitehead said to MacIntyre.

"I was in on the operation from the first. At least, when Dad was first approached about it."

Santo realized that they were speaking cryptically. "Why don't you guys tell me what's going on?"

MacIntyre bit deeply into his cheeseburger and avoided answering.

"Don't you know who Matt's father is?" Whitehead asked Santo. He glanced back at MacIntyre. "He's never told you?"

Santo regarded the red flush of MacIntyre's face. "He's never told any of us about his family. We'd always kind of wondered about that."

Whitehead excused himself to the latrine. It was better for Matt to explain. After Santo let Whitehead out of the booth, MacIntyre gulped down his first bite and took a slug out of his beer.

"So what gives, Boss?"

"Dustbowl Enterprises."

"Dustbowl Enterprises? What's . . . ? Hey, you're not talking about—"

"A three-billion-dollar corporation. My old man owns it. Wayne MacIntyre."

"*Wayne* MacIntyre?" Santo's eyes lit up. "*That's* your old man?"

"Yep."

Santo let out a low whistle. He remembered something he'd heard in the news about the mega-wealthy Wayne MacIntyre. Lately. *Of course!* The emergency leave the kid had gone on, the news . . . "Your little brother, he was hit in the JFK massacre, right? That's why you were on emergency leave, to be with your family, right?"

MacIntyre stared hard at his cheeseburger and felt his throat constrict. "Yeah."

"Jesus, Matt. I'm sorry. I didn't realize."

"It's okay, Manny. David's getting around now. His arm's a little messed up. . . ."

"We all wondered why you've been so quiet since you came back. I mean, you left so quick we knew you were on some type of emergency leave. You never talked about it—hell, you've never even talked about your family. Your father. Why?"

"C'mon, Manny. It's not too hard to figure out. Evidently, you know Charlie here," MacIntyre said, bypassing Santo's question. "Dad's sent him out to recruit."

Santo realized that MacIntyre wasn't going to talk much

about his father. Then he realized why: It was the same thing for junior officers whose fathers were generals. They were either always having to measure up, or they were getting some kind of special treatment, whether they deserved it or not. MacIntyre didn't want to play that game. "Recruit for what?" he asked.

Matt MacIntyre settled back into his seat and took another long pull from his beer.

"Were you a good history student in high school? College?"

"Cut the rhetoric and get to the point."

MacIntyre grinned, knowing that Santo had gotten his master's in international relations two years ago. "Okay, Professor. Remember during the Revolutionary War when no one could make their minds up about the American flag, and we went through a whole series of them?"

"Yeah, so?"

"One of those flags had a big old rattlesnake emblazoned on it, getting ready to strike, with a real pissed-off look on its face. The caption below read in big capital letters, 'DON'T TREAD ON ME.'"

"What's that got to do with Whitehead or your father?" Now it was Santo's turn to take a long pull from the frosty mug of Bud sitting before him.

"Charlie Whitehead's here to talk to you, Manny. I didn't know he was coming, but it makes perfect sense, and I think you're right for the job. If you'll take it, that is."

"Sounds like *you're* sold. Why aren't you on the team, whatever it is?"

"You know why."

"Lucky boy," Santo grumbled, envious of MacIntyre's pending reassignment to Germany.

Whitehead exited the latrine and rejoined them at the table. MacIntyre, finished with his cheeseburger, got up and said, "You two catch up on everything. I'm outta here."

Whitehead looked Santo hard in the eyes. "Let's go shoot a few more rounds, Manny. We don't have to talk over supper tonight."

"That's good, Charlie. Hell, I'm ready, you old buffalo-fucker."

"Case of beer this time?"

"Case a beer."

CHAPTER EIGHT

A Porsche 911 Carerra ripped through the last stoplight on Yadkin Road en route to a condominium development not far from Ft. Bragg. Seconds later, it pulled to a stop in the condominium's parking lot. Inside the 911, sixties-vintage rock and roll from the Alpine disk player blasted one of the owner's favorite golden oldies: "L.A. Woman," by Jim Morrison (his idol) and the Doors. As the owner parked his car, he tried his damnedest to keep his mood upbeat by jamming to the Mojo risin' before turning off the ignition.

This did not work. After a moment, Randy Hanlon wearily hauled his six-foot-two-inch frame out of the Porsche's driver's seat and pocketed his keys for what would surely be one of the last times. He gazed at his image where it was reflected off his condo's glass window and stood there for a moment, taking stock. He used to keep his thick, blond hair short, tapered and clipped on the back and sides of his head. Professional. Now it hung past the top of his ears. His clothes consisted of Polo and Calvin Klein, which he only used to wear on his nights out or during weekends. Now, he wore them full time. Staring down at his feet, he saw not the spit-shined jungle boots he used to wear around Group; Christ, no, now he wore Docksiders.

What the fuck had happened?

No, he didn't want to answer *that* question again. He still hadn't forgiven himself.

During any given noontime period, back when he was still in Group, Sergeant First Class Randall Hanlon could be found pumping max iron in the Tucker Field House Gym on Bragg. He had a physique men envied and women loved to brush against. Then there was his face. It used to piss him off that the guys on the team gave him so much shit about a face that belonged more on a Marlboro Man cigarette poster than a steely-eyed snake-eater type. And to top all that off, he was from California—San Francisco, no less. He'd even spent a couple years as an undergrad at Berkeley, and had he ever caught a continual ration of shit from his teammates about that. He'd put up with it all, no sweat. Randy Hanlon was not just another pretty-boy and all the razzing had been in good humor. But those days were over. Days when he had been a cash-paying *customer* at *Jim's*, not the resident civilian expert. Not the druggie who'd been kicked out of Group.

Why?

Because he'd been a dumb shit last Christmas.

As he walked through the foyer and into the den, he automatically reached up for the beret that used to perch on top of his head to place it on top of the TV . . . but then remembered he no longer wore his beret. When he'd been booted out in January, the clerks typing up his paperwork for the less-than-honorable discharge had also confirmed his disqualification for both Airborne and Special Forces status, relegating him back to leg status. A bar to reenlistment was the coup de grace.

No, he no longer wore a beret, and even if by some wild quirk he was allowed to reeneter the Army, he would not be allowed to return to Special Forces.

He remembered how it had happened. His newest girlfriend had taken him to a New Year's Eve party. She was a senior at the University of North Carolina at Chapel Hill. He'd driven her up to the party and, once there, she had passed him a smoking joint two hours after the party had started. Thoroughly drunk and like a fool, he'd taken two puffs, then realizing that it was a cardinal sin in Special Forces to partake of the weed, he had immediately crushed it inside the nearest available ashtray. He'd rushed to the bathroom to gargle and rinse out the marijuana taste.

Sergeant First Class Randy Hanlon prayed all weekend long that he would not be found out, should an unannounced spot-check be initiated within the unit. But even if one did happen, hell, he'd only taken two puffs. That wasn't going to show up in a piss test, was it?

His beret was hung on a frame occupying a spot on the wall,

a wall crowded with awards, certificates, and decorations from his service days.

He reached for his beret and put it on, snugging it down with the Group's flash over his left eye and canting the beret exactly one inch above his eyebrows. He nudged the award frame back in place, returning its plane to a horizontal position.

It was a Meritorious Service Medal. His eyes focused on a snapshot of his team, stuck in the lower left corner of the decoration's certificate. They were posing on a hillside in southern New Mexico, where they had deployed for desert training that year. They were all grinning, mustaches grown out, hair past regulation length, their boonie hats reflecting each individual's own deployment fashion statement. There was MacIntyre, Santo, himself, Maslow. The guys squatting in front were killed just a week after the picture was taken . . . Barkowitz and Greeley . . .

Hanlon was standing in the back, his arm draped around Santo's shoulders. He was grinning hugely at the camera, and looked as if he held the key to the biggest goddam beer box in the world.

Well, peacetime award or not, he'd been decorated for valor in combat the previous year while deployed to the White Sands Missile Range. The narrative on the MSM Hanlon now stared at was simply a cryptic, vague summary proclaiming glorious *administrative* feats of derring-do while temporarily assigned to the Drug Enforcement Administration.

Hanlon pulled off his green beret and hung it back on the top corner of the decoration's frame. It was time to fire up the grill. Santo was coming over tonight, just to shoot the shit. He'd stopped by Jim's earlier in the day for some small talk and they'd decided to have dinner.

Hanlon sighed. How much longer would his friends hang around—those on active duty? How much longer would it take for them to abandon the druggie who'd been kicked out of Group?

Santo knocked on the condo's door.

The door swung open. "Manny! C'mon in!"

Santo walked in. A cold Coors was thrust into his hand while Hanlon walked back out to the patio, where the T-bones alerting every dog's snout in the neighborhood were crackling on the barbecue.

"Want a job?"

Hanlon walked back inside, carrying a plate full of surface-blackened, raw meat. "What kind of job?"

"Security."

"Does it pay?"

"Enough to keep that bug-eyed monster of yours in the driveway."

"I don't know." Hanlon set the steaks on his table and proceeded to spear two baked potatoes with a fork in each hand. "Security, huh?"

"Remember ol' Charlie Whitehead?" Santo drained half the beer out of the shiny silver aluminum can he held.

"Yeah," Hanlon replied, gesturing toward the dinner table. "Wasn't he a company commander a few years ago in Group?"

"That's right." Santo sat down before his T-bone, his mouth watering. "Need some more brew."

Instantly, another silver bullet appeared before him. Hanlon rejoined him at the table.

"Whitehead's been lurking around, recruiting. I've agreed to see his boss, the guy who's doing the hiring."

"What kind of security job?"

Santo hesitated before answering. Whitehead had given him permission to find a good demo man cross-trained in communications and operations/intelligence for the team he had proposed forming. Hanlon was the man, and Whitehead would find out sooner or later why he was not still in the Army. Still, though, this was *not* the Army. This was the real world. Whitehead would take a man on with Santo's recommendation. But he had to be a man with no family. A man with drive and dedication, sure professionalism. And he had to have maturity. Did Randy have enough maturity?

He thought of a time when he had once let his head loll on one side of Hanlon's bull-corded neck while the big man had slung him in a fireman's carry, hauling his bloody, shot-up ass out the line of fire in the high desert of New Mexico. . . .

Yeah. He also remembered the time when they all stood inside a latrine, pissing into tiny specimen bottles, joking about what strange molecules the yooourine experts would find, and the unexpected look of panic and shame in Randy's eyes when he handed his bottle to the spec-four from headquarters.

"What kind of security job, Manny?" Hanlon garbled through a mouth full of T-bone.

"It's classified, Randy. It's also civilian. It has nothing to do with the government, that much I can tell you. I'm going to leave in a few days. If everything pans out, I'm putting in my papers. I'm going to spend the next weeks with Whitehead out in Oklahoma on some kind of orientation seminar for my final decision. We're going to be at a cattle ranch in the southeastern part of the state. Do you want to come?"

"My job—"

"You'll get two grand up front just for making the trip."

Hanlon knew he could get his boss at *Jim's* to let him go for a week. Two grand? He needed it.

"Count me in."

The two men ate in silence for a moment.

"Manny?"

"Yes, Randy?"

"Are you gonna contact Wintz Maslow about this?"

CHAPTER NINE

Vilseck, Germany

A young staff sergeant in his mid twenties—homely with a small, round potbelly that puckered the buttons of his uniform blouse—nervously glanced at his watch inside the kaserne's snack bar not far from the main gate. It was time. Images flashed through his mind from the night before, when he'd taken Inge home. Howard Lumpkin's rubbery moon face and pencil-thin arms and legs had never made him attractive to women much in the past. But Inge had taken a sudden, inexplicable liking to him the night before at Jodie's—the only country and western music hangout this side of Nuremberg—and had miraculously invited him home with her. Howard had been flushed with glory as he strutted past his peers with the tall German blonde on his arm and escorted her to the cab of his Silverado. In no time at all they'd been at her cottage on the edge of town and in her bed.

Everything had been perfect. At least until the intruders had shown up and booted them out from underneath Inge's luxurious down comforter—intruders who had broken down Inge's door, and had beaten her for hanging out with, in their words *Ami Schwein*. Howard could still remember her pitiful cries in the other room as he was left alone in the dark, shivering, crying in his impotent rage.

He looked at the cheap Casio strapped tightly on his left wrist. It was time. Swallowing, Howard gingerly touched his face and rose from the snack bar table, where he'd been listening to Merle Haggard sing the prison blues on the jukebox. Except for one swollen lip, the only blows he'd received were those that didn't leave marks. He shivered. He would meet the others as planned, do what they told him to do, cooperate, and get Inge back—without taking their money.

At 2200 hours, the scared sergeant met them at the entrance driveway of Building 102, headquarters for the chemical warfare training unit to which Howard was assigned.

Two people: A captain and a driver who, as far as he could tell, was a woman. Wordlessly, they got out of the CUCV they had driven onto the post, pulled their seats forward, and removed a layer of gunny sacks in the rear of the vehicle hiding two other uniformed people, who quickly joined their comrades outside.

Inge. He was doing it for Inge. Well, also . . . there was one whole hell of a lot of money involved. . . .

No. No, goddammit. No money. Just do what they tell you to do, get Inge out of trouble, and then inform post security. Besides, they were here. They could kill him just like that. And after the drugs and alcohol and the beatings from the night before had worn off, he'd already been too compromised to go to the authorities. He had gone to Inge's house, made love to her; then they'd held him for hours and beat him and hurt her and . . . and then they'd told him what to do and what would happen if he didn't in no uncertain terms . . . Christ, he was in trouble.

The captain strode silently up to Howard where he stood compliantly in the doorway. Howard watched the other three fan out and around the building.

"Are you ready?" the blond man asked him.

"Where are those others going?"

"I said, are you ready?"

"Yes."

"Do not ask me any questions, Staff Sergeant Howard Lumpkin. You will do as you are told. Or else you will have on your conscience the life of the German whore you slept with last night and whoever else is in this building."

"Don't—"

"You are in no position to say or do anything." The blond man pulled a suppressed H&K 9-millimeter out from beneath the U.S. Army field jacket he wore. "And if you have set us up . . ."

"I—I didn't do that. No one knows."

They entered the silent hallways of Building 102. In the

daytime, it was used as a school for nuclear, biological, and chemical training for soldiers sent there by units from all over American Forces Europe. In the hallways in glass display cases stood mannequins dressed in chemical-protection suits and gas masks. Mannequins wearing Soviet chemical suits stood silent watch alongside them, each a gloomy forecast of a form of warfare that was hideous and forgotten . . . forgotten since World War I, when soldiers from all sides choked to death on chlorine gas and mustard gas, veterans dying years later from coughing black liquid out of their lungs from chemical exposure. The mannequins wearing these modern suits foretold of the time when all that would happen again, and Central and Western Europe would become a poisoned countryside, replete with bloated, blistered corpses putrefying in their own excrement.

Howard Lumpkin had always hated running guard detail in these hallways. Especially knowing what it was he guarded. The Microcystin. It had been a mistake to send it here. But when the shipment from the States came two weeks early, before the special cache site was ready outside Bad Hersfeld, there'd been no choice but to store it where Europe's chemical experts were headquartered: in Vilseck, at Harrison Kaserne's chemical tactics, research, and instruction center.

In the vault. In Staff Sergeant Howard Lumpkin's vault, of which only he and his immediate chain of command knew the combination.

The blond man striding silently behind him, dressed as a captain in the United States Army, knew these things as well, based on what Howard had told him under the influence of last night's injection.

As they approached the end of the hallway, Howard could see that one of his men was nodding off at his position behind a small field table with a TA-312 field telephone resting on it. In all, he had four men inside the building, each one posted at the ends of the hallways on both floors, another man by the vault, and a roving guard who patrolled the grounds outside. He himself roved the inside floors, and checked with each man every thirty minutes.

Howard glanced at his watch. At 0200 in the morning they'd be relieved by the graveyard shift. They had another four hours to go.

"Remember what I told you," the blond man whispered in

Howard's ear, as they approached the guard at the end of the hallway.

Howard drew in a deep breath and swallowed, as they came to a stop before the guard. "How's it going, Woljinski?" he said.

A young private snapped up his head upon hearing the sergeant and jumped to his feet, knowing he'd been caught napping. "Uh . . . fine, Sarge. It's real quiet." The private's eyes caught the gleam of the captain bars on the blond man's hat, and he assumed the position of attention.

"Relax, Woljinski," Howard told him, amazed at the calmness in his voice. "Me'n the captain here are just making the rounds, that's all. He's inspecting security tonight, so keep on your toes."

"Clear, Sergeant," came back a snappy reply.

They walked up the flight of stairs to the second floor, and the process was repeated with the other guard. Minutes later, after sweeping the building, they met the other three cell members.

After letting them inside, the blond man quietly led everyone into an adjacent hallway just inside the entrance of a classroom. He touched one of them lightly by the sleeve. "Report."

The other man answered with a Gallic shrug. "There was one guard leaning against the parking lot street lamp, smoking. He had no radio. I put him out and dragged him off into the trees. There is no one else."

"What did you do to—" Howard protested.

"Shut up!" the blond man hissed, shoving his pistol into Howard's gut. Howard's jaw relaxed and the pit of his stomach fell out under the pressure of gunmetal in his solar plexus.

"But you said there would be no killing," he said weakly.

"Continue to do as you are told, and there will be none." The blond man turned his attention back to his assistant, who spoke with a French accent.

"And the phone lines here are now cut," the Frenchman finished. "Nothing else." The blond man turned to his other helper.

"I have the whole area checked out. It's a tiny post. The movie theater, snack bar, and club are all full."

German, this time, Howard thought to himself. *One Frenchman, and two Germans along with the asshole here pretending he's a captain. Can't make the other one out . . .*

"Good. Leave, now, and complete your work."

Howard watched the last man who had spoken—the other German—walk back outside. Through the office window of the room they were in, he watched the man open the door of the CUCV and strap a huge, Army-issue rucksack on his back. Then, he disappeared into the night.

The blond man checked his watch. "Time is now . . . 2205." He glanced up at Howard. "Take me to the vault."

Howard shifted uneasily, and then began to walk toward the flight of stairs down the adjacent hallway that led to the basement vault. There was nothing else he could do. The blond man paused, looking at his comrades.

"Wait two minutes . . . then move."

And then they left.

Private Steven Woljinski, young, only three months out of Basic and AIT, stretched his legs out underneath the small wooden table before him and yawned. It would be a long night, but he'd get to sleep in the following morning. He'd even get to catch up on some of his letters, work out in the gym, maybe even call Sally back home. . . .

The sound of bootsteps. Growing louder. Someone in the hallway.

Private Woljinski straightened up in his chair. *Hope it ain't Sarge again,* he thought.

The creaking grew louder, slow, measured, the squeak of rubber sole against the newly waxed floor echoing throughout the hallway.

That's not Sarge. . . .

"Who are you?" he said, standing up. He tried to remember the procedure they'd taught him in Basic Training on the challenge and password. He'd forgotten. Hell, they never paid any attention to that security stuff around here anyway.

The figure approached him, closer, Why didn't he answer? Woljinski's heart picked up a beat. He could tell by the person's silhouette that he was in uniform. *Had* to be from the unit. Maybe to relieve him early, maybe a different schedule had been worked out. But whoever it was hadn't answered.

"Who's there?" Woljinski demanded. He glanced to his left where an ax handle rested against the wall next to his chair. A thought flashed through his mind just then, about how ridiculous it was for the Army to send you to guard duty with just an ax handle, when they should have given you a .45. Now why in Christ's name would they do that?

"It's only me," a female voice answered him, almost upon him.

Woljinski breathed a sigh of relief. Allison—one of the five women assigned in his NBC support section here at Vilseck.

He watched her silhouette come close. "Why didn't you say so earlier, Big Al? You almost had me—" He broke off when the woman's silhouette became a face in the moonlight that shone through the huge hallway window by his desk. A woman with short, blond hair. Allison was a brunette. "Hey. *Hey! You're not—*"

Private Steven Woljinski stared in disbelief at the blackjack the tall blond woman held as it came whipping across his temple.

She did a good job, knocking him out. Woljinski didn't feel a thing as she broke his neck.

On the second floor, Specialist Andrew Thurman also heard bootsteps creaking down the hallway toward him.

Located just above Woljinski, thirty feet below, he'd heard strange sounds. He'd heard Woljinski call out to someone twice, then start to talk, and then . . . and then nothing. What gives?

Bootsteps.

He hated the goddam dark hallway. Why the fuck had Sarge told them earlier to keep the lights off? Didn't make any sense. He flipped the switch on. Down the hallway, coming closer, was a very disorderly-looking soldier dressed in BDUs, with long black hair and a mustache, both way too long for regulation, and a great big, shit-eating grin on his face.

Weird.

"Identify yourself," Specialist Thurman ordered, reaching for his ax handle.

"Oui, m'sieur."

Sergeant Stanley Tanner looked up from his desk by the vault downstairs in the basement, secreted away from the rest of the world in a tiny cubicle, and saw his section sergeant, Staff Sergeant Howard Lumpkin, enter. Normally, he would have rolled his eyes at the incompetent sonofabitch whose job *he* should have had, but instead, he jumped to the position of attention when he saw a slender, blond-haired captain with hollow cheeks and dark-circled eyes enter the cubicle with him.

"Good evening, sir," Tanner said crisply, his short-cropped black hair shaved to a Ranger's high and tight standard, his muscles tensing slightly underneath his immaculately pressed fatigues, and his power-lifter's chest expanding. He suddenly found himself staring at the bore of a suppressed automatic.

The "captain" drilled him between the eyes with that suppressed automatic.

Howard Lumpkin stood there, shocked, aghast. One second, Tanner had just stood there, big and uppity, like every other nigger he'd ever come across, and the next . . . now . . . the NCO lay tumbled into a heap on the concrete floor by his ax handle, staining the floor with the back of his head, arterial spouts of blood pooling at the foot of the vault. Suddenly, Howard Lumpkin felt the warm, loose wetness of urine stain the crotch of his fatigues. He stood there, paralyzed, wanting to scream.

The blond man wrinkled his nose in distaste. "Open it."

Howard swallowed and tried to say something.

"Open it!" The man reached out and slapped Howard on the face, galvanizing the NCO into action.

Howard stumbled forward as blood gushed from his nose, tripped against Tanner. He fumbled for the digital combination hidden by a metal screen.

"Move him first," the blond man ordered. "He'll be in the way."

Breathing in short, rapid bursts, Howard dragged Tanner away from the vault, the back of Tanner's head painting a broad red streak along the floor. Howard walked gingerly back to the vault, careful not to step in the blood and the gray matter mixed with it. He stuck his hand back behind the metal screen over the combination digital display and began to punch the digit sequence.

Seconds later, they were inside the vault. It was about the size of a small bedroom. Inside were ceramic vials, banded tightly with lead seals; inspection receipts hung off the handles for initialing. Some vials were colored blue, with red lettering.

Most were colored yellow, with red lettering. The blond man arched an eyebrow at Howard. "Well?"

Howard walked to the rear of the vault and opened a footlocker. He withdrew a metal vial that resembled the others, only this one had a series of numbers on it in groups of four. He gave it to the blond man.

"Go back to the rear of the vault."

Howard walked back.

"On your knees and clasp your hands behind your head."

Seconds passed as the blond man inspected the vial Howard handed him. "This is not the formula. You now have exactly ten seconds to give me the correct one."

Howard scrambled to his feet and turned around, his uniform askew, thinning hair falling down into his eyes, his gut bulging and puckering his uniform blouse. The blond man was stuffing a small piece of paper back into his pocket. Well, he had tried. . . .

He reached back down into the footlocker and gave the blond man a second vial.

"Get back to the wall."

Howard resigned himself to his fate. Surely they would kill him now. And he had helped them! *Inge, oh, Inge. They'll kill you too.* . . .

"Okay, Sergeant Lumpkin. This will do quite nicely. You have earned your money tonight."

Howard swallowed. Yeah. Right.

The sound of footsteps, light and quick.

The blond man wheeled around. Howard kept his nose pressed against the wall, his back to his captor. "Oh, it's you," he heard the blond man say. "Are things ready?"

Howard heard no answer. Evidently they were.

"And I take it you want the coup de grace?" The blond man repeated.

"Yes. Very much so."

The bottom of the world fell out from underneath Howard Lumpkin, and he wanted very much to throw up.

Footsteps, approaching.

"Turn around, Howard."

Wincing, Howard Lumpkin turned around on his knees away from the footlocker and saw Inge standing before him, dressed in BDUs, holding the blond man's suppressed H&K in her hand before his face. Her long, blond hair hung in a thick, loose rope over her left shoulder.

"Inge," Howard rasped between sobs.

"Yes."

"No," Howard whimpered, his shoulders shaking as tears erupted in his eye sockets. "No, *please*, Inge. I did it for you. . . ."

Inge reached out with her left hand and pulled down on Howard's chin. "Enough of that. Now open wide. That's right. That's my Howard."

Minutes later, they were back in the CUCV.

Bombs, digitally wired, in Building 102. Bombs in the theater. Bombs in the snack bar and in the community club. All digitally wired for remote detonation. All set to go off at 2300 hours, just another ten minutes away.

They waved at the MP guarding the gate, on the way out of the kaserne.

Explosions rumbled through the night, and the man standing by the side of the country road intersection listened to them and nodded his head grimly. The mission to steal the American chemical and toxin formulas had evidently been a success. Or was it? His plant within the Latino drug world had informed him about a potential sellout by Stern's old gang—which happened to be the cell executing the mission against the American garrison at Vilseck and now inbound to meet him.

The man turned back to face his car, which was embedded hub-deep in muck, the kind only wet German winters can produce. The persistent, day-long rainfall was now changing into snow. Twenty meters behind his Volvo, he had erected a triangle roadside signal device which would warn motorists to watch out for his mired auto.

It also served as a signal for the RAF cell which was supposed to be delivering the Microcystin.

Headlights cut through night fog, reflecting against huge, wet snowflakes. Valdimir Bolivar Marighella Rozo, known to his contacts as Simon, drew in a deep breath. Was it them? When he heard the sound of a diesel engine, and saw the silhouette of an American Chevrolet Blazer approach, he let his breath out.

The Blazer slowed. Simon opened the trunk of the Volvo and put his right foot on the rear bumper.

With the near-term recognition signal validated, the Blazer pulled up ahead of the Volvo and stopped, where the tree line of the forest met the road.

A soldier exited the passenger side of the Blazer and walked toward Simon. Simon noted that the man, a slender Army captain, judging by the twin silver bars on his cap, kept his right hand in his field jacket pocket. It took no imagination to figure out why, and his suspicions of a sellout deepened.

"Where might I find the church in Bad Hersfeld?" the Army captain asked Simon.

Simon's mouth twitched. "It's too late for the service," he replied, completing the bonafides. He recognized the RAF cell leader. It was Ludwig Genscher, Monika Stern's second in command in the Munich cell.

"Then I am at your service," the Army captain said, keeping his hand in the pocket of his field jacket.

"Judging by the explosions back on the kaserne, you were successful." A snowflake landed on Simon's upper lip and he brushed it away, as he stood shivering in the chill German night.

"We were." Genscher made no move to hand over the Microcystin.

Simon arched an eyebrow, trying not to show his concern. "Where is the Microcystin?"

"Where is our money?"

Simon's eyes narrowed. So. He had suspected as much. Damn the Russians and their stupidity! You do not bankroll operations on credit, and you certainly do not bankroll operations with rubles, which were worthless outside the USSR—and nearly so inside too! Simon thought for a moment. Then he said, carefully, "Are you telling me you did not retrieve the Microcystin?"

The RAF terrorist cell leader thumbed back the H&K's safety inside his field jacket pocket, knowing that Simon saw the slight movement and interpreted it correctly.

Simon took a step back. So. He *had* been sold out.

Ludwig smiled thinly. "Moscow pays poorly these days," he said, "and you may tell them we are finished working for them. We cached the Microcystin before meeting you here, Simon."

"Who bribed you, Ludwig? The Palestinians? The Colombians?"

"The highest bidder," Ludwig replied after a moment. "The RAF does not operate on flames of revolutionary passion for a future Marxist utopia any longer. The old days are over, Simon."

"I will have the money tomorrow," Simon lied. Who had stolen these operators from him? Surely they had been the ones to approach their current employer. He could probably rule out the PLO, who would of course love to possess the Microcystin, but even the RAF would not do business with those Arab madmen and their Muslim unpredictability. Totally unreliable. No. Better it was to do business with a man or a group of men who were now waging a terror campaign against the U.S. and their puppet government in Bogotá. The Extraditables. The Colombians.

Strictly from an RAF perspective it made sense. That way, the Microcystin would most likely be used against U.S. targets alone. No messy affairs in German airports and railway stations.

And when it came to the European theater, that meant one man—the ex-Medellín cartel member who was currently on trial in Spain for bull smuggling, of all things.

Smiling, Simon faced the Army captain who was no Army captain and clapped a hand on his shoulder. "I think you are a capitalist at heart, Ludwig. You have the Microcystin I need, and simply want to be paid for your efforts. I understand completely. When shall we meet again, so that I may pay you?"

They discussed a rendezvous plan Simon had no intention of fulfilling. A few minutes later, after they had reached an agreement, Simon pointed at his Volvo in the mud. "Come, get the others and lend me a hand. *Mein auto . . .*"

"The message said you would be stuck in the mud," Ludwig said, bending over to examine the rear of the Volvo, "but I am afraid you overdid it." He walked back to the Blazer. "Everybody out," Simon heard him say. "He's stuck."

Minutes later, Simon waved them off and reentered his Volvo. It had taken all four members of the cell straining at the bumper while he steered to get the car back onto the road. He had tried not to let it be too easy a job, and could still remember the insolent Frenchman cursing beneath the mud caking his face, the result of Simon's heavy foot punching the accelerator. He had done it on purpose, never having liked the Gallic frog on loan from Action Directe.

Simon grinned, and the corners of his mouth twitched as he shook with quiet laughter. He opened the glove box of the Volvo and retrieved a tiny transmitter. He extended the antenna and then climbed back out of the car in time to see the departing Blazer's taillights approach the crest of a hill in the road to his front.

Before they crested the hill Simon blew them up. Simon watched the Blazer's roof skyrocket into the drizzle and the rest of the flaming vehicle careen downslope into a stream bed where it continued to burn.

A noise on his right. He turned and shoved the transmitter in his trousers pocket, as another man, his features made indistinguishable with black greasepaint, exited the woods by the roadside. After entering the Volvo together, the night's work done, they drove down the adjacent road away from the intersection, away from the scene before the Polizei arrived.

"You did well, Siegfried, for a freelance," Simon offered. "Who knows? Maybe someday you can lead one of my cells."

"*Nein,*" the man replied, wiping his nose with his sleeve. "Freelance only. Did they get the toxin?"

"Yes and no. Their mission against the American garrison in Vilseck was successful, but they betrayed us by delivering the goods to another party. I figured as much, and that is why I wanted you to assist me tonight."

Siegfried fell silent.

"And did you emplace *our* toxin before attaching the explosive?"

"It's a good thing you took so long to get unstuck," Siegfried replied. "I had just crawled back into the woods when they came back from helping you. Those damned *Amerikanische* diesels," he muttered.

"Eh?"

Siegfried grinned. "Ever try to tape a receiver and plastique and a vial of your evil liquid underneath the engine block of an American Army vehicle? *In three minutes,* comrade? You'll get oil on your face."

Simon laughed, his mood improving, and he stepped the

Volvo up to a hundred and twenty kilometers an hour. It was good to be back in the field, away from gray, unhappy Moscow, back in Deutschland. Working. Using people he could trust, such as Siegfried. The operators he had just killed? That had served two purposes. One, to erase all traces of Monika Stern's old team, which evidently had sold out to the Colombians once the iron presence of their leader had departed. Two, to make it look like a Red Army Faction terror op gone bad to placate American authorities searching for the terrorists who had bombed their garrison and stolen, unsuccessfully, it would seem, one of their most dangerous toxins.

The Soviet toxin Siegfried had tagged onto the Blazer was just as lethal as the Microcystin, and for a while could be mistaken for the American formula they had just stolen and now apparently had given to their new sponsor. There was plenty to draw from the Soviet arsenal. All kinds—palytoxins, genetically engineered for lethal depolarization of nerve and muscle tissues; venom toxins—concentrated into doses hundreds of milligrams more than what was needed to kill a large man . . . the list was endless.

But the American Microcystin had *their* signature; it was their formula. An American toxin formula turned loose on their own population was a powerful political lever in the hands of the team he was forming in Aden. But now, this renegade RAF team he'd just executed had fouled things up.

Siegfried said something, and Simon snapped out of his thoughts.

"What?"

"I said, think about Humberto Werner-Miranda."

"Or it can just as easily be the Ochoa family or Pablo Escobar," Simon countered rhetorically as he drove. As a freelance operator, Siegfried Brandt had conducted execution operations such as the one he'd just carried out for Simon over the past five years. Siegfried therefore came into contact with numerous revolutionaries and their sponsors, whose operations dovetailed increasingly with the continually expanding drug cartels. The money was simply that good. "You still think this betrayal was motivated by someone in the drug world?" Simon continued. "There are over twenty odd Colombian cartel members with business contacts in Europe. So which one would it be?"

"Werner-Miranda. It was not hard for Stern's old team to contact him."

"You know Stern?"

"I trained her in Aden myself, ten, eleven years ago."

"Werner-Miranda?"

"I am quite sure. You see, Humberto Werner-Miranda thinks he's a German. The fact that he employs half the RAF for his own special operations illustrates that point completely."

That made sense to Simon. The short, affected Colombian-German drug lord loved dressing in battle fatigues, quoting Nietzsche and Hitler, wearing German paratrooper boots, and preaching to anyone who would listen about Colombia becoming a force to be reckoned with against the exploitation of Yankee imperialism. He would be the one most interested in stealing an American chemical toxin.

Throughout the seventies and eighties, as part of a unilateral Soviet-Latino policy to make money and subvert the U.S., Soviet GRU and KGB agents had trained Latino operatives mounting drug-smuggling activities along the American southwestern border. The resulting flow of marijuana, heroin, and cocaine tied down U.S. security assets, made money to finance Soviet and Cuban intelligence operations within the Western Hemisphere, and in the long run, demoralized and subverted an increasingly despondent, drug-addicted American society.

Simon had expanded business with Werner-Miranda and others like him in the late eighties by mounting drug operations along the U.S. southwestern border with Mexico, which in turn rejuvenated empty Soviet coffers that financed terror operations within the European theater of operations. In return for Werner-Miranda's money, Simon used RAF and other Western European terrorists to advise and assist the drug lord's smuggling infrastructure. There was always a judge in Bogotá to be assassinated, an American DEA agent assigned to Medellín to be taken out, members within his own organization to be disposed of when they became reckless or untrustworthy.

But perhaps now those early seeds of mutual cooperation were proving troublesome. Werner-Miranda was currently seething in the prison of his Madrid hacienda, while awaiting the outcome of an American extradition attempt with Spanish judicial authorities. Bull smuggling was a rather serious matter for Spaniards. Where would he escape after it was over? Simon wondered. Back to Colombia? Surely not. Perhaps to the ski resort in the Dolomites Werner-Miranda owned. Italian authorities were among the more lax, and possibly willing to help him in order to protect their interests in his investments in Selva-Wolkenstein.

"As you and I both know, Werner-Miranda employs RAF mercenaries for his personal security force," Siegfried said. "Perhaps he wishes to expand his operations. He certainly has the money."

Simon nodded his head. "I think you are right." He thought of Monika Stern, when he had once watched her dispatch an entire officers' club in Munich with such cold-blooded efficiency. He thought of her now, in the desert, in Aden, Yemen, with the finest operators under her command he could possibly have assembled. From five different countries and organizations, freedom fighters all, each had skills—in multi-linguality, the martial arts, clandestine communications, explosives, and small arms—that made other operatives, even the GRU specialists he had worked with in Lebanon, pale by comparison.

Microcystin.

"When was the last time you saw Aden, Siegfried?"

Siegfried pulled off his black watch cap and stared at Simon in the moonlight as they sped down the road. "Twelve years ago," he replied.

Simon nodded his head. Siegfried. The mark of a professional freelancer such as him was the secrets he kept. Simon only knew that Siegfried had never let him down. He was one RAF operator he could trust, a good-looking man with steel-gray eyes, an intellectual's gaunt face, and nerves of steel. Cool, cold, even. A martial artist.

"There are not many people I trust, as tonight's activities have demonstrated. But you and Monika Stern I can depend upon," Simon said carefully.

A moment's silence as Simon drove on into the night. Finally, Siegfried spoke. "We should contrive a plan to counter this intrusion from Humberto Werner-Miranda, no?"

Simon nodded his head. "Yes, but it will involve a much larger operation I shall brief you on later, at a place where I can have both you and Monika Stern together."

"A reunion?"

"Of sorts. I am assembling one of the best teams in Western

Europe. I'll need your help with Werner-Miranda, of course, if in fact he's the one who has possession of the Microcystin. Otherwise, my entire plan has just gone to hell."

"Then where do we go to begin planning?"

"Aden."

PART II

"As a school for choosing the guerrilla, urban guerrilla warfare prepares and places at the same level of responsibility and efficiency the men and women who share the same dangers fighting, rounding up supplies, serving as messengers or runners, as drivers, sailors, or airplane pilots, obtaining secret information, and helping with propaganda and the task of indoctrination."

—Carlos Marighella, June 1969

The Minimanual of the Urban Guerrilla

"Cocaine has become and marijuana has become a revolutionary weapon in the struggle against North American imperialism. Stimulants from Colombia are the Achilles' heel of imperialism. That's why the persecution against us is not legal, it is political."

—Carlos Lehder, Medellín drug cartel chieftain

CHAPTER TEN

Pushmataha County, Southeastern Oklahoma

Charlie Whitehead's '91 Bronco had driven down the Indian Nations Turnpike at a calm, legal sixty-five miles per hour, but when he turned off at the Clayton exit, and started barreling up a dirt mountain road, all hell broke loose and his passenger, a slender black man wearing an immense Stetson, tore the hat off his head and roared.

"Slow the fuck down!"

Charlie Whitehead slowed down, remembering the last time Winston Eugene Maslow the Third had gotten a case of the ass at him. They had been back at Bragg a hundred years ago, and Captain Charles Whitehead, commander of the Military Free Fall team, had been quietly told, "Sir, your plan for linkup after infiltration stinks. Here's why . . ." And Maslow had proceeded to tear his plan for sneaking into an Air Force base in New Mexico to conduct a reconnaissance operation all apart.

Whitehead, a Vietnam veteran, an experienced enlisted man and officer who was older than Maslow, hadn't listened. And their entire team had been caught by base security on the DZ. After the operation, Maslow in no uncertain terms had "re-explained" to Whitehead the importance of listening to his people, even if they were one, new to the team, and two, born and raised in the area in which an operation was to be conducted.

Charlie grinned at Maslow, who in turn grinned back as they whipped on down the highway to Clayton, Oklahoma. Yes, Charlie remembered how Maslow the enigma, Maslow the only black cowboy he'd ever known, Maslow his team operations and intelligence NCO, had helped turn his free-fall team into one of the Group's star performers. That had been over eleven years ago, back in 1980.

The years passed. Charlie went on to become a company commander, served his twenty by 1983, and retired from active duty. Winston Maslow attended Warrant Officer School, served as a team technician for a number of years in the "peacetime" Special Forces, and finally retired a year ago.

Having recruited Santo and Hanlon back at Bragg just two weeks ago, Charlie had decided a trip to Alamogordo, New Mexico, was worth it, to see if Maslow was interested. The retired warrant officer came highly recommended by Santo, and in view of his own experiences with Maslow, Whitehead enthusiastically agreed.

"Charlie, *please* slow this vehicle down," Maslow told him, carefully setting the Stetson back on his shiny bald dome.

That shiny bald dome had surprised the hell out of Whitehead when he'd first located Maslow at his computer store in Alamogordo. "Wintz," he said, exchanging glances between the highway and his partner, "how in the hell did you get so damned bald?"

Maslow rolled his eyes. "Too many U-turns underneath the sheets. You need a haircut, Injun."

Whitehead laughed. "Still the same old Wintz. Don't see how Janie ever put up with you in the first place."

Maslow grew quiet and slunk down into his seat.

"What's the matter now?"

"Janie and I aren't divorced like I told you back in New Mexico, Charlie."

"Huh?" Whitehead wondered what *that* was supposed to mean. After all, it only made sense. When Wintz had taken the offer he'd made two weeks ago for the meeting here at MacIntyre's ranch, Whitehead had just figured that Wintz's marriage had hit the rocks, like those of so many other SF guys, whether they were still on active duty or retired. It was just too damned easy when you stayed in SF for so long. Charlie had been one of the lucky ones.

"We," Maslow began, "were skiing last year up at Sierra Blanca. You know, the ski resort the Navajos run not too far away from Alamogordo?"

"Yeah."

"We were coming off this one slope that was kind of a cross

between intermediate and advanced . . . she lost control and broke her neck inside the tree line."

Charlie Whitehead did not know what to say. First Santo's wife, and now Maslow's as well. Coincidence? Was this what was drawing these men back together into a team?

Perhaps it was the only family they had left.

"She died over a year ago," Maslow said.

"Jesus, Wintz, why didn't you tell me?"

Maslow said nothing for several moments. Then: "I'm glad you made the offer, Charlie. About this MacIntyre business. I'll at least listen to what the guy has to say, but I'll be up front. This better not be a macho-mercenary type of thing. Those kind of people scare me."

"I've already told you I'm MacIntyre's chief of security."

"And that's why I came, pard. Who knows? Maybe it'll be like old times. I let a friend of mine run the shop back in Alamogordo. He might even buy it from me if this thing you're talking about has any substance to it."

Whitehead appreciated his old friend's comments. Too many other security organizations already existed in the country that could easily impress civilian security-conscious corporations even with old, outdated skills. Christ, it was an industry. But of what caliber? Replete with gung-ho soldiers of fantasy who had never been in combat, save for the wistful dreams and imaginings brought on by a few old war stories from burned-out vets and maybe a couple of years of good training with the 82nd, Rangers, Special Forces, or Delta.

Damned if the organization he and MacIntyre had in mind would turn out that way. They had purposefully avoided soliciting from outside security organizations already in existence. For something like this—conducting deniable drug-interdiction operations with a small and dependable unit—the best way was through personal knowledge and recruitment from a pool of men who had earned their reputations the hard way, through word of mouth and nothing else. The men they selected had to be honorable men, not afraid to lay it on the line for something they believed in. Mature men, who could devote their time and energies to the unit even more than to their own families. That is, if they still had families to go home to.

Charlie Whitehead glanced at Maslow, who was staring at the countryside rushing past him. He actually hadn't known about Maslow's personal life over the past several years. He damned sure didn't know about his wife. Maslow had always been a quiet one. Like Santo, he was one of the finest soldiers he'd ever known.

Thirty minutes later, they had traveled the dozen bumpy miles up the mountain road accessing MacIntyre's ranch. Already, long shadows had crossed the valleys and were crawling up the ridgelines like black fingers. The temperature started to cool as the day wore on toward evening. Whitehead drove the Bronco past a barbed-wire gate, and they approached two old log cabins sequestered among the pines and hardwoods.

Whitehead had always liked coming here, and once a year, he'd take his boys deer hunting. The ranch was the best place to hunt throughout the Kiamichis, and not just every Tom, Dick, and Harry could hunt on MacIntyre's reservation, only his employees. Whitehead remembered the past four seasons, while one boy was in high school and the younger in junior high. All those crisp Novembers when the schools would shut down for a week around Thanksgiving . . . the smell of roast venison at night, and mashed potatoes with deer meat gravy and fried okra . . . a little Jack Daniel's Black Label and thick, black coffee to wash it all down with . . .

These mountains reminded Whitehead of damned good times. He remembered the time when he and Wayne had taken their sons—his two and MacIntyre's Matt and Donny—and ambushed a herd of whitetail loose in a deep, bush-covered ravine half a morning's walk up in the hills. God, they'd all eaten well that night, and the rest of the winter.

MacIntyre had come up here quite often with his boys. Once. Now things were different. Matt had shipped off for the 1st of the 10th in Germany, shortly after he'd recruited Santo. Donny was dead. After the incident in JFK a month ago, Wayne had packed David off to an exclusive school in Maryland—exclusive for the security, that is. Now he was lonely for the company of his sons.

As they drove up to the main cabin, Whitehead saw two men dressed in camouflaged fatigue trousers, jungle boots, and black T-shirts exit one of the smaller cabins. Charlie slowed his Bronco to a halt. He glanced at Maslow for a reaction. The retired warrant officer was speechless for a second, and then he leaped out of the four-wheeler.

"Santo! Manny Santo! You ugly motherfucker!"

"Well, I'll be a sonofa—" Manny Santo gave Randy Hanlon the quarter of vension he'd just cut off a buck hung in the smokehouse and met Maslow on the rock sidewalk approaching the main cabin door. They pumped each other's hands furiously, and backslaps mingled with insults and belly-laughs. Whitehead joined the confusion.

"It's the James Brown cowboy himself," Santo said, holding Maslow at arm's length. "Check it out, Randy!"

Hanlon approached the group, holding a buck knife in one bloody hand and the hindquarter of vension in the other. He stuck the knife in the scabbard on his belt, wiped his bloody hand on his trouser leg, and extended it to Winston Maslow. "Hiya, Chief. Been a long time."

Maslow took it and matched Hanlon's hard grip. He studied Hanlon's face. "Heard you got out of Group a while back, Randy."

Hanlon looked away. "Yeah. Good to see you again, Wintz."

Maslow exchanged looks with Santo, and knew the rumor about Hanlon was true. Too bad.

Whitehead guided them toward the door. "Manny," he said, grinning, "who's doing the cooking around here? I hope it's not you." They walked inside.

"Whattya trying to do, Charlie, hurt my feelings?"

"Didn't know you had any."

"There's an old cowboy in here cooking tonight. He just sent us out to the smokehouse to get some deer meat. Randy, where's that deer meat?"

"Right behind you, Boss," Hanlon said, bringing up the rear as the men entered the cabin.

"Whew."

The three ranchers who ran the MacIntyre spread met them inside, and amenities were exchanged. The other people consisted of two brothers and an old, broken-down cowboy Wayne MacIntyre employed. The Alderidge brothers, Larry and Barry, were both the quiet sort. One was small and thin, and the other was big and hammy. Larry seemed to use his brain a little more, and Barry complemented the team with his skills as a mechanic and handyman. They both ranged about four hundred cattle for MacIntyre. Claudie, the old fart, generally tended the cabin and did all the cooking, since he was getting on in years. Whitehead had known Claudie ever since he'd gone to work for MacIntyre. Claudie's idea of a good time was a jar of snuff, a *Penthouse* magazine, a hot meal, and maybe once in a blue moon, a little poon down at the senior citizens' center in beautiful downtown Clayton. But only after he'd taken his weekly bath.

After dinner, they all broke out the Jack Daniel's and talked over hot coffee and whiskey, and Claudie surprised them all with hot apple pie. Larry and Barry said their good-byes and departed for their houses and wives back in Clayton, their sixteen-hour day over. The crisp late February night air turned cold, and Claudie stoked up the wood-burning stove inside the cabin's kitchen where they ate. The talk grew quiet.

"He'll be here in the morning," Whitehead announced after a moment's silence, and everyone knew that it was time to get down to business. "I've told you what this was all about." He glanced over to the adjacent room, where Claudie had stretched out along a weathered mohair couch, fast asleep and snoring.

"Surely not just us three," Maslow said, cupping a hot mug of coffee around both hands.

"No," Whitehead replied. "He's bringing another man with him, temporarily on loan from an outside agency that's coordinating with Wayne on this."

"Wayne?" Santo interjected, recalling the initial shock upon finding out that Matt's father was in fact one of the wealthiest men in the country.

"Wayne MacIntyre. Your ex-team leader's father," Whitehead added for the others' benefit. "He's flying in early tomorrow morning. A word about Wayne MacIntyre. You don't attain his stature in the Fortune 500 club without having political contacts. In no small way, he influenced the outcome of the last election with the bucks he donated to the present Administration's campaign."

Hanlon scooted back from the table, a disbelieving smirk on his face. "Right, Charlie."

Whitehead's poker face wiped Hanlon's grin away. "Then believe it tomorrow when he flies his private Sikorsky in. He's got a couple of Blackhawks for our use, gentlemen," Whitehead said, pouring another shot of J.D. into his coffee mug. Whitehead glanced back up at Hanlon, who was now paying full attention again. "Your challenge is to make a decision on whether or not you want to work for a private citizen outside the government. In other words, you all are going to be Wayne

MacIntyre's own personal band of—well, hell, may as well say it—mercenaries. Guns for hire. Whatever you want to call it."

Maslow snorted. The others looked at each other in embarrassment. There were too many commando magazines out there glorifying the concept, and there were too many would-be SF and 82nd Airborne types all too eager to take on proffered "merc" jobs that were more often than not facades for rip-off security scams, drug-running, or messy divorce cases in search of permanent solutions.

"At any rate," Whitehead continued, "the bottom line is that Wayne MacIntyre needs good men to carry out drug-interdiction jobs the Administration won't go near with a ten-foot pole."

"And we're supposed to be above the law," Santo said quietly.

Whitehead returned Santo's hard look stare. "That's right."

"I don't know, Charlie."

"Wayne's bringing a guy from the National Security Council with him. He's a specialist in narco-terrorism."

All four men fell silent for a moment as the word *terrorism* sank in, each pondering the meaning and the implication of what Wayne MacIntyre was going to ask them to do. Hanlon then broke the silence, as he leaned forward to pour himself a new shot of coffee from the pot.

"What's he paying, Mr. Whitehead?"

"Charlie."

"Charlie. If I'm going to be a merc, then what's Wayne MacIntyre paying?"

"He'll talk to you about that tomorrow, Randy. It'll be enough." Whitehead leaned back in his chair, studying his coffee cup of ice cubes and Jack Daniel's straight. He swirled the contents around for a second and then leaned forward again over the tabletop and said, "I just didn't want there to be any false illusions about why Wayne MacIntyre wants you here. When he flies in tomorrow, you'll receive the benefit of a full-blown ops briefing from the NSC guy he's bringing with him. You'll meet the fourth member of your cell at the same time, the pilot flying in the Blackhawk.

"One thing to remember, though, gentlemen: Wayne MacIntyre has entrusted me to find and recommend good people for him. People of honor, and people of trust. It wasn't hard to decide on you guys. Besides, you've worked together before."

"MacIntyre wants to get even with the people who shot his son," Maslow said abruptly.

Whitehead examined his old friend. "Right, Wintz. But it's not the only reason, though he's highly keen on getting that *particular* group."

"You mean there's more than one group he's after?"

"Yeah, you could say that. Be flexible."

Santo pondered what Whitehead meant. He'd been flexible all his life. Problem was, was he ready to go underground? This operation had all the signs of requiring that. He scanned the faces before him: Whitehead, a man he hadn't worked with in over eleven years; Hanlon, busted out of the Army on dope charges, but whom he knew he could trust as a man who had saved his life on more than one occasion during the battle they'd fought at the White Sands Missile Range the previous year. Santo took in Maslow's black countenance. Maslow was sprouting gray at his temples, yet the sinewy strength of his forearms and biceps reflected a man in his mid-forties who had stayed in shape. He'd been in on the operation last year in New Mexico as well. But how was his mental attitude? Whitehead had already taken Santo aside and explained the situation with Janie's death. Maslow hadn't talked to anyone about it. Yet. Santo remembered how *he'd* felt, knowing full well the impact of a spouse's death, whether you were getting along or not. When Sally and Sarah were killed by that drunken driver, Maslow was the one who'd helped him cling to sanity, and to overcome his own guilt-ridden drinking problem at the time. Now it was Wintz's turn to go through that exorcism of guilt and pain. Santo would draw him aside later.

And then there was the wild card of Matt MacIntyre's father. Up until recently, Manny Santo hadn't known anything about his ex-team leader's father, except that he was a wealthy businessman from Tulsa, Oklahoma.

Wayne MacIntyre. Those two words translated into Daddy Warbucks. What kind of man was Wayne MacIntyre? And who else was Wayne MacIntyre bringing to this rendezvous to round out the core of a team that he, Hanlon, and Maslow were forming?

Bottom line: Who else did he have to trust?

CHAPTER ELEVEN

Madrid, Spain

Valdimir Bolivar Marighella Rozo cruised his rented Mercedes through the suburbs of one of Madrid's most fashionable districts. Mansions, swimming pools, tennis courts, and discotheques proliferated throughout every tract of privately owned land; the very feel and sunset ambience of Spain's monied elite in this neighborhood gave the Iberian peninsula's climate the crispness and appeal of a brand-new American hundred-dollar bill.

As he thought that, Simon's right nostril began to itch, and he picked at it with a ragged thumbnail. He took a deep breath and forced himself to relax. He examined his thumbnail. That, his day's growth of beard, and his wrinkled linen suit had turned him into a seedy man. Simon wished he'd taken the time to shower at the airport. But there was no more time. He had to leave for Aden the following day, and there was another, more important meeting to attend later that night. And the one now was no cakewalk.

He rounded a corner and spotted a sprawling stucco manor with a long driveway, a guard shack, and baby trees that spoke of recently developed land. Slowing down to forty kilometers an hour, Simon pulled the Mercedes 580 SL up to Casa Werner-Miranda's gateway. A security guard stepped out. His Aryan appearance indicated that few things had changed. Humberto Werner-Miranda—one of the "Extraditables," as the U.S. Drug Enforcement Administration had labeled him, undergoing self-imposed exile from his native Colombia—had always employed "independent contractors" needing a break

119

from Red Army Faction operations. Many times Simon himself had agented such contracts for the drug lord. Werner-Miranda, himself half-German, loved the affectation of things Aryan. He read Nietzsche, studied biographies of Hitler, and listened to Beethoven. He loved dressing up in various paramilitary costumes, accompanied by large-bore handguns strapped to his hip which Simon thought exposed the short Colombian's subliminal desire to enlarge his penis.

Simon braked the Mercedes to a halt and glanced to his left. A gate guard waited for him to lower the driver's window. He did so.

"Pass, please?" the guard said in Spanish.

Simon stared at the bore of the MP5 submachine gun draped casually over the guard's shoulder and leaning on his hip. Simon flashed the guard the papers Werner-Miranda had planted in the dead-letter drop at Madrid International. *"Mein Pass,"* he replied in German. *"Ja, gut?"*

"Sehr gut, mein Herr," the guard replied, his lips compressing into a thin smile, as he waved him up the driveway with the muzzle of his submachine gun. *"Geradeaus, bitte."*

Simon raised the window and pressed his foot on the accelerator, his heart quickening. He could almost taste it, the sudden pop of clarity, the way his heart would speed up, his bloodstream mixing comfortably with adrenaline in preparation for a conversation with Humberto Werner-Miranda.

More perspiration popped out on Simon's forehead. His ears itched. He hated it when his ears itched, because now was not the time to scratch them.

After he pulled up before his and her sets of Mercedes and Jaguars and a Rolls—all of which were parked in Werner-Miranda's open six-car garage—another guard met him at the foyer and gave Simon the customary but thorough frisking. Simon resisted a smile. The faint strains of a Wagnerian symphony filtered through the open door, and Simon wondered if his host was following his custom of damaging his hearing with his favorite German composer.

Moments later Simon was led into Werner-Miranda's library, a room smelling of old leather, dusty books, felt tablecloths, and Scotch. A bluish haze of cigar smoke hung overhead, and the source of that smoke, a smallish man dressed in fatigues and boots, sprang up from his leather recliner and strode quickly toward the door, a grin splitting his cherubic face, which had never lost its baby fat, even though Werner-Miranda had just turned forty the previous day.

"Paisano!" he piped in an effeminately high voice.

"Humberto, *wie geht's*?" Simon stepped forward and exchanged a warm, moist grip with the other man. Inwardly, he wanted to shrink about six inches, because Humberto Werner-Miranda was a full head shorter than Simon, and Simon was no tall man at five-foot-ten. A fat, black Joya de Nicaragua was shoved in front of his face, taken from the breast pocket of Werner-Miranda's sweat-stained fatigue shirt. Simon reached for the cigar, then found himself staring at a flame four inches from his nose. He started puffing.

"Paisano," Werner-Miranda repeated, "it has been such a long time, *amigo*. But it is good you could catch me here. I have been cooped up too long. But of course, you heard about the court hearings yesterday. . . ."

Simon smiled and tried not to snort with laughter at the shorter, fatter man standing before him. Spotting Werner-Miranda's Casill .454 magnum hanging from his hip, the most powerful handgun in the world, Simon lost all desire to grin. He'd seen the man who would be King of Colombia shoot too many people in the face with the Casill. "Humberto," Simon said in a serious voice, "I read the news just two hours ago upon touching down in Madrid. The Americans shall never have you."

Humberto Werner-Miranda's face transformed suddenly into the cold-blooded killer's countenance he'd been born with, and Simon's blood chilled a degree. "The *yanqui* bastards. The DEA. The CIA. The FBI. The motherfucking acronym upon acronym! They tried to convince the Audiencia Nacionale that the charge of smuggling bulls from Madrid to my Medellín estate wasn't grounds to have me stand trial in Colombia. No grounds! No, they tried to sway the court to ignore that, so they could extradite me to Miami!"

Werner-Miranda spat on the polished hardwood floor, and managed to hit the taxidermist's eyeball of a polar bearskin rug he'd poached two years before. "Of course, Spanish authorities saw the light, after a conversation or two I had with a judge or two," Werner-Miranda added with a chuckle and a nudge into Simon's ribs. "So fuck those imperialist bastards. I'll just go back to my native country and stand trial there. For smuggling bulls. Ha!"

Simon grinned and walked toward a wingback upright upholstered in the same color and texture leather as the recliner Werner-Miranda had been sitting in. It was rather hard to imagine the little man before him actually donning a matador's finery and proceeding to slaughter a horned, bovine beast weighing nearly a ton. That he'd been caught smuggling some of Spain's finest into Colombia was all that had saved him from extradition directly to the United States when Spanish officials had finally caught up with his forged passport, wild parties, and excessive spending. The man had simply refused to maintain a quiet, clandestine existence.

Of course Simon had already known, rehearsed even, what he'd say to Werner-Miranda about his court victory and the bait he'd use to lure the Colombian to his Italian resort. The drug lord's dangerous machismo had to be stopped.

Simon regarded the close-cropped, Hessian bullet head of Werner-Miranda's biggest guard, posted in the library's back shadows. Sitting on the wingback, Simon accepted the Johnny Walker Black Label Werner-Miranda had poured for him at the bar. He swirled two ice cubes around his glass and let the Scotch give him the warm-up he needed, as Werner-Miranda sat across from him and sipped on his own Scotch. One never underestimated a drug lord with a short man's complex.

Simon cast a look over the Colombian's shoulder and eyed the guard watching him back. "Can we talk, Humberto?" Simon began carefully.

Werner-Miranda stared back wordlessly for a second. Then, positioning his recliner upright, he scooted forward and sat on the edge of his seat as he would a piano bench. He raised his right hand in the air and snapped his fingers with one, loud pop. The guard stood up, and after staring a second longer at Simon, left the room, affording Simon a look at the automatic tucked in the back of his Levi's.

"Friedrich is extremely loyal," Werner-Miranda informed Simon.

"Loyalty is usually predicated on cash, Humberto."

"So you've often told me, paisano. Things are different now that I have a reason to go back to Colombia. Besides, I miss home. It has been two years."

"Of course, Humberto. And now, you would like nothing better than to get back at the *yanqui* bastards who forced you to stay here, no?"

Werner-Miranda squinted. "What have you in mind?"

Simon's eyes wandered over to the shelf of books closest to Werner-Miranda's recliner, and found what he was looking for. Standing up, he strolled over to the bookshelf and picked it out, Machiavelli's *The Prince*, standing guard next to Hitler's *Mein Kampf,* Plato's *The Republic*, and Hemingway's *For Whom the Bell Tolls*. He placed Machiavelli in Werner-Miranda's hands.

"Humberto, I believe that you have intercepted a chemical weapon I sent some colleagues of mine to retrieve."

Werner-Miranda raised an eyebrow.

Simon smiled and swirled his Scotch. It was always such a game. "Of course, should you retain this poor man's atom bomb, you will never again have to rely on incompetents like retired members of the Weather Underground or flighty revolutionaries from the FALN."

Werner-Miranda slammed Machiavelli onto the hardwood floor and jumped to his feet. "I don't want to be reminded of that goddam JFK fiasco!" he ranted. "Is this why you came? You can tell your goddam Cuban friends to go straight to fucking hell!"

With all the self-control he could muster, Simon wiped the spittle off his face and strolled over to Werner-Miranda's liquor cabinet, where he poured himself another Johnny Walker. "Nor will you have to rely on people like Luis Munoz," he calmly added, "who ran your operation in southern New Mexico two years ago with the incompetents from the KGB." He turned around and regarded Werner-Miranda with scorn. "That was very sloppy, Humberto."

Mouth twisting, the Colombian angrily slammed his glass down on the cabinet next to Simon's. Amazed that it hadn't shattered into a thousand pieces, Simon calmly poured four fingers of Scotch into Werner-Miranda's glass to match his own and tumbled in another pair of ice cubes from the compact refrigerator beneath the bar. A fleeting moment of panic convinced Simon that the Colombian was on the verge of yanking out his .454 and blowing his head off. Werner-Miranda did not react well to bravado, but timidity set him off like a shark going after baby blood. It was better, prodding him this way. All that was needed now was a little nose candy.

Handing the Scotch to the Colombian, Simon retreated back to his chair. After a moment's hesitation, Werner-Miranda followed. Sitting, they faced one another again, composure reestablished. Simon's eyes traveled to an ornate silver box adorning the lamp stand near Werner-Miranda's recliner. Simon estimated it to be of Inca orgin, hand-crafted, circa 14th century. "You still indulge, Humberto?" he asked, knowing full well that the Colombian packed his nose on quite a regular basis.

"Of course. It is nothing."

"There are those who say it has made you sloppy. I have countered those accusations, as I partake a little myself."

Humberto Werner-Miranda grabbed the silver box from its tray, flipped open its lid, and shoved it in front of Simon's face. Simon licked his lips and stared at the box's mirrored bottom, where a half-dozen lines of white powder and a nose straw made of sterling silver waited.

"I've always admired your integrity in producing and distributing only the finest product," Simon said, taking the box in his hands. Laying it on his lap, he put the nose straw in his left nostril and snorted a line. He repeated the process with his right nostril, and then forced himself to turn the box over to the Colombian, who promptly finished the other four lines off in ten seconds flat.

Wiping his nose with the back of his hand, Werner-Miranda took a deep breath and sat up straighter in his chair, his eyes sparkling. Remembering his Scotch, he retrieved it and sipped it. "You pay your people poorly, Simon. It is why they came to me."

Simon forgot about any further misgivings. One got nowhere without boldness and audacity. Snorting the toot had been a good idea. Made him think better. He began expansively.

"With drugs, Humberto—despite your earlier mishaps with our Cuban allies and friends within the KGB—you can control Colombia. Our Soviet friends can no longer support your networks along the American Southwest; they're bankrupt anyway, and want to distance themselves from their President's wrath. But you, *amigo*. You can *buy* Colombia's politicians. Your people work for and support you. Your government doesn't take care of them. *You* do. And the Americans will always buy your product, despite their corrupt government's pious hosannahs about this so-called drug war. The terrorists will guard it for you. You can lead."

"What do you think, I'm stupid or something? I know all that. Get on with it."

"But the weapon you intercepted from me . . . whatever plan you have for its use won't work for you, *amigo*."

"Eh?"

"Cars, buildings, newspaper offices, universities, courtrooms—Humberto, my friend, already your bombings are creating a groundswell of support for the Colombian government by the very people you employ. Your bombs are too messy. You level a building. So what? Twenty innocent bystanders, wiped out. Have you furthered your cause? No. Juan Valdez, who used to pick coffee beans, whose son can now go to school because Juan now picks coca leaves, does he identify with your cause? No. His son was killed in the blast. Now what do you suppose will happen by employing—"

"A poor man's atom bomb, as you put it?"

Simon's eyes widened. It was one thing to talk about possession of a lethal toxin capable of creating hundreds of thousands of casualties, simply by dumping it into a city's water supply. It was another thing to hear it admitted. The Microcystin was every bit as powerful as a portable nuclear weapon. He found his voice again.

"The Americans will mobilize, hunt you down, and their Administration will convince their populace of the need to take over Colombia and hunt down every cartel member with whom you work. Use that toxin, Humberto, and you will regret it."

Humberto Werner-Miranda absently rubbed the heel of his hand against the butt of his revolver and stared at the toe of his German Jump boots.

"Humberto, you use your men wrong." Simon tossed his head in the direction of the doorway. "Señor Bullet-Head out there, he's a fine Aryan product. Tell him what to do, who to kill, who to maim and torture, and like a good doberman he will see his task through to completion."

"I'm an Aryan. You have something to say about that?"

Simon remembered the copy of *Mein Kampf* on Werner-Miranda's bookshelf and repressed a grin. "I meant that as a compliment. All I am saying, is that you should refine your process."

"So get to the goddam point! What about the toxin?"

"Humberto, you no longer need it. The courts awarded you

the extradition victory you sought. Don't make trouble for yourself."

Werner-Miranda thought about what Simon was saying. Simon pressed on.

"You wanted the toxin as a revenge weapon for any successful extradition the Americans wished to levy against you, correct?"

No answer.

"And did they succeed?"

Again, no answer, save the sucking sound Werner-Miranda made as he drained his Scotch.

"I have a deal for you, paisano," Simon said, ready to trade favors for the operations Monika Stern would execute within the next month. It was simply the way things worked. "I have always admired your fabulous resort in Selva-Wolkenstein. . . ."

The line was cast. Simon reeled him in. Thirty minutes later, after establishing a time and place to meet two weeks later in April to accept delivery of the toxin, Simon was shown the door by "Señor Bullet-Head," and found his car in the driveway, pointed in the exit direction. Evidently, someone had searched it for listening devices, papers, anything that would speak of clandestine communications. Simon's eyes automatically traced the outline of the engine's hood to see if the scotch tape he'd stuck on the hood line was still there. It was.

Still buzzing from a final toot of Humberto's best, Simon climbed behind the wheel of his Merc and drove away, smiling broadly. The transmitter Werner-Miranda's men had been looking for wasn't in the car.

He pounded the side of his head with his right hand, as if he were shaking water out of his ear after finishing a swim. A tiny hearing aid—the kind that can be hidden inside an ear canal—tumbled into the palm of his hand. He spoke to it.

"Copy all transmissions, Siegfried?"

"*Ja*," the hearing aid in his left ear replied. "Looks like we'll be skiing in northern Italy within the month. I've always liked the Dolomites, Simon."

After telling his contact to service his next dead-letter drop, which would include air fare to Aden, Yemen, Simon allowed himself a hearty laugh, astounded at the excellence of German electronics.

CHAPTER TWELVE

Pushmataha County, Southeastern Oklahoma

A Blackhawk shot over the mountain ridges and treetops, and began its spiral down to the mountain clearing before the cabin.

Given the pilot's flaxen, Nordic good looks, her aerobicized body, and overall cover-girl appeal, Rene Burchette didn't mind at all being the Old Man's babe. Or bimbo. Squeeze. Mistress. Hot piece. All of the above.

It was in her job description, and besides, she really admired Wayne MacIntyre— respect she gave to few men—because she'd been hired by him four years ago exactly for the attributes she'd had to offer the president and chief executive officer of Dustbowl Enterprises. And others: both fixed and rotary wing pilot's licenses; a third-degree black belt in Tae-kwon-do; a sharp eye and steady trigger finger from her biathlete college days; linguistic flexibility in German and Spanish . . . There were many reasons Wayne MacIntyre had hired Rene Burchette on as one of his personal bodyguards.

As well as his pilot. Rene concentrated on rolling the Old Man's Sikorsky UH-60 in a goose-egged orbit around his southeastern Oklahoma ranch, her eyes darting about the periphery of the camp below for any signal, any giveaway of danger—the flash of metal or glass in the tree line from a would-be sniper, the faces of the men outside the cabin below who were dressed in camouflaged fatigues, black T-shirts, and jungle boots.

Rene spotted Charlie Whitehead below. Satisfied, she told her boss, "We're clear to land, Wayne."

MacIntyre grinned at her from the copilot's chair on her left, then turned around and gave a thumbs-up to the man sitting in the command passenger seat to his rear. "Welcome to Push County, Lonnie," he said to the man from the National Security Council.

"Straight out of *Deliverance*," Wilkerson said simply, reaching for the chin strap of his flight helmet. He was a studious-looking man in his mid-forties, attractive in an intellectual sort of way. Maybe it was the granny glasses he wore and the sharp widow's peak of his brown hair, which he swept back upon removing his flight helmet. The Levi's, hiking boots, and black and red plaid flannel shirt he was wearing did not look out of place on a man who was equally comfortable in Brooks Brothers and Saville Row attire. What did look out of place was the cable and handcuff locked around his wrist that bound him to the briefcase he carried.

"Bet you didn't know that Oklahoma was this beautiful," said MacIntyre.

"That I didn't," agreed Wilkerson in his rather fastidious, deliberate manner that was beginning to annoy MacIntyre. "I really expected something else."

"You'll find it," MacIntyre replied after a deep breath. "It's all in the evaluation the DEA boys forwarded your department before you came down. I need help, Lonnie. I hope this weekend will do all of us some good."

"If you've got the men, Wayne, we can do many things."

Rene hovered over the mountain clearing fifty meters to the cabin's front. She eased the Blackhawk down until the wheels touched the ground, settled for a moment, then began shut-down procedures. Wayne MacIntyre and the man from the NSC slid open the passenger door.

"Lonnie," Wayne MacIntyre shouted over the beat and whine of the rotor blades, "we will truly see about that, because it looks like everyone's present." He clapped a hand around Wilkerson's shoulder and led him toward the cabin. Charlie Whitehead met them halfway. They paused, waiting for Rene to catch up after she finished post-flight and shut down the bird. "Meet Charlie Whitehead, here, my chief of security."

"My pleasure," offered Whitehead, hand outstretched. Wilkerson took it, and the two men sized each other up. Wilkerson regarded the tall, lanky Indian with his big easy smile and Oklahoma country accent with faint distaste. Wilk-

erson peered over Whitehead's shoulder and noted the others.
"Your men?"

Whitehead and MacIntyre exchanged looks. "Our guests,"
Whitehead answered, growing serious. Then he saw Rene
Burchette approach them from the now-quiet Blackhawk. She
unfastened the chin-strap of her flight helmet and swung her
head to free the tangle of her brown hair. He suppressed a grin,
knowing that Santo, Hanlon, and Maslow behind them were
now giving the group their full attention. They strolled toward
the cabin.

"Check it out," Hanlon muttered to the others.

"Down, boy," Santo replied.

"Now, children," Maslow intoned gravely, "be good."

"She's hot," Hanlon reiterated for the third time, quieter
now as the group approached them.

"Shut up," Santo said. "Keep that Irish dick of yours in
check, and be polite like the Chief says."

The two groups met.

Wayne MacIntyre stuck out his hand, singling Santo out
first. "Sergeant Santo," he said, grinning.

"Sir," Santo replied, taking it. He smiled at the larger man,
an older replica of his ex-team leader, Matt MacIntyre: black
hair, bright blue eyes, athletic frame.

"Matt told me a lot about you, Sergeant Santo."

"Manny."

"Why sure, Manny. Just call me Wayne. I don't like sir too
much." MacIntyre proffered his hand to Maslow next. "Let's
see, you're the Chief. Winston Maslow the Third."

The others laughed, Hanlon the loudest. "The James Brown
Cowboy," Santo added, breaking the ice further.

Maslow looked embarrassed, and he matched iron grips with
Wayne MacIntyre. "Uh, sir—Wayne—just can the 'third' part.
I'm Wintz. As a matter of fact, we all like to operate on a
first-name basis." He jerked a thumb at Hanlon, towering
behind him. "Except for Lurch, here. He's our team rottweiler.
Pat him on the head, give him a bone, and he's your friend for
life."

MacIntyre and Hanlon shook hands, MacIntyre evaluating
Randy Hanlon with inquisitive eyes. "I've heard a lot about
you," he said.

Hanlon's grin faded.

"Good things," MacIntyre added, keeping Hanlon's grip. "I'm proud to meet you."

The smile came back to Randy Hanlon's face, and he nodded. "Very pleased, sir. Your son was one of our team's best captains."

MacIntyre motioned for Wilkerson and Rene Burchette to step forward. "Gentlemen, my pilot Rene Burchette and Mr. Lonnie Wilkerson from the National Security Council."

Amenities were exchanged. MacIntyre watched Rene carefully. Her reactions and blending with these men were important. As always, she smiled while maintaining a cool aloofness to keep the distance. It was her business. Men couldn't help but take in her countenance and figure a second longer than necessary. On one hand, it tended to piss him off. But on the other . . . Rene's profession came first. He would never, ever let personal concern override the fact that she was his bodyguard first and foremost. Some women considered good looks necessary, part of their tool kit. Others couldn't handle it. For Rene, the natural camouflage of her beauty was a large asset.

MacIntyre saw Claudie waving an iron skillet at them from the doorway, and the crow's feet around his eyes deepened. "Claudie!"

"Y'all c'mon in'n get the grits while they're hot," the old man ordered. "Got some flapjacks'n scrambled eggs too." Claudie spat a foot-long stream of amber juice from his toothless mouth for emphasis, which splattered against a river rock next to the porch.

"Got some chew, Claudie?" MacIntyre asked him, walking for the door.

"Shore 'nuff." Claudie fished deep inside his overalls.

MacIntyre caught a tar-black twist of home chew from the old, broken-down cowboy and bit off the end. Everyone watched, a little open-mouthed. He offered some to Rene, who declined with an embarrassed grin. As did Wilkerson and all the rest, except for Maslow. MacIntyre tossed the chew back to his ranch cook, who shoved it back into his overalls, which looked like they hadn't been washed in two weeks. Venison grease had given them a shiny veneer. "Well, c'mon inside!" he said, disappearing back into the kitchen with his iron skillet.

While Claudie cleaned up the dishes later, Wayne MacIntyre and Charlie Whitehead led their guests to one of the cabin's back rooms, where the touch of a panel opened up an entranceway to the basement downstairs.

It was an underground command and control center, replete with computers, videos, telephones, and radios.

Manny Santo let out a low whistle as they entered. Hanlon's mouth hung open. Maslow's eyes glinted at the abundance of silicon, switches, and buttons.

MacIntyre smiled as the door shut and locked behind them. "Matt told me once that this was sort of like a military TOC—I forget what the acronym means."

"Tactical Operations Center," Santo finished for MacIntyre in an awed, hushed voice. "Man, you could control World War III from inside this place."

"Let's hope we don't ever have to."

Santo realized that MacIntyre was serious.

Charlie Whitehead walked up to another door and punched in the number combination to the code lock. The steel-reinforced doorway slowly swung open. He hit the lights, illuminating another room dedicated as a private council chamber cum briefing center with screens, a podium, and a mini-auditorium. Whitehead entered first, as MacIntyre paused before the doorway to let the others pass. Computerized images and videos could be shown against a special laser-receptive wall screen that enhanced images to a life-sized scale with the touch of a button. All screening automation was controlled by the switches and LED displays covering the broad armrests of a center chair at the front of the other seats.

Hanlon paused at the entrance before Rene Burchette. "Beauty before beast," he said, smiling what he hoped was his most charming smile.

Rene regarded him with a poker face for a moment and walked in. Hanlon glanced back at Santo and shrugged.

As the group filed in, MacIntyre motioned at the seats, and Whitehead hit the switches of the control chair he occupied. Projectors at the rear of the room hummed to life, as Whitehead monitored the controls and the others took their seats. The viewing screen suddenly illuminated into a global map. Red dots indicated port towns and capitals across the world: a scattering in Europe, fewer in Africa and the Middle East. A few lights in Thailand and Australia. More in South America, and a light in practically every state in the U.S. and province in Canada. Finally, a digitized logo of Dustbowl Enterprises appeared at the top of the screen.

MacIntyre cleared his throat and motioned for Lonnie Wilkerson to join him at the podium. He picked up a pointer and waved it at the global display. "I've, uh, got a few shops set up in different places as you can see," he said, almost embarrassed.

"You're a modest man, Mr. MacIntyre," Maslow commented.

"Wayne, dammit. It's *Wayne*."

"Import-export?"

"Yes. That, and computers and oil. Computers and software are the bread and butter of Dustbowl Enterprises, though. We've let oil take a back seat over the past few years. Gentlemen, I'll be frank with you. I'm proud of what I've produced in life because I started with nothing. And I also take pride in the fact that I've contributed to the world something born of production. Never made any money on hostile take-overs and junk bonds like some of those idiots on Wall Street.

"Let it just suffice to say that members of my organization and I can travel virtually anywhere in the world, communicate throughout the entire spectrum of the international economic community, and . . ." Wayne MacIntyre took a deep breath and fixed the group before him with an intense look. "And front clandestine and covert activities as I have for the government already."

"That's a bold statement, Wayne," Santo said evenly, glancing at the man MacIntyre had introduced as Lonnie Wilkerson. He distrusted most government men of his type. National Security Council. Now *that* was a multi-faceted organization.

MacIntyre noted Santo's look and nodded at Wilkerson, who laid his handcuff-cabled briefcase on a table adjacent to MacIntyre's podium and started to dial its combination. MacIntyre nodded at Whitehead, who touched a button on the arm-rest of the screening room's control chair. The screen changed from a global display to one of the United States, highlighting all Dustbowl Enterprises offices across the country. Another touch of a button enlarged the state of Oklahoma, which in turn enhanced and enlarged Pushmataha County until a 1:50,000-scale map of the ranch and its surrounding area filled the entire wall screen. A red dot indicated the cabin housing them, set away by at least twenty kilometers north and west of the town of Clayton.

A moment's silence. MacIntyre had wanted to deliberately impress upon the group the high degree of state-of-the-art computerization and laser optics his TOC possessed.

By now, Lonnie Wilkerson had retrieved a folder and a roll of slides from his briefcase. With a key that had been locked inside the briefcase he unlocked the wrist cuff. He handed the roll of slides to Whitehead and then took a seat close to the podium. All eyes were on MacIntyre.

"Again, thank you for coming, gentlemen," MacIntyre said. He eyed Rene Burchette. "All of you," he added. A few glances were directed her way, and Rene maintained her cool, poised stare at MacIntyre. MacIntyre looked back at Santo. "You're right, Sergeant Santo. To say that I've been responsible for intelligence-gathering operations for the government *is* a bold statement. It's also the truth. I put together a recon team once to find our boys who were left in Southeast Asia. To say that relations between my intelligence apparatus and that of the past four Administrations have been rosy and good-willed would be a lie. It would be a lie because the fine efforts of my recon team were ignored, and I became rather embittered because of it. It was explained to me later that it was not politically expedient to stage a rescue operation in Southeast Asia."

A stony silence filled the room as MacIntyre paused. How many times, Santo thought to himself, had he seen those black and white "You Are Not Forgotten" flags of a POW's silhouette back at Ft. Bragg? Seemed like every mercenary magazine and pawn shop back in Fayetteville sold those flags and T-shirts. Where were those men now, those poor bastards who had their F-105s and F-4s shot out from underneath them while knocking out MiGs and ADA sites over Hanoi's deadly skies?

Amputees, lunatics, slaves. By now, anyway. Ten years ago a rescue operation might have been feasible. There might have been someone to rescue. What was it that had happened to the integrity of his country and its elected leaders that would allow its finest men to rot in *nuc-mam* sauce for the rest of their lives? Small wonder that many officers and NCOs in the Army were more interested in their careers as opposed to duty, honor, and country.

Duty, honor, country, Santo thought, words that MacArthur had made famous at West Point with the bright, shining faces of the graduating class of '64 who later on led men into Southeast Asian combat.

Santo's face clouded. MacArthur had meant those words. But what about his country's leaders? Santo examined Wayne MacIntyre standing before him and saw the same cloud. There too was a disappointed man, disappointed in the system, its leaders, the route his country was taking into economic chaos, greed, materialism, and decay.

"And because I was told that it was not politically expedient to rescue those men," MacIntyre went on to say, "I stopped all further extracurricular activity with the government." MacIntyre glanced at the NSC man, Lonnie Wilkerson, who stood by at the desk adjacent to MacIntyre's podium. "Until most recently."

MacIntyre stepped away from the podium and stood directly before the group. The skin on his forehead was taut, shiny. His thick, black hair seemed more shot through with gray. The quaver in his voice betrayed his true age of fifty-nine years, where usually he acted, sounded, and looked a generation younger. Charlie Whitehead, still monitoring the screening controls, looked away. He knew what was coming.

"I have three boys, gentlemen, Rene. Or had, rather. One of them is dead. Donny, my eldest. My middle son Matthew, you all know. He's now serving with the Special Forces battalion in Germany," MacIntyre broke off, confusion clouding his eyes.

"Bad Toelz, sir," Santo said gently. "Matt's assigned to 1st of the 10th over there. It's a good assignment. Unfortunately, however, they're about to move to Stuttgart."

MacIntyre nodded his head, hitched up his Levi's, and sat on the mini-auditorium's stage before the group, his shoulders slumped. "My eldest son killed my wife in a boating accident three years ago. He was addicted to crack cocaine. We were in the water, Maria and I. We were water-skiing at Tenkiller Lake, and Maria and I had just fallen, because Donny was speeding the boat up more than necessary and taking sharp turns. I didn't know that he'd been getting high, sucking that damned shit into his lungs and ruining his body, his mind, Lord God. . . ." MacIntyre's voice cracked, and he made himself take a deep breath.

Then MacIntyre straightened up, his eyes glinting suddenly

with a hard light, and he bored those eyes into his audience. "My son was high. He brought the boat around recklessly fast, dangerously close to my wife and me, at too great a speed. It had twin Mercury 150-horsepower engines. He was always trying to impress me, that boy. At the last minute, he failed to shut down the throttle. He tried to swerve."

MacIntyre swallowed suddenly, and looked away.

Charlie Whitehead reached out and touched MacIntyre's knee. "Boss, you don't have to do this."

MacIntyre gripped Whitehead's hand hard, and he looked up at the others. Twin streaks ran into the deepening creases of his leathery face, which had been robust and handsome earlier, and was now just plain old. "My wife was decapitated by my son," he said simply. "I buried Donny one month later to the day, after he'd committed suicide. They're both up on my family's plot in the Tulsa cemetery. I plant oak saplings out there every now and then."

MacIntyre stood back up and breathed deeply. He wiped his face with his sleeve. "Sorry about that," he told them. "It's embarrassing to see an old man cry." He cleared his throat. "Well then, that's my story, and that's the reason you all are here. Drugs ruined my family. It's almost a cliche these days, hearing and saying, 'Drugs ruined my family.' Fact of the matter is, that's the case. Doesn't matter if you're rich or poor. Drugs will mess up any family. It's an equal-opportunity vice. I might have let it go at that and thanked my lucky stars for the Good Lord having spared my other two boys, Matt and David, but you know what?"

Everyone knew what was coming next.

"David had to go and get shot at the JFK International Airport last month. He got shot by terrorists. They used to be members of the Weathermen, a radical '60s group that went around bombing federal buildings." MacIntyre shot another look at Lonnie Wilkerson. "Those same bastards—excuse me, Rene—or at least, a couple of them, tried to stage a hijacking at JFK, and my son was caught in the middle of the cross fire that erupted in the airport. The kid was just going to a Boy Scout convention in Munich. He saw his bodyguard die in front of him. And David, all fourteen years old of him, absorbed four 7.65-millimeter submachine gun rounds in his right arm. The doctors wanted to take it off. I wouldn't let them. He barely survived."

Wayne MacIntyre paused again, while Lonnie Wilkerson handed him the manila folder the NSC man had retrieved from his briefcase. Inside were pictures, eight-and-a-half-by-eleven black and white glossies. MacIntyre handed the pictures around to the group before him. "Those are the terrorists," he said. "They were trained to hijack a jet, pull the hostage routine, and demand freedom for some Latino terrorists imprisoned in Peru. Name of the group was Light of the Shining Path—Sendero Luminoso. For Christ's sake. Can you imagine that? What kind of bullshit name is that? They say they're Maoist-Leninist revolutionaries funding their campaign with drug money. Kind of like the Cartel's Mafia controlling their coca fields in Bolivia and Peru. They hire out to the Cartel as bodyguards, assassins, and hit men.

"At any rate, Lonnie here will fill you in on the details about all that later. The bottom line is that narco-terrorists killed seventeen people at the JFK International Airport last month, and one of my employees was killed. My youngest son was maimed." MacIntyre added softly, "He'll be lucky to ever get full use of his right arm again."

Santo contemplated the tension in the air. Everyone sat forward in their chairs, keyed in to the emotion in Wayne MacIntyre's voice.

"So I've come to a decision about what I intend to do. Key people in the Administration, recognizing my all-too-apparent lust for vengeance, have played upon this. I'm not so naive not to figure it out. My decision is to take the war to the drug lords themselves, to exterminate their kind. In short, I intend to have selected targets captured or assassinated."

MacIntyre's jaw set suddenly, and the hard look returned to his eyes. "And that is why I invited you all here. My son Matt recommended you after I told him that under no circumstances would I allow him to participate. I told him I wanted the names of the best people he'd ever worked with. And he gave me yours, Master Sergeant Timothy Santo, Chief Warrant Officer Winston Maslow, Sergeant First Class Randy Hanlon." MacIntyre glanced at his pilot. "And you, Rene. I trust that you and these men can come together as a team."

MacIntyre swept them all in with his penetrating stare. "Years ago this country had a different flag, one of a rattle snake poised and ready to strike. It said, 'Don't tread on me.' Well I'm tired of being stepped on by these drug lords. I want you all to help me get rid of them, and any other person or organization that seeks to enforce their trafficking through narco-terrorism."

Another silence filled the screening room. Santo, glancing around, could see a sort of wistful look in the woman pilot's eyes, like she was savoring the promise of vengeance for hire. For what reason, Santo couldn't fathom. He could also see the trace of guilt that permeated Hanlon's countenance at every mention of drugs, and that made Santo wonder if this mission would make Randy seek absolution, a way to wipe out his own self-contempt. Santo turned toward his old executive officer. He saw the look of anticipation in Maslow's face, as if the transference of emotion and feeling for what MacIntyre was going to ask them to do would vent the immense sorrow at the loss of Maslow's own wife in another type of skiing accident.

They were all primed and ready. MacIntyre knew how to persuade. Santo knew what the others in this room would do.

MacIntyre nodded at Whitehead and Wilkerson, and they quietly exited the screening room. He faced the others. "As I have now reached the point of directly asking the four of you to engage in illegal activities for what essentially is my personal vendetta, regardless of whether it's right or wrong, it is time for the four of you to come together and discuss things before I go on any further. You may interpret what I have just discussed as my own vision of a 'higher morality.' It may not be for you. After talking, if you decide you want no part of what I ask, then you will be free to go with my signature on your checks and tickets home."

MacIntyre stepped away from the podium and walked outside. Santo, Hanlon, Maslow, and Rene Burchette looked at each other in the silence that followed. Then Santo moved his chair around, starting to make a circle. The others did the same. Rene joined the circle. They faced each other.

"DTM," Santo said, spelling out the acronym. "Don't Tread on Me. Well, the name of this organization fits. Question is, do *we* fit?" Santo regarded Rene Burchette with an even, frank look. "Looks like we all have a decision to make." He consciously tried to disregard her natural beauty, and knew he would have trouble doing so.

Rene returned Santo's look with a level stare. "Wayne asked me to attend this briefing. He didn't give me any details, other than the fact he was forming a new branch within his security organization. It didn't take much reasoning to figure out why."

Maslow smiled at her disarmingly. It caught her off guard. "You flew that Blackhawk in quite nicely, Rene."

Hanlon snorted, and tried to suppress a laugh of contempt. "Hey, the Army pins wings on a lotta female pilots—"

Rene stopped him short with another of her cool, unsmiling looks. "I'm a civilian pilot. I have no military training."

"Oh."

Santo cleared his throat. "Rene, I don't know you. Neither do these guys, so please try to ignore any verbal diarrhea from Mr. Big Mouth." He smiled, hoping for a response, as did Maslow and Hanlon with a hurt-puppy look. Rene Burchette gave them a Mona Lisa smile and tilt of her chin in return.

Santo's grin faded. "In other words, I hope you left your ego at the door. I also hope you're not a radical feminist type ready to prove herself to three men she doesn't know."

"Just as I hope not to be pre-judged by three strangers."

"Touché." Santo paused. She was right. "Well put, Rene. But the point I'm making here is that it's time for frank talk, if we're to come together on a decision for Mr. MacIntyre." He nodded at Hanlon and Maslow. "I know these men. I don't know you. One thing is, if we decide to work for Mr. MacIntyre as some sort of counterterrorist team against druggies and the like, then I'm the one in charge. On the ground, that is. I'm the cell leader."

"I understand that."

"So why does Mr. MacIntyre want you on this team, Rene?" Maslow interjected in a gentle, inquisitive voice. "What skills can you bring to the team other than piloting a Blackhawk?"

"Linguistics and shooting skills."

"Explain that," Hanlon said.

"I was an Air Force brat growing up. My mother is German; in fact, my father's last assignment was in West Germany as the attaché there. Prior to that, my family had pulled tours in Latin America, Mexico, and Honduras, to be exact. Naturally, I picked up the languages and dialects. I enhanced them by becoming a linguistics major in college. My hobby has always been flying. I ended up with two degrees, aviation and linguistics, by the time I graduated school seven years ago, hoping to end up with an organization such as Wayne's. I did. Here I am."

"So what about your shooting skills then?" Hanlon prodded, a smirk on his face.

Rene ignored his edge of sarcasm. "I was a biathlete in school—skiing and shooting. When I joined Dustbowl Enterprises, Wayne and Charlie Whitehead recognized my additional potential for security work, and I learned various other shooting skills: quick-draw, house-clearing techniques, et cetera. Not so much unlike what you do in Special Forces. Charlie ran a pretty good shooter's course based on his own experiences."

Santo warmed to the cool, mature woman sitting before him. She couldn't have been more than in her late twenties. She seemed level-headed enough. He realized that Maslow and Hanlon were playing an old game, the Mutt and Jeff routine. Good guy, bad guy. What was interesting was that she seemed to know it.

Santo's mind was made up. He stared hard at Hanlon and Maslow. "You guys have any objections toward working with Rene here?"

Maslow shook his head, his eyes twinkling at Rene. Hanlon bit the inside of his cheek, glanced at Rene, then looked back at Santo. "No objection, Manny. At least not for now." He looked back at Rene.

Santo wondered if the two could work together. Personalities were everything in this business. Time would tell. That, and the gamut of shooting drills, patrols, sleep deprivation, thinking under stress, and a couple of practice runs against the local druggies here in Pushmataha County.

"There's a shooting range about a hundred meters away from the ranch," Santo announced. "Charlie Whitehead told me that we can qualify on over a dozen different pistols and submachine guns out there."

The new cell leader of DTM stood up. "So let's go to work."

CHAPTER THIRTEEN

Dhofar Province, Yemen

The early morning sun peeked over the Dhofar mountain range and spilled its brittle March light into the chilled, barren gray of the desert valley below, illuminating a Soviet air base. The wasteland surrounding the air base, and for that matter, over ninety percent of the country of Yemen, was alkaline. Nothing grew. Rocks rotted, expanding and contracting with temperatures which at night plummeted to the forties and fifties, and in the day boiled the mercury up a hundred degrees. Few animals, other than snakes and scorpions, stirred in their rocky habitats to greet the sun's rays, and the only vegetation was mottled greenish-gray lichen growing despondently on the north face of occasional boulders and cliff walls.

The land was poor. Even the Middle Eastern sea of black gold floating their Moslem brother countries along the Yemeni periphery had neglected to bless this portion of the world, until recently, when North and South Yemen had united after the northern fields were discovered and tapped. And so the region had suffered for centuries, until South Yemen became a charge of the Soviet Union in the late sixties. South Yemen had only one asset: its strategic location overlooking the Red Sea where the southern approaches to Bab el Mandeb controlled one of the world's most active shipping lanes, and the Soviets were more than willing to take advantage of it.

The Dhofar Air Base was inhospitable to anything but the man-made and man-occupied presence of the Soviet war machine, a war machine now in decline; the once-robust Dhofar Air Base was now only a facsimile of its original self.

It was now a boomtown gone bust, with no more rubles to sustain it. Indeed, the occasional roar of an Ilyushin heavy freight transport jet rent the dawn quiet with its four 26,455-pound-thrust turbofans, a steady reminder of the Soviet Union's shrinking presence on the Yemeni Peninsula. For the past several days, transport craft had airlifted the air base's complement of vehicles, cannon, dismantled fighters, and munitions, including the deadly nerve and blister-agent gas cannisters used for chemical warfare the Soviets had proliferated throughout the Middle East over the past decade. Heavy-lift Mi-26 helicopters straddled semi-trailers in their characteristic long-legged stance of a praying mantis.

The airfield and Army encampment were at once busy and dead. It depended on which end of the airfield's loosely rectangular expanse one looked at. Contained in a broad, rocky valley between the Dhofar and Kurdistani mountain ranges, the airfield's axis shot like an arrow toward the southwestern tip of the Yemeni Peninsula in the direction of the tiny country's capital of Aden. Yemeni soldiers and airmen, stationed at the Dhofar airfield, slept quietly through the dawn hour, while their Soviet taskmasters left them "unsupervised" for once, now that the country's fifteen-year-long civil war had finally ceased and North and South Yemen had united under one flag. Now there were other, much more economically important priorities taking place within the Dhofar Air Base that did not necessitate Soviet war-machine advice for their Yemeni comrades.

The loudly publicized Soviet military de-escalation camouflaged another activity in a remote portion of the air base, along the northeastern access to the base closest to the mountain ranges beyond, bordered by a myriad of trails and ravines. A barbed-wire-encircled complex of barracks and desert-tan colored concrete buildings formed an aquarium-like enclosure there, where early morning grunts, curses, and yells signaled a routine of calisthenics in a sawdust exercise pit centered inside an enclosed area. A three-bird pack of Mi-24 Hind-D gunships intimidated any would-be explorers and snoops hoping to answer the riddle hidden behind the barbed wire and gate surrounding the periphery of this part of the Dhofar airfield.

This portion of Dhofar Air Base was closest to the firing and demolitions ranges freckling the northern outskirts; it was closest to the northern access of the base where occasional visitors from West Europe, young men and women in their twenties and early thirties, were closely monitored and chaperoned by the officers and senior sergeants assigned to the lone battalion of Soviet Signal Corps soldiers. It was here, at this portion of the Dhofar airfield, where only Soviet access was permitted. It was almost an embassy unto itself.

Centered in the sawdust pit, a Soviet senior sergeant and first lieutenant monitored the calisthenics of six people: two women and four men. They were of different colors and races. Each spoke several languages, a critical skill for the trade and life-style they lived. Late evening conversation within the barracks housing them easily switched back and forth among Arabic, French, and Spanish, but each spoke a common language, English, and it was in English that they now conversed for their early morning drill of calisthenics and hand-to-hand combat techniques.

"Pair off!" the lieutenant barked at the group in harsh and broken English. His sandy-brown hair was a stiff brush of crew-cut authority, defying the desert breeze to blow it about.

His assistant, a compact and blocky senior sergeant with lank black hair, eyed the lieutenant's desert camouflage uniform, sterile of any unit patches and qualifying badges, and noted the faint smell of starch filtering through the cool desert morning air. In contrast, the battle-hardened senior sergeant's mottled gray and tan desert uniform was faded with wear and patched at the elbows and knees, and the smell of his previous day's sweat was more befitting the circumstances.

The group of men and women before them paired off as the Soviet officer ordered.

The senior sergeant suppressed a sardonic grin and told the lieutenant, "Time to separate the *stariki* from the *salagi*, eh?" To separate the men from the boys. It was always a game to insult the junior officer and make him think it was at someone else's expense.

"They have much to learn and we have much to teach, Sergeant," came the officer's reply.

The senior sergeant bit off the chortle threatening to escape his lips. The officer thought they were *amateurs*? Well, Comrade Bristle-Hair was new, if anything. The sergeant turned his attention to the group and regarded their leader, the German woman with pony-tailed, honey-blond hair, and the proud tilt of her chin. She looked familiar. He remembered her lithe and graceful body, which could be as strong and threatening as the angular structure of her face, yet was also as becoming as the sensuality that always simmered behind her cool, jade-green eyes. Yes, she had been here before.

In the pit, Monika Stern picked the most muscular of the men in the group and approached him in what she knew was a graceful, feminine gait. There was a point to be made. Out of the corner of her eye, she saw that Yuko was watching. The Japanese woman had paired off again with the Irishman, and she wondered if there was something going on between them.

"Phillipe," Monika Stern said, smiling seductively at her hand-to-hand partner. "You know how I despise you pig Frenchmen."

Phillipe Marceau shifted his two-hundred-pound bulk in her direction, and tried not to chew the inside of his cheek. He was a large, balding man with an intellectual's round-lensed wire-frame glasses and a short-trimmed beard. He was dressed in the same combination of desert camouflage the Soviets had supplied the team with, a mixture of mottled gray and tan. Marceau smiled thinly and ignored the adrenaline shooting inside his stomach. *To mess with this one,* he thought, *is not so good.* He'd been told he'd have a woman leader upon notification of this mission, whatever it was. Marceau and Feltrinelli, the Italian, had discovered this fact upon linking up with the Irishman and Palestinian at rendezvous in Beirut, shortly before their arrival in Aden last week on the Air France shuttle.

It had been easy enough to recognize the others, and why they were in Aden. They had all heard about this German woman. After all, their trade was a large and deadly fraternity fractionalized by myriad networks and cells. Sooner or later, one pieced the puzzle together and learned that one was *really* working for the PFLP, or the Shi'ites, or the Abu Nidal organization with their rich Libyan sponsors, all through a series of cutouts. It was always the damned Arabs that had enough money. It seemed that the Western European organizations—Red Army Faction, Red Brigades, Combat Communist Cells—were now as bankrupt as their Eastern Bloc sponsors, not to mention the utter chaos that had ensued that winter the wall came down in Berlin.

He wondered why *this* team, a mixture of races and organizations, was being assembled. *As the snake twists,*

Marceau thought, bracing himself before his group leader for the throw technique to follow, *so we shall all conform*. The chauvinist in him said to bash her face good. The professional in him said to beware and let her keep the upper hand. A resounding thump in the sawdust would do for now.

"Okay, Monika Stern, we shall dance," Marceau found himself saying, his eyes glittering at Stern's figure. Yes, he wouldn't mind putting his hands on her.

From where he stood in the center of the sawdust pit, the Soviet lieutenant snapped, "Take-down drills! First is practice!"

The senior sergeant faced his new lieutenant, weary of the routine.

"One!" the lieutenant commanded. The senior sergeant struck an imaginary blow to the younger man's face, which was energetically blocked by the lieutenant's left forearm. The others before them choreographed the movement in tandem. The senior sergeant noted that the German woman had allowed the Frenchman to be the thrower, and he awaited the next step.

"Two!" The lieutenant pulled his sergeant's hand over his shoulder while socking his hip deep into the sergeant's lower abdomen. The others followed suit with their respective partners.

Now the sergeant saw that the Frenchman had lifted the German woman off the ground, and that she was draped over his back like a rag doll. He grinned, seeing her relaxed, feline calm.

"Three!" the lieutenant snapped again, and suddenly the sergeant was flipped over the lieutenant's back and slammed onto the ground to the accompaniment of three other thuds. He coughed; his breath had been knocked out from the force of the throw. His forty-one-year-old spine protested from one too many throws, one too many parachute drops, and way too many mountain rucks. The throw didn't have to be *that* fucking hard.

The lieutenant leaned over him. "Comrade Senior Sergeant! You are all right, comrade?"

The others in the group tittered. The senior sergeant picked himself up and noted that the German woman too was trying to catch her breath, and was brushing the sawdust off her back. "Fine, sir," he replied patiently.

The lieutenant jerked his head towards the others. "Switch!"

He faced back to the senior sergeant, who was grinning at him. "What is it?"

"One!" the senior sergeant replied.

The lieutenant tried to punch him in the face, and the older man easily blocked it, feeling the energy of the younger man's blow travel up his forearm with a numbing sting.

Monika Stern's eyes glinted at the Frenchman, as she blocked Marceau's blow.

"Two!" Hips thudded into abdomens.

"Three!" Four bodies pounded in the sawdust pit. The senior sergeant cleared his throat. The lieutenant wasn't getting up. He glanced back at the German woman. Neither was the Frenchman, who stirred, moaning, on his back. He exchanged grins with the German woman, then dragged his officer-in-charge to the side of the pit. The officer started to come to, sputtering and protesting. Marceau joined him on the perimeter, kneading the small of his back and trying to stretch out the kinks Stern had twisted into him.

"Switch partners, practice the move, and conduct the other throws we showed you yesterday," the senior sergeant told the group in a voice bordering on equality. The men and women in the sawdust pit complied thankfully, relieved of the Soviet officer's diatribes for the while.

Monika Stern contemplated the Japanese and Irish members of her team. Yuko Suzuki and Liam O'Brien. She pondered the implications of this international team. In a word: *why?* Why join forces between the Japanese Red Army, the Provos of Ireland, her own Red Army Faction, the Italian Red Brigades, the Palestine Liberation Front, and France's Action Directe? She knew enough to be patient. Her case officer would explain when he arrived in Aden.

For now, however, there was discipline to be established, recognition from the others of her command and authority.

Stern approached Yuko Suzuki and the Irishman. "Switch off," she told them. Liam O'Brien squared off to Stern. "Okay, lass. Let's go to it," he told her with his easy grin. Monika caught Yuko looking at her in that way she thought she had seen earlier.

"No," she told O'Brien. She tossed her head in the Italian's direction. "You pair off with Feltrinelli. Come, Yuko."

"I have heard of you," Yuko told her softly in perfect English, as they moved away from the others. Stern took in the other woman's figure. Yuko Suzuki was slim and rather plain in the face, which was a good trait for a terrorist, since it ensured anonymity in a crowd. Yet her rounded breasts, flat belly, and strong hips were very appealing. Her conditioning was reflected in strong legs that tapered delicately to her ankles but that also highlighted the smooth, hard half-spheres of her calf muscles. Her voice was clear and pure, a child's voice locked in a killer's heart with Shogun assertiveness.

"You have been quiet the past year. It is interesting with the events in Eastern Europe that you organization hasn't been—"

"Now isn't the time for discussions," Monika bristled, gripping Suzuki's arm firmly. She applied a firm and steady grip on the Japanese woman's upper arm, excited by the svelte warmth of her skin.

The Japanese woman's arms flashed in a blur, and suddenly Monika's world was upside down. She stared at Suzuki's feet for a moment. Stern pulled her face out of the sawdust, and noted that her fatigue shirt had hiked up to her chest. The others were looking at her. Jerking her fatigue shirt down, Monika jumped to her feet and squared off, concentrating hard on keeping her composure. The two women circled each other.

Suzuki moved gracefully, the hard muscles of her legs pumping claw-like against the sawdust of the hand-to-hand pit. The others gathered to watch. Monika moved in, prowling closer to Yuko like a caged panther.

Suzuki struck first, the knife edge of her left hand slicing through the air for a strike at the side of Stern's neck. Monika blocked it, smashed the flat of her palm against Yuko's face, stepped in, and scissored her legs around the other woman's legs. Then, deliberately falling, she straddled the Japanese woman between her thighs and raised her fist.

The Japanese woman lay on the ground in surrender. Monika considered the blow a moment longer. How to punish her? Monika then felt Yuko's hips and pubis rise and press against her crotch. It was a subtle movement. Monika saw her smile, and reached down with her hand and wiped a strand of black hair away from Yuko's eyes.

"Nice throw," she told her, climbing off. She extended her hand. Yuko took it and got to her feet.

Yuko smiled again at Monika. "Yes," she reasserted, looking deeply into Monika's green eyes. "I have heard of you." She bowed slightly, then glanced quickly at the others, noting their attention.

Monika wheeled about at them. "Practice your drills," she ordered in a tight voice. The others changed partners and resumed training. The group practiced various punches, blocks, and throws in a deadly mixture of various arts they had been taught over the years. Now was nothing more than a warm-up and review of old skills. After a while, the Soviet lieutenant and the Frenchman rejoined the group. This time the lieutenant was more mellowed and unassuming.

Stern caught the Soviet senior sergeant's eye from where he stood in the center of the sawdust pit and approached him. "I think we are ready for an advance in this area of training."

"I think you are right." The senior sergeant got his lieutenant's attention. "Sir! Shall we introduce our house pets to the group? I think it is time."

"Yes, of course," the lieutenant replied to the senior sergeant with an eager nod of his head. The lieutenant had regained the color in his face, and he was wise enough this time to realize there was much more for him to learn, and that the senior sergeant before him had much to teach. He also had some face to save. "Select two of them. Fetch the knives and clubs as well."

"Come with me," the sergeant told Monika Stern. "You may help if you like."

Stern complied, the corners of her mouth upturned, as the two walked toward the corner of the compound. The bars on the windows of their destination signaled that it was the blockhouse.

"I remember you," Stern told the senior sergeant in Russian. "You are the *starik* of this place. That puppy officer you threw, how do you put up with him?" Dust picked up around her booted ankles. The morning sun had by now raised the temperature to the seventies, and Monika Stern wiped the back of her hand across her forehead.

"*Salagi* like him come and go," replied the senior sergeant dryly. "I remember you too" he added, changing the subject. "How long has it been?"

"I first came here twelve years ago. Other times as well."

"Never mind the details, I know you cannot say. I can tell you have a good team this time. Better than I've seen in a while."

"Thank you. Of course, they have not come together yet. The Frenchman needs to be humbled more."

"That you have done already, I see," the senior sergeant chuckled. Neither spoke again for the next few moments as they approached the blockhouse. Operational security mandated that they did not exchange names, nor reminisce too deeply on past experiences and locations. It was an anonymous camaraderie, this rare esprit between the terrorist and sponsor.

Upon arrival, the senior sergeant yanked open the door and kicked awake the guard dozing in his chair guarding the cell block's entranceway. Protesting his innocence, the guard reached deeply inside his pocket for the keys and handed them over.

"Make the tea," the senior sergeant snarled to the cell block guard, "and have it piping hot within the next five minutes."

"Yes, Senior Sergeant!" The guard scampered away in search of a teapot.

Monika Stern followed the senior sergeant into the cell block's hallway, where the stale stench of urine and feces mingled with the coppery taste of blood in the air. She contemplated the row of bars before her, cells containing sleeping men, bearded and wasted with captivity. Most were Yemenis, with a scattering of Soviet soldiers or airmen serving time for drunkeness on duty or petty thievery. Her empty stomach rebelled and she tried not to let her face react to the smell of vomit permeating the cell block.

"The filth of these swine is fitting," the senior sergeant informed her, his canvas and leather boots thudding softly into the rough concrete floor with each step they took into the dimly lit corridor. "Yet believe it or not, there are worse conditions. If you can possibly imagine, there is worse depravity. They send us about four or five of the hard cases a month from the *Rodina*, when the KGB are finished with them. By then their minds are gone. Lately, they've been sending more. For what reason I cannot tell you."

"Moscow faces many problems these days." Stern offered, eager to make conversation to better numb her sense of smell. "That is why."

"*Da,*" the senior sergeant mumbled in reply. They stopped before another doorway. "Lithuania, Latvia, Estonia, they present many, many problems. Of course, I am only a humble sergeant. What do I know of political challenges facing the *Rodina*?"

"You are Spetsialnoye Nazhacheniye," Stern said softly, a knowing smile returning to her mouth. "Spetsnaz. You cannot be an ignoramus and make it in your organization. I have worked with Spetsnaz before."

Opening the barred door with another key, the senior sergeant swung it open. For a moment, the two of them stood there and considered the dusty stairs leading down into the blockhouse's dungeon. Neither of them said anything. From somewhere down below, a scream greeted their ears in what sounded like a mixture of surprise and resignation. "It is hell down there," the senior sergeant finally told Stern, ignoring what she'd just said to him. "And that is where the hard cases stay until we are ready for them. Today, they see light for maybe the first time in twenty, thirty days."

A kerosene lamp mounted inside the door cast a gray, liquid pallor on the cold stone wall lining the hallway. Silently, the senior sergeant led the way. His booted feet echoed like hollow totems on the dusty stairs as they descended into the dark. Another scream shattered the cold quiet when they reached the bottom.

"The perverts," the senior sergeant muttered under his breath. "They deserve each other."

Approaching the scream, Stern and the senior sergeant came upon another row of grimy cells, where lighter-complexioned prisoners imported from the USSR either stared at them with the manic glint of insanity behind their eyes or glared at them in hate behind the brooding masks of filth and hair that hid their faces.

The screaming grew louder. As they turned a corner, Monika Stern saw that one man was being brutally assaulted by a huge, darkly bearded man who had sunk his nails into his victim's hips, while two others held the screaming man's legs apart. Monika Stern riveted her attention on the scene. Sensing their arrival, the bearded prisoner raping the younger man saw them, and his thrusts became more rapid. He threw his head back in a scream as he came.

The senior sergeant simply looked at Monika Stern and said, "So. Pick two of them."

Stern was mesmerized. The victim, his rapist spent and through with him, had coiled into the fetal position on the concrete floor. The others had shrunk back against the wall. The rapist pulled up his baggy gray canvas trousers and secured them to his waist with a loop of hemp rope. He glared at Stern and the senior sergeant, a smile twisting crazily on his lips.

"That one is a murderer," the senior sergeant said to Stern. "An animal motivated only by instincts and his perversion." The senior sergeant removed a brick-like object hooked on the back of his waistband and walked toward the cell door with his keys. It was a stun gun, which could send enough voltage into a man to make him convulse and pass out. The crazy man's face twisted and he shrunk against the back wall with the others, babbling incoherently. The senior sergeant opened the door.

Monika Stern walked in first, much to her escort's surprise. Something in her eyes told the crazies lined up against the wall to stay there. She toed her boot against the blubbering man on the floor, who was still coiled in a combination of shame and outrage. "How many, Sergeant? Two, three?"

"My lieutenant said to bring back two."

"This one."

The sergeant looked at the man on the floor. His features, which had once been smooth and fair, were now a mixture of scabs, missing teeth, and bruises. One eye had been sealed completely shut. His scraggly dirt-blond hair and weak beard were patchy and teeming with lice.

"Poor bugger," the senior sergeant said under his breath. "He, I think, is a political prisoner. Probably a university student from Lithuania caught distributing an underground newspaper." The senior sergeant glanced sharply at Stern. "I was about to move him upstairs with the others. Why do you want him?"

"For those who have yet to kill with their hands," she explained. "One must crawl before they can walk."

The senior sergeant shrugged and hoisted the bloody man to his feet. In moments the prisoner was cuffed and propelled out the cell door. All too aware of the consequences if he tried to run, he stuck to the corridor wall as if it were made of flypaper.

"And the big bastard that raped him," Stern added with a tight smile.

The senior sergeant whipped out another pair of handcuffs from his belt and walked toward the big bearded prisoner, who started screaming. The senior sergeant jolted him with his stun gun, and the crazy man howled and groveled at the soldier's feet. The senior sergeant booted him in the face and then handcuffed him. Then he shoved the rapist out the cell. The young blond man started kicking his erstwhile tormentor, and the senior sergeant had to pull him away. He waited for Stern to exit the cell.

Monika Stern gazed longingly at the other men left inside. Her eyes traveled up and down their gaunt and clawed bodies. Her cheeks flushed, and her breathing picked up. Her eyes shone, and the senior sergeant put his hand on her shoulder to lead her away.

He felt cold marble and shuddered quietly inside. "Come," he said to her, releasing her shoulder as if it were contagious. "The others are waiting."

"I . . . I want to come back here."

Five minutes later found the four of them back at the sawdust pit.

It was the lieutenant's moment. Selecting the blond man first, he led the prisoner into the center of the sawdust pit, while the others circled around to watch. The senior sergeant kept his stun gun pressed lightly against the crazy prisoner's back to hold him still.

"Today you will learn to kill with your hands," the lieutenant explained to the group.

The younger prisoner became cognizant of his fate. He bolted out of the perimeter of the sawdust pit. Machine-gun bullets from one of the guard towers plowed the dirt in front of his feet before he could sprint twenty meters, and he froze in place, weaving crazily back and forth on his bare feet, while holding up his loose canvas pants with the other hand.

"Come!" the lieutenant ordered, grinning. He nodded at the senior sergeant, who clawed inside a bag he'd retrieved from the blockhouse before he and Monika Stern had returned to the group. The senior sergeant pulled out a commando knife and threw it, scabbard and all, at the prisoner's feet.

The young prisoner stared at the black heavy leather encasing the knife. He looked up at the lieutenant. Then he picked up the knife and yanked the blade out of its scabbard. He screamed something unintelligible at the Soviet officer.

"What did he say?" asked Stern, who stood next to the senior sergeant.

"I don't understand Lithuanian," the senior sergeant replied.

"He probably told our fine young officer to copulate with his mother." The senior sergeant examined the bright light in the crazy prisoner's eyes. "Isn't that right?"

"*Da!* Give me the knife! I will help!" It was the first intelligible utterance the big, bearded prisoner had made. The Soviet NCO reached for the handcuffs key in his trousers pocket.

Stern smiled, knowing what the senior sergeant was up to.

The prisoner and lieutenant circled one another while the others watched. "You must never underestimate your opponent," the lieutenant preached, his sharp White Russian face razored with what he hoped was a convincing look of killer's intent. The prisoner's mouth twitched, and slashed the air before the lieutenant's face with the commando knife he'd been given. The lieutenant jerked his head to the side, the whizzing blade before him missing his nose by centimeters. Out of the corner of his eye, he saw the bored stares of his students.

"Finish 'im off, mate," the Irishman yelled out.

The prisoner slashed again, this time nicking the lieutenant's forearm.

The lieutenant screamed and clamped his hand over the laceration. The blond prisoner charged. The lieutenant ducked and thudded his fist deeply into the prisoner's gut.

Stepping back, the Soviet officer then side-kicked the prisoner's right leg at the knee joint. The bone cracked with sickening clarity, like a pine knot exploding in a fire. The prisoner went down with a shriek.

"Always go for the knee first," the lieutenant lectured, his masculinity saved. The young prisoner writhed in the sawdust and howled. The lieutenant strutted toward the perimeter. "Someone go in there and demonstrate a pressure point blow underneath his forearm."

Still screaming, the prisoner crabbed away and managed to hobble upright onto his good leg. His eyes darted in all directions, blue diamonds flashing panic.

Phillipe Marceau stepped out, grabbed the screaming man by his wrist, twisted it up and away, and slammed his bony fist into the side of the young man's rib cage. The prisoner dropped onto the sawdust, choking for breath. Marceau returned to the perimeter, noting that Monika Stern had been watching him closely. Her eyes betrayed neither approval nor disapproval.

The lieutenant pointed his finger at the Palestinian member

of Stern's team two heads down from him. "You. Demonstrate another pressure point. Do in his collar bone."

The Palestinian, the youngest man in the group, no more than twenty-four, shrugged. "He is finished," he told the Soviet officer in husky, Arabic-accented English. The Palestinian regarded the moaning, semi-conscious prisoner for a moment, then looked back at the lieutenant. His jawline pumped as he worked his jaw muscles. "There is no challenge. Only shame." He did not see Monika Stern glaring at him from across the sawdust pit.

The lieutenant puffed up and, walking up to the Palestinian, thumped his forefinger into the slender man's chest. "Ahmet Habashi, right? They say you are the cream of the crop back at the PFLP. What would your superiors say if—"

"Sir!" the senior sergeant barked, his unseen hands locked on his bigger prisoner's wrists behind the prisoner's back.

The lieutenant wheeled around. "What is it?"

The Palestinian coiled, ready to strike out at the Soviet officer. Then he saw Monika Stern watching him with an expression of contempt. That, from a woman. Ahmet Habashi reexamined the prisoner twisting in the sawdust before them.

"We are not to mention anything about our guests' home organizations," the senior sergeant told his officer patiently.

The lieutenant bristled, his lips pressed together in parallel blue lines.

Ahmet Habashi walked quietly into the center of the sawdust pit and, encircling the blond man's head in a full nelson with his right hand nestled into the crook of his left elbow, snapped the prisoner's neck against his right forearm. The Lithuanian collapsed and lay very quiet and still. Habashi glanced back at Monika Stern, who gave him a smile and a nod of her head. Habashi returned to the perimeter. The lieutenant confronted him like an angry farm rooster.

"I said to break his collarbone, not kill him!" The lieutenant yanked the Palestinian into the center of the sawdust pit. Habashi squared off with the Soviet officer.

The senior sergeant looked at the prisoner he restrained. Then he twisted the key in his prisoner's cuffs and loosened them. The prisoner looked incredulously at the senior sergeant. "I have my stun gun in the small of your back," the senior sergeant muttered. "You have only one direction to go. Understand?"

The prisoner nodded his head excitedly.

"Then pick your target."

The lieutenant never saw the bigger prisoner barrel toward him like an unleashed steer. All he felt was the force of a sledgehammer in the center of his back and he was out cold. The prisoner scrambled in the dust for the knife the Lithuanian had dropped earlier. Ahmet Habashi remained inside the sawdust pit. Before the prisoner could launch another attack with his newfound weapon, the senior sergeant tossed Habashi a commando knife.

"You'll probably need that."

Ahmet Habashi flashed the senior sergeant a grin and reversed the point of his knife blade, holding it to his forearm with the cutting edge facing outward. In that manner, he could fight with his fists and leave a cut behind each strike with his right.

Monika Stern smiled tightly at Habashi with an approving nod. The Palestinian at least, had her respect. He was the lone one of them with balls enough to face the big bastard he was now knife-fighting. While Habashi and the prisoner circled each other, slashing and jabbing, Stern took in the rest of them. The Frenchman, predictably enough, merely watched. He was a demolitions expert who had delicate hands and long skinny fingers to protect. She would push him no further. The Irishman, standing next to Yuko Suzuki was the cell's driver and communications expert. He could imitate American or English accents, where and whenever needed. Other than that it was too early to tell about his sense of will, his sense of purpose, what Ahmet Habashi was proving in the sawdust pit now. Stern's gaze next found Yuko Suzuki. Yuko had different attributes. . . .

And that left the Italian from the Red Brigades, who viewed the spectacle in the sawdust pit with large, strangely opaque eyes. Stern contemplated the handsome, slender Italian on her team, one Marcello Feltrinelli. Even his hand-me-down Soviet desert camouflage uniform seemed tailor-made for his frame. Marcello Feltrinelli. In this business, one's reputation preceded one. He was the rich son of an Italian publisher whose contacts within the Red Brigades had engineered the kidnapping of an American general ten years before in protest of U.S. forces stationed in Europe. Feltrinelli's rise in the Red Brigades since that time had earned him a reputation for plans and operations.

He knew the U.S. order of battle and their counterterrorist capabilities inside and out. Yes, she thought. He would be a good one to size up before the others.

Habashi deflected another charge of the prisoner's knife by ducking underneath a clumsy slash, designed for hopeful decapitation, and sliced the prisoner's pectoral muscles open with his return strike. He followed the slash with a boot into the larger man's groin that sent him reeling back toward the center of the sawdust pit. The crazed prisoner roared in outrage, the wound serving to madden him rather than cripple him.

"You!" Stern shouted, pointing at the Italian she had been examining.

Marcello Feltrinelli casually looked her way, condescending to acknowledge his new cell leader.

"Inside the pit, Marcello," Monika ordered.

Feltrinelli shook his head.

"I said—"

"I know what you said," Feltrinelli replied in broken English. He gestured toward the two knife-fighting men in the pit. "This is barbaric."

Monika's eyes flashed. Exactly as she had expected. Italians, Frenchmen, always they were the worst. Chauvinist pigs.

She entered the pit. Ahmet Habashi, seeing her, paused in mid-strike. The moment's hesitation allowed the crazed prisoner a chance to rush him, and Habashi took a slash along his rib cage. Leaping away, Habashi tripped over his feet and rolled over in the sawdust. The prisoner lunged to finish him off.

Stern's flying boot caught him in the crown of his head, and the prisoner plowed into the sawdust, just short of the Palestinian.

"Excuse my interference," Stern told Habashi. "You did well."

Shaken, the Palestinian handed Stern his knife. Clamping his hand to his bleeding side, he returned to the perimeter. Stern, arms crossed, waited for her opponent. She glanced at the Italian, who had paired up with Marceau, the Frenchman, and flashed both a look of contempt. Certainly, an example had to be set.

The stunned prisoner sat up in the sawdust, his face clouded. Then, realizing his predicament, he riffled through the sawdust with his fingers, hunting for his own knife. Finding it, he faced his new opponent. His initial look of incredulity at facing the woman who had "selected" him from the cell he'd rotted in for the past three weeks turned into one of amusement. The prisoner threw his head back and roared with laughter.

"Come, pig," Monika Stern taunted, her eyes glazing over. The image of the prisoner laughing before her turned into one of her father long ago. The crazed man's tangled thatch of thick brown hair, his eyebrows grown together between his eyes, the rough, wild tangle of his beard, the roll of flesh distending over the waistband of his baggy canvas trousers—the whole sum of his disgusting appearance—revolted her and somehow she enjoyed it; she enjoyed the sight of this prisoner who, not half an hour before, had been raping the Lithuanian who now lay in a crumpled, bloody heap on the side of the sawdust pit.

He was more than evil, she reasoned, a pig who laughed at her the way her father had once taunted and laughed at her when she, Monika Stern, had suffered abuse at his hand no young girl her age should ever know. Her eyes fell to his crotch.

The prisoner followed her gaze and quit laughing. Instead, his upper lip curled with a sneer, and he advanced slowly on Monika Stern.

The senior sergeant stepped up alongside Stern and told her, "Easy now, miss, you've made your point." He waved his stun gun at the prisoner, who stopped short and glowered at them both like a caged animal before the whip.

"Get away," Stern snarled at the senior sergeant. She hefted her knife and assumed a fighting stance before the prisoner.

"Yes, let her have her way," the Italian said to the senior sergeant with laughing eyes.

Backing away, the senior sergeant realized that the group of people before him were different in method than any he had ever seen before; different than even his fellow Spetsnaz, who were not afraid to file a victim's teeth to the gums with a mill bastard file as an interrogation technique, march kilometer after kilometer with a fifty-kilo rucksack through Afghanistan's range of ridges, valleys, peaks, and endless rocks, then conduct a raid against a guerrilla holdout, including the wholesale slaughter of civilians, if they were in the way. The villages, after all, housed and fed the Mujahideen.

Always, there had been a purpose for the killing and even torture, and he and his type were not afraid to step inside the fray and make it happen. Yes, he'd seen more than his share of blood and inhumanity, but always there was a sense of purpose behind it, and the men he had served with in the past were men he would have died for if the situation warranted it.

The senior sergeant returned to the periphery of the hand-to-hand pit. Even this, he reasoned, the execution of prisoners who had committed atrocities back in the *Rodina* against their fellow man, rapists, murderers, thieves all, even in this bloody and distasteful exercise to execute those who deserved it, there had been a purpose: instill the killing instinct into those who would have to someday kill with their hands.

But the light behind the eyes of these Western Europeans was no different than that of the prisoners in the bowels of the Dhofar airfield's blockhouse. They were crazy, every one of them. Inhuman. Evil.

The senior sergeant shook his head and mentally washed his hands of the situation. What was it he had told the cell leader earlier in the dungeon? Yes, that the perverts deserved each other.

Monika Stern and the sneering prisoner before her circled one another with knives poised. Like the Palestinian, Stern held the blade of her knife parallel to her forearm with the business edge facing out. The prisoner lunged. Stern weaved to the right and slashed the prisoner's nose, flaying it open. A spray of blood misted the desert morning air.

The members of the cell surrounding the knife fight fell completely silent. Even the guards in the towers monitoring the access to this portion of the airfield watched. Yelling in outrage, the prisoner slashed the air before Stern with a combination of jabs and angry waves, as if he were holding a fly-swatter. Stern weaved back and forth, light on her feet, graceful as a cat of prey, the strands of her honey-blond hair wisping in the wind and setting a strange contrast against the taut, hard lines of her face. She streaked around to his side and caught him with a right thrust that opened up his ribs. As the prisoner whirled, trying to find her, she then ducked and backhanded her knife across the prisoner's Achilles tendon above his right heel.

The prisoner bellowed like a bull before the matador. His slashes and thrusts grew fewer, more exaggerated, with less power. Monika Stern, one hundred pounds lighter than her opponent, continued to dart in, back and forth, this time nicking the prisoner's eye, blinding him, only to fly away before the answering sweep of his thrust could find her hard, sinewy body. She was numb to his screams and ranting, only conscious of the sawdust plying underneath the soles of her bare feet as she darted in and out, creating a rhythm of crimson and spray, laceration and sharp metal and the pull and tug of knife fighting an opponent one hundred pounds to her disadvantage.

She loved it. She loved doing it in front of the Frenchman and the Italian. And she loved doing it in front of Yuko Suzuki. There was a point to be made.

The prisoner swayed before her, a tower of sweat and blood and cut marks all over his face and body. He was blind now. Tears streaked his cheeks and mixed with blood, dripping into his roaring mouth and onto the sawdust into a puddle at his feet.

Stern moved in and kicked out the side of the prisoner's knee. It popped, and the prisoner's screech rose an octave. He fell on all fours, a Goliath to Stern's David. A flash, a cut on the prisoner's wrist, and his knife hand was useless. Stern straddled his back, grabbed the prisoner's tangle of thick brown and bloody hair, and yanked his head back, exposing his grimy throat before the others so they could see. She poised the tip of her black commando knife at the tip of the prisoner's bluish jugular vein where it pulsated next to his carotid artery. She glowered at the Frenchman before her, her breath hoarse with adrenaline, her crotch warm and moist and her nipples hardened with arousal. She dug the tip of her knife into the prisoner's neck and it bled down the anodized finish of the blade into the grip, slowly at first, and then faster.

"Come here," she told the Italian quietly, fixing him with a hard look.

The Italian obeyed. As he stepped inside the hand-to-hand pit, the faint but angry whir of a Mi-24 Hind helicopter disrupted the desert morning air and grew louder as it approached the airfield.

"Never disobey me again. Do you understand?"

A moment's silence. Then; "Yes. I understand."

Stern climbed off the prisoner and let him flop facedown into the sawdust. "Finish him off," she said, walking away, brushing past the senior sergeant, who stared after her.

Monika Stern faced the morning breeze and watched the sun

as it crawled over the mountain peaks blocking this valley from the civilized world. The roar of the approaching helicopter grew louder, and it came into view like a mutated hornet hovering over an anthill. She could see the faces inside. She could feel the others' attention riveted on her back. She could smell her sweat and her scent mix with the alkaline taste of the desert air in her mouth and the smell of spilled blood, and she nodded with approval.

Behind her, the Italian perfunctorily slit the prisoner's throat.

The helicopter set down inside the compound, whirling sand into the air. Squinting her eyes, Monika Stern let the particles sting her face, choosing not to cower before the helicopter's onslaught like the others. Two men in civilian outdoor clothes of canvas safari pants and khaki shirts stepped out, one of whom who was immediately familiar, with his straight, swept-back hair, pockmarked face, and casual, cosmopolitan gait. The other was blond and hard, and walked, or rather marched, with military bearing. He too looked familiar. Monika's eyes narrowed. Business. Orders. Her gut contracted, and she inhaled deeply, knowing it wouldn't be long until she received her orders.

This six-person cell consisted of representatives from six different revolutionary organizations. Was she honored to have been chosen as their leader? What money was there in honor?

There was only the kill, and that was what counted. To kill well, and to kill with a plan and to kill with a purpose. Facing the others before the newcomers could approach her, Monika Stern knew they had accepted her as their leader. Always, there was an example to provide, she thought. Particularly with the men. In their faces, she saw respect, and if not respect, then she saw fear.

She regarded the blood pooling in the sawdust pit.

She nodded. This cell was ready to be led.

CHAPTER FOURTEEN

Pushmataha County, Southeastern Oklahoma

A whippoorwill called out its eerily repetitive warning to those who would be spooked at zero-dark-thirty, and Rene Burchette answered it with a shiver that started down in the small of her back and crawled up her spine to the nape of her neck. As she crept silently forward, the strands of a spider's web brushed against and stuck to her face, caught in her eyelashes. She froze in mid-step, unsettled, fighting back her desire to thrash wildly, to bat away the silk. Gritting her teeth, she carefully picked away the spider crawling up her cheek, and wiped the web from her eyelashes.

Calming down, she contemplated her surroundings. The rush and gurgle of the river they were following blended hauntingly with the occasional hoot of an owl and the whippoorwill repeating its lonely call, a song beckoning to all other night predators in the forest.

Sweat from Rene's forehead ran into her eyes and stung them. Mosquitos whined around her ears, and she had to resist slapping them away. After straining to hear any other noises in the Kaimichi wilderness that might be out of place, she focused on the moving figure to her front, a chameleon who blended into the woods with his camouflaged fatigues, face-paint, and jungle boots. It was her partner, Maslow, threading carefully through the wait-a-minute vines. Following his intended path with her eyes, she spotted the glint of a wire stretched across a splash of moonlight on the ground carpeted with pine needles.

"Pssst."

Winston Maslow turned around and saw Rene's finger pointing at his feet. He saw the wire and traced its path to the trunk of an oak tree to his left. Stepping quietly toward it, he found the wire's terminal—a hand grenade. Maslow knelt down and leaned his suppressed Sterling 9-millimeter submachine gun against the tree trunk. With its built-on suppressor, the weapon was as long as an M-16, and Maslow had to be alert to keep it from getting entangled in the myriad of wait-a-minute vines strapping the mountain forest to its wet, decaying floor.

On cue, Rene Burchette crept up next to him and faced outward, her CAR-15 pointed north. Their target was just another hundred meters away on the next ridgeline. Rene gently pulled out a brick-like Motorola radio from an ammo pouch on her web belt and pressed the talk button. "Dustbowl One, this is Bravo-Mike, over."

"This is Dustbowl One," came back the tinny reply. Rene recognized the voice of the NSC man, Lonnie Wilkerson.

"Entering the objective's primeter," Rene whispered, wasting no words.

"Roger that," Wilkerson replied from where he and Wayne MacIntyre overwatched the infiltration of the objective from their vantage point across the river.

"Sierra-Hotel-Whiskey doing same, over," said another transmission over Rene's Motorola, the voice this time belonging to Manny Santo.

Wilkerson acknowledged that Santo, Hanlon, and Whitehead were on-site at their objective infiltration point and broke off contact. Rene returned her radio to its ammo pouch. After scanning the tree line to her front, Rene returned her attention to Maslow, whose fingers gently caressed the wire before them. The wire was taut, but not that taut. She knew that Maslow was inspecting the trip-wire to see if it was rigged for double-action triggering, enabling the grenade to blow if the wire was cut. She looked upwards at the pine and oak boughs providing their scattered forest canopy before the moonlight, searching for any of the itinerant deer stands prevalent in the area. Only the hunters in this neck of the woods wouldn't be looking for deer.

Maslow retrieved a Leatherman knife from his pocket that held an amazingly compact array of survival tools including wire cutters and pliers. He quietly snipped the wire attached to the grenade's pin locking its spoon in place.

"Thanks," Maslow whispered, winking at the strange woman he had come to regard as a friend. For the past two weeks, he had shot weapons with her, exercised with her, rappeled out of helicopters with her, and in general, served as her mentor while DTM trained on the basics necessary for an urban guerrilla combat team. Now, they were on their field-training phase, and Rene had a lot to learn. Maslow had taken her under his wing when it came to teaching her dismounted patrolling, hand and arm signals, and knowing how to spot danger areas and booby traps.

"You would have seen it," Rene told him, holding her CAR-15 purposefully in place.

"Maybe. Maybe not."

A northern breeze stirred the treetops and rustled the leaves before them. Following the wind was a sharp, ammoniated odor.

"Smell that?" Maslow whispered.

Rene's nostrils flared, and she nodded her head. "Yes."

"Like a baby's mattress, right? Like it hasn't been cleaned in a long, long time. You can't forget that smell once you've been around it. Third World toilets don't even come close."

Rene's fingers flickered on Maslow's forearm. "Wintz, listen."

The wind had suddenly died down. The whippoorwill ceased calling its song of despair. The area before her blackened. Maslow looked for the moon, and saw that it had sunk behind the ridgelines to his west. Only the river they followed, fifty meters downslope and to the left, continued with its consistent rush of fast water cascading over rapids. But there was a new sound, now, a low, muffled humming.

Maslow readied his suppressed Sterling, his thumb caressing its selector switch. Reaching back, he felt for the stick-like object strapped around his back, over his web gear. After touching the cold, black metal tube he was reassured. "Generators," he whispered, nodding in the direction of the humming sound. "We're close, Rene."

Maslow opened one of his web belt's ammo pouches and ran his fingers across the row of darts contained there. Everything was accounted for. He leaned closely toward Rene's ear, warming to the scent of her. It was good to enjoy a woman's scent, but the professional in him said to quit getting off on it, and never to patronize this woman. "Okay, let's move out. Can't be more than another fifty, hundred meters, max. Watch out for other booby traps."

Rene nodded.

"You got any questions, girl?"

Rene shook her head and forced a smile. Maslow squeezed her shoulder and grinned. Then he glanced at his watch. 0450 hours. He estimated that they'd only have a few important moments of inky black before the illuminating gray of BMNT—before-morning nautical twilight—would commence.

As would their attack.

Lonnie Wilkerson returned his radio to the wooden shelf supporting his rifle and gave his attention to the thermos of coffee he'd brought along.

"Burchette and Maslow are on site, Mr. MacIntyre," Wilkerson told the man next to him, who scanned the river below with a pair of binoculars. They were camouflaged from the opposite side of the river gorge by expertly thinned tree boughs, making up the concealment of their elaborate tree stand. "The other guys should be floating down the river any sec now."

"Fine," the older man replied. The president, owner, and chief executive officer of Dustbowl Enterprises, Inc., ran his hand over the M249 SAW—Squad Automatic Weapon— propped up on the wooden shelf before him and licked his lips. It had been almost forty years since he'd last seen combat, and the adrenaline in his gut spurred his breathing and tightened his sphincter muscles. Some things never changed.

Except for weaponry. The SAW could fire a cyclic rate of over nine hundred rounds per minute, and each plastic drum feeding the chamber contained a total of over two hundred rounds of 5.56-mm ammunition. It was a lot of lead to throw downrange. Wilkerson, scanning the objective to their front, could pick off a target with his sniper rifle at five hundred meters in the dark with his night-scoped Remington. These night scopes he'd had Whitehead buy for the team were something else. Some of them could sense heat and pick out moving bodies at night that way; others merely enhanced all available starlight or moonlight and brightened things up into an eerie, phosphorous-green glow. State of the art.

MacIntyre focused his binoculars on the dark, oblong object in the shadows across the river's gorge about seventy-five meters away as the crow flies from his vantage point up in the tree stand. Rene and Wintz Maslow would be somewhere in those shadows, somewhere near the crank lab itself, which was fifty meters west of the relief-shift cabin located near the summit of the river bluff.

Shifting his binoculars from the objective to the cliff, MacIntyre contemplated the eighty-foot drop-off denying direct access from the river. The limestone cliff was eroded at the base where the Kaimichi River had cut into the bluff for Lord knows how long. Much of it was overhanging, and would present one hell of a challenge for the boys about to climb it.

He spotted movement. Three blackened and face-painted heads bobbed next to the poncho raft floating downriver toward the bluff. Just before they swept into the splash and roar of the rapids boiling below the cliff, the three swimmers exited the river into a tiny eddy and a small bank of rocks and sand near the base of the cliff. Pulling the poncho raft onto the riverbank, the swimmers unslung their weapons and immediately broke their gear out of the raft.

Setting the binoculars down, MacIntyre fished out a twist of chewing tobacco Claudie had give him the day before and bit off a chew. The warm, sweet smell of coffee accompanied the sound of someone unscrewing a thermos to his right.

Lonnie Wilkerson handed MacIntyre a cup of the brew. "Wish you would have let me establish some kind of backup for you, Mr. MacIntyre. You've got no business being out here."

MacIntyre watched Wilkerson resume a good firing position with his Remington Model 700, a homely, yet deadly accurate bolt-action Marine Corps sniper rifle equipped with an AN/PVS-4 night-observation scope. "They just got to the cliff," MacIntyre told him, ignoring the younger man's remark. Hell, he'd been throwing M1 rounds downrange in the middle of a Chinese wave attack on the Yalu when Wilkerson was still painting a rich mustard in his diapers.

"Yeah. I see'em. Hanlon's crazy."

"You should lay off the coffee, Lonnie. You boys in Washington worry too much and the caffeine's doing you no good."

"You ever take down a crank lab before, Mr. MacIntyre?"

"I've watched these bastards and their supply boats run chemicals and dope in and out of this area since last deer season," MacIntyre said, evading the answer. "They pretend they're running trotlines. Catfish'll get up to ninety pounds in this river, you know."

"That's something, Mr. MacIntyre, but have you ever taken down a crank lab before?"

MacIntyre smiled. Decorated Vietnam vet or not, Wilkerson was a little too uptight. Hell, *he* was too uptight. Why not? It was DTM's trial run. "Nope," he said finally. "Primary rule of leadership, though, is that the boss-man don't tell his people to do something he himself won't or can't do."

Wilkerson pulled his face away from the lens of his night scope and rubbed his eyes, feeling the onslaught of a headache. "Mr. MacIntyre, you're a public figure, not to mention a billionaire. These people are weird. They get wired up on crank and wig out. No telling what kind of stuff they're armed with. I'm telling, you, I wish that—"

"*Shhh . . .*"

Both men heard the sound at once. A metallic clinking.

MacIntyre returned the binoculars to his eyes. It was almost too dark to see, now that the moon had set. Then he heard the faint tinkle of climbing gear again, and knew that Randy Hanlon was ready for the cliff. Peering intently at the base of the cliff, MacIntyre could barely make out two other dark forms. One of them, Santo, fed out Hanlon's rope from the base of the cliff. Whitehead secured the area by scanning the tree line with his night-scoped M16A2, which was also equipped with an M203 40-millimeter grenade launcher. The three of them looked like panthers, blending into the river's edge as they began the tarantula's ascent into the treeline capping the cliff eighty feet above.

Wilkerson glanced quickly back at MacIntyre. "Whitehead just switched the infrared mode of his night scope on and off a couple of times at me."

MacIntyre grunted. "Guess they're okay then," he muttered. "How do you reckon Maslow and Rene are doing?"

Wilkerson fingered back his widow's peak and pressed against the rubber eyepiece of his night scope, sweeping the muzzle of the Remington along the southern ravines leading up to the ridgeline comprising the objective. After a moment he glanced back at MacIntyre. "There's another tree stand across the gorge from here," he said. "They're somewhere near the base of it. It's too dark to tell, even with the night scope. Look, I gotta tell you, I don't know if these people you hired are going to be able to pull this off."

MacIntyre ignored the comment by staring through his binoculars. Time would tell soon enough about that, but Wilkerson was starting to get on his nerves. He glanced at his watch, which told him things would start happening within the next ten minutes. He reexamined the cliff wall straight across the gorge. Hanlon had begun his climb.

Randy Hanlon laid his hands on the lichen-covered, slick limestone before him and shuddered inwardly. The cliff loomed in an overhang for the first thirty feet above him. *Greasy, slick damn rock,* he thought. *Rotten.* Hanlon then tried to psych himself up for the climb, forgetting about the 12-gauge Autoloader strapped across his back, the waist-constricting climber's harness he wore, the array of chocks and carabiners hanging off his right shoulder harness, and the rope joining him to Santo, who belayed him from his position a few feet away.

Taking several deep breaths, Hanlon thought about his route, the overhang, the rotten moss and lichen-covered limestone he'd have to contend with, and tried to ignore the slippery coils of fear twisting in his stomach.

Santo padded quietly up next to Hanlon. "Do it, wild man. Got you on belay."

Hanlon's eyes found his first handhold, a wet block of rock just out of reach. He jumped for it, and his tall, lean body swung out underneath the overhang, the metallic clinking of aluminum chocks becoming lost in the sound of the river rapids rushing just a few feet away. Hanlon muscled up the first few feet of the overhang to a point where his feet could get a purchase on what were his initial handholds. Then, quick-drawing a carabiner, sling, and chock assembly fastened to his climbing rack, he emplaced his first running belay by wedging chock, an aluminum, tapered wedge, into the shallow vertical crack fracturing the cliff face before him. Santo fed him extra rope, so Hanlon could clip it into the chock sling's carabiner. In this manner, if he fell, the rope and carabiner-chock assembly would act as a running belay, and keep Hanlon from bottoming out on the river rocks below. That is, if the chock stayed in place.

Securing the climbing site in the bushes and rocks by the river's edge, Charlie Whitehead, dressed like the others in water-darkened camouflaged fatigues, peered downstream with his AN/PVS-4 night-scope-mounted M16A2, which also had an M203 grenade launcher attached to the forearm grip assembly. Nothing. No engines, cigarette trails, nothing. He aimed at Wilkerson and MacIntyre's position across the river, and flashed them two flicks of the switch on the infrared mode of his night scope, signaling that all was well and that Hanlon had begun his climb.

That done, Whitehead then sidled up to Master Sergeant Manny Santo, who continued to feed out rope to Hanlon. "Weird," he whispered.

Santo's eyes followed Hanlon's every movement, lost in concentration. "Yeah."

"Chancy, this."

Santo considered this vertical approach to the objective, and had to agree with Whitehead. "Audacious, though. Druggies will never figure out what hit 'em."

In a sense, the team was holding the objective by the nose while creeping up from behind to kick it in the ass. The aerial photo shots the team had reviewed the day before revealed that the crank lab and cabin housing the dope cooks and security element were located near the summit of a ridgeline that abruptly dropped off into the Kiamichi River below. Vegetation was so thick on either side of the ridgeline that it was best to scale the eighty-foot cliff face and surprise the druggies that way, as opposed to the entire team trying to infiltrate the objective from the tree line above, as Maslow and Burchette were doing. The whole group of them would have made too much noise. MacIntyre and the NSC man were observing from their overwatch position across the river up in their tree stand, and if need be, would provide suppressive fires if the shit hit the fan.

Whitehead craned his neck upward and saw that Hanlon had resumed climbing. He'd already gone fifteen feet. At this rate, they'd be up and over in the next ten minutes. Whitehead brought his night scope back up to his face and contemplated the swirling river, its pre-dawn color gray and unforgiving.

* * *

Creeping forward on all fours, Winston Maslow and Rene Burchette approached the tiny building they'd spotted five minutes ago. They melted into the early morning shadows offered by a huge, gently swaying pine ten meters away from the cabin. On cue, Rene Burchette strapped her CAR-15 to her back, pulled out her Browning Hi-Power from the holster on her web belt, and screwed on its suppressor.

The cabin's stench was overpowering. A strong, ammoniated smell, like cooked piss. Maslow looked at Rene and winked. He pointed at an oak tree about twenty meters away. Rene followed the aim of his finger and spotted the tree stand about fifty feet up. Bringing her night-observation goggles up to her face, she spotted the figure of a sniper dozing on the job. She glanced back at Maslow and nodded.

Maslow leaned close to her ear, exhaled, and whispered gently, "I'll take him out with the blowgun. There might be another sniper up by the relief shift's cabin farther up the ridgeline, so keep a lookout for him too. Cover the lab door for now while I take care of this one."

"Okay, Wintz," Rene said, nodding. She glanced back at the crank lab. The windows had been sealed shut with thick black plastic, and she could dimly hear a television set inside. That meant that at least two people were awake. She then assumed a good kneeling shooter's position behind the tree while Maslow loaded a dart from his ammo pouch into the mouthpiece of his blowgun. The dart was tipped with a powerful knockout drug that would keep the sniper asleep for the next several hours.

"Just don't make any pygmy jokes, wench," Maslow said, grinning. "Keep me covered." Maslow gave Rene a thumbs-up and then crawled to the next tree a few meters away. Seconds later, he was padding silently across the small open area toward the sniper's tree stand.

Then the crank lab's cabin door banged open, spilling light into the forest and exposing him.

Thirty feet up the cliff, Hanlon pondered his next move. His white-knuckled grip on the slimy rock before him was starting to weaken, and he knew if he stayed in this crazy, backwards-leaning position at the crux of the overhang much longer, he'd fall.

And he didn't want to do that. He'd only been able to set up three running belays, and this last chock at waist level was only a size-four stopper slotted loosely into a diagonal, shallow crack.

Fuck it, he thought.

Hanlon toed his right foot up to a half-inch-wide foothold at knee level. The only handholds he had were two diagonal ones slanted together at the bottom, forming a V. Opposing them with both his hands, as if trying to tear the tiny ledges apart at his chest, Hanlon gingerly toed his left foot up to a granule of quartzite, then lunged for a foot-wide shelf just out of reach with his right. He grabbed it, and silently cursed the river slime greasing the palms of his sweaty hands. His gear clinked softly like aluminum chimes, their sound lost in the roar of the rapids below, as he clung to the hold.

Dangle city. The crux. Thirty-five feet of overhang sloped like a concave hourglass from the tiny ledge Hanlon clung to, and as he fought for a better grip on the hold, he could smell the sweat in his armpits grow pungent with fear. He tried to pull up onto the ledge, his jungle-booted feet scraping uselessly on the cliff face for a purchase.

Any kind of purchase at all.

"Wayne, I think he's in trouble. He's just hanging there."

MacIntyre shifted his binoculars to the cliff face. He'd been looking upstream, where he thought he'd heard the sound of a boat engine a moment before. As he found Hanlon, his heart quickened. Hanlon seemed to be kicking and clawing at the rock face with his feet, while hanging onto something with both his hands.

MacIntyre glanced back at Wilkerson on his left, who studied the cliff face with the night scope mounted on his Remington. "Think he'll make it?"

Before Wilkerson could answer, the far-off but unmistakable sound of a gunning boat engine filled the early morning quiet as dawn broke.

Rene Burchette trained her suppressed Browning Hi-Power on the man who had just exited the crank lab not ten meters to her front. Probably the crank cook's gofer. Maslow had immediately fallen to the prone next to a decaying log just inside the treeline when the door had suddenly opened, as if he were reacting to a flare. She felt sweat running in rivulets down her side from her armpits. The gofer, a bearded, anorexic man dressed in ragged Levi's, secondhand combat boots, and a blue denim work shirt, walked over to the tree line to relieve himself, close to where Maslow lay.

Rene switched her gaze to Maslow. The gofer was headed straight for him. With his back to her, Rene spotted a stainless-steel revolver packed inside the waistband of his Levis, probably a .357.

The gofer froze suddenly in mid-step. Rene quietly thumbed her Hi-Power's hammer back, and trained its luminous front sight piece on the man's head. Then she heard the faint sound of an engine, growing louder. The gofer started to walk back for the cabin door and reaching it, yanked it open.

"Hey Joe-Don," he yelled to the cook inside. "C'mere."

A potbellied fellow in a faded yellow T-shirt and baggy shorts stuck his head out the door, guzzling the remains of a Schlitz. "What?"

"Listen."

The cook stepped outside.

Rene wrinkled her nose. The stench of chemicals, a mix of acetone, hydrochloric acid, and ammonia, was overpowering. From her vantage point behind the tree, she was afforded a quick look inside. Shelves everywhere. Amber bottles and cellophane packets. A huge glass ball with spigots adorning its top sitting inside a ceramic heater. The glass ball's spigots were rubber-nosed and connected to other glass paraphernalia. She returned her attention to the two men, who were conversing quietly.

"Resupply, it sounds like," the cook informed his gofer. "They like to come early. It's time for the daytime shift to get up anyway," he added, tossing his head in the direction of the ridgeline sloping up behind the cabin. The cook returned to the cabin. Rene breathed a sigh of relief.

The gofer made for the tree line, fumbling with the fly of his Levi's.

And that was when Maslow took aim with his blowgun and popped a dart into the gofer's neck.

Hanlon fought the cliff face before him, his hands continually slipping on the moss and lichen covering the ledge he was trying to climb onto. Beads of sweat had popped out all over, mixing with the scent of fear that only panic-spawned adrenaline could produce.

He had to get on top. As he pulled the ledge down with all his might, his feet began to find a purchase on the cliff wall, and catching the toe of his jungle-boot on a brittle, tiny flake of rotten rock threatening to peel away from the cliff face, he committed to the hold and managed to toe his left boot up to the ledge. Then came the balancing act as he tried to do a one-legged stand-up with his face pressed against the damp limestone to his front.

Then there was noise, engine noise.

Below, Santo wheeled around. Whitehead had heard it at the same time. A boat rounded the river's bend and came into view.

"Jesus H. Christ!" Whitehead exclaimed in a hiss, scrambling behind a rock.

Santo froze in place. Any sudden movement would pull Hanlon away from the rock face because of the rope. If he stayed, he'd be seen. Santo started to feed slack out to Hanlon so he could at least lay in the prone and one-arm his weapon in the direction of the river while keeping his belay hand cinched around the belay plate that was all that kept Hanlon from bottoming out if he fell.

From where he lay in the rocks along the bank of the river, Whitehead unscrewed the night scope attached to his M16A2 and quietly laid it down. The sound of the engine grew louder. He saw the boat first as it came around the riverbend. It was about fifty meters away. Whitehead injected a 40-millimeter heat round into the breech of the M203 grenade launcher attached to the forearm assembly of his M16 and locked it home. He crawled a little way into the cattails and shore rocks five feet into the river and flipped up his M203 sight.

Santo desperately fed out more rope for Hanlon, and knelt behind the only boulder along the base of the cliff large enough to hide him. He quickly unstrapped the MP5 from his back and laid it to his side. He tossed a quick glance upwards at Hanlon. Somehow, Hanlon was hanging on to the cliff. He prayed the boat's occupants wouldn't see Hanlon three quarters of the way up the cliff.

Then Santo spotted the bass boat, as it approached the

riverbank from about twenty, thirty meters away. From its bow one man swiveled a spotlight along the banks of the river. The boat floated closer and nosed toward Santo's direction.

Sixty feet above the riverbank, his feet slipping on the moss-covered ledge, Hanlon clawed at the quick-draws on his climbing rack to set a final piece of protection into the rock wall before him, before committing for the easy jug-holds overhead that were just out of reach. Hanlon prayed for his strength to hold out. He crammed a number-two stopper into a lichen-covered crack and somehow managed to clip his rope into the carabiner attached to the stopper's sling.

Relieved, he scrambled upwards toward the easy holds jutting out like jug handles. The angle of the climb was still slightly overhanging, but the holds were there.

Then there was a sudden pop, like the sound of dry wood snapping.

Hanlon flew backward, his arms windmilling, his right hand still clutching a chunk of rotten limestone the size of his head.

Rene Burchette sprinted across the tiny clearing as the gofer passed out and crumpled to the ground. Kneeling before the unconscious man, Maslow immediately popped another dart into the mouthpiece of his blowgun, and then dashed ahead of Rene into the tree line.

"Oh, *fuck!*" Rene heard Maslow hiss, as she flew into the treeline behind him.

Immediately, pain seared into Rene's cheek. It was a sharp, incredibly sharp, barbed pain gouging deeply into her right cheek only centimeters below her eyelid, penetrating her cheek and lodging into the gum above her molars. She choked back a scream as her right hand flew up to her face, and she felt where the line had fishhooked her.

Maslow had been snagged by three fishhooks—one in the ear, one in his arm, and one in his calf muscle. His knife flashed, once, twice, three times and he was free. Dropping his blowgun, he unstrapped the suppressed Sterling from around his back and weaved around the other fishhooks hanging from the tree limbs toward his partner. Booby traps for perimeter security, unseen and devastatingly painful.

Hands shaking, Rene waited for Maslow to cut her loose, tears streaking silently down her cheeks. She fought to get a grip back on herself and on the Browning Hi-Power she'd almost dropped from her hands a moment ago when she was snagged. The world, which had become a crazy, violent gray, was breaking into a new dawn, and all she felt was pain, a sharp, searing pain in her cheek. Maslow hovered overhead to cut the line holding her in place.

Over her shoulder, she spotted the sentry in the tree stand above taking aim at Maslow's back.

Her pistol spit once, twice. The sentry grunted in surprise as he wheeled around from the force of the 9-millimeter slugs tearing into his neck and chest. Then he pinwheeled over the front armrest of his tree stand, smacked into a tree limb going down, and was already dead before Rene popped another slug into his head on the way down to the forest floor at their feet.

Both Maslow and Rene wheeled around in time to catch the cook as he rushed out the front door of his crank lab with a double-barreled 12-gauge.

Rene automatically assumed a shooter's stance. The cook, squinting into the early morning light, paused, his eyes finding the unconscious body of his gofer and the corpse of his guard. His double-barrel thumped softly onto the pine needles, and he raised his hands up in surrender.

"You okay?" Maslow breathed, fumbling for the plastic cufflets he'd stuck inside his trouser cargo pockets earlier.

Rene kept a steady grip on her Hi-Power, wanting more than anything to sneeze from where the fishhook gouged her cheek. "I think so, Wintz. You?"

"Nice piece of work there, Rene," Maslow told her, moving toward the cook, who stared at them in bewilderment.

"Ya'll's Effa-Bee-Eye, ain't ye?" exclaimed the cook, a grizzled, potbellied good ol' boy in his forties. A thick wad of H&H snuff bubbled out his lower lip, and he wiped his nose with the back of his hand.

Maslow pushed the cook facedown into the pine needles and bound his hands behind his back with the cufflets. "Something like that, Bubba." Maslow then bound the cook's ankles.

Rene's radio crackled to life, and she retrieved it from her web belt.

"Bravo-Mike, this is Dustbowl One," said Lonnie Wilkerson. *"We've got company. Resupply boat floating in from the north. Climbing team's in trouble. Take down the relief-shift cabins pronto, you copy?"*

"This is Bravo-Mike," Rene said into the transmit speaker, her face twisted in pain. "We're on our way to the cabins now."

With no time to waste and ignoring the fishhook in Rene's cheek, Rene and Maslow ran up the ridgeline for the cabins by the river bluff.

Horrified at the sight of Hanlon plunging twenty feet from his last stance on the cliff, and then bouncing on his rope as if he were attached to a rubber band, MacIntyre grabbed the loudspeaker lying by his feet and faced the bass-fishing boat that had entered the area. Santo and Whitehead trained their assault rifles on the boat's every move. "You people in the boat, put your hands in the air, or we'll open fire." The loudspeaker magnified MacIntyre's voice in an empty boom that shattered the pre-dawn hour's nocturnal quiet.

Wilkerson had had his radio cupped to his ear while receiving a transmission, and now set it down. "Burchette and Maslow are right behind the cabins on the objective, Boss," he said, socking the butt of his sniper rifle back into his shoulder socket, drawing a bead on the bass boat below.

MacIntyre kept his right hand on the SAW's pistol grip and peered intently at the boat through the mist. Other than a huge tarpaulin-covered bundle centered in the bass boat, MacIntyre could see no visible weapons. His order seemed suspended by the dawn's humidity, pregnant with impending reaction; the bass boat's occupants glanced in different directions, searching for the source of the order that had just boomed out to them. The boat drifted toward the riverbank by Santo.

MacIntyre exchanged quick looks with Wilkerson. It was too early to tell what they'd do.

Hanlon had barely kept himself from yelling when the rope caught him between the legs and gave his balls a good squeeze during the fall. He hung upside down, dazed and disoriented, the horizon spinning wildly. He stopped the spin and spotted Santo, who had belayed his fall and somehow managed to train his submachine gun on the boat that had just floated into the objective area from upstream.

Hanlon righted himself and examined the running relays he'd emplaced during his climb. His blood chilled. He was supported only by the one hastily wired stopper stuck into the highest point he'd attained on the cliff before falling. The rest of his running belays had zippered out of place with the force of his plunge. That stopper was the only thing keeping him from a sixty-foot free-fall without a parachute.

"For Chrisakes, Randy," Santo called out from below, "*move* your ass."

Hanlon grabbed the rope with both hands and started pulling upwards, his eyes riveted on the thin aluminum wedge above that had saved his life.

Below, Whitehead waved his M16A2 and M203 grenade launcher at the bass boat. The occupants, a man in his forties and a teenager, probably his son, both had kept their hands at waist level, unsure of the situation. Their boat started to drift downstream toward the white water. Whitehead knew that the Mercury 100-horse motor could zip them out of the area quickly. "You boys just come on over here," Whitehead told them in a calm voice.

The older man manning the stern of the bass boat revved the idle of the motor, and threw a quick glance downriver.

"Do it now, asshole!"

The bass boat motored slowly toward them and shored up on the riverbank. Whitehead threw a quick look at Santo. "How's Randy doin'?"

Santo craned his head up. Hanlon had just reached the point where he had fallen. "About another minute, and he'll be up and over."

Above them, Hanlon rested for a moment on a ledge, breathing a prayer of thanks. Quickly, he inserted two more stoppers into a flaring, vertical crack, knowing already that they probably wouldn't hold if he took another fall, but that he needed the psychological support anyway.

"Let's get that fishhook out of your face," Maslow whispered to Rene as they approached the cabins, careful to remain in the trees and whatever shadow they still offered in the morning gray. They knelt behind a stand of pines about halfway there, careful to watch out for any other trip-wires or fishhooks in the area.

He wondered how she was taking the pain. There was about a foot of fishing line trailing behind the fishhook, which, if it caught on anything, would imbed the hook deeper into the bed of nerves networked between her cheek and gum. A streak of blood and mucus had dribbled down her cheek, underneath her swollen, angry red eye.

Rene shuddered, biting back the pain, and said, "We don't have time, Wintz. I can make it to the cabins."

As the teenager in the bow of the bass boat stepped onto the riverbank, Whitehead moved out of his way to let him tie the boat to the shore. For the moment, the teenager was between Whitehead and the man in the stern of the boat. It was all the older man needed to whip out the MAC-10 lying in his lap.

"Get down, Manny!" Whitehead yelled, lunging out of the way, knocking the teenager down at the same time. A stream of .45 caliber slugs spat into the cliff wall behind him. Suddenly, a well-aimed sniper round from Wilkerson's overwatch position in the tree stand across the river caught the man between the shoulder blades. The drug runner, arching his back, hooked his spray of bullets up the cliff.

The barrage of .45 rounds chipped at the limestone by Hanlon's feet and walked up the cliff along his side. Splinters of rock bit into his face, as he lunged for the final jug-handle holds between him and the summit.

The barrage stopped as suddenly as it had begun. Hanlon crested the cliff face, his rope trailing behind him. Rope drag—friction from where his climbing rope rubbed against the rock and his running belays below—threw him off balance, trying to pull him back over the edge.

The cabins! He saw them now, about twenty meters into the treeline. They lay squat and dark before him, overhead canopies of camouflaged netting concealing them from aerial observation. He heard movement from inside, people banging around, awakened by the blast of the MAC-10 from seconds before.

Unslinging his shotgun, Hanlon dropped behind a cluster of boulders at the cliff's summit. There were too many things for him to do at once. He had to tie off the climbing rope so Santo could climb up. He had to be ready for the people inside the cabins. He had to . . .

Two men suddenly ran out the front door. Hanlon thought he heard another door open and slam back shut, but couldn't see it. The men before him were armed, one with an M16, the other with a Smith & Wesson .357.

"Freeze!" Hanlon yelled, holding his shotgun on them as if they were clay pigeons. "Drop your weapons, *now*!"

The two men skidded to a stop and saw a tall, blond man, his shoulders draped with an odd assortment of ropes, webbing, and climbing gear, aiming a shotgun at them. He seemed to be shaking, and the skin on his face and arms had been scraped raw. He was bleeding in places. Their weapons did not leave their hands.

"I said—"

"What you gonna do, fella?" one of them snarled back, finding his voice. He was a tall, lanky man with hollow cheeks and a gaunt frame. "Get us both with your first shot? Better hope you do."

Hanlon licked his lips, tugging uncomfortably against the rope drag trying to pull him back over the cliff, the front sight post of his 12-gauge Autoloader switching back and forth between the two men.

Then, to his immense relief, Maslow appeared out of the treeline behind the two men, and took cover behind a tree.

"You two drug addicts just get on down," Maslow told them in his best drill-sergeant voice.

Hanlon grinned. "That's right. My good buddy behind you is about to fire your asses up if you don't do as he says." Hanlon quit grinning. "So drop your weapons and just get on down like he says!" He walked closer, to give them a better look at the 12-gauge bore facing them. They did as they were told.

Maslow darted forward. "Keep these guys covered while I cuff them, Randy." Maslow's bony black hand flashed inside his fatigue trousers cargo pocket and retrieved a fistful of plastic cufflets. He then began to bind wrists and ankles.

"Where's Burchette?"

"In a safe place back in the treeline. She got hurt."

"Ain't that just like a wench?" Hanlon was feeling his oats, and for him, a little cockiness and adrenaline went well together.

Maslow glanced up from where he was securing the crank lab's relief-shift personnel. "Don't be so quick to judge. She saved my life."

Rene Burchette exited the treeline just then with another man to her front, her CAR-15's muzzle jammed securely into his back. "Hey, guys," she said, with some difficulty. "Found this one trying to sneak up on you from behind the cabins."

Hanlon stared at the slender, athletic woman bringing in another prisoner. The left side of her face was swollen, her eye purple. Tears flowed from it, and mucousy blood trickled from the puncture in her cheek. A fishing line trailed behind her head, and Hanlon knew that she must have run straight on into the booby trap. She walked the prisoner toward the others, where they were lying prone and cuffed on the ground. Reaching the group, she stopped, her prisoner obedient and silent. He stared at Hanlon and Maslow in rage, saying nothing. Rene swayed on her feet, and Hanlon could tell she was close to passing out.

Hanlon opened and closed his mouth. Then he opened it again. "How many more of these assholes are there?"

Maslow took her prisoner, ready to secure his wrists and ankles with the cufflets, like he'd done with the others. Hanlon approached Rene. She wavered and sank to one knee.

It was all the time the remaining sniper in the trees above the cabin needed. His first round plowed through her shoulder-length hair, barely grazing her neck, and lodged into the thigh of one of the prisoners Maslow had cuffed earlier. He started screaming.

Chaos!

Rene spun around and fell to the ground. The prisoner she'd just brought in took advantage of the melee to grab her CAR-15. Two other rounds cracked from the treetops, one of them blasting Hanlon's 12-gauge out of his hands, miraculously missing his heart. The shock of the slug that ricocheted off the receiver of his autoloader numbed his hands, and a chip of plastic gouged deeply into his forearm. He and Maslow lunged for cover. Hanlon yanked at his shoulder holster for his Browning Hi-Power.

From across the river, MacIntyre let loose with a long SAW burst that chopped into the treetops from where the shot came. Bark, pine needles, limbs flew. Maslow injected a magazine of 9-millimeter slugs into the treetops with his Sterling. The gunfire ceased. Filling the void was the wailing of the prisoner who'd been shot by his own sniper.

The sniper tumbled from his perch and slammed into the ground.

The prisoner Rene had brought in now had her CAR-15 and had locked his forearm around her throat, his hand clenched tightly around the fishing line trailing from where it was hooked into her cheek. He used the fishhook and line to lever her around, and had scrubbed the muzzle of Rene's CAR-15 against her scalp, while he walked slowly away from them. The man's eyes were fired up, an angry red flush lighting up the cherubic features of his face, his athlete's body oddly different from the bearded and anorexic appearances of his partners at the crank lab. This man was different. Possibly the shift leader, maybe even one of the district distributors, responsible for getting the crank down to Texarkana for transnational distribution.

"Let her go," Hanlon told him, squeezing out his words between the vice-like contractions of his jaw as he gritted his teeth. He trained his Hi-Power between the other man's eyes, and noted how a bead of sweat was rolling slowly down the bridge of his nose. They were separated by a mere fifteen feet.

"No!" Rene screamed suddenly, her voice wavering on the edge of hysteria. "Oh, Jesus, it hurts. Randy, get away from him. *Please!*"

Her captor sneered at Hanlon. "Ya'll put your guns down, or else the bitch gets it." By now Maslow had slammed a fresh magazine into his Sterling and had leveled it at the man holding Rene. The man continued walking back for the tree line, keeping his eyes on Hanlon. "Just play it cool, Rambo."

Hanlon's eyes found Rene's, and found what he had expected in her all along—the look of a frightened, panicked female. Rabbit eyes. Whatever remained of her inner control must have succumbed to the incredible pain she was suffering—especially in light of the way the man holding her twitched every now and then yanking on the fishing line hooked to her face.

Hanlon knew what he had to do. Wanting desperately to swallow, he thumbed the hammer back. He swallowed anyway. He couldn't keep the front sight post lined up on the other man's nose. He tried not to shake.

"Randy," Rene said in a choked, tight voice, "I know what you're thinking. Don't do it. Please don't do it." Her voice cracked, and sudden tears erupted from both eyes.

Hanlon saw the other man's eyes widen slightly. Testosterone dictated otherwise. Hanlon inhaled deeply, and hot, beaded sweat poured off his forehead into his vision. His finger began to depress the trigger.

"Randy, no! *Please* . . ."

The man holding her stopped moving, and began to level the muzzle of Rene's CAR-15 against her temple for a better shot. Hanlon saw the look of disbelief enter his eyes. He also saw how Rene had brought her hands up, fingers interlocked, praying, sobbing openly, that bloody mucus still trailing down her left cheek, her body trembling, her shoulders quaking. . . .

The knife edge of her hand suddenly sliced the air into her captor's crotch.

Simultaneously, she twisted her head away from the muzzle of the weapon and grabbed its barrel, while a three-round burst split the branches above. The man howled and clutched his balls. Rene jerked the CAR-15 away from him, and ignoring how the fishhook lodged in her cheek and upper jaw threatened to rip out of her face with the drug runner's sudden tug on the line, she slammed the butt of the CAR-15 into his head and knocked him to the ground.

Hanlon, with Rene temporarily masking his aim, lurched forward for a two-round kill shot.

It was too late. The smuggler was down and out for the count.

CHAPTER FIFTEEN

Dhofar Province, Yemen

Monika Stern rose from where she had been sitting in the spartan briefing room inside the Spetsnaz garrison and walked toward the only window. Remaining at the table were the Uruguayan and his guest, a German she thought she knew. But she could not remember his name, and this unsettled her. It unsettled her more than at first when she had realized that the Uruguayan was the same man who had accompanied her when they bombed the American Army *kaserne* together in Kaiserslautern the previous fall.

Simon.

She knew him simply as Simon—the Uruguayan who apparently was the case officer she had worked for over the past eight years. Only the past fall had she met him for the first time, and unwittingly at that. Stern had been in the business long enough to know that her case officer actually worked for the Russians, and she was not so naive as to believe that she wasn't ultimately working for the Russians as well. That a man who was supposed to be her case officer had brought along another German whose name she could not recall unsettled her.

Stern graviated to the window of the briefing room, pulled aside its blackout curtain, and stared through the dust-grimed glass at the brewing dust storm outside. In half an hour, she would join the others comprising her international team and take them on a twenty-kilometer hike through the desert. She would see then how they fared under the discipline of a heavy rucksack and little water, and sand that would bite through your lips and chip away at your teeth in the kind of dust storms only poor, misbegotten Yemen could produce. Another few days would bring the team together.

But apparently, judging from what the Uruguayan had just told her, the timetable was to be stepped up.

Simon knew many people. People who could pay. He didn't care about timetables, only results. Results that demanded prompt payment.

But where had the money come for their last operation together? The Greens? Perhaps. Now that reunification was complete, their howls demanding an American military exodus from Deutschland were growing by the day.

Or perhaps Moscow had paid for their Kaiserslautern operation in a last, heaving gasp of Cold War animosity, before acknowledging to the world the Berlin Wall's demise, and thus implying that a reunified Deutschland should determine its own destiny. Surely, even as bankrupt as they had become, the Soviet Union's intelligence apparatus—the KGB or GRU—could piss away some rubles for the dispatch of senior American Army officials, so juicily enjoined together at their pathetic tradition of formal dinners.

She smiled, warming to the memory. There had been the elderly maitre d' and the leverage of his granddaughter which had coerced the maitre d' to secrete Monika's briefcase inside the pie cart at the officers' club during the formal dinner. Monika had wired the briefcase herself, lining it with gelignate and arming it with her trademark radio receiver, courtesy of one of her cell members who worked for Siemens Electronics. The operation had been a success, and Monika Stern's eyes glazed over as she stared at the glass window of the briefing room and saw instead the tongues of flame bursting from the windows of the officers' club as she and the Uruguayan sped away in their Volvo.

Finally, she turned away from the window and regarded Simon, whose face had become more pale since she had seen him last, his gut more filled out, his black, curly hair receding higher toward the crown of his head—a once-attractive man now on the verge of bland middle age. He was repulsive.

"You make a mockery of procedure," she told him, jerking her head in the direction of the German who had accompanied him.

Simon toyed with the photographs and files he had spread out on the table, and very carefully lined them up in a row. "I dictated procedure—how and when we met, where and how often we communicate—long before you saw me for the first time."

"The American officers' club in Kaiserslautern."

Simon nodded. "Your test. Your, shall we say, leadership evaluation."

Monika Stern grinned her wry half grin and approached the table where the other two men sat opposite each other. Her chair had been placed in the middle. She gripped the wooden backrest of her chair and leaned on it, holding Simon with a cool, level gaze.

"Why is he here?" she asked simply.

Before answering, Simon found himself admiring the tawny strength of Stern's arms, bared by the black, cotton tank top she wore hiding an athletic brassiere binding her firm breasts; the way her strong hips filled out the tight waist and thighs of her fatigue trousers. Even her field boots, scuffed and worn with use, seemed to mold to her sturdy ankles as if Stern had been born with them.

This was the woman, the Spetsnaz senior sergeant had informed him upon landing here hours ago, who had engaged in hand-to-hand combat with a giant of a man, a prisoner from the Soviet's blockhouse used for "training purposes," while demonstrating kill-blows to her other cell members—and no doubt assuring them of her ascendancy as their cell leader as well. Simon remembered briefing old Ishutin, his Soviet taskmaster back at the Aquarium. What had he called her then? A snow leopard?

Yes. The description fit. Stern was ruthless, a woman with no conscience. A lesbian with sadomasochistic tendencies.

"I know this man from somewhere before," Stern prompted, impatient with Simon's reticence. "Tell me who he is and why he is here."

Simon exchanged looks with the other man. His erect, military bearing and Aryan good looks had made Stern edgy. For good reason. Their paths had crossed once before.

"You don't have a need to know."

"Can't he speak for himself?" Stern asked mockingly. "He hasn't said a word for the past hour you have briefed me on this—this absurd ski vacation in the Dolomites." Her hand slid down to the leather belt encircling her waist, and hung on the metal buckle.

Simon's eyes followed the movement and saw her fingers press a button on the buckle that allowed the edge of the buckle to separate from the rest of it. His heart skipped a beat.

Stern yanked the push-knife out of her belt buckle and spun around toward the other man at the table. She darted the point of the two-inch double-edge blade in the hollow of his neck underneath his right earlobe, and cupped her other hand around the back of his head. He was one quick jab away from death. The room became very quiet, save for the tympani booms of Simon's beating heart in his ears.

"Stern!" Simon bellowed, finding his voice. "Put it away!"

Monika Stern twisted the left corner of her mouth into her characteristic half grin, and let her cold, jade-green eyes match stares with the man whose life she now commanded. He made no move to defend himself.

Rather, he smiled coldly back at her. "You don't remember Siegfried?" the man said simply. "Monika?"

"Stern!"

"Shut up, you Latin playboy," Stern spat at Simon, sudden laughter bubbling to the surface. "I don't like people who think they know who I am and then don't have the manners to introduce themselves. Especially people I've seen before." Then, staring back at the German before her, she found herself remembering how once, a very long time ago, when she had first traveled to Aden for her terrorist apprenticeship, she had known a martial arts instructor, a lawyer from Bonn, a youngish man in his late twenties who now was nearing forty—the man who sat before her this instant. She remembered his strong jaw, the way his high cheekbones braced immediately underneath his gunmetal gray eyes, and how occasionally he wore round wire-framed intellectual's glasses when he read.

Calmly, Siegfried raised his left hand up and locked his fingers around Monika's wrist. The tip of the push-knife gouged his neck as he increased the pressure on her hand and pushed the knife away.

She let him do it, her eyes crinkling at the corners. "It has been a long time, Siegfried."

"Yes. You have done well since we first met each other. Here." He released her hand.

"Yes, here," Stern said, sticking her push-knife back into her belt buckle.

"Are you now quite finished?" Simon asked her, glowering, his hands clenched into fists as he leaned over the table.

Monika Stern flashed Simon a look of contempt, and swept her hand over the photographs and papers scattered before them. "Your plan is awkward, defies procedure, and opens my cell up for compromise. You are bringing together too many variables."

"I want this man dead."

"Then kill him."

"I cannot do that unless I use the right people to penetrate his security force. They consist of former Red Army Faction members such as yourself. It will not be easy."

Monika Stern bristled and looked again at Siegfried. "Where do you come in?"

Siegfried said, "I used to work for Humberto Werner-Miranda."

Stern picked one of the photographs out of the drug lord's dossier and stared at it. She saw a rather plump, affected man dressed in a paramilitary outfit and wearing a monstrosity of a revolver on his hip. His pouty face made her laugh. "Him? A drug lord?"

"One of the godfathers of the Medellín cartel," Simon explained. "He's gotten careless. His relentless bombing of his own country's capital, and his involvement with the JFK Airport massacre last winter, has ultimately disrupted his distribution network in the States, his clientele, and it's ruining his market. The American Administration is labeling him, justly so, as a prime target for their drug war. He has most recently escaped extradition from Spain, and is returning back to Colombia to be tried for lesser charges—chiefly, bull smuggling."

"And what is your other reason? Where do I come in?" Stern asked, wondering why Siegfried had once again lapsed into silence. She jerked her head at her old acquaintance. "And him? Why are we here, Simon?"

Simon waved his hand toward a videotape recorder and closed-circuit television set occupying a desk by the wall. Retrieving a remote from his front pocket, he punched the play switch. A grainy black and white home movie started rolling, and Monika Stern and Siegfried viewed a crowd of men milling about inside a bare concrete room. A caption below read, simply, "Before Exposure," in Russian. The men's gray and white striped uniforms indicated that they were prisoners, apparently slaving away in a Soviet gulag somewhere in Siberia. The looks on their faces were of bland disinterest; they seemed resigned to the fact that they were herded together like cattle into close quarters, ostensibly to go through their quarterly delousing.

The television screen then showed a close-up of an aerosol cannister suspended overhead, which apparently no one paid much attention to. Simon hit the pause button of his remote. The aerosol cannister remained in place on the television screen. He picked through a manila folder on the desk and pulled out an eight-by-ten glossy. He handed it to Monika Stern.

"It is called Microcystin," he explained to her.

"Microcystin," Stern repeated, forming the syllables of the word carefully in her mouth. She stared at the picture Simon had handed her, and saw a blue-and-yellow-colored vial with a skull and crossbones emblazoned on the front. English lettering on the skull-and-crossbones label indicated that it was highly toxic and would cause immediate death. A list of its molecular characteristics were detailed in a handwritten legend below the label. "A chemical?"

"A toxin," Siegfried explained, discontinuing his earlier reticence. "An organization within the fold liberated it from the American garrison in Vilseck last month," he said, thinking how Stern's old team had been neatly dispatched for their treason. "Essentially, they coerced an American Army sergeant into allowing us access to their controlled-substance facility. They were disguised as American soldiers going about their business. After dispatching their guards, they procured several vials of the toxin, created a diversion in the kaserne with a number of timed explosions, then departed the area."

"Biological and chemical warfare was outlawed by the Geneva Protocol of 1925," Simon said, taking up where Siegfried left off. "Then, in 1972, the Biological Weapons Convention prohibited each signatory, quote, 'in any circumstances to develop, produce, stockpile, or otherwise acquire or retain microbial or other biological agents or toxins whatever their origin or method of production, of types and in quantities that have no justification for prophylactic, protective, or peaceful purposes.'"

Simon's voice trailed off. "End quote," he said after a

moment. "Simply put, both the Soviet Union and the United States have invented insidious strains of toxins and other biological weapons despite the fact that they both signed the treaty. Then, upon agreeing to the START talks with the Soviets in late 1987, followed by mutual disarmament proceedings in Western Europe by late 1989, both countries have secretly edged up their chemical and biological warfare capabilities by increasing toxin and biological agent production. The United States apparently is using sophisticated chemical and biological agents to fill the strategic void in the defense of Central Europe created by the withdrawal of their medium-range Pershing and Cruise missiles."

"No doubt the Soviets are doing the same," Stern sneered. "So tell me, Comrade Case Officer, what has this to do with Humberto Werner-Miranda?"

Ignoring her question, Simon hit the play button on the VCR's remote, and his audience saw the paused close-up of the aerosol cannister hanging above the heads of the Russian gulag prisoners suddenly activate. The bursting munition discharged an aerosol cloud that formed a greasy blanket of a grayish drizzle that fell slowly downward on shaved, human scarecrow heads.

Immediately, the prisoners convulsed with a violent shivering, as if the thermometer had plummeted fifty degrees. Open mouths gasped for breath, eyes winked, cheeks twitched, arms, elbows, and knees shot about in spastic lack of control.

"It took these men between one to three hours to die," Simon informed Stern. "Microcystin deforms and disrupts cell membranes in the liver, leading to circulatory collapse, nerve damage, and total incapacitation within the first thirty minutes after exposure. Death is certain to follow, regardless of decontamination efforts after the first fifteen minutes of exposure."

The film dissolved into the next scene, in which the Russian caption read, "Two hours later." Stern, mesmerized, sat very still in her chair. The occasional knee twitched on screen. Faces had become frozen masks of surprised outrage.

"An ugly, distasteful death," Simon said. "Needless to say, the release of a toxin such as this would be psychologically ruinous to any target population. Some call it a poor man's atom bomb."

Monika Stern nodded her head, a smile forming on her lips. Such a weapon!

The second scene dissolved into a third that read, "Three hours later," in the caption below. No movement at all. Simon hit the stop button and rewound the video. He returned his attention to the others.

"I thought you said the toxin was American-made," Stern said. "That film was Soviet."

"Each property has its own molecular structure," Simon explained, relieved that he had finally captured Stern's undivided attention. "The Soviets have their formula for essentially the same thing, the Americans have theirs. If you were to release this formula in a certain part of the world, Monika, it could be typed back to reflect U.S. manufacture."

"We begin with exposure in our homeland," Siegfried interjected with enthusiasm. Stern swiveled a glance in his direction. "American chemical spill murders innocent German citizens," he intoned, his voice reflecting the stern indignation of a German newscaster. "The Greens would have a field day. U.S. occupation, regardless of how they term their presence on Deutsch soil would cease as the rest of the world would demand their policymakers' heads."

"Ah, yes," Simon replied, nodding "It will be a successful operation. . . ."

Monika Stern held her hand in the air. Simon quit talking. She fixed him with a level stare, and Simon could not see past the opaque jade of her eyes. "Why are you trying to sell me on this weapon, Simon? You knew it would appeal to me."

Simon scratched his nose with a ragged thumbnail. "Because Humberto Werner-Miranda has it. He bought the RAF cell I recruited to liberate the toxin. They betrayed me."

"You or Moscow?"

Red-faced, Simon responded with, "They were awarded the appropriate punishment. They didn't know that I've had dealings with Werner-Miranda before. But his kind work better in the drug world. He's transcended that barrier into things political, and now he has become a nuisance. I want him dead, of course, but more importantly, I want my Microcystin back."

The corners of Monika's Stern's mouth slowly upturned. "Yes," she told him. "You could say I want this opportunity."

"Old times, Monika," Siegfried added. He glanced at

Simon. "And old friends. The two make for auspicious beginnings."

Simon nodded his head, unable to return Stern's cold smile. The skin on Monika Stern's face had seemed to stretch thin and taut, translucent with beaded sweat, highlighting a blood vessel high up in her forehead. Suddenly alarmed, he saw how Stern had unconsciously dug her fingernails into the soft flesh of her inner forearms, drawing a trickle of blood.

Then, when Simon saw Siegfried smiling icily back at him, a queer light glinting in his gray eyes, he wondered why the intensity of the two terrorists before him unsettled him so. Were they all nihilists, these Western Europeans? These two were no freedom fighters. He had seen these same looks in the French and the Dutch organizations—the look of anarchy, nihilism, even madness. Death for death's sake. Anarchy for the sheer pleasure of watching fire trucks and ambulances. Disruptiveness for the sake of a headline, a sense of some kind of twisted accomplishment. Things were different than they were back in the seventies.

Perhaps the roots were found in some kind of twisted upper middle-class guilt complex, repressed homosexuality, or prolific promiscuity. At least the Irish and the Palestinians had causes to motivate them. Even the religious fervor and the fanaticism of the Shi'ites made more sense compared to the two before him.

But then again, for what he was asking them to do, they were right for the job. Only a certain mindset could release Microcystin in a nursery or a crowded shopping center. Madness and carnage *worked*.

And in the end, terrorists, despite their political platitudes, simply didn't care *who* paid them.

Chapter Sixteen

Pushmataha County, Southeastern Oklahoma

"Hey, c'mon, Manny, what is this shit?" Hanlon whined. "Wintz, why are you two fucking me over like this? I thought we were all going on a ruck march."

Santo and Maslow brushed past Hanlon heading for the cabin's front door. Santo paused by Hanlon before exiting.

"Quit sniveling, glory-boy. Look, you scaled Mount Everest and then led the raid on Entebbe—"

"With, ahem, some outside assistance," Maslow enjoined.

"Yeah, well, ya done good, pard, but look," Santo said, his face growing serious, "you've still got a problem with a member of this team. On orders from your cell leader— namely, *me*—fix it!"

Hanlon inhaled sharply. "How many times I got to tell you guys I got no problem working with a woman?"

"The same *woman* who was *the* contributing factor toward our taking down the crank lab, that is," Maslow corrected.

Hanlon wanted to give the skinny warrant officer's leathery neck a squeeze. "She was whinning like a baby on the objective when that one druggie got ahold of her."

Maslow and Santo exchanged disbelieving looks. Shaking their heads, they exited the cabin. It was too good of a late March spring day to screw it up without catching some of the channel cat proliferating in the Kiamichi River—and listening to any more of Hanlon's bullshit platitudes.

"Randy," Santo told him on the way out the door, "look, man, it takes four people to pull together as an effective team. Thing work better as a meritocracy. Mr. MacIntyre and Mr.

193

Wilkerson, when they return from Washington tomorrow, expect to find us all in agreement before we sign the contract. I trust MacIntyre, just like we all trusted his son when Matt was our team leader. The key word here, knucklehead, is *trust*. Look me in the eye, Randy."

Hanlon squared off to his old team sergeant, the veins in his forehead purpling with blood pressure. "What?"

"Wintz and I accept Rene. We both can see what you don't. Don't know what your problem is, but before we sign anything, or do anything else for Mr. MacIntyre outside of that little not-so-spiffy crank lab op we just pulled, we expect you to make peace with Rene."

"I got no problem with her, Manny. How many times do I have to tell you?"

Maslow said, "C'mon, Manny. Fish are biting."

Santo and Maslow headed off for the river, leaving Hanlon opening and closing his fists and grinding his teeth.

Goddammit, he hated being alone! Fucking teammates he'd lived with for the past six years together in Group, telling him to get his act together. They hadn't been on the sharp end of the rope the other night! Santo was the one who'd lost control of the operation! It'd been Randy himself, climbing up that slick damn greasy cliff, who had taken down the relief shift's cabin, and Maslow who had turned the tables on the Mexican standoff that followed when the shit hit the fan.

Then the wench had had to go and get captured. Another goddam Mexican standoff. So she'd sucker-punched her captor in the balls, so what?

You were just as unprepared, asshole, his innermost voice countered.

Still, a woman on the team's a problem.

What's your problem?

Not a damn thing.

Got kicked out of Group for smokin' dope, little man, that's your problem.

The sound of slapping rotor blades informed Hanlon that he'd soon have company. Moments later, he walked to the door and watched Rene Burchette shut down MacIntyre's Blackhawk. Evidently, she'd soloed back from Tulsa, where the team's employer had had her check in with the best plastic surgeon in town.

"Fuckit," he said aloud. He walked out into the early March

sunshine to settle everything, once and for all. If Santo and Maslow wanted him to kiss her ass, then so fucking be it. *Only she'll kiss mine first.*

Rene Burchette glanced up at Randy Hanlon as she placed the final chock block underneath the Blackhawk's wheels. The lazy spin of the rotor blades overhead slowed with each cycle, and its passing shadow crossed the quick-time step of Hanlon's marching feet as he stomped toward her. Catching his movement out of the corner of her eye, she glanced up.

"Hi." Burchette then returned her attention to the shut-down checklist on the kneepad strapped to her thigh.

"Hello," Hanlon responded formally, feeling suddenly awkward, like an eighth-grader before his first big date. He tried to remember that he was a professional and that she was a professional, and as professionals, they should be able to break the ice and learn how to work together. "How's your face?" he asked, his voice bordering on the edge of smart-ass.

Burchette looked up from her pad, and he saw how the swelling had gone down. The skin under her left eye was still purplish, and she had an inch-square gauze pad taped to her upper left cheek, where the fishhook had gone in. Now it looked as if she'd just been stung by a wasp. "Better," she replied. "Going on a run?"

Hanlon compared her flight suit to his odd combination of running shorts, Vuarnet tank top, Ray-ban sunglasses, and jungle boots. He'd been about to go on a ruck march before Santo and Maslow had abruptly departed on their little fishing spree just moments ago. How he'd been set up; they'd known she was only seconds inbound when they left! Then an idea came to him.

"Yeah, I'm going on a little hike in the woods," he said expansively. "Mr. MacIntyre mentioned the other day that there's a twelve-mile trail along the perimeter of the state park nearby."

Rene Burchette unclasped the barrette binding her shoulder-length brown hair behind the crown of her head, and shook it free. Hanon's mouth hung open a little, and he promptly shut it. Rene attempted a smile, winced, and brought a hand up to her cheek. "Where are the others?"

"Gone fishing. Mr. MacIntyre and the NSC guy are coming in from D.C. tomorrow sometime. Charlie Whitehead's spending the day home with his family."

"And you're here by yourself?"

"Yeah. Uh, look, we gotta talk."

"Okay."

She's been expecting this. Hanlon remembered his plan. He began to choose his words carefully. " 'Course, I'd ask you to take a hike along with me, as I was just about to leave, but . . ."

"Sure."

"Oh?" *Reel 'er in, Hanlon.*

"I'll go," she said, smiling sweetly. "Just give me a moment to change and get my rucksack."

Before Hanlon could say anything, Rene Burchette walked back to the Blackhawk's cabin door, retrieved her rucksack, and shrugged it on. Hanlon noted how the straps bit into the flesh of her shoulders. Wasn't exactly a nerf ruck. Burchette tossed her head at the ranch Bronco parked outside the cabin. "Better change, first. I'll just be a minute."

Breathing heavily, Hanlon paused at the crest of the saddle separating the trailhead from the sprawl of boxcar-sized granite boulders and moraine leading down into the valley below. The afternoon heat—hot even for March—had cooked the mercury up to the mid-seventies. That and Oklahoma's humidity made things a bit uncomfortable. Rene walked up beside him, perspiration dripping off the sides of her face and forming a point on her chin.

"They call it the Boulder Graveyard," she announced.

"You've hiked this route before?" he asked, seeing the mockery in her eyes. They'd only gone about three miles, and already, he was feeling it. Of course, his rucksack always weighed fifty pounds, minimum.

"Whenever Mr. MacIntyre wants to fly down to the ranch, I usually come here to give this trail a go."

Hanlon's respect meter began to climb. When they had parked the Bronco at the park headquarters parking lot half an hour ago, Rene had gone to the latrine and shower point to fill her canteens. He'd picked up her rucksack when she wasn't looking. It had to be forty, forty-five pounds.

"Want some water?" Burchette offered him her canteen.

"No."

Hanlon immediately started the descent into the Boulder Graveyard, a half-mile climb down boulders and scree slopes they had to negotiate before reaching the forested valley below.

Hanlon passed the back of his hand over his forehead. *That was stupid. Of course you need water.* He made an effort to yank his canteen out from his rucksack's side pocket. She pulled it out for him.

"I can get my own damn—" Hanlon broke off in midsentence. "Sorry." He reached for the canteen.

She yanked it angrily away. "Listen, motherfucker, I've had about enough of your shit!"

Hanlon stared at her. Gone was the prim little ice-queen. She was boiling hot.

"You wanted a little walk-a-thon? You got it. I'll hike your ass into the ground!"

Hanlon chuckled. "Well. Bust my balls."

"You got a chip on your shoulder about me? About women in general, perhaps? You've been doing nothing but getting on my case since this team came together! You say you want to talk?" Rene Burchette thumped Randy Hanlon hard in the chest with her forefinger, and he almost lost his balance on the loose gravel and scree underfoot. "Okay! So *talk* to me, big man."

Hanlon stared at her, not knowing quite what to say.

"If you don't have the balls to say what's on your mind, then get off my ass and *stay* off! *Capice?*" Rene Burchette glowered at Hanlon, who didn't know whether to smirk, snarl, push her back, or shut up.

Rene stepped out ahead of him. He followed a moment later, anger surfacing from the delayed reaction. Five minutes later found them at the bottom of the Boulder Graveyard, where a broad rock- and cactus-spined valley paralleled the chain of mountains they were hiking around.

Striding ahead of him, Rene increased her pace. Hanlon riveted his eyes on her ass while he dogged her heels. He tried not to admire the copper tone of her thighs, how they narrowed ar her crotch, swelled at mid-thigh, narrowed at the knee. How her calves bulged just above her sturdy ankles, topped by a well-broken-in pair of Vasque hiking boots. The rest of her body . . . tight was the word, her breasts firm and bound tightly against her chest with an athletic brassiere; her hard, sturdy hips gently caressed by the sheer, nylon fabric of her running shorts. Her tank top billowed in the mountain breeze, and the knot she'd tied above the midriff to let the breeze cool her flanks displayed her smooth, hard abdomen.

He wanted to fuck her. He wanted to throw her down on the ground and fuck her good and hard. She had no right to say that to him earlier. Typical feminist ball-busting bitch out to assert her dykehood. Well, he'd see about that.

Then the cotton in Randy Hanlon's mouth informed him that this woman *was* in shape—and he could certainly be in better. He made it a point to catch up with her.

The valley was splashed with sunshine, and the odd Oklahoma terrain blended cactus with pine trees and oaks; the creek bottom was strapped down with wait-a-minute vines and running water, clear and clean, feeding the Kiamichi River farther east. Exiting the valley, they started climbing again to the next saddle marking the halfway point. Here, scattered oaks displayed greening buds of new life as spring pollinated and grew more lush with each passing day.

Their route led them toward a pass, where the trailhead horseshoed around a rocky bend. Hanlon regarded a jumbled mass of cliffs and boulders dominating the left rim of a canyon they would soon enter.

Rene saw it at the same time. They both began an unspoken race for the top of the saddle near the base of the cliffs. Each one's stride matched the other's as their pace increased. Then they confronted another scree slope of loose gravel. Hanlon led out first, scrambling and slipping on the rocks and cactus. Rene passed him. Hanlon fought the slope harder. The weight of his ruck bore down on his back, and his lungs pumped like bellows. Salty sweat poured from his forehead and stung his eyes. Glancing at the woman climbing next to him, he saw that she was in no worse shape.

By the time they reached the saddle by the cliffs, the rest of the valley spread before them like a green and brown tablecloth of gravel and trails and trees and cactus. Since entering the Boulder Graveyard forty-five minutes earlier, they had rollercoastered over a thousand feet in elevation, during the six miles it had taken them to reach the cliffs and saddle. It was the halfway point.

"Ready for a break?" Hanlon gasped.

"If you want," Rene replied, her voice in neutral. She gingerly traversed a shelf of granite that overwatched the valley below in its splendid display of coming spring. Locating a spot underneath the shade of an oak, she did a rucksack flop and began to suck on her canteen. A moment later, Hanlon followed and parked his ruck next to hers. She dug back into her rucksack. "Want a power bar?"

"Sure."

She handed him a foil-wrapped candy bar, the kind cyclists use for quick energy, that contained no fat and max calories. "Thanks," Hanlon said, meaning it.

"You wanted to talk."

"Forget it."

"No, let's not forget it. You're uncomfortable about a woman being on the team. I could see that in your eyes the first day we all met."

"I can be an asshole sometimes. Wintz and Manny'll tell you that. So I'm sorry if I . . ." He couldn't continue. He couldn't continue saying something he didn't mean.

Rene Burchette took a bite out of her own power bar and chewed on it during the next few silent moments. "Okay," she said finally. "Then get this: I have things to contribute to the team that you don't. Mr. MacIntyre uses my looks as camouflage. No one knows, or assumes, for that matter, that I have a Ruger .380 tucked away in my handbag when we go to formals together, or that I've got an Uzi in my briefcase when I fly him around in the Blackhawk or his Lear jet. You know why? Because people just don't take women seriously when it comes to security work and clandestine operations. People like you."

Hanlon shook his head with a grin. He had her figured out now. Maybe something had happened to her years back, something that made her want to feel like she could get the best of men. Who knows, maybe she was just one of those feminists who had something to prove. *That's it*.

"So you think you have to prove yourself, then," he said. "Something from your past motivates you to be Rene Burchette, winsome bodyguard, pilot, martial artist, and dead-eye shot for Mr. Dustbowl Enterprises, Inc., himself, Wayne MacIntyre. Well, I'll have to hand it to you, Rene, you're a stronger woman than many I've met. No, really, you are."

Rene snorted with disbelief. Shaking her head, she put her canteen back in her rucksack and climbed to her feet. Hanlon followed suit.

"Am I right?"

Rene gave him a look of resignation. "You know, for a moment there I thought you were going to say something that would make sense. Not that patronizing bullshit about something I have to prove. Would it make any difference if I told you that I'm my daddy's girl, that I'm an Air Force brat whose fighter-jock father turned his daughter into a tomboy with pilot lessons and skiing lessons and week-long deer hunts with high-powered rifles? Give me a fucking break!"

Hanlon said nothing.

She gave him a look of dismissal. "I guess what Chief told me was right," she muttered, shrugging on her rucksack. She returned to the trailhead for the hike back. Hanlon chased her down and pulled hard on her shoulder, spinning her around. Rene tensed up, ready to put her fist in his throat.

"What'd Wintz tell you?" Hanlon croaked.

"That you were busted out of Group on drug charges."

"One motherfucking joint!" Hanlon screamed. "What the *fuck* does Maslow have any goddam business to tell you—"

"And that the Group's assistant personnel officer—who happened to be a *female* lieutenant—was the one who administered your urinalysis test and wrote up your subsequent discharge papers."

Hanlon deflated. He stood there, feeling empty. A greasy, lead ball of shame and defeat sagged his guts.

"The fact that you blew a little dope and got caught," she added, not unkindly, "doesn't make you an incompetent ass, Randy. But the fact that you're taking out your own neurotic crap on me makes my life hard and life hard for the rest of the team. Give it a rest."

Rene hiked down the trail and, quietly, Randy Hanlon followed her, late afternoon shadows from the pines swaying overhead reaching for the soles of his boots. The rest of the hike passed by in silence, save for the gentle scuff of leather on granite and the crunch of winter-dried leaves. The trail eventually leveled off, upon entering the lush valley containing the park's headquarters, parking lot, and shower and latrine facilities. The sun had almost set. Burchette slowed her pace, and she and Hanlon walked side by side toward the parking lot. He stopped suddenly. She turned around.

Hanlon took a deep breath and stuck out his hand. "I guess . . . I guess . . ."

She shook hands with him. "Truce. C'mon, let's go."

Hanlon let go the deep breath he'd been holding. " 'Kay. Gotta hit the latrine, then I'll be ready."

Rene Burchette let his hand go. As he turned away, her eyes lingered.

Approaching the riverstone-masoned-latrine—fashioned in the same manner as MacIntyre's ranch cabin—Hanlon saw a middle-aged man in a wheelchair doing his best to roll his wheelchair out of the latrine. His face was beet-red, and brownish smudges on his hands and shirt informed Hanlon that the poor guy hadn't had the best luck in the world maintaining basic hygiene.

The man in the wheelchair looked up at Hanlon as he got closer. "H-heyyy."

To Hanlon, it sounded like he was retarded. His heart sank. "M-missterrr. Would . . . youuu h-help . . . meee?"

Walking up slowly to the crippled man, Hanlon saw how he'd unsuccessfully tried to empty his colostomy bag. Or maybe the tube broke off. There was shit everywhere: in his long, stringy hair, in his face. . . . Judging by the smallish gym bag laying on the ground near his wheelchair, the poor guy had been trying to use the shower facility.

Hanlon remembered cleaning up his father when he was so far gone that he could pick him up in his hands like a sack of potatoes and wipe his bony, decayed butt with one clean swipe.

"Sure, man," Hanlon replied with a fake, but enigmatic smile. "You trying to take a shower?" The bright tone in his voice made the man in the wheelchair grin back in embarrassed relief.

"I-I-I come . . . out heeere . . . on my owwn alot," the man replied, as Hanlon wheeled him inside the shower point. Hanlon gently pulled at the quadriplegic's Army field jacket, reaching for the zipper. He regarded the Combat Infantryman's Badge and airborne wings sewn just above the crippled man's left breast pocket and the 173rd Airborne unit combat patch on his right shoulder. "But . . . today is . . . just . . . not . . . mydayIguess . . ."

Tears flooded warm and hot in Hanlon's eyes. The poor guy's mind was there, all right. Judging by his age and his long hair and his old and faded olive-drab field jacket, a land mine in 'Nam had probably blown his body out from under him, not to mention that little extra bit of scrap that must have penetrated his cranium in the process. That would explain his slowed speech.

An hour later, after wheeling the veteran back to his camp, where others in the vet's group welcomed Hanlon with their shamed and impotent smiles, he and Rene were halfway back to MacIntyre's ranch. Hanlon was behind the wheel, lost in his thoughts. Rene broke the silence that had accompanied the trip.

"That was a nice thing you did, Randy."

Hanlon made a noncommittal sound in his throat.

"Not just anyone would clean up somebody whose colostomy bag had burst."

"Chauvinists have feelings too, you know."

"Smart-ass. Here." She handed him a Kleenex tissue.

When they parked the Bronco outside MacIntyre's ranch cabin, they saw that another helo was parked next to Rene's Blackhawk. Smoke billowed out of the cabin's chimney, and the smell of Claudie the cook's fried potatoes and onions wafted in the early evening air. Opening the door, they realized that dinner that night also included roast venison, cornmealed catfish, fried okra, corn on the cob, and generous helpings of Jack Daniel's Black Label. Seated at the kitchen table, Santo and Maslow were arguing about the size of catfish.

Randy Hanlon propelled Rene Burchette through the door and clapped his paw around her shoulders. *"Hey, you mother-fuckers!"*

The room fell silent, save for the sizzle of frying potatoes. Manny Santo, swirling ice cubes in his mug of Black Jack, stared hard at Hanlon.

"I just want you prying, nosy sons of bitches to know that this here *wench* knocked my dick in the dirt today on a rucksack march. So are you satisfied now, or what?"

Rene, trying not to grin, removed Hanlon's hand from her shoulder and joined the others at the kitchen table.

Manny Santo shook his head, and observed, "Always did think you were a pussy, Randy."

A noise behind him made Hanlon turn around. Lonnie Wilkerson had just exited the cabin's underground command and control center. Charlie Whitehead followed on his heels, after locking the entrance. The second helicopter parked outside explained the fact that Wilkerson was back twenty-four hours ahead of schedule from his trip to D.C. Hanlon looked back at Santo.

"Well, what do you think? We're just out here for fun and games? We got a mission," Santo explained.

Wilkerson gave Hanlon a thin smile as he shook hands and walked past him for the kitchen. "Good to see you Randy. As I've already told the others, Mr. MacIntyre sends his regards from Washington, where he's wrapping up some personal business. I've . . . returned a little early to deliver your first mission brief for an overseas operation that is to commence immediately." Wilkerson then gave the entire group a searching look. "That is, if you feel ready."

On cue, Charlie Whitehead produced a contract from his briefcase, and spread it out on the table. The others gathered around, save Hanlon, who nodded to Santo after a moment's silence.

Santo chuckled and waved Hanlon over. "Quit standing there like a dumb rottweiler and grab some chow, Randy," Santo told him. "Claudie's venison is getting cold."

Santo then informed Lonnie Wilkerson of the National Security Council, "DTM's ready, Mr. Wilkerson. You say you wanted one of those scumbag Extraditables snatched?"

CHAPTER SEVENTEEN

Montgomery County, Maryland

A late-model Lincoln Continental—the stretched-limo version—cruised through the heavily forested Maryland countryside, en route to a boarding school where only the privileged could afford to send their children for a higher education.

The limousine's two occupants were oblivious to the two Mercedes driving approximately fifty meters front and back of their vehicle—each Mercedes containing four Secret Service men apiece, armed with an assortment of submachine guns, assault rifles, and grenade launchers.

Because one of the passengers inside the center limo was the Vice President of the United States.

Inside, Wayne MacIntyre, Vice President Stuart Lawson's guest, regarded the Maryland countryside with resigned indifference. Trips to Washington always depressed him.

Lawson reached for the partition button that prevented the driver from overhearing conversations with his guest, who was getting more than a little tight. Ever since MacIntyre's son David had gotten shot by terrorists at JFK the previous December, he'd become increasingly irascible, increasingly critical of the very Administration he'd helped ascend to power during the past election. And MacIntyre's stunt of actually participating in his clandestine organization's crank lab raid last week had been the icing on the cake. Wealthy businessmen, leaders of the country's economic community, simply had no business indulging in such activities!

And that made Lawson wonder if the deniable cell he'd asked MacIntyre to form up shortly after his son's encounter with airport terrorists would prove to become an unbridled wild card, an organization destined for dismantling before it could even be used.

He thought of MacIntyre's name for the counterterrorist cell: DTM—Don't Tread on Me. Lawson recalled the picture of a flag from History 101 with a rattlesnake coiled and ready to strike with that logo emblazoned on it. An overly independent, reactionary philosophy on the surface. He hoped the people MacIntyre had recruited were as competent as Wilkerson from the National Security Council said they were. Time would tell.

Lawson chose his next words carefully. "You said that you never wanted David to look at the business end of a submachine gun again, Wayne. Well, I feel the same way about my granddaughter, who, I believe, shares some of your affection for your son."

MacIntyre gave the vice president a sardonic grin. "Our privileged children." The vice president's granddaughter and his son attending the same school had afforded Lawson this excuse to "bullshit about old times" during the trip from D.C.

Lawson dismissed MacIntyre's last remark and plowed on. "When DTM grabs Humberto Werner-Miranda—"

"*If* they manage to do it."

"You can regard it as step one toward solving the problem. There will be other opportunities."

"What problem, Stu? The terrorist problem? The drug problem?"

"You're in a fine mood today."

MacIntyre shook his head, and reached for the Scotch. Lawson assisted by refilling both their glasses with ice cubes from the bucket. "Sorry."

"Forget it." Lawson clapped his old friend on the shoulder. "You've every reason to be bitter."

"I've just sent four good men and one of my most capable bodyguards, who also happens to be my most capable pilot, to Europe on their first deniable operation together. I wanted more time for their preparation. The only information about the target's security is what little your man Wilkerson was able to supply from the NSC's data banks."

Lawson leaned back in his seat and contemplated the rolling, tree-infested countryside undulating before the window, and spotted the guard shack monitoring perimeter security for the school. The leading Secret Service Mercedes had just stopped before the gate, which was promptly raised for their pass-through.

"Wilkerson's info about Werner-Miranda is dead-on, Wayne," Lawson said. "We intercepted his itinerary through Bonn from their plant inside the RAF—that's the Red Army Faction—Germany's most notorious terrorist gang. Apparently, there's something going on between the drug cartel and various Western European terrorist organizations. We believe that Moscow has traded conventional power with their demobilization in Eastern Europe for increased involvement in terrorism and the drug trade. Conducting deniable terrorist ops of their own to influence world events is much more economical than making more tanks and rockets, or struggling to keep up with the arms race."

Now it was MacIntyre's turn to arch an eyebrow. "And Bonn just offered you that information on a silver platter."

"We've always known that the Soviets have sponsored—"

"I'm talking about this plant of theirs in the Red Army Faction."

A moment's silence, as their limo passed through the gate.

"The Germans are sensitive about world opinion these days, what with the reunification. Old fears half a century old are resurfacing throughout the European community, and the Germans want continued U.S. approval. When their RAF plant—"

"Who is . . . ?"

"A rather intrepid fellow from GSG9, Germany's counterterrorist organization. He's forwarded information about Werner-Miranda's pending vacation in northern Italy, and naturally, Bonn told us about it. Simple enough."

MacIntyre's gut twisted into a knot. Lawson was a professional liar. He remembered the time the Administration wanted him to send those men he sponsored into Laos, staging them out of his Bangkok offices for cover. That those men found American POWs and died on the way back in after communicating the fact was an outstanding feat of heroism; that the Administration buried the POW verification data was criminal.

MacIntyre considered what had happened after he and Wilkerson had briefed Lawson and the National Security Council on DTM's readiness. The news about Werner-Miranda had come as a shock, a mission readily available on the heels of DTM's graduation exercise. Was DTM ready? Truly?

Last-minute intelligence. A plant in the RAF. Drug lords and extradition treaties. DTM and a mission.

Something just didn't jibe, and his brain was tired. What he's been wanting to say all along to an old friend he'd known all too well over the past four decades finally came out.

A shocked response. *"What?"*

MacIntyre cleared his throat. "I said don't double-cross me, Stu. You fuck me around on this, and it'll come back to haunt your ass."

Lawson's brittle laugh cackled nervously in the car. "You're joking."

"I assure you that I am not."

"Why are you looking at me like that?"

"Just remember Thailand and Laos, Stu. And remember the game you threw in high school, when we had Hugo down by a field goal in the fourth quarter. Remember how you got married just before they called up the reserves when the shit hit the fan in Korea."

"I resent that, Wayne."

"And I resent the way you wanted me to take this ride with you to see our privileged children, so that you could remind me who calls the shots with DTM. I resent the way you wanted them to leave on this immediate mission concerning Humberto Werner-Miranda, and how everything concerning this mission seems a little too pat. I just hope you realize that DTM is not to be considered as an expendable asset."

"Wilkerson said they were ready!" the Vice President of the United States protested. "And I don't like what you're implying in the least, Wayne!"

It didn't matter if DTM was ready or not, Wayne MacIntyre thought, glancing at his watch, which read the 29th of March. They were gone.

They were in Italy.

And he had a plane to catch.

PART III

"I like good food and good cigars. I like to sleep in a good bed freshly made. I like to walk in good shoes. I like to play poker and blackjack. I like parties, and dances, and going to see a dramatic play from time to time. I know I'm going to be assassinated someday, so I like living to the hilt."

—**Ilyich Ramirez Sanchez, aka "Carlos, the Jackal"**

But if the cause be not good, the king himself hath a heavy reckoning to make, when all those legs, and arms, and heads, chopped off in battle, shall join together at the latter day, and cry all "We died at such a place"; some swearing, some crying for a surgeon; some upon their wives, left poor behind them; some upon the debts they owe; some upon their children rawly left. I am afeard there are few die well, that die in a battle: for how can they charitably dispose of any thing, when blood is their argument? Now, if these men do not die well, it will be a black matter for the king, that led them to it; who to disobey were against all proportion of subjection.

—**Shakespeare,** *Henry V*

Chapter Eighteen

Selva-Wolkenstein, Northern Italy

Manny Santo and Wintz Maslow sat side by side on a swaying gondola that was gaining altitude by the second, as they traveled from the base of Monte Selva to the summit bowl. It was nine o'clock in the morning and they were on one of the first few ski lifts.

"Never did care that much for heights," Maslow gravely intoned in the calmest voice he could muster.

Santo hooted. "That's a good one, Wintz." Santo was itching for the feel of his K-2 slats slicing through good snow and the adrenaline rush he always felt when skiing. It was recon time, and he fully intended to enjoy it. He was groomed for the part with dark, nondescript ski clothes—a bland, charcoal-gray set of coveralls, a wine-red Chamonix guide sweater, a black knit watch cap, and black gloves.

"These Italian gondolas scare the hell out of me."

Santo pondered that. Yes, it was true. Ski-related deaths and accidents were much more commonplace in Europe than in the U.S. Particularly in Italy. He craned his neck up and regarded the suspension cable and trolley above their seat. Then, looking down, he saw they were at least seventy-five feet above the mountain slopes. Ahead, the cable shot through an Alpine valley before terminating at the summit. The temperature dropped a few degrees.

As their gondola neared the top of the summit bowl, the brisk early April wind breezed icily across Santo's face. The altitude and carefully groomed thirty-five-inch snow base still allowed for excellent skiing. Nearby was the *hutte* servicing

211

the summit-bowl skiers. Smoke from the Austrian-styled heavy-timbered and stucco mountain chalet curled loosely into the sapphire sky.

They lifted the guard rail and scooted to the edge of their seat. A mound of snow and a lift-keeper greeted them at the lift's terminus. The two men hopped out of their seat and schussed down the exit mound. A level spot allowed them to review the initial ski run leading to a *hutte* about two hundred feet down. It was a chic place, with state-of-the-art fashion statements posing about in the latest ski-wear and equipment. The smell of roasting wurst, espresso, and the babble of at least a half dozen languages mixed agreeably in the morning air.

"Check out the alcohol igloo," Maslow said.

Santo spotted a snow dome below, adjacent to the *hutte*, bristling with two dozen bottles of varying brands of liquid courage. "I see it," he said. An Italian bartender was serving steaming mugs of something or other to two men. A scattering of couples and groups dotted the veranda overwatching the summit bowl.

"Then you also see one each Captain Matt MacIntyre and a pal of his."

"What?"

"You're one blind Cuban, Santo. C'mon, we've got supplies to pick up." Maslow jumped off the lip of the run and headed straight for a small mogul field that would lead them directly to the drink igloo. Following him, Santo concentrated on weaving through the moguls and getting his ski-legs back into shape. Schussing down to the bottom of the run, he found himself admiring Maslow's parallel slat technique and form. Maslow side-chopped to an abrupt halt before the two men at the ice igloo, where he immediately placed an order for some hot espresso.

The two men they'd spotted at the top of the run glanced at Maslow. Santo followed closely behind, and immediately recognized his ex-team leader, Matt MacIntyre, obviously a younger version of his old man, Wayne. Santo grinned, but refrained from greeting him. The plan was to link up discreetly.

Maslow ordered two espressos, ski-skated to a vacant outdoor table twenty feet away, and deposited the drinks there. On cue, Santo moved up to a ski rack, where other skiers had stuck their slats into the snow, and began removing the skis from his boots. Matt MacIntyre and the man he was with approached Santo, and stopped to adjust their bindings before beginning a run.

"Hiya, Manny," Matt said quietly.

"Matt. Good to see you."

"Meet Sergeant Corky Cortez. We've got an update for you. Corky did some intel work on the Panamanian-Colombian border last year with the 7th before coming to Germany. You could say your target is one of his main interests in life."

Santo glanced up and regarded the Hispanic face of a well-built Latino roughly his own age. He nodded, resumed adjusting his bindings, and out of the corner of his eye saw that Maslow was still waiting for him at their table.

"Take the black run heading across that ridgeline to your right," MacIntyre said, stomping his skis in the snow and ensuring his bindings were tight. "Number Thirteen. They call it that on purpose, it's one of the hardest routes on the mountain. Randy and Rene are one of the couples mixing with the rest of the tourists outside the *hutte*."

Santo discreetly looked in the direction of the *hutte*. Sure enough, Hanlon and Burchette were talking and smiling together, like the other beautiful people jet-setting that morning at one of northern Italy's premier ski resorts.

"We'll meet you at the hairy part of the slope. Act like you've fallen. We'll be there to help you back on your feet and give you some data on Werner-Miranda."

Santo gave MacIntyre a sharp look. He'd thought the boss's son wasn't supposed to be in on this operation. Or any DTM operation for that matter. "Matt—"

But it was too late. He and Cortez had already left. Santo joined Maslow at his table.

"Message pickup time?" the retired warrant officer asked him.

"Yeah. Can you say Route Thirteen?"

"I thought ski resorts didn't use that number."

"Apparently this one does."

"Oh, boy. Let's go."

Two minutes later, the two men had drained their espressos, copped the desired caffeine buzz, and were schussing smoothly by the entrance of the *hutte* with all the beautiful people. Maslow spotted Burchette and Hanlon and suppressed a grin. Santo brought up the rear. "Let's do Thirteen," he said to Maslow for Burchette and Hanlon's benefit.

Seconds later brought them to a knife-edged ridgeline. To the right, the mountain sheared downward in a three-thousand-foot drop-off. All the way down below the snowline. At the bottom of the valley was the lush green of Italian spring. To the left were the twisting equally steep slopes groomed for the most experienced—or most foolhardy—skiers. Maslow paused before a black signpost that, in bold relief, was numbered 13.

"Oh, Gawd," Santo said, catching up with him.

"Exposure, my man," Maslow jumped off the lip of the run. Santo swallowed and did the same.

"C'mon." Randy Hanlon touched Rene Burchette's arm, back at their table.

"Going to show off some more, Randy?" she said, smiling.

Grinning, Hanlon rose from their table and headed for their skis. Burchette followed. They began to step into them.

"Mission time, babe," Hanlon Bogarted.

"Quit calling me babe."

"Okay, wench."

Without waiting for her, Hanlon ski-skated down the knife-edged ridgeline leading toward the black runs. Rene stepped into her right ski, and prepared to follow him. Then she felt a warm, creeping feeling along the base of her neck. She turned around. A blond-haired woman, athletic, similar to her in frame, was staring at her. She and an Asian woman had been sitting two tables away from her and Hanlon. Even behind her mirrored Vuarnet sunglasses, Burchette could tell that . . .

She was being examined. She felt naked. Rene stomped her right foot into the clip binding, made herself ignore the blond woman staring at her, and skied toward the ridgeline connecting to the black runs, where Hanlon had gone. She met him in front of a signpost listing the number thirteen. Hanlon was concentrating very hard on the drop-off before them.

"Damn."

Rene Burchette grinned. Then it faded, as she remembered the woman who had stared at her. "Randy, we need to be careful here."

"No shit."

"I'm not talking about this run. I think we're being watched."

"Yeah?" Hanlon rocked back on his skis, and started hyperventilating on purpose. Rene knew that he wasn't listening to her. Before them twisted the steepest run they'd encountered on the mountain yet. It bent sharply through a narrow, twisting cut through the fir trees clustered all along the mountain.

It was time to go. Rene led out, beating Hanlon to the punch.

Santo's balls climbed up into his lower intestine, as he tried to let his legs absorb the moguls that seemed to grab his slats, turn him left, right, left, right . . . he missed one. Headed straight for it. The forty-five degree angle—downward, that is—was designed for maximum takeoff.

He skyrocketed into the air, just as he'd seen Maslow do a second earlier.

And like Maslow, he crashed and burned into a snowbank signaling the end of their first run on Route Thirteen. Two skiers waiting by the tree line ski-skated toward them to help them out of the snow.

"You okay, Manny?" Matt MacIntyre asked him. Santo could barely hear him, as he had executed a snowplow with his face, and had become buried headfirst in the snowbank.

"Never better," Santo garbled through the freezing snow. He felt two strong hands underneath his armpits and was righted. Miraculously, the skis had remained on his feet. He turned around. It was the other guy MacIntyre had brought with him. "Thanks. Cortez, isn't it?"

"Yeah."

Santo thought he'd seen the man before. In the SF community, one usually got to know practically everyone worth a shit sooner or later in their respective careers. But there was no time for amenities now. Santo felt a tug on his parka pocket and, looking up, saw that Maslow was skiing toward them. Glancing back at MacIntyre, he saw that his ex-team leader had shoved a package into his pocket.

"Here's a packet of intel from Corky. We also set up an equipment cache just outside of town—snowmobiles and a ski-touring package for each member of the team, demolitions, radios, and a basic load of weapons and ammo." MacIntyre glanced upslope for a second and looked back at Santo. "Hanlon and the woman on your team just started the route," MacIntyre said. "Tell them where to meet as they pass by. Dad, Charlie Whitehead, and the NSC guy are waiting for you at Hotel Sudtyrol. It's a four-star joint in the center of town. Room 338. Remember that."

Santo grunted his approval. The team had prearranged a number of meeting places to rendezvous, pending initial reconnaissance activities, which they were all doing today. Evidently Matt MacIntyre had informed his father of an intelligence boon, and that was where Cortez fit in. He patted his pocket and zipped it up. "Okay, Matt. See you then."

MacIntyre grinned at Santo and Maslow, who had joined them by now. "One thing more, Wintz."

"Check."

"That bag of magic tricks you wanted. Wilkerson cached it for you at Hotel Sudtyrol. It's in a locker in the health spa. Number Twenty-five. The key is in that packet I gave Manny. Any questions?"

No one spoke. MacIntyre glanced at his watch. "Okay. Time is now 1030 hours. You guys take it easy. We're outta here."

MacIntyre and Cortez schussed away, and soon had disappeared. A soft melting touched Santo's face. Looking up, he saw that it had begun to snow. He also saw two skiers rocketing toward them.

"Jesus!" Maslow moved out of the way, trying to avoid getting hit by the two oncoming blurs. Hanlon and Burchette braked to a halt, sending a snow plume into Santo's face.

"Hey, Team Daddy!" Hanlon said with cocky enthusiasm. Behind him, Burchette rolled her eyes.

"Don't stick around," Santo told them. "Hotel Sudtyrol, 1800. Room 338. For now, drive on with your recon and be prepared to report on any of the target's goon squads you see, bodyguard activity, and whether or not you've spotted Werner-Miranda."

Half an hour later found Santo and Maslow at the bottom of the run, aching, bruised, and humbled. A long, easy main run sloped back toward the gondola line where they'd started earlier in the morning. As they skied side by side along the gentle slope Maslow grinned hugely and said, "Well, Manny, did you be all you could be this morning?"

"Fuck you."

"You're so coarse."

"No, I just want to get to work. All I can see around here are ski bums and tourists."

"Pay closer attention to detail, then." Maslow ski-skated to the side of the run, where the treeline paralleled an icy mountain road separating the slope from Selva's outskirts. From his vantage point, Maslow could see the outline of the village below, dotted with Alpine chalet-style ski lodges, chapels, nightclubs, and restaurants. The village was enclosed in a circle of high mountains, sequestering Selva like an Alpine Shangri-la, an island of a ski resort cut from the ordinary Italian system of roadways linking resort with resort from the Austrian border all the way to Cortina.

Maslow's finger traced the village's outline for Santo's benefit. "I stayed at Hotel Dorfer last night. See it?"

"Kind of rough."

"Three-star hotel."

"I prefer four stars."

"Who wouldn't? But it's the clientele there that made me do a little thinking. Mostly men, as a matter of fact. Just a few women. Young and in shape. What does that tell you?"

"I see what you're getting at." Santo squinted harder at Selva, wishing he had a pair of binoculars. He and Maslow were trying to blend in as a couple of GIs from Germany just out having a good time. "Hotel Dorfer's pretty much along the outskirts of town, situated on the ridgeline opposite this one. Across the valley itself."

"Now if you were a drug lord, who happened to like laundering his money through a private resort in the Italian Alps, where would you put your command and control center?"

Santo's eyes swept across the town to the opposite ridgeline that formed the valley. He found the hotel where Maslow had spent the previous night. Looking at it from their present perspective, he saw that it was situated on a pretty broad ridgeline, one that was not too steep. Level enough for a helicopter, even. A screen of mountains just one kilometer behind it opened up into a canyon, forming an escape route through the mountains. "Hotel Dorfer would be my bet," Santo replied. "That way you could overwatch all the other resorts you happened to own, not to mention any unwanted activity brewing in town."

"Would you live there when you were in town?"

"Nope. I'd stay out in the woods somewhere. Werner-Miranda's got to have his own private lodging, which could be easily defended with good routes of ingress and egress. It wouldn't be in town." Santo nodded his head in the direction of Hotel Dorfer and the mountains enclosing the canyon a kilometer behind it. "I'd say he'd want a place somewhere near that canyon, Wintz."

"Roger that. There's a cross-country ski route along the mountain massif in that direction. We ought to give it a recon."

Santo remembered what Matt MacIntyre had told them earlier, about Maslow's "bag of magic tricks." Maslow knew his shit when it came to computers, listening and surveillance devices. "Know what I think, Wintz?"

"You're a thinking man?"

"Fuck you," Santo said for the second time that day. "Let's service the cache—"

"And wire Hotel Dorfer for sound," Maslow finished for him. "I agree." Maslow stopped speaking suddenly, as something caught his eye. Touching Santo's arm, he nodded toward the main lift area about a hundred meters downslope next to a *hutte*, where tourists were getting on the main gondola. It was a boxcar affair lifting hundreds of feet into the air for a direct ascent back to the summit bowl where they'd been earlier.

A half-dozen young Latino men, mixed with a couple of broad-shouldered Aryan types, were escorting a rather short and plump Latino in his mid-forties onto the main lift gondola.

"Bingo," Santo said, stabbing his ski poles into the snow.

CHAPTER NINETEEN

"So he just kind of stood there outside the latrine, butt-naked, and watched his towel make like a tumbleweed." Hanlon laughed, telling an old desert-training war story to Rene where they sat outside the *hutte* servicing the main gondola lift line. "It finally plastered up alongside the perimeter fence, dirty and shot through with cactus needles. Manny chased after in his birthday suit and thongs. Me and Wintz howled like Third World shamans, watching him. I'm here to tell you, Rene, Orfice-Grande winds just don't let up—"

Hanlon broke off in mid-sentence as Burchette bent over their table to kiss him on the ear.

"Hey!"

"Shut up," Burchette muttered, "and don't turn around." She continued to make love to Hanlon's ear.

"I like that."

"Don't flatter yourself," Burchette told him through clenched teeth. "I'm trying to tell you that our target has just arrived. I'm going to the ladies' room. Turn around to watch me, and I'll intersect their line of sight." She kissed Hanlon full on the lips and then rose to leave the table.

Hanlon was nonplussed, and he would have turned around to watch her leave anyway. When she did, he saw Humberto Werner-Miranda walking toward the gondola with a half-dozen bodyguards, all dressed in the latest ski fashions.

He also saw Manny Santo and Wintz Maslow ski down the entry slope toward the target. Rene's visit to the restroom was brief, and she exited the *hutte* in time to catch their eye. Hanlon tossed some liras on the table and strode casually toward the racks where he and Burchette had stuck their skis in the snow near the lift line's gateway.

Santo and Maslow snowplowed to a halt, preparing to enter the line with the others waiting to join the drug lord and proprietor of one of Monte Selva's premier ski resorts. Out of the corner of his eye, Santo saw that Hanlon had seen the target too and was headed their way for his skis. Santo lost control of his snowplow on purpose, and managed to fall down and bump into Burchette. Both of them hit the snow.

"Excuse me!" Santo got to his feet first.

"It's all right," Rene responded quietly. She allowed Santo to pull her up.

"See them?" Santo muttered.

"Yes."

"You and Randy keep a tail on them." Then louder, "You okay, miss?"

"Honey?" Hanlon announced, joining them. He threw Santo his best jealous-lover look.

Rene came fully to her feet and smiled sunnily at Hanlon. "Fine! Come on, I want to catch the gondola before it leaves." She tugged at his arm, and tiptoed up to kiss him.

Santo spotted Werner-Miranda and his gang as they entered the main lift gondola. It was getting full. Suddenly, one of his escorts exited the gondola, striding purposefully back for the *hutte*. He reached a pay phone and hastily punched a touch-tone sequence. Santo looked at Maslow and moved his head in the direction away from the lift line. Slowly, they ski-skated toward the *hutte* to order coffee, careful to stay in line of sight with the bodyguard making the phone call.

After binding on their skis, Burchette and Hanlon joined the lift line, keeping an eye on Humberto Werner-Miranda and his escorts. The suspension car was getting packed. Somehow, they managed to squeeze in.

"Check him out," Maslow said quietly, sipping on black Italian espresso.

"Looks like he's getting his butt chewed," Santo said, pretending to be leaning back in his chair where they sat outside, soaking up the spring sun glaring brightly over Alpine snow. He surveilled the Latino escort from the corner of his Rayban Wayfarers. The Latino was a slim, good-looking man with thick black hair and an animated expression on his face. He was also a very scared-looking man. Something was up.

The sound of beating helicopter blades mixed with the other sounds of skis, the trolley of the gondola, and the happy buzz of tourists. Glancing up, Santo saw a helicopter pass overhead and circle the resort town beneath the mountain. He looked back at the Latino and saw that he'd watched the inbound helicopter as well.

Maslow was watching the crew-served gondola. The doors started to swing shut. Suddenly the doors reopened for another couple. Two women. One of them was Asian.

Santo tapped his arm. Looking back at the phone, Maslow saw that the Latino had hung up and was striding away as fast as his stiff ski boots would allow.

"Check out the bird that just flew in," Santo said.

Maslow saw that the helicopter had overflown the town and was now rolling in on the far ridgeline.

"Let's go," Santo said.

They followed the Latino to his car, and casually snowplowed next to another vehicle, pretending it was theirs. Santo looked at the license plate number of the Latino's black BMW and memorized it for future reference. Later on that night the number might come in handy, when the team rendezvoused at the head shed MacIntyre and Wilkerson and Whitehead were rigging up at Hotel Sudtyrol. Wilkerson could downlink the data trail on the license plate through the array of modems and fax machines he had remoted into NSA computer terminals. The thought reminded Santo about what Matt MacIntyre mentioned earlier about Maslow's "bag of magic tricks."

The Latino drove away. The helicopter, a civilian Bell Ranger, settled down onto a helipad behind Hotel Dorfer.

"I bet I know where he's going," Maslow declared.

"Figure the odds," Santo said with a grin.

"Good odds, my man."

They skied down the parking lot to a point along Monte Selva where they could watch the Latino drive his BMW down into Selva.

They watched him drive through Selva.

And they saw him take the opposite ridgeline toward Hotel Dorfer and the helicopter.

"Bingo," Santo said again, pleased with their luck, as he and Maslow skied down toward the center of town. "Looks like Hotel Dorfer's Werner-Miranda's command and control center, Wintz. Just like you said."

"Then what do you say we go hit the cache of lucky charms Matthew told us about earlier?" Maslow said.

"My sentiments exactly."

They reached Hotel Sudtyrol's health spa twenty minutes later.

Smiling, Siegfried shouldered past ski vacationers packing the lunchtime crowd inside the summit bowl's *hutte*, and found the Colombian's table right where Simon told him it would be: on the upper deck of the *hutte*, where semi-private booths capable of holding a dozen people could view the Dolomites' glaciated and rock-tipped vista of ice and snow and rock, while watching skiers plummet down the slopes below. At sunset, the view was spectacular, what with golden-red sky fire igniting the rocky periphery into an Alpine phoenix. Service on the upper level of Monte Selva's summit bowl was the best, and paying customers could therefore avoid the crush of humanity downstairs, while mere commoners swilled grappa and espresso.

Even so, Werner-Miranda's ostentatious display of bodyguards spoke frankly of the drug lord's terrible sense of operational security. The Colombian's arrogance would do him in. *As it has already,* Siegfried thought with a smirk.

Seeing him, the plump, short man greeted the RAF terrorist with a grin. "Welcome to Monte Selva," Werner-Miranda cried. "You are . . . Herr Brandt, no?"

"Horst," Siegfried corrected, giving Werner-Miranda his cover name as he pumped his fat, moist palm.

"You have a message for me, I believe."

"Should I convey it to you now?"

"No, no," Werner-Miranda clucked, sweeping his hand before the array of wurst, pasta, beer, and mineral water occupying the table before his stone-faced bodyguards. "Please avail yourself of my hospitality."

Siegfried concealed a smile of contempt and noted, while looking over Werner-Miranda's shoulder, that Monika Stern and Yuko Suzuki were occupying the next booth over. He hoped they would execute their part of the operation—Werner-Miranda's demise—with some degree of finesse and not jump the gun. That is, *if* things were timed right. Sitting at his booth, he casually opened a notepad and showed two names to Werner-Miranda.

"This will be our payment for the product we came for, señor," Siegfried said quietly. He politely took a sip from the glass of mineral water one of Werner-Miranda's thugs poured for him.

Werner-Miranda sat silently, munching on the sausage-like, mustard-covered wurst link protruding from his mouth. He burped, took a swig of beer, and chuckled. "You are telling me you can erase those names easily enough with your organization?"

"And anyone else you wish to see dead within the U.S. Treasury Department and/or the DEA," Siegfried quietly assured him. He nodded at the two names on the notepad. "Their children as well," Siegfried spoke in quicksilver High German, an accent he knew would appeal to Werner-Miranda's Aryan affectation.

"I would have preferred that Simon came here to visit me himself," Werner-Miranda pouted, clutching the notepad.

"He awaits you at the Hotel Dorfer even as we speak."

Humberto Werner-Miranda nodded gravely. "I know. I sent one of my men back there to receive him. Simon is always such a stickler for . . . how do you call it?"

"Operational security," Siegfried said quietly, regarding Werner-Miranda's closest bodyguard. He noted for the first time that the bodyguard had a plastic earplug in his right ear with a wire, barely visible, running into his neckline, where evidently a radio was strapped beneath his armpit. Siegfried surmised correctly that Werner-Miranda had been notified that Simon had landed long before he himself had arrived at the drug lord's table. *Perhaps his security is not so bad after all.*

"Operational security, why, yes, of course." Werner-Miranda drained his beer and rose. On cue, so did his bodyguards.

Siegfried swallowed, and rising, saw that Stern and Suzuki had already left.

"Well," Werner-Miranda added, "Comrade Simon shall simply have to wait until I finish my favorite ski run on Monte Selva. Tell me, Horst, have you ever tried Route Thirteen before?"

At fifteen-thirty hours, Wintz Maslow and Manny Santo drove their rented Alfa Romeo up the ridgeline leading toward Hotel Dorfer and entered the parking lot. The mid-afternoon sun was already sinking toward the high horizon of the Dolomites' enclave separating the tiny resort village of Selva from the rest of the world. Golden rays draped the broad shoulder of the ridgeline in a gentle, warm hue. Santo stared at the beauty with a thousand-yard stare brought on by a full day of skiing.

"Drowsy?" Maslow asked him.

Santo jerked upright like a Ranger School student caught sleeping on patrol. "No!"

"Your nose is growing. Here we are."

Santo regarded Hotel Dorfer as they pulled into the parking lot. It was on the outskirts of the village, high enough up to overwatch anything going on in town. It was a three-star affair, a simple, mountain-chalet-styled rectangular structure of two stories, framed in heavy timber and white stucco. But on the other side, Santo knew that Hotel Dorfer had something many of the other resorts in Selva didn't—a helipad, currently occupied by the Bell Ranger they'd seen earlier from the Monte Selva main lift line.

Maslow parked the car backwards midway into the parking lot, so the nose of the vehicle pointed toward the exit. Just in case. Both men looked at the day-pack resting on the back seat. They had picked it up from locker number 25 in Hotel Sudtyrol's health spa an hour ago. After inventorying it for completeness, and ensuring all equipment inside worked, they had then taken off for the ten-minute ride that now had them parked outside Hotel Dorfer.

Maslow retrieved the day-pack from the back seat and pulled out a Sony Walkman. Seconds later, he had it adjusted and tuned the way he wanted it. He hooked the earphones around his neck and ensured the Walkman was fastened securely to his belt.

"You're some computer nerd, Wintz," Santo said softly.

Maslow gripped the door latch and gritted his teeth. "Yeah. Janie used to bitch to me about that."

"I miss her too, Wintz." The two men exited the Alfa after a moment's silence. Walking over, Santo put his arm around Maslow's shoulders. "Don't let the spiders freak you out, while your jammin' with that Walkman."

"I'll give you a call in an hour."

"That'll be around 1630 hours then. I'll be downstairs in the restaurant."

"That's a rog."

"Be careful, Wintz."

"Uh-huh."

As they walked up the entrance stairway and entered Hotel Dorfer's smallish lobby, Santo's eyes and mind formulated a mental blueprint of the building. Maslow had spent the night here, as had Hanlon and Burchette, so they already knew the layout of the place. He'd spent the night in Hotel Sudtyrol, readying the head shed with all the electronics and silicon magic Wilkerson and Whitehead had brought to Selva with them. The layout of Hotel Dorfer was simple enough.

As they walked into the warm, rough-hewn wood ambience of the lobby, Santo spotted a disco on the left. The front desk was directly ahead, an enclosed loft with mirrors—two-way mirrors, that is—directly above it: today's objective. To his right was a small restaurant, its outside glass panes allowing a magnificent view of the Dolomites in the throes of the mid-afternoon's setting sun. This and two stories of suites in two wings were all that comprised Hotel Dorfer. Maslow would have a simple enough time installing the surveillance equipment they sought to wire in with his bag of magic tricks.

But then again, nothing in this business was simple; Murphy's Law was always in effect.

They approached the staircase near the front desk. A doe-eyed Italian woman with blond hair revealing her Austrian heritage smiled at them. Not bad-looking. In her mid-twenties. Maslow said, for her benefit: "Thanks for the ride, John." Maslow yanked out the heavy pewter room key out of his pocket and made for the first floor corridor.

"No sweat, Ben," said John Reed, aka Manny Santo. "The girls are meeting us here, right?"

"Yeah, in about an hour," replied Ben Jackson, aka Winston Eugene Maslow the Third. "Gawd, I need a shower."

"Be back then, buddy."

"Check."

As he turned to head back for the car, Santo saw that the receptionist was trying very hard not to appear like she'd been paying attention. Exactly as he and Maslow had anticipated. The receptionist was only a cover for whoever occupied the enclosed loft directly above her head. What was in there?

Maslow was about to find out.

Santo pushed open the front door and left to spend a very slow-moving hour in the village.

Maslow passed a maid cart and the open door of the room next to his. Glancing in, he saw that the maid, or rather, an orderly, was fluffing pillows and making the bed inside. The smell of disinfectant reeked of German efficiency. Maslow stuck his key in his door and twisted it.

He was in a good location, only six or seven doors separated him from where he needed to go to penetrate the loft above the lobby. As he entered his room, Maslow's eyes searched for and found wiring leading across the top of his door frame, down to the hardwood floor, and along the wall to a telephone. Was that all there was to it? There had to be a camera eye somewhere. Where?

The room's layout was heavily influenced with Germanic overtones—a heavy down-comforter-shrouded bed, simply carved blond wood furnishings, a shower, a television set. It wasn't unlike most hotel rooms, except for the South Tyrolean furnishings. Maslow pulled his modified Walkman's earphones over his ears and flicked on the operating switch. Only a flatline wail, no varying degree in pitch. It didn't make sense. There had to be some type of electronic eavesdropping or surveillance device somewhere. He turned on the television set, and turned the volume way up. He thought about the only logical place a camera could be and glanced up. Seconds later he'd found the camera hidden behind the ceiling hook suspending the corner lamp. A quick check informed him that it wasn't running. Whoever was pulling security today wasn't doing a very good job.

So, Maslow thought, if he climbed into the air ducts above his room, he might be monitored, and then again, he might not. There was a possibility of capture by whoever secured this hotel, and that meant any number of the young athletic men and women he'd observed frequenting it. Maybe even one of the servants on maintenance detail. How many of them belonged to the Red Brigades or the RAF?

There had to be another way.

And then he thought of it. Who would monitor an empty room? One that was being cleaned perhaps?

He shrugged off his parka and threw it on the bed. The bathroom was conveniently located adjacent to the next room over. In fact, another door allowed his neighbor, if he had one, to share his bathroom. Not good for a tourist's privacy and convenience, but then three-star hotels were three-star hotels.

He entered, pack and all. No camera this time, the earphones on his Walkman informed him. He marveled at the gadgetry Wilkerson had provided him. The Walkman was both a microwave and transmitter signal detector. With it he could identify and avoid all security systems with microwave and electronic signatures, and that included about all of them.

He listened to the sounds the cleaning man made next door. After a moment, Maslow heard the door close. Grunting with satisfaction, he removed his jacket, revealing the modified ammunition vest he wore underneath. Strapped to his body by way of the vest were the tools of his trade: Around his neck hung miniaturized infrared goggles with an infrared spotlight, similar to a miner's lamp; underneath his left arm, an MP5-K submachine gun, small enough to fire with one hand; underneath his right arm a suppressed H&K P7; a locksmith kit was strapped around his waist, containing two palm-sized magnets, wire clippers, and an assortment of Allen wrenches and screwdrivers, all machined out of titanium for light weight; and two CO_2 mister cartridges occupied shotgun-shell loops over the right breast pocket of his ammunition vest. Tucked inside two pouches over his kidneys were other tools of the eaves-dropping and surveillance trade. Special equipment. He'd use it all later. First he had to reach the objective. He fished surgeon's rubber gloves from the front pocket of the chinos he wore and pulled them on.

Maslow started by examining the door connecting with the next room. A thin wire was sloppily painted over the top of the doorjamb. It led to a security device implanted underneath the doorjamb encasing the top of the door. Maslow picked the lock, then with his left hand held one of his magnets near the top right of the door. This deflected a metal lever intended to spring up and connect with the metal tape underneath the top of the doorjamb, signaling illicit entry into the next room. He twisted the doorknob with his right hand and slowly opened the door. He then fished out his other magnet and put it on the other side of the doorway opposite the magnet he held in his left hand. So far, so good. He afforded himself the luxury of a quick glance in the other room. His Walkman's silence informed him that no cameras were running in there.

Moments later, he had re-locked the door from the side next door and had silently climbed into the air duct connecting every room on the wing.

Including his target.

An hour later, Santo had returned to Hotel Dorfer and was ordering from the menu inside the restaurant.

"Ich mochte ein Pils, bitte," he ordered in German to the South Tyrolean blonde waiting on him.

"Dankeschön," the waitress replied, swishing away. Having chosen a middle table, Santo gazed through the glass wall allowing for one hell of a view, and watched the sunset nuking the range of peaks and glaciers before him in a rich reddish-gold. The restaurant was deserted, save himself and the maitre d' and cook chatting in the rear, but that wouldn't last long. Already, skiers were starting to return to their hotels.

Two men, dressed in expensive clothes, entered the restaurant. One was of medium height, with a rather pouchy face with a fish-belly complexion and a receding black hairline. Somewhat of a gut. Reptilian. Santo's eyes found the menu again after spotting the first man's partner.

It was the Latino Maslow had first spotted back at the ski lift. Evidently, he was escorting someone who wanted to meet Humberto Werner-Miranda.

The two men sat at one of the tables close to the back of the restaurant. Santo's eye caught the bulge of the pistols tucked inside the waistbands of their trousers.

Santo pressed the button of the Sonics Type-87 transmitter/receiver hidden inside his right trousers pocket. Now was not the appropriate time to speak into the whisper-mike threaded through the collar of his sports shirt. Seconds later, two answering beeps piped loud and clear inside the Siemens Electronics hearing aid in his left ear canal. Santo examined his menu, hoping Maslow was all right. A few moments later, the waitress returned with his beer.

"You are Signore Reed?"

Santo gave her a bland smile and felt the newcomers' eyes on the back of his neck. "Yes."

"We received a phone call from your friend, Signore Ben Jackson."

Santo sipped on the Pils lager the waitress had brought to him.

"He conveys his regrets that he and the two ladies you were to meet tonight are unable to come tonight."

"What?"

"I'm sorry."

"Dammit!"

"Mr. Reed, there is no need to—"

"Bring me another beer!"

The waitress departed. Just another ugly American. Santo watched her seek out the receptionist in the lobby and quickly converse. He didn't have to see the receptionist glance at him to know that he'd been watched the entire time. From the corner of his eye, he also noted that any suspicion of who he was had been dismissed by the newcomers. So far, so good. Turning the "incoming" dial of the Sonics Type-87 transmitter inside his right trousers pocket, he managed to pick up their conversation from thirty feet away.

Santo's heart rate climbed as he listened.

Perched in the rafters near the edge of the target room and draped in inky darkness, Maslow unhooked the cable connecting one of the hotel's phone lines to the telephone repairman's portable connection checker with which he had just conveyed his "regrets" to Santo's receptionist, not thirty feet downstairs and to the right of where he was now. *Fucking Santo,* he thought, his lips compressed into a tight grin. *Probably drinking beer and having a good time.* He pulled the infrared goggles and spotlight back over his eyes and examined the rafter system above the command and control room overwatching the lobby below. Twenty feet away, a generator and a multitude of electrical wiring and black boxes networked above his target, a virtual Medusa of technology.

He'd install the Fly-Eye there. Maslow glanced to the rear, where the air duct he'd crawled through led to the rafter system he was now negotiating. His gut told him not to go any further. He always obeyed that feeling in his gut, the little voice deep inside his mind, always a clarion warning.

Pulling one of the CO_2 mister cartridges from his belt, he sprayed the rafter space before him with it, and then switched his infrared spotlight on.

He was only two feet away from a greenish laser crisscrossing the rafters. It was simple enough to step over, but if he hadn't misted the target first . . .

Maslow pressed the on switch of the modified Walkman strapped to his utility belt, this time switching it to the microwave mode. Another high-pitched whining greeted his ears. Maslow's respect grew for whoever had installed Werner-Miranda's hotel security. His infrared-enhanced eyes panned the perimeter of the room until he spotted a transmitter— nothing fancy, just a tiny black box—mounted two feet off the ceiling. Switching his gaze opposite the black box to his left, he found its partner mounted on the right wall. They were microwave transmitters, designed to back up the laser trip-wire to his front.

He'd have to step over the laser and crawl under the microwave. He did so. Moments later he had arrived at the network of black boxes and wire terminating over the target. Now he was ready to go to work.

His eyes found the generator along the left wall, where the cables and electrical wiring were bound together into a stalk adjacent to the generator and connected to the equipment downstairs. He tried to remember the dimensions of the lobby. About fifteen feet long by twenty-five feet wide. Assuming the same dimensions for the command and control center, he performed mental geometry. Simply put, he needed to crawl ahead about another ten feet. Glancing that way, he found another cable and wiring mount strapped over one of the rafters. That would be the ceiling light.

Maslow crawled to it. When he got there, he quietly reinstalled the audio jack to the phone lines and installed the first of his own black boxes on the nearest rafter. It was a phone line transmitter remote, which could pick up all incoming and outgoing phone calls and fax messages. Putting that in place was the easy part. Next came the hard part. Maslow gently retrieved the sound-suppressed, battery-operated, hand-held drill from the kidney pouch hooked to his ammo vest.

Five minutes later found his face glued to a tiny periscope he pushed through the hole he'd drilled through the ceiling. Muted, Italian voices filtered through the hole. Twirling the periscope, Maslow spotted banks of computer and video monitors, a couple of fax machines, a copier, and several telephones, all neatly arranged. Two monitor watchers talked inside, smoking hashish and drinking grappa.

Santo glanced at his watch. 1715 hours. Maslow had been at work for the past hour and three quarters. He himself had been inside the restaurant for the past forty-five minutes.

He wasn't the only one inside the restaurant who was impatient, his Siemens Electronics hearing aid informed him.

"You told me he'd be here fifteen minutes ago," one tinny voice scolded inside Santo's left ear. He tried not to glance at the two men five tables down near the rear of the restaurant.

"Signore Rozo," the griping man's escort said in soft, earnest tones, "the *jefe* is coming. He is simply late. You must wait here."

"I wait for no one. Not even Humberto Werner-Miranda!"

Even though the voices were mute, muffled to the ear, Santo's hearing aid picked it all up. They were dead on target. The receptionist entered the restaurant, casting a look of dismissal toward Santo as she passed him.

"Signore Rozo," she told one of the Latinos softly, "you have a call waiting at the front desk."

Santo departed for the men's room.

Maslow took what looked like an aluminum cigar container out of his left kidney pocket, connected the cable from the Fly-Eye's power generator—nothing more than a palm-sized battery box—and turned it on to check the circuits.

The audio signal cabled between his audio transmitter remote and the hotel's main phone line picked up. The eavesdropped phone call was clearly relayed into Maslow's left ear, where he monitored the phone calls while working.

"*Gruss Gott, Hotel Dorfer,*" he heard the receptionist say with Teutonic crispness.

"*Signore Rozo.*" A Germanic voice. Somewhat strained.

"*Einen moment, bitte.*" Maslow hummed away at his work while waiting for the "guest" to answer the front desk's phone. Holding the metal tube up to his face, he unscrewed the middle and gently pushed up from the bottom. The Fly-Eye became a sea anemone as twenty delicate laser optic fibers blossomed out of the top with Maslow's telescoping effect, each end glowing softly from the signal they were receiving from the generator. When he pulled back down on the bottom, the tentacles of the Fly-Eye receded back inside their chamber.

The hole Maslow had drilled was three quarters of an inch wide, just wide enough for the Fly-Eye to fit snugly. He inserted the business end into the hole and pushed the laser optics back out. Inside the target room, one would have to know what he was looking for in order to spot it. The delicate strands of laser optics were transparent in color, and you could only see the lasers they emitted if you wore infrared goggles, such as the ones Maslow was wearing. Blossomed out, each of the twenty tentacles of the Fly-Eye viewed an eighteen-degree-by-nine-degree sector of the surveillance target. Back at the safe room at Hotel Sudtyrol, Wilkerson and Whitehead would have a number of monitors set up to simultaneously view the Fly-Eye's surveillance for real-time transmissions. There would also be scrambled phone communications relayed back to NSA and NSC channels via the Satcom radio Wilkerson would have rigged up as well, for instantaneous processing of all message traffic emanating from the surveillance target, whether it be fax, audio, or visual.

Maslow checked the Fly-Eye's audio reception/transmission by connecting another cable to its generator box, and then hooked the other end to the "signal in" port of his Walkman. As he looked at its front cover, a miniaturized monitor sprang to life. Now he had his own closed-circuit television set. The room directly below him was now in full view, and he was able to catch varying angles by tuning the Walkman's frequency dial.

Check. Disconnecting the Fly-Eye cable from his Walkman, Maslow gathered his equipment and prepared to leave.

Santo's whisper-mike transmission suddenly crackled in Maslow's right ear. *"Wintz!"*

"Yo," Maslow breathed. What was up?

"Wintz, I'm in the restaurant's men's room. You got a phone tap on yet?"

"That's a rog."

"This is Señor Rozo," Maslow's left ear crackled, via his Walkman headphones, overriding Santo's whisper mike. "Wait one, Manny," Maslow said, ready to listen.

"He is on his way." The Germanic voice again. What about the other voice? Maslow wondered, eavesdropping. Spanish-sounding.

"Then you know what to do."

"Ja."

The phone line clicked. Maslow spoke into his whisper mike. "Manny?"

"Yeah."

"Looks like we're about to have company."

"It's more than that, Wintz. I'll brief you later. Look, we may have to step things up a little and—"

Santo's transmission abruptly broke off.

"Manny?"

No answer. Maslow's guts slipped around inside him.

• • •

From where he sat inside the toilet booth, Santo quietly thumbed back the hammer of his suppressed Browning, while watching a shiny pair of patent-leather Guccis step into the men's room. The click of heels on tile echoed hollow and deadly on the spotless floor. The shoes paused before his booth.

Sweat beaded Santo's forehead. He reached for the commode's flush chain. Pulled it. The flush roar came, and Maslow flapped open the newspaper over his lap, hiding his Browning.

The Guccis stopped in front of his stall. Santo heard the rustle of clothing and knew a pistol was being pulled.

"Do you mind?" Santo said irritably, thumbing back the hammer of his 9-millimeter from behind his newspaper.

The Latino said in perfect English, "I will shoot you unless you do exactly as I say."

"Why can't you just let a man take a crap in peace?"

The door slowly opened. Santo found himself staring at two pistol bores. He fought back a desire to laugh. The Latino was holding two Berettas on him. A regular two-gun cowboy. Santo saw the cords of the Latino's jaw tighten, and he knew he was about to be shot. Then things happened very quickly. Santo's finger tightened on his own trigger, as he reflexively brought his left hand up to block the bullet he knew would plow through his face.

The Latino pulled the trigger first, and Santo heard the suppressed *pop!* of the Latino's Beretta and felt a dart stick him in the heel of his upraised palm. Its needle lodged in the bone, sending a shock wave of pain in the heel of his hand. He pulled his own trigger, and hit the Latino between the eyes. He fell to the floor, already dead. Santo turned his palm around and saw a dart sticking out of the heel of his hand. Seeing the needle lodged inside one of the bones made him feel nauseous.

"Maslow," he rasped into his whisper mike. "I've been hit. A fuckin' dart . . ."

No answer. Why? No time to think. Had to move.

He blinked. Spots. Everything was spots. He had to retard the drug he knew was inside him. Probably only seconds left. Lurching out of the stall, he reached out for the Latino's neck and loosened his necktie and pulled it off. Santo slipped the noose above his elbow and tightened the Windsor knot with one hand while he pulled the other end of the tie with his teeth.

A tourniquet. His eyes wanted to close now. Would the tourniquet work?

At least he was still in control of his body. For the time being, anyway. At best the tourniquet would afford him only seconds before the tranquilizer he'd been injected with took effect and put him out. It explained the reason for the Latino's two guns. One had been loaded with darts, the other with actual rounds, for backup.

Santo dragged the dead man into the stall and stuck his feet into the toilet. He propped the dead man up against the wall to keep him in place. There hadn't been much blood, since his bullet hadn't blown through the Latino's cranium. A few drops on the floor. Now the dead man was hidden. Santo exited the stall and closed the door.

He scrubbed at the floor hastily with a hand towel. When he got to his feet, the world seemed to tip at an angle. There wasn't much time left. He walked for the door as much in control as he could muster, and found it very hard to keep his mouth closed as the muscles in his jaw started to relax. There was some type of paralyzing agent in the dart, now working on his system. It was being kept at bay only with his tourniquet. But still, a little of the tranquilizer was slipping into his bloodstream with each passing second.

Santo pulled the men's room door open with a drunken stagger and paused in the hallway. Somehow he remembered to put the Browning back in his shoulder holster. His knees felt very weak, and now his fingers were starting to tingle. He glanced around, trying to remain as alert as he could. No chaos. No one racing about. Still pretty quiet. Even the receptionist in the lobby was hunched over her paperwork. He licked his lips and concentrated very hard on putting one foot in front of the other as he stepped out from the slick, cold tile of the men's room onto the carpet of the hallway. His arms felt numb, like they'd once felt when he'd almost passed out from shallow water blackout in his pre-SCUBA days back at Bragg. Seconds left. He entered the lobby, the world tilted at an angle. If only he could make it outside, to the car, to Maslow. *There's no time, where's Mas—*

Footsteps padding softly from behind. It was over. *Nice try, Manny,* he thought. *Nice fuckin'* . . .

Powerful hands grabbed him underneath the armpits just as his knees gave out.

CHAPTER TWENTY

Wayne MacIntyre checked his watch for the fifth time in as many minutes and realized that Santo and Maslow were entirely too late. But how late was late? Five minutes, even ten? Things happened, Murphy's Law was always in effect. But forty-five minutes meant that something was wrong. Dead wrong. He leaned back against his chair where Whitehead and Wilkerson had set up the conference roundtable in the room adjoining the situation room in their Hotel Sudtyrol suite, and surveyed the faces waiting for him to speak. He hadn't wanted to bring his son Matt in on the operation. The fact that DTM had needed some auxiliary support, however, and any intelligence on Werner-Miranda that the NCO sitting beside Matt had to offer, warranted Matt's being there. That and the equipment they had cached just outside of town. Randy Hanlon and Rene Burchette were in the room as well; they'd tailed Werner-Miranda all afternoon, and seemed convinced that some sort of exchange was up with a third party—drugs, weaponry, who could say?

"Sir." A head popped in the doorway.

MacIntyre glanced up from the ash buildup on the end of his cigar. "Yeah, Lonnie?"

Wilkerson said, "Sir, I really don't think it's quite appropriate at this junction to bring Sergeant Cortez into this—"

"Mister Wilkerson, if I say he sits in on this brief, that's exactly what will happen."

Wilkerson stood in the doorway, exhaled, and ran his long, skinny fingers through the widow's peak of his hairline. MacIntyre fought to control his temper. Wilkerson had tried to convince him to return to the States today. Again. He'd had it with the NSC man.

"You got something for me?" MacIntyre snapped.

Wilkerson glanced sharply upward. "Maslow installed the Fly-Eye a couple of minutes ago. It's why they're running a little late."

"We'll be with you in a moment," MacIntyre told him, speaking in a very deliberate voice. Wilkerson returned to his monitors in the other room.

"Okay," MacIntyre told the others at his table, "now we can breathe a little easier. Rene, Randy, please go over what you found today again."

Hanlon spoke first. "Rene and I followed Werner-Miranda up to the *hutte* at the summit bowl of Monte Selva, where we then observed him talking to a German male in his mid-thirties. Seemed like Werner-Miranda was staging a rendezvous there at the *hutte* with this guy."

"They were discussing a meeting place and time with another party, someone named Simon," Rene Burchette said, placing her hand on Randy's to interrupt. MacIntyre noted the movement, and Rene followed his eyes to her hand and moved it back. Calmly, she added, "There was sort of a breakdown in communications, as if the German fellow was being led on by Werner-Miranda. There wasn't much he could gripe about, since Werner-Miranda had about six of his thugs escorting him around."

"Where's the rendezvous?" MacIntyre said impatiently. Burchette stiffened. MacIntyre glanced at his son Matt, sitting silently beside the NCO who had accompanied him during the day's events. Now he saw reproach in his own son's eyes. MacIntyre knew he was being an asshole. Too much strain. Too little sleep.

"Dad."

"Yeah, I know." MacIntyre sighed. "Sorry, Rene, please go on."

"As far as we know, sir," she told him, "he's supposed to receive another party tonight for an important meeting. We think the meeting place is Hotel Dorfer, as Manny and Wintz assumed earlier."

"That makes sense," Sergeant First Class Corky Cortez announced, speaking for the first time since the debrief began fifteen minutes ago. All eyes turned to Cortez. He was a large, stocky man with a barrel chest, and steady black eyes that looked like they knew something you didn't.

"What's that?" Wayne MacIntyre said.

"Makes sense, sir. Werner-Miranda wouldn't stay overnight in Selva, unless he was at a lodge he owned and could personally secure. My vote's cast for Hotel Dorfer."

"Why didn't you say something earlier?"

Matt MacIntyre shifted in his seat. "Because," he informed his father with an edge in his voice, "Sergeant Cortez doesn't talk a hell of a lot about the same guy whose outfit he watched in Colombia for the better part of six months."

"You told me you had a resident expert on Werner-Miranda."

Matt MacIntyre glanced at Cortez, who nodded and opened his mouth to speak.

"I pulled some border narco-intel ops for the CIA a couple of years ago in Panama, before we made our incursion down there to put Noriega out of business." Cortez examined his fingernails for a moment before going on. "The Darien Gap. A rain forest like you wouldn't believe. That's where we staged from. There is a gulf on the Caribbean side along the Panamanian and Colombian border that bites into the isthmus on the Colombian border, called the Gulf of Turbo. My team would cross over the border into Colombia and watch the druggies do their thing, primarily cocaine refinement and packaging for distribution. A lot of seaplanes landed and flew out of the gulf, circulating coke and cash in and out of Colombia. Most of the operations we surveilled, we trailed back to Humberto Werner-Miranda and his employees. He's got a real paramilitary outfit down there, largely recruited out of the Panamanian Defense Forces when Noriega was still in charge."

MacIntyre sucked on the end of his cigar until it glowed bright red. Exhaling, he said, "Go on, Sergeant Cortez."

"We spotted Pineapple-Face himself a couple of times, and relayed the intel we gathered back to a CIA case officer in El Corrizal we were working for, but nothing ever really happened." Cortez chewed the inside of his cheek for a moment and then added, "I kind of gathered by the end of my tour that maybe our own spooks were involved in the drug trade as well. Anything to fund the Contras, right? At any rate, after six months, I came up on levy for Bad Toelz, so here I am."

"Get to the point about 'making sense' out of what Hanlon and Burchette saw with Werner-Miranda."

"He *owns* Hotel Dorfer, Mr. MacIntyre. If Werner-Miranda had business to conduct in Selva, then that's where he'd do it: where he's surrounded by his own people who staff the hotel when he's in town. Guarantee you one thing, though, he won't be staying long."

"Why didn't you say something earlier?"

Corky Cortez leaned across the table. "Because I don't trust too many people," he said quietly, matching MacIntyre's steely gaze.

MacIntyre considered what Cortez said for a moment. Then he stood up. "Well. I hope we've passed your test, Sergeant Cortez." Without waiting for a reply, he announced, "Let's go see the pictures Lonnie's waiting to show us." The group cleared the room in moments. Cortez and Matt MacIntyre lingered. MacIntyre knew that Cortez wanted to say something else, and nodded his head to prod him on. Cortez glanced in Wilkerson's direction in the other room, where the others crowded around him and Whitehead and their array of technology.

"That guy Wilkerson hasn't," Cortez said. "Earned my trust, that is."

"Why?"

"Call it prejudice against spooks, Mr. MacIntyre. I've been burned before." Cortez exited the room, leaving Matt MacIntyre alone with his father.

"You shouldn't have come to Italy, Dad."

"So now *you* want to tell me what to do."

"Just like you told me to stay out of this operation. Did you really expect to keep me away from a team I'd been with over the past four years?"

"You set up the arms cache for the equipment Wilkerson brought across the borders and arranged for Cortez's meeting with the team for an intel brief. That's *all* you're doing."

Matt MacIntyre put his hand on his father's shoulder. "Dad, you couldn't have kept me from doing this anyway. Look, I know you want to be involved. But you've got to leave this thing up to the people you hired. Take Mr. Wilkerson's advice and leave Selva. Let us handle this."

Wayne MacIntyre said in no uncertain terms, "I'm staying and that's the last of it." He glanced at the door. "I respect what you're telling me, Matt, and I suppose you're right. But this is the way it's going to be."

Matt grabbed his father's arm. "Bullshit! You're doing this out of some sort of revenge trip, Dad! What is it you really want to do? Pull the trigger yourself when the target goes down? You really think you're going to get off on that?"

"Let—goddamn you, Matt, let go of me!"

Silence. Matt had never heard his father swear at him before, and his face registered the shock he felt. He began to realize what Wayne MacIntyre had become over the past several weeks, no, the past several years: an old man, lonely and bitter with rage, with an obsessive thirst for revenge.

"I'm sorry."

Matt saw tears fill his father's eyes.

"I'm so terribly . . ."

"Dad. . . ."

They embraced. Wayne's shoulders trembled, and Matt hugged his father very hard. Then he heard his father's voice, weak and choked with emotion, saying, "These kinds of bastards took my wife and my eldest son. They crippled my youngest son for life. What have I got left, son, but you and David? Dustbowl Enterprises?"

Matt MacIntyre said nothing.

Clearing his throat, Wayne MacIntyre wiped at his eyes with the back of his hand and straightened up. He nodded at the others in the adjacent room, who, fortunately, were out of earshot. Wayne nodded toward them. "So what am I supposed to do? Tell them to kill my enemies for me while my feet are safely planted on a desktop back in Tulsa?"

A hard glint suddenly sparked from Matt MacIntyre's eyes, leveled dead on his father's. "Yes, Dad. That's *exactly* what you should do. And you know it."

Matt exited and joined the others in the war room. After a moment, Wayne followed. An array of video monitors beamed varying images of the office Maslow's Fly-Eye had penetrated. Charlie Whitehead and Wilkerson, each with earphones wrapped around their heads and plugged into their respective monitor jacks, were typing data into the two computer terminals beside the monitors. On their right, the suite's vista window had been curtained and padded with foam to prevent any audio pickup lasers from eavesdropping on their activities. Another technology bank completed the horseshoe that

Wilkerson and Whitehead monitored, consisting of a fax machine, modem, and another black box that received transmissions and receptions from the satellite radio mounted on the hotel's rooftop. The black box automatically broke down incoming message traffic from Wilkerson's liaison in the NSA exchange between Selva and Washington D.C. It was surveillance and eavesdropping, live, against Humberto Werner-Miranda's lair at Hotel Dorfer.

A laser printer suddenly hummed to life, and Wilkerson grabbed the paper being spit out. After scanning it, he handed the message to Wayne MacIntyre, who took a seat next to Wilkerson. A fax from Washington. As MacIntyre struggled through the complex message format, Wilkerson spoke.

"We're getting wonderful pictures from the Fly-Eye. So far we've found out our target has some sort of activity going on with another organization, probably his European coke connection. What you're reading there is updated data from NSA computer banks on Werner-Miranda's itinerary and frequency of travel between Spain and Italy. This is the first time he's visited his own resort in at least a year, but at any rate, that itinerary says he's catching a red-eye flight out of Innsbruck back to Colombia in the morning."

"So the sooner we pick him up, the better," Cortez grunted.

MacIntyre glanced at his son and Sergeant Cortez. Both of them moved toward the wall, where a 1:24,000 acetate-covered map of the area surrounding Selva had been plastered. He glanced at Wilkerson. "Can you get me a blowup of the town?"

Moments later, a new map was posted on the wall. The group huddled around the map, Hanlon and Burchette side by side with Matt MacIntyre and Cortez. Hanlon traced the outline of Hotel Dorfer with his finger, and began to construct a mental concept of the operation for the snatch. He directed his comments to the group. "With Manny and Wintz away, there won't be much time for a full-blown op order," he said. He traced a finger from Hotel Dorfer's parking lot down the kilometer it took to reach downtown Selva. "It's a pretty isolated roadway, lined with trees. We could ambush his vehicle and make the snatch along the road. Use the snowmobiles at the cache to skijor him and the rest of the team into the countryside. Someone meets us at a rendezvous with the van;

then drives him across the Italian and Austrian borders and hands him off at the American Consulate in Munich."

"That's all well and good, folks, but maybe it's time we found out what the hell happened to Manny and Wintz." All eyes turned onto Matt, who glanced sharply at Wilkerson. "They should have been in contact by now." Matt switched his look to Whitehead. "Try to reach them, Charlie."

Wayne MacIntyre contemplated the increasing suspicion aimed toward Wilkerson. Why was the NSC man still being treated as an outsider?

Reaching over to the black box sitting next to the fax machine, Whitehead pressed a button in rapid succession three times. The room fell silent. After a moment, Whitehead repeated the transmission. A voice, tinny and distorted, then crackled over the loudspeaker mounted overhead. *". . . awaiting . . . pickup, over."*

"He's transmitting in the clear," Wilkerson said, his voice edged with urgency. "Break out the FM." Whitehead reached to his right and flicked the on switch to the same frequency as Maslow's Walkman. "Mike Sierra, Mike Sierra, this is Delta-Tango-Mike, over."

This time the reply was more clear, as Maslow's tinny voice responded, *"Move out ASAP to the cache. We've got a code six, over."*

"They're still inside the hotel!" Matt exploded, walking over to the wall map. "Christ!"

"Roger that," Whitehead responded to Maslow's transmission, his voice even with forced control. "I copy immediate rendezvous at the cache, code six, over."

Maslow's voice carried on through the loudspeaker. *"Sierra element and I are still inside the hotel, Room Number 5. Can't leave now . . . tranquilizer . . . Santo . . . may have to . . . fight . . ."*

"We're losing him!" Whitehead said, his hands gripping the radio, as if trying to squeeze the message out.

Matt MacIntyre strode quickly to the window and peered outside from behind the blackout curtain and foam padding. "It'll be dark in another few minutes." He threw a glance at Randy Hanlon. "They're in trouble. We've got to step this entire operation up, and you need extra bodies to pull it off. Me and Corky volunteer."

The look he gave to Wayne MacIntyre left no doubt in his father's mind that he would indeed.

Immediately, parkas were zipped, boots laced, weapons charged and concealed.

Before they left, Wayne MacIntyre touched Matt's shoulder. "Son."

Matt MacIntyre shrugged off his father's hand. "We've got to go, Dad."

"I . . ."

"What?" Impatience, urgency. Matt MacIntyre's eyes kindled the fire of the moment.

His father shrunk an inch, feeling much smaller. What had he gotten them into? He was no covert operator. "Nothing. Just . . . good luck. Lonnie and I will monitor Hotel Dorfer and any further transmissions from here."

"That's good, Dad." Another moment of silence. Then, simultaneously, both men embraced.

"Just be careful, you cocky kid," Wayne MacIntyre said, breaking the bear hug and wiping at his eyes.

After a quick review and frag order five minutes later, the team left, en route to the cache. Only Wayne MacIntyre and Lonnie Wilkerson remained behind, taking transmission notes from Maslow's Fly-Eye.

Back in his room, Winston Maslow returned his brick-sized radio to the holster on his utility belt and redirected his attention to Manny Santo, whose hand was plunged elbow-deep inside an ice bucket on the bedside. He'd propped Santo upright against the headboard, and opened the window to allow frigid evening air to breeze into their room. He had re-stuffed his day-pack, disconnected the surveillance camera he'd found earlier to keep it from recording, and administered first aid to Santo, trying to contain the effects of the tranquilizer drug.

Santo was concentrating very hard on keeping his head upright and his eyelids open. His entire body wanted to go to sleep, but somehow, his mental facilities were perfectly intact and conscious. "How much time, Wintz?" Santo asked, slurring his words.

Maslow kept the earpiece of his modified Walkman glued to his ear, alert for the contact the rest of the team would make as soon as they hit the cache. Walking over to where Santo lay propped up against the headrest of the bed, he pressed his index and middle fingers of his right hand just to the side of Santo's Adam's apple. Santo's pulse registered a calm fifty-eight beats per minute. "You're a real triathlete, Manny," Maslow announced, loosening Santo's necktie tourniquet. "Not much longer."

"Hey, Wintz, how about a better frigging answer than that?"

"You've got to let your system beat back the tranquilizer you absorbed, Manny. If you were out cold and put on a respirator, you'd wake back up in about twenty minutes, but we don't have that kind of time." Pulling Santo's hand out of the ice bucket, he inspected the dart lodged in the heel of Santo's palm. Glancing at his watch, he realized it was time to pull it out and did so with a distinct lack of ceremony.

Santo bit his lip and swallowed to keep from yelling out. As weak as Santo felt, he could still at least think coherently. It had been ten minutes since he'd been hit. Fortunately, Maslow had grabbed him out in the lobby before he collapsed, gotten him back into his room, and shoved his hand in the ice bucket to cool it down, slowing circulation and keeping the tranquilizer from spreading any faster than it already had.

"Just tell me how much longer, Wintz."

Maslow shrugged. "You'll be up and about in another half hour. I don't know if my commo shot got through to the safe house or not. Hopefully, they're on the way. At any rate, we've got to sit still and quiet."

"We don't have that kind of time. Christ, as soon as that body is found—"

Maslow sprung up from the bed and plastered his ear on the door. "Please shut the fuck up. I hear voices in the lobby." Maslow turned a switch on his modified Walkman and pulled the earphones over his ears.

"Picking up anything?" Santo slurred through relaxed, numbed jaws. Maslow was able to monitor all activities going on in the office he'd bugged with the Fly-Eye. Real-time intelligence was invaluable. Maslow nodded his head after a moment.

"I'm picking up a babble of voices up in their head shed. Sounds like they're upgrading their security." Maslow looked up at Santo. "The *jefe*'s on his way."

"Werner-Miranda?"

"That's a big rog."

"Oh, shit."

"Sounds like that particular commodity has definitely hit the fan."

"They've found the body in the men's room."

"Maybe not." Maslow glanced quickly around the room, as he considered the air duct he'd used earlier to sneak the Fly-Eye into place. His eyes fell on the dead camera eye he'd disconnected earlier. Santo followed his gaze.

"How are they gonna react to faulty surveillance equipment when the Big Cheese gets here, Wintz?"

Maslow shook his head. "How are you feeling?"

"Relaxed. Too relaxed. Breathing's getting a little difficult."

Maslow returned to Santo's bedside and re-tightened the tourniquet. "Wiggle your fingers."

"What?"

"Wiggle your goddam fingers, you stupid Cuban!"

Santo wiggled his fingers. It surprised him. Maslow's eyes shot twin ebony sparks as he got Santo's undivided attention.

"I don't want to hear that defeatist crap in your voice anymore. Got that? You just better hope you ate your mother-fucking Wheaties this morning."

Santo slumped back in silence, knowing that everything was up to Maslow, and that he'd just have to work the drug out of his system before anything else. Santo also knew the retired Special Forces warrant officer would never leave.

Maslow's Walkman crackled to life. *"Mike-Sierra, this is Delta-Tango-Mike, we're at the cache site, over."*

The two men exchanged looks.

"They're heeere," Maslow singsonged with a grin.

Matt MacIntyre, Corky Cortez, Rene Burchette, and Charlie Whitehead buzzed around the thicket where MacIntyre and Cortez had cached the snowmobile and akhio sled containing their supplies for the operation, while Randy Hanlon established contact with Maslow. Their initial plan had been pretty straightforward: Snatch Humberto Werner-Miranda at the most opportune moment, stash him in the akhio, cross-country skijor him to a rendezvous with the team's van down the valley fifteen kilometers away, and then drive him across the Italian and Austrian borders to the American Consulate in Munich. Simple enough. But nothing was ever simple when Murphy paid a visit.

They had skied away from Hotel Sudtyrol's midtown ice-

and snow-covered streets to the outskirts of Selva, where another snowmobile parked innocently enough at a ski lift parking area had provided them all transportation to the cache, located about a kilometer away in the forest separating the Monte Selva massif from the broad ridgeline across the valley where Hotel Dorfer perched in its overwatch position over Selva itself. With Cortez driving, MacIntyre, Whitehead, Hanlon, and Burchette had wrapped their ski poles around the one-hundred-and-twenty-foot nylon rope trailing the snowmobile as it skijored into the treeline. Cortez had worn night-vision goggles while driving, to see the trail of infrared chem-lights he and MacIntyre had rigged earlier in the day to guide them toward the cache. Now, as the team uncovered branches and swept away the snow hiding their equipment, the first thing they did was rig up the brick-sized radio to reestablish contact with Maslow.

"This is Mike-Sierra," Maslow's deep voice grated through the static hissing inside Hanlon's ear. Hanlon repressed a whoop of joy. They were all right after all. MacIntyre and Cortez had attached the akhio to the back of their snowmobile and had issued arms and magazines to the team for the snatch. It was only a matter of time.

"This is the hotel element," Hanlon spoke quietly into the radio's mike. "Be advised we're booking from the cache now, en route to your location, over."

"Affirmative," Maslow replied over the radio. *"Things are cooking up on my end. Be advised the target is inbound to this location. He should enter the hotel in about ten minutes. Have the Sierra-Hotel element establish line-of-sight overwatch with the NODs from their position and keep us all informed on incoming and outgoing traffic. The sooner you people get into position, the better. Sierra element and I will try to snatch the target from the inside and bring him out to the Bell Ranger parked on the helipad. Can Rene handle flying it? Over."*

Hanlon glanced at Rene Burchette, who had already put on a pair of the camouflaged overwhites waiting for them at the cache. "Wintz says there's a bird on the helipad," he told her. "The same one that flew over the resort today, remember?"

"Yes."

"Wanna fly it?"

Rene quickly nodded her head. "I can handle that." Hanlon stared at her a moment longer than necessary.

"I said *yes*."

Hanlon pressed the mike button. "Roger that. Bravo element is prepared to fly the bird on order from you guys. We'll have the snowmobile in the tree line as backup transportation for the exfil, just in case."

"Roger," Maslow replied. *"Keep posted to the radio. Things are pretty much touch and go. Check your flash-bangs at the cache. Everyone should have two per man. Break in contact here likely, over."*

"Wilco," Hanlon responded, flipping back a canvas tarp on the end of the akhio, revealing a smallish crate of the devices Maslow had mentioned. The flash-bang was an explosive device designed to disorient and confuse, rather than kill. No larger than a palm-sized frisbee, the black disk packed enough of a charge to blind and deafen its target with a brilliant flash and thunderous roar. They were invaluable for hostage rescue. By the same token, they were equally as valuable for snatch missions. Hanlon nodded at Burchette, and she began passing them out to everyone on the team who had already taken their places by the skijor rope. Hanlon keyed his mike and said softly, "Good luck, Wintz."

"Whiskey-Mike, out."

Hanlon returned the brick radio to his utility belt, shrugged off his web gear, quickly donned the overwhites Burchette handed him, then strapped his web gear back on. He quickly jacked a hearing plug into the radio and stuck it inside his ear, so his hands could be free. A group huddle surrounded him for a mission update. Everyone was equipped roughly the same. MP5s, overwhites, web gear, and a radio wired to each ear with a jack and earplug. In this manner, the team could communicate with each other on whisper-mikes and hear other elements on the same net for quick reaction to any contingency occurring during the snatch.

"Manny and Wintz are okay for now," Hanlon began. He glanced quickly up at MacIntyre and Cortez. *"Dai-uy*, Corky, you guys have already done more than what was needed for this mission—"

"Drive on, Big Sarge," MacIntyre interrupted. "Me'n Corky's taking orders from you. Hell, someone's gotta grade this patrol, so it might as well be us."

"Ditto that," Cortez added.

Hanlon exchanged looks with MacIntyre and a grin came to

his face. Things were back to normal now. Just like the old days. He thought of Jim's Pawn Shop back in Fayetteville and was glad that he would never have to go back there again. "All right, then. Manny and Wintz are still holed up at the hotel. The plan's simple. We stay in contact with them through the radios. Everyone's checked out on FM, right?"

They all nodded. Everyone was wired for sound. Hanlon continued. "So we establish point surveillance on Hotel Dorfer, which is about fifty meters away from the parking lot inside the treeline. Once there, Rene and I will sneak around to the helipad and get ready to fly it and the target out of the AO. *Dai-uy,* you and Corky link up with Maslow and Santo at the hotel. They'll conduct the actual snatch, so you guys provide cover for them and everyone get back to the helipad behind the hotel. Charlie . . ." Hanlon fumbled with the acetate-covered map he'd stuck in his trousers cargo pocket earlier and pulled it out.

Whitehead moved in closer. "Yo."

Hanlon pointed at the map. "Link back up with Wilkerson and Mr. MacIntyre. Drive the van down to grid coordinates NS 169834." Whitehead inspected the pickup zone Hanlon had indicated. "Be there no more than two hours from now. If we're not there by 2300, it'll mean that we couldn't use the bird, and are skijoring to the rendezvous, so be prepared to wait. If everything works out all right, you'll hear the bird coming in. Have the van revved up and ready to sky outta there."

Whitehead nodded his head. The plan was simple. He glanced at his watch. It was 1930 hours. And dark. They'd have Werner-Miranda in Munich by midnight. He glanced up at Hanlon. "Check."

The frag order was complete, and everyone knew what to do. It was just a matter of doing it. Before firing up the snowmobiles, one final radio contact was made back to the safe room at Hotel Sudtyrol. Matt MacIntyre made it.

"Sierra-Hotel, this is Delta-Tango-Mike, over."

"This is Sierra-Hotel, over."

Matt MacIntyre was surprised at the sound of his father's voice over the radio. He'd expected Wilkerson. A moment passed. Then he squeezed the talk button again. "Did you copy all last transmissions with the Sierra-Mike element at the hotel, over?"

"Yes, I did. Over."

"Be advised that the Charlie element is inbound your location for mission update and coordination, over."

"Okay. We'll be waiting for him. The, uh . . . Whiskey element is going to rig up the night-vision device on the rooftop for overwatch update. Okay?"

MacIntyre grinned at his father's lack of radio procedure knowledge. "Okay, Dad," he said softly. "Just wanted to let you know that we're on our way."

"Be careful, son. Son?"

Momentary static filled Matt MacIntyre's ear. He wondered if the transmission was going out. Then he heard his father's voice again.

"Know that I love you, Matt."

MacIntyre bit his lip and blinked several times. "Roger that, Dad. Out."

"Over and out."

Swallowing, Matt MacIntyre stuck the radio back into his web gear and assumed his position on the skijor line behind Cortez's snowmobile.

Everyone was ready. Up front, Hanlon made a thumbs-up. Behind him, Burchette did the same with Whitehead, who bit his ski poles into the snow and started back for the Hotel Sudtyrol. Trailing the end of the skijor rope, Matt MacIntyre passed the thumbs-up to Cortez, who turned the snowmobile's ignition switch.

And then a covert group of operators skijored through the firs and pines en route to a three-star hotel housing the drug lord they'd come to snatch.

Wayne MacIntyre put down the microphone he'd used to communicate with Matt, and stared at the monitors before him with a thousand-yard stare. The command and control center he was manning with Lonnie Wilkerson had become very quiet since the team had departed. DTM was now totally and irreversibly commited. An illegal covert operation was underway inside Italian borders, and he was personally responsible.

Clearing his throat, Wilkerson stood up from his seat. "Well, sir, looks like everything's checking out. I'd better go up to the roof and inspect the Satcom and the night-observation scope. Maybe the antenna linking us with Santo and Maslow has problems, and that's why we're not communicating with them too well on their frequency."

"Sure," MacIntyre said, fighting despondency. "I'll just hold down the fort."

Wilkerson walked out the door.

Wayne MacIntyre remained at his seat in the lonely room, wondering if this, the first real-world deployment of DTM, would also be its last one.

He also wondered if another son would die.

CHAPTER TWENTY-ONE

From Lonnie Wilkerson's vantage point on Hotel Sudtyrol's third-story rooftop in the center of Selva, he was separated from Hotel Dorfer as the crow flies by only five hundred meters. Given the climb in elevation from where Hotel Dorfer overwatched Selva, and from Wilkerson's vantage point, the view provided unobstructed surveillance. Clear and precise. It had been planned that way, of course.

This position afforded the AN/TVS-7 night-observation telescope Wilkerson was training on the Hotel Dorfer parking lot clear surveillance, and the chill Alpine air of the Dolomites complemented the brilliance of the Milky Way overhead and the crystal white of the ground snow the stars reflected upon, to add that much more to the light-enhancing starlight technology inside the AN/TVS-7. Wilkerson's view of the parking lot was equally as discerning as if he had been watching the objective with the same-power telescope in the daytime.

Next came the radio. The one DTM didn't know about. It was a beacon/transponder equipped with an FM transmitter/receiver capability for voice communications. It had been miniaturized for easy concealment. Wilkerson pulled the black oblong device out of his down jacket and fastened it to the bracket on top of the night-observation telescope. He jacked an earplug into it.

A noise from behind. A door closing. Drawing his Beretta, Wilkerson glanced back in the direction of the rooftop access doorway. He had left it cracked open, and the wind had simply blown it shut. He glanced back at Hotel Dorfer and saw that a car was entering its parking lot. Another followed it. Shivering in the fifteen-degree weather, exacerbated by the steady wind chill generated by twenty knots, Wilkerson returned his attention to the night-observation telescope.

Siegfried drove his armor-plated Mercedes-Benz into Hotel Dorfer's parking lot and saw that the van containing Stern's team was parked nose-downward, facing the exit, on the left side of the parking lot. This far-side signal—the fact that the van was arranged in this direction, not twenty meters from the hotel's entrance—indicated that Stern's gang was ready, and that no mission compromise was in effect.

And that meant, of course, that once the toxin exchange was effected between Humberto Werner-Miranda and Simon, the Colombian's life could be dispatched with RAF efficiency.

But these things were to occur within the next half hour, provided things went well, and anything could happen within half an hour. There were many players in this operation. Too many.

Siegfried parked his armored Mercedes in the middle row of vehicles beside the van. From all outward appearances, the van was empty. But the smily-face sticker plastered on the driver's window was the near-side signal, indicating the terrorists inside the back of the van were ready and waiting.

He frowned. Where was Stern? She and Suzuki should have been dressed to the nines and waiting for him in their Volvo somewhere in the parking lot. They were to walk inside shortly after he did and take their position in the dining area. The Volvo wasn't here.

He returned his attention to the smily-face sticker on the van, which despite Stern's absence indicated that the hit was still in effect. Evidently things had changed somewhat.

Glancing at his rearview mirror, Siegfried saw that the car that had followed him to the hotel had parked a few spaces behind him and that the two bodyguards Werner-Miranda had dispatched to watch him were waiting for him to get out first. Naturally.

Siegfried climbed out from behind the driver's wheel and gazed across the valley into Selva.

Lonnie Wilkerson trained his night-observation telescope on the blond German male exiting the Mercedes he had parked beside the van near the entrance of Hotel Dorfer. As if knowing he was being watched, the man gazed in Wilkerson's direction for several moments, and this reminded him how the naked human eye transcended all things technical and extraordinary. Gut instinct and alert vision superseded silicon, micro-chip circuitry, and laser optics anytime.

The contact was good. The plan, despite Wayne MacIntyre's presence in Italy, was good.

Of course, one needed state-of-the-art surveillance equipment, for clear and precise identification of one's fellow operator.

Entering the lobby, Siegfried found Simon waiting for him by the front desk with a cup of coffee and an ashtray full of cigarette stubs.

The Uruguayan jumped to his feet and met him at the door. "Where is he?"

"Where is your guard?" Siegfried responded, regarding the beads of perspiration dotting the fish-belly white of Simon's forehead, and how his thinning, curly black hair seemed gelled to his scalp. Simon was even sweating through his Saville Row suit, contrasting sharply with Siegfried's simpler, more functional winter trousers, sweater, down parka, and functional Vibram-soled hiking boots.

Simon took Siegfried by the arm and led him past the receptionist's desk into the restaurant, where three couples already inside the restaurant occupied their posts in scattered locations around the dining area. "He left about half an hour ago. He hasn't returned. I don't why."

Siegfried wondered if Monika Stern was inside the hotel. She could be anywhere. Sometimes she was as unpredictable as the Muslim fanatics who had trained her throughout her career. As they sat at their table, a commotion was heard back in the lobby.

Humberto Werner-Miranda entered the lobby from the parking lot. His loud, booming voice greeted the receptionist with the same enthusiasm that he slapped her bottom with.

"I thought he wasn't to arrive for another fifteen, twenty minutes yet," Simon muttered, watching the other "couples" inside the restaurant watching him.

"He must have been in the car following me here."

"Odd."

"No. It means he wishes not to set a pattern. Besides, he's protected well enough."

"The others—"

"Know exactly what to do," Siegfried hissed, cutting Simon off. Simon was simply too nervous, out of sorts. It was unprofessional. The hit on Werner-Miranda was to happen only after the toxin exchange was effected and Siegfried and Simon were airborne in the Bell Ranger parked on the helipad behind the restaurant. In theory at least.

There were many other events to happen that night superseding anything Simon had planned with Monika Stern.

Humberto Werner-Miranda entered the restaurant, dressed resplendently in his "uniform" of German jump boots, corduroy knickers, knee-high wool socks, and a thick, red Chamonix guide sweater.

"*Paisano,*" he exclaimed, spotting Simon and walking toward their table with arms outstretched.

Simon got to his feet and forced a smile. "You are well, yes?"

"It has been a long day, Humberto."

Werner-Miranda swiveled a look at Siegfried's direction, and the German caught the Colombian's ice-filled blue eyes, his German heritage. His swarthy skin was flushed with crimson from the day's skiing. "Both of you, welcome to my humble establishment."

A pregnant pause. Minds, calculating. Smiles, forced. Werner-Miranda broke the silence first. "Please sit, *sit!*" He snapped his fingers. "Grappa," he yelled at the maitre d' hovering by their table.

Simon and Siegfried considered for a moment how the other couples in the restaurant seemed to close in on the center table. Their table.

"My very good friend Simon," Werner-Miranda expostulated, slapping Simon on the back, "you should have seen our German comrade here zipping down Slope Thirteen this afternoon."

"I'm sure I missed out on quite an enjoyable time, Humberto."

"I sent you an invitation to join us."

"Why, yes . . ." The greasy ball of adrenaline already occupying Simon's guts began to weigh heavier. Simon's escort had disappeared over an hour ago.

"So why did Chico not bring you out to join us?"

"He . . . he . . ."

Werner-Miranda's eyes turned opaque. "Where *is* Chico, Simon?"

Simon shrugged his shoulders.

"You are starting some intrigue with me, eh?"

"I don't know where the hell your man went. You are too distrusting, Humberto."

Werner-Miranda glanced sharply at Siegfried. "Perhaps." He snapped his fingers. One of the bodyguards left his post at the dining room's bar and came to his side. "Find Chico," Werner-Miranda muttered. He resumed smiling at his two guests. "And we shall conduct the remainder of our business upstairs, gentlemen." Werner-Miranda got to his feet, Siegfried and Simon following suit.

On the way back to the lobby, Siegfried saw how the rooms along the bottom floor were being opened methodically by Werner-Miranda's men. The hotel security forces were mobilizing. Before walking upstairs into Werner-Miranda's council chamber, Siegfried excused himself for the men's room.

"Why, certainly," Werner-Miranda boomed. "Too much *grappa* on the slopes today, eh?" The Colombian nodded at one of the bodyguards escorting them. "Show our German comrade where the men's room is, Jorge."

Siegfried allowed himself to be escorted. He had no choice.

Two Colombians left Room Four, walked down the hallway, and knocked on Room Five's door.

"What is it?" came an American voice from inside.

"Hotel security," one of the Colombians replied, drawing his Colt Python .357.

"Oh. Come on in."

They entered, finding a swarthy American, a fellow Latino, slumped in an easy chair watching rock and roll on television. Manny Santo managed to twist his head to look at them. "What's up, Doc?" he said, managing a grin.

The door closed. The two Colombians approached Santo's chair. "The guest list says a black man is spending the night in this room."

"So?"

The other Colombian drew his automatic and screwed on a suppressor. "So why don't you tell us where your friend is?"

The room door swung back, revealing Maslow, who had his

suppressed MP5K leveled at the two Colombians. "Why, here I am, boys."

Siegfried entered the men's room and started counting booths: one, two, three. He entered the third stall, conscious of the bodyguard Werner-Miranda had dispatched to cover him. As he eyed the wall tank feeding the toilet, Siegfried's heartbeat picked up. Everything hinged on whether or not the technical assistance department had done their job. His fingers searched the space behind the wall flush tank.

And found the oblong plastic and metal box waiting for him there. A miniaturized beacon/transponder. That wasn't all. A suppressed Beretta .22 waited for him there as well. He stuck the Beretta in the waistband of his trousers. Siegfried sat on the stool and punched a digital code into the beacon/transponder, sending a burst communications to the safe house in Selva, and relaying half the needed transmission to headquarters in Munich for mission activation.

As he concentrated on keying in the activation code, a soft, plopping sound, delicate yet persistent, greeted his ears. The sound of a leaky tap. Siegfried's eyes fell on the floor.

Blood. A small pool of blood expanding on the floor the next stall over.

Bending down, Siegfried peered into the next stall to see a man with his feet stuffed in the toilet and propped upright with a small bullet hole between his wide-open eyes.

Siegfried licked his lips and tried to still the trip-hammer in his heart. Now how was this? Werner-Miranda's escort for Simon. Dead. Had Simon killed him? What about Stern? Was she *inside* the hotel? Anything was possible.

"What's holding you?" his guard grumbled from outside the stall.

"Just a moment, please," Siegfried replied, keying in the rest of the beacon/transponder's activation sequence. He reached up and pulled the flush chain. A relieving roar of water cascaded into the toilet. Hastily, he stuck the beacon/transponder back behind the wall flush tank.

He exited the stall and confronted the stony countenance of his guard. "You may now take me to your leader," he intoned with an uneasy smile, remembering an old American Grade B outer-space movie.

• • •

Lonnie Wilkerson's ear plug beeped, as it received the transmission from Hotel Dorfer's men's room. Checking where the ear jack was plugged into the FM-equipped beacon/transponder affixed to the AN/TVS-7 night-observation telescope he had trained on Hotel Dorfer, he then started typing in a code to the burst-radio-transmission device, known as a Digital Message Device Group (DMDG), he had cabled to the FM assembly. Moments later, it read: BRER RABBIT RUNNING. GOLDILOCKS, SNOW-WEASEL, AND SCHATZ, ALL ASSEMBLED AT VALHALLA. GO.

Wilkerson's fingers hovered over the transmit button. He bit his lower lip. His career was made.

A scraping sound from behind. Wilkerson wheeled around.

A woman aimed a suppressed automatic at him. His mouth opened.

"You," he breathed.

A spit and a dart of flame. Then an explosion in his head, followed by numbness and dark.

Lonnie Wilkerson died, his finger frozen on the transmit button of the DMDG.

Siegfried and his escort walked up the spiral staircase adjacent to the receptionist's office. Moments later, they entered Humberto Werner-Miranda's "office," a sort of command and control center for the drug lord's communiques and surveillance over the ski resort he owned. Computers, video terminals, twenty-four-hour news channel, faxes, copiers, radios. The technology inside the office overlooking the lobby of Hotel Dorfer was state-of-the-art.

Only now it was one of confusion. Two Italians sat in one corner, bound and gagged with duct tape. An open bottle of *grappa* sat on a tray beside them, next to a baggie of dope. The smell of hashish permeated the air. Siegfried's heartbeat increased. Something was up. He returned his attention to Simon and Werner-Miranda.

On one end of the office by a desk, one of Humberto Werner-Miranda's bodyguards had propped open a briefcase containing vials. Humberto Werner-Miranda held one of the vials up toward the ceiling light, peering at it closely. The Colombian had strapped on his favorite revolver, Siegfried noted. A Casill .454. The cartridges were large enough for big game. An elephant gun. His eyes wandered back to the briefcase on the desk.

Vials of Microcystin. Siegfried's throat went dry. The grin on Werner-Miranda's face was too huge. His heart flopped into his mouth like a netted fish.

"Herr Horst!" Werner-Miranda called, seeing him enter. He waved Siegfried over to join them.

Siegfried approached the two cautiously. Simon had a hangdog look on his face, and Siegfried knew then and there that Simon's days as an operator for the Soviets were over, completely over. A mounting rage boiled inside. That meant that Simon's usefulness for the RAF and Deutschland was over as well.

Werner-Miranda beamed at them both with knowing eyes. "My present to you both," he said with an evil grin, waving his hand at the briefcase full of Microcystin.

Siegfried walked boldly to the briefcase and inspected the vials. They were real. He suppressed a cold chill stealing up his spine. He closed the briefcase and glanced at Simon, who opened his mouth to speak.

"Then we shall be leaving," Simon said hopefully, feathering back his thinning hair with his fingers. "Unless you have further questions for us, Humberto."

The little Colombian maintained his huge grin. "Yes. I have a few questions. But please bear with me for a moment." He drew the Casill hanging off his hip and swiveled the huge bore in Siegfried's direction.

Siegfried knew he was a dead man, and his blood ceased to flow.

"Move out of the way, if you please."

Siegfried moved out of the way.

A deafening roar. Siegfried's ears rung with the blast. He glanced to see what Werner-Miranda had shot. It was one of the Italians he'd seen bound and gagged. The man's head was obliterated. The Italian next to him began screaming.

"Let him talk," Werner-Miranda said casually, holstering his Casill and walking slowly toward the Italian. One of his Colombian bodyguards ripped the duct tape off the Italian's face.

"We found these two sleeping on the job, so to speak," Werner-Miranda explained to Siegfried with a grin. "Drunk and high. I don't particularly like it when my security people sleep on the job. Why, anything could have transpired here this afternoon while I was out skiing, see?"

"Mike-Sierra, this is Delta-Tango-Mike, over," Hanlon breathed into his whisper mike.

"This is Mike-Sierra," Maslow replied from inside the hotel.

Hanlon gripped Rene Burchette's shoulder hard, and they made eye contact. Hanlon gave her a thumbs-up. From their vantage point just outside Hotel Dorfer's rear accessway, where the tree line afforded them the closest route of approach toward the helipad, they were still somewhat in an exposed position. They were kneeling inside the evergreen shrubbery lining the perimeter of the hotel, next to the exit door closest to the helipad. No one guarded the Bell Ranger that had flown in earlier that afternoon. The situation was tense, chancy. Now a gunshot had been fired.

"What's going on?" Hanlon asked Maslow.

"Don't know."

"Still in Room Five?"

"Roger that, over."

"Be advised that Mac and Corky are working their way toward the front door to cover that position. Rene and I are at the back door by the helipad. Let me know when you're ready for the snatch, over."

"Rog-o," Maslow breathed.

Back on the snowy, wind-chilled rooftop of Hotel Sudtyrol, two figures hovered over the lifeless body of Lonnie Wilkerson.

One of them, Yuko Suzuki, rifled her fingers through the NSC man's pockets, searching for slips of paper, data, anything that would clue her in on why there was an American presence in Selva, with eavesdropping and surveillance technology trained on the location of their target, Humberto Werner-Miranda.

Monika Stern, on the other hand, was more interested in the squarish computer device resembling a chiclet-punch typewriter in her hands. Encoded on the view screen was the message BRER RABBIT RUNNING. GOLDILOCKS, SNOW-WEASEL, AND SCHATZ, ALL ASSEMBLED AT VALHALLA. GO. Stern felt very uneasy.

"He is sterile," Suzuki told her, finishing up with Wilkerson's pockets and finding nothing. She stood by Monika's side.

Monika Stern handed her the DMDG. "It's a burst-transmission device," she said.

"So we were correct in following the American couple to this place," Suzuki said. "But why would the Americans be here in the first place?"

"There's only one way to find out," Monika told her, dropping the DMDG onto the rooftop. She turned toward the access door. "Come, Yuko. We haven't much time."

One of Werner-Miranda's bodyguards was waving an elongated, mesh-covered microphone around the room while he carried a briefcase in his other hand and listened closely to the earphones clamped around his head. His attention drifted toward the ceiling.

Siegfried exchanged glances with Simon, wanting more than anything to ask him what he and Monika Stern had done to foul up a simple toxin exchange by leaving a body in the latrine and now, apparently, by giving Humberto Werner-Miranda reason to believe that his head security office had been breached. The scene unfolding before them was unpleasant enough. Werner-Miranda had the muzzle of his .454 Casill planted deeply in the remaining Italian office monitor's mouth. But were he and Simon able to do anything at all? No. Two of Werner-Miranda's goons watched from the rear, waiting for any sudden move.

"*Jefe*, I've got something here," the bodyguard informed Werner-Miranda, his microphone sweeping up the wall toward the ceiling.

Werner-Miranda turned his head, and thumbed back the hammer of his Casill. The Italian office monitor's doe-brown eyes widened with terror, and they crossed, staring at the bore of the handgun Werner-Miranda had planted in his mouth. He began to emit a hoarse moan.

"What?" Werner-Miranda hissed, his trigger finger tightening on the trigger of his Casill.

The bodyguard's microphone found the Fly-Eye Maslow had installed two hours earlier near the center ceiling light. "Hey! Boss!"

"What, what!"

"Look!"

Tearing off his headphones and tossing his electronic eavesdropping sensor equipment onto the nearest table, the bodyguard ripped away Maslow's Fly-Eye assembly. Werner-Miranda ripped his Casill out of the Italian office monitor's mouth, chipping his teeth in the process with the revolver's front sight post. The Italian cried out in pain. The bodyguard handed the Fly-Eye to Werner-Miranda's outstretched hand. The Colombian snorted and squinted his eyes at the strange laser-optic tentacles sprouting from the cabled cylinder.

"Looks like a goddam sea anemone," he said. He handed it to Simon, who was perspiring heavily. "Did you bug my office today, *paisano?*"

Simon looked like he wanted to throw up. "No! Goddammit, Humberto, I simply came here to make an exchange and offer you—"

"Or did *you*," Werner-Miranda hissed, shoving the Fly-Eye in Siegfried's face, "decide to bug my office today?"

Wayne MacIntyre sat straight up in his chair. The video terminal servicing the drug lord's command and control center had suddenly gone blank, and the monitor was now only a field of snow. Something had gone wrong. Had Wilkerson screwed up the reception somehow on the roof? What was taking him so long, anyway?

Rising from his chair, he started for the suite's front door, then paused. It was very quiet. He was alone. The team was deployed. Maslow and Santo were holed up in Hotel Dorfer. He had to make radio contact with them.

Where was Wilkerson?

Wayne MacIntyre's senses suddenly sharpened. He became alert and wary of every noise in the suite. Nothing out of the ordinary. But Wilkerson had been up on the roof now for fifteen minutes.

That was too long.

Checking the safety of the Browning Charlie Whitehead had given him earlier before moving out, Wayne MacIntyre reached for the door knob.

The door suddenly banged open, barking his left hand away. Stabs of pain shot up MacIntyre's wrist and forearm.

An Oriental woman before him leveled a suppressed pistol from where she stood in the hallway.

The first round Wayne MacIntyre absorbed plowed through his upper left arm. The second spit from the Oriental woman's handgun punched through his right shoulder, as if she were crippling him on purpose. Crying out, Wayne MacIntyre toppled over a sofa adjacent to the doorway and was temporarily masked from her view.

She began rapid-firing through the couch. MacIntyre crabbed away, hoarse with pain. His arms were practically useless, but somehow he managed to hold onto the Browning. His eyes widened as rounds shot through the sofa, sending tufts of foam padding and dust into the air; 9-millimeter slugs thunked into the carpeted floor between his legs.

Enough was enough!

Yelling, Wayne MacIntyre raised his pistol to shoot as best he could.

Hearing the gunfire, Charlie Whitehead raced upstairs, snow still clinging to his head and shoulders from the cross-country ski run he'd just made to return to the safe house. His hands were in motion, years of training never having left him. He flipped the safety off his Browning while taking the stairs two and three at a time. His eyes found the top stair and the floor level.

A woman came into view, blond and screaming in the hallway, emptying a magazine from a machine pistol into the suite Wayne was manning. Noise! Chaos!

Wayne!

Whitehead dove for the floor, his Browning two-fisted out to his front, nostrils flaring from the acrid gunsmoke filling the hallway. He returned fire at the screaming blond woman. A spray of machine-pistol rounds arced in his direction, then stopped, as her clip ran dry. Whitehead continued firing in rapid succession at the blond woman. One of them spun her around, and she ran, limping heavily, down the hallway.

Another woman burst out of the suite's front door, masking his fire. An Oriental woman. Only this one was being shot out the door. Round after round plowed through her chest, her abdomen, her legs. She slumped against the hallway wall opposite the suite's front door, sagged to the floor, and died, leaving a broad red smear on the wall.

"Wayne!" Charlie Whitehead roared. Ejecting the empty, he slammed another into the pistol grip of his Browning, sprang to his feet, and raced for the suite's front door. He paused, wanting to enter, but knowing he had to find the blond woman,

whoever she was. Christ, what had gone wrong? He couldn't take the time now to find out. He couldn't take the time, even if his friend and employer was dead or dying somewhere in the chaos of their command center.

The blond woman! Where was she? Whitehead raced passed the front door and on down the hallway.

Two-fisting his pistol in a quick-fire stance, he shuffled toward the corner of the hallway and bobbed around the corner for a quick look, then followed through the corner, ready to fire.

Nothing. Only a broken window where she had broken through to the . . .

Outside? At three stories high?

Cautiously, Whitehead moved toward the window. Kicking away the glass, he made the aperture larger. He thumbed back the hammer of his Browning. Snow swirled inside the hallway. It was freezing.

Charlie Whitehead found a ledge encircling the floor, just wide enough for toeholds. Footprints, where the snow had been scraped off the ledge. Blood, crimsoning the snow and the brick of the hotel's exterior. The footprints and blood led toward the next corner of the building and then ceased.

She would have jumped off there. Or more likely, fallen off.

Whitehead pondered the void below. Black, swirling with snow.

He felt nauseous and pulled his head back inside the hallway. He got to his feet and stood upright. Wearily, he quick-stepped back to the suite, not wanting to see what he knew he would see. Nothing would have stood up to the barrage of automatic fire the blond woman had pumped into the suite just moments before.

Whitehead paused by the dead Oriental woman and gave her an absent look. Why?

A moan.

"Wayne!" Whitehead burst inside the suite. He found MacIntyre propped up against the wall. Blood everywhere. "Oh, sweet Jesus, Wayne."

"Hey, Charlie . . . you old . . . buffalo-fucker . . ."

CHAPTER TWENTY-TWO

Liam O'Brien chain-smoked the American Camels he was so fond of and said to Marcello Feltrinelli, who surveilled the entrance of Hotel Dorfer from the back of the van with the Frenchman, Phillipe Marceau, "Time grows late for Fraülein Stern."

"And her Japanese lover," Marceau grumbled, wiping the rear window with his gloved hand. "They should have returned from town by now. They haven't. It means something has gone wrong." Everything was cold. His head was cold, the black metal of the Heckler and Koch submachine gun he held was cold, this fucking van sitting in the middle of this fucking snowbound parking lot was cold.

"Ah, yes, her Japanese lover, the inscrutably lovely Miss Yuko Suzuki. Now there's one charming lass." O'Brien stubbed out one Camel and lit another.

Marceau twisted his rubbery face in the direction of the Irishman, their cell driver, and mimicked, "Her Japanese lover. You are jealous of a lesbian then?"

Next to him, Feltrinelli snarled. "Quiet! This place is ridden with Werner-Miranda's men. Stern will contact us soon enough." Feltrinelli shivered and checked the action on his submachine gun. Peering outside where the Palestinian was posted, he fumbled inside his pocket for the radio. Ahmet Habashi, the loner of the team, was nowhere to be found. He was a ghost somewhere in the shadows. Chills methodically stroked Feltrinelli's shoulder blades as another hour crept toward eight o'clock in the evening. It was time for Stern to arrive. Past time, in fact. And where had Habashi gone? He'd been told to stay in the shadows, to cover the van in case it was approached. As for Stern and Şuzuki, they should have returned from the village already.

Up in the front seat, O'Brien grinned his easy grin. It was too much of an easy grin for what the situation warranted, but O'Brien had learned long ago that the lads were always too uptight before an operation went down, and humor was the best antidote. "Did I ever tell you the one about the leprechaun and the Provo at Heathrow, lads?"

Marceau and Feltrinelli exchanged disbelieving looks. Mediterranean shrugs. Feltrinelli pulled his radio out of the deep cargo pocket of his ski pants and turned it on. "We have no time for jokes, Irish. Turn your vehicle over."

Liam O'Brien obediently twisted the key in the ignition. The van coughed to life, and soon, the heater started warming them. Then, from his vantage point in the front seat, he spotted a car's headlights downhill about to negotiate the S-roll up the long ridgeline toward Hotel Dorfer's parking lot.

"That's her, mate," O'Brien called out softly to the Italian.

Feltrinelli keyed the mike on his radio. "This is Hound, come in, come in, Fox."

". . . them all! Kill . . . all!"

"Is that Stern?" Marceau muttered, gripping his submachine gun. Returning his attention to the frost-rimmed rear window of the van, he squinted through the glass for any sign of the Palestinian. Where was Habashi? Then he saw something in the lobby door of the hotel that made his blood run cold.

"Quiet!" Feltrinelli snapped, gluing the radio to his ear. He twisted the volume knob.

"Kill them all!" Stern's voice shrilled into the still of the van's cold quiet. *"Go in now and kill every goddamn one of them!"*

"That's her BMW driving up the hill," O'Brien informed Feltrinelli. "She's lost control of her senses, man."

Marceau tugged on Feltrinelli's sleeve and pointed in the direction of the hotel lobby. "Marcello! Werner-Miranda's men! Two of them approach our van!"

Glancing around in different directions, Feltrinelli fought to think clearly. The Alpine cold had numbed his mind. What was Siegfried doing inside with Simon? There was no use trying to communicate with him. If either Simon or Siegfried had met with Werner-Miranda with a wire on, they'd have been frisked, caught, and executed. He glanced at his watch. It was only seconds away from eight o'clock. Now Stern had radioed in this crazy message. A crazy message from a madwoman. What had gone wrong in Selva?

"Marcello," Phillipe Marceau hissed. "They come. Get ready."

"All right on this end, mate," O'Brien said, calm and even. "I see 'em too." Glancing at the van's rearview mirrors, he spotted the two security guards walking in his direction, one flanking each side of the van. They had both drawn automatics, held discreetly against the outside of their trousers.

O'Brien reached inside his shoulder holster for his pistol and kept his eyes trained on the rearview mirror.

Marceau flipped off the safety of his Heckler and Koch submachine gun and shivered in his down parka.

Feltrinelli screwed a suppressor onto the muzzle of his Beretta.

From where they lay on the hard-packed snow between the exterior of Hotel Dorfer and the shrubs lining the perimeter, Captain Matt MacIntyre and Master Sergeant Corky Cortez squinted at the van in the parking lot through the peep sights of the submachine guns they'd picked up at the cache site. The cold was unbearable, at least fifteen degrees outside, with a wind chill making it seem at least twenty degrees colder. But now, both men possessed a presence of mind that only years of training could induce, a knowledge of the intensity of the moment before sparks flew that made only blood, adrenaline, the edge of their breathing, and their own headspace and timing upstairs in whatever gray matter they possessed count.

Right now their gut instincts told them that something was up with the dark van poised at the entrance of Hotel Dorfer.

"What do you think, Corky?" MacIntyre checked the web belt slung on his overwhites, and ensured the flaps of his ammo pouches were open, so he could grab another magazine quickly. Immediately to his front, a flash-bang lay on the snow, ready for action.

"I think we got a suspicious vehicle to our front, Boss. I think we got two of Werner-Miranda's men walking out there to check it out." Cortez then raised his head, his black watch cap a black bob in the Italian night. He peered downslope, held his gaze for a moment, then squeezed MacIntyre's arm. He nodded in the direction of the parking lot's exit. "See that inbound vehicle?"

MacIntyre swung his attention from the two goons approaching the van to the road accessing Hotel Dorfer's parking lot. He saw a black BMW fishtailing its way toward the parking lot, its wheels racing and spinning twin plumes of snow behind the car's exhaust. "Yeah. I see it. Mario Andretti's obviously at the wheel."

Cortex spotted another movement, sudden and fluid, a dark shadow darting from evergreen bush to evergreen bush as it stalked the two men approaching the van. Voices. He lowered his head and checked the safety on his MP5. *Shhh . . ."*

A ring-knuckled rap on the door window. Dragging deeply on a Camel, Liam O'Brien swiveled a bored glance at the Colombian. Petulantly, he rolled the window down. "Yes?"

The security guard, a big beefy sort dressed in a bulky guide sweater and woolen ski patrol trousers, curled his upper lip in what was supposed to be a smile. O'Brien spotted many gold teeth. There was another guard watching him through the passenger-door window, but he couldn't let on about it or seem nervous. "Coming inside?" the security guard asked.

O'Brien saw a shadow rise up behind the security guard, and grinned. "Well, no, mate, as a matter of fact, I was just sitting here thinking about the time this Provo was on his way to the men's room at Heathrow, see, and this leprechaun—"

"What is your business here?"

O'Brien thumbed back the hammer of the suppressed automatic in his lap and said, "Right, just a minute, lad. Anyway, just before the Provo sets out to do in the Iron Lady, he—"

The guard's eyes suddenly widened and he made choking sounds. The pistol he'd been holding on O'Brien sank noiselessly into the snow at his feet, as he brought his hands up to get a purchase on the wire loop cutting through his neck.

O'Brien whipped the pistol out of his lap and fired through the passenger window at the other security guard. The glass shattered and the guard was blown backward into the snow, a neat bullet hole centered between his already lifeless eyes.

"What the fuck? Corky—"
   "Stay cool, Boss."

Both men reached for their flash-bangs and flipped the selector switch on their MP5s to the fire mode. The black BMW careening up the access road now entered the parking lot, recklessly banged against the bumper of another car, and spun toward the van.

Three figures jumped out of the van and dragged the dead guard to the concealment of a nearby snowdrift. The two SF soldiers became silent sentinels in the shadows, not daring to breathe. The three men who exited the van then dogtrotted through the knee-deep snow toward the front of their vehicle, where a fourth man was sawing his garrote back and forth into the bloody neck of the guard who had accosted the van's driver.

Muted voices in the night. "Ahmet! Let him go!" One man helped the man with the garrote haul the choked guard into the snowbank, while the other two dispersed to the flanks of the main entrance of the hotel with drawn submachine guns.

The sound of the BMW's driver door opening and being slammed shut filtered through the crystalline Alpine air as an athletic blond woman ran—limped, rather—toward the two men remaining by the van.

"You got me by the balls on what the fuck's going on," Cortez breathed, now that the flurry of activity was centered back at the van.

"Those people are—"

"Some kind of hit team," Cortez answered, reaching for his radio. "Terrorists. Question is, who are they hitting?"

"All elements, this is Mike-Charlie. Be advised there are five unidentified operators located outside the main entrance by a black van, over. We just spotted them taking out a couple of the target's guards."

Santo glanced at the two bound and gagged bodyguards he and Maslow had secured earlier, then exchanged glances with Maslow, who had just peered out into the hallway.

"You hear that, Wintz? That was Cortez. Werner-Miranda's men are crawling all around the place."

"At least everyone's in position now. How you feelin'?"

"Better."

"Respond then, Manny. Murphy's in effect and this whole thing is about to blow."

Santo keyed the mike on his radio. "This is Sierra-Mike,

roger last transmission, Mike-Charlie. We've got two of the local trolls secured in Room Five. The target's upstairs above the lobby in his C & C center. Shots were fired about two minutes ago. We'll snatch Miranda on the way out. You continue to cover the front. Over."

"Got you loud'n clear, Sierra-Mike," Santo heard Cortez reply softly over the radio, while Maslow got out his locksmith tools from one of the pouches on his utility vest. *"Break. Hotel-Bravo, you copy last transmission?"*

The ex-warrant officer nodded at Maslow. "Cover me, Manny. We've got to find a better position."

"Hotel-Bravo, come in."

Santo made a fist, stared at it, and then released it. He took a deep breath and shuffled weakly toward Maslow, almost willing the tranquilizer out of his system. He turned the volume down on his radio. Hotel-Bravo—Hanlon and Burchette— were not responding to Cortez's transmission. Why?

Maslow read Santo's thoughts. "C'mon, man. Randy and Rene are all right. You've got to believe that."

Santo shoved the radio into the cargo pocket of his ski pants and nodded his head.

Maslow popped his head back out the room's door. The hallway was clear, and he gave Santo a thumbs-up.

"So let's do the shadow dance, my man," Santo told him.

The two men crept out into the hallway.

"Hotel-Bravo, Hotel-Bravo . . ."

Randy Hanlon's ears thundered with the hiss of the last transmission and its answering response. Mike-Charlie was calling him, but he couldn't answer. His heart was in his mouth, and he could not call out to Rene. Two men had just floated down from the sky in black ram-air parachutes—free-fall rigs—and landed not fifty feet away from the helicopter. They were dressed in helmets and overwhites. After bundling their gear, they hustled for the bird near where Rene had been steadily creeping while he guarded the rear access door. Now what was this?

At least he had a suppressed MP5. Better to use it than to let Rene try to take both of them out. Exposing himself, Hanlon stepped out into the snow between his position near the access door and the helipad.

Rene watched him from the bushes along the perimeter of the hotel, and knew she'd have to make a move.

The two men got closer. She heard urgent whispers in German. Walking past her, they reached the helicopter. They were armed with submachine guns. Removing their helmets, one of them climbed into the cockpit to conduct pre-flight checks, while the other inspected the exterior of the aircraft. Rene crept up behind him and chopped him in the neck with the edge of her forearm. The blow staggered the man into the snow. Rene put him out with another blow to his temple.

Hearing the noise, the pilot reached for a shoulder-holstered pistol and tumbled out of the bird, rolling onto the snow and bringing his pistol up for a shot. Rene's foot roundhoused a glancing blow and the intruder's shot went wild.

Hanlon's suppressed MP5 shuddered a three-round burst in the snow before the man's face. The newcomer slowly raised his hands. Rene automatically climbed up into the pilot's seat and began pre-flight procedures.

Moments later, Hanlon had secured the two parachutists with plastic cufflets and deposited them in the bushes. Upon trotting back to the bird, he leaned into the cockpit. "You okay?"

Rene nodded her head, her face a mask of concentration. "They'll make noise when they come to."

"Nah, I put the one out with a sleeper hold. You pretty much cold-cocked the other."

"They had parachutes and were wearing uniforms."

Hanlon did not want to answer.

"They were military, Randy. German commandos."

"Yeah. Just do your job, wench, and stay out of trouble." Hanlon returned to the rear access door of Hotel Dorfer. He reached for his radio. He squeezed the radio's mike. "This is Hotel-Bravo," he announced to the remainder of the team. "We're up on this end, and are in possession of the Bell Ranger. By the way, we've got uniforms in the AO. German. My guess is that the GSG9 is paying this place a visit."

And then, as if in reply, the distant cacophony of helicopter blades filled the snowbound quiet with the impending arrival of more uniformed men dressed in overwhites.

"Start it up, Rene!" Hanlon yelled, sudden adrenaline surging through his veins.

The answering whine and purr of the Bell Ranger mixed

with the increasing clamor surrounding Hotel Dorfer in the chaos of desperate operatives getting in each other's way.

"So what is the meaning of this?" Humberto Werner-Miranda roared, shoving the Fly-Eye in Siegfried's face. He turned to Simon. "You incompetent ass. To think we could continue to do business." He nodded at one of his bodyguards, who walked over to the table near the window overlooking the lobby where the briefcase containing the Microcystin vials lay open for inspection. The bodyguard closed the briefcase and rotated the locks underneath the handle.

"You disappoint me, Simon," Werner-Miranda said, his .454 Casill held loosely in his right hand with his arms akimbo. His right hip and foot were jutted out in a cocky display of self-mastery over the situation. It was grim enough. All was silent in the room, save the tearful moaning of the office monitor awaiting his fate at the hands of Werner-Miranda's rage, as he sat bound and at the mercy of his employer.

Siegfried calculated the odds of getting out of here alive. There were six people in the office. The remaining office monitor, two guards, Werner-Miranda, Simon, and himself. And everyone was thinking at once.

Simon thought of how this would be his last mission.

Siegfried thought of the Beretta .22 stashed in his waistband.

Werner-Miranda thought of the Casill he enjoyed using. Waving his bodyguards aside, he swiveled the bore in the office monitor's direction. "You are the first to pay, you miserable, drunken sonofabitch."

"No!" the Italian screamed.

Werner-Miranda's Casill roared, and the Italian's face mushroomed into a bloody pulp against the wall behind him.

Simon stepped forward, his hands outstretched. "Humberto . . ."

Then the Casill found *his* face.

"You goddam fool! Don't you see what's going on here?" Werner-Miranda shouted.

Suddenly the windows rattled from something vibrating outside, something larger than the Bell Ranger Simon had arrived with, something like several large dragonflies filled with men intent on everyone's destruction.

Then Simon knew.

"Think of it, Simon," Werner-Miranda said. "We happen to

be having a wonderful meeting between a Colombian cartel chief, you—a master case officer with agents throughout Europe—and this," he nodded at Siegfried. "Someone who is not whom he portrays."

Werner-Miranda thumbed back the Casill's hammer. Simon paled.

Werner-Miranda jerked his head to the left, signaling for Simon to move out of the way.

"Did you copy Hanlon's last transmission?" Santo asked Maslow, incredulous with the news.

"No time for that, Manny," Maslow hissed, fumbling with the locksmith tools he had jammed inside the remaining flanking door nearest the lobby. They were trying to establish a cross-fire position by getting in position behind the two doors flanking the hallway. In that manner, they could cover anyone coming and going from Hotel Dorfer, while Cortez and MacIntyre covered the front and Hanlon and Burchette covered the back and the helicopter. There were German uniforms in the AO and things were cooking up outside in the parking lot. What fucking else?

Maslow tripped the lock and opened the door. Santo plopped down into position and covered the lobby. "How you feeling?" Maslow asked him, fishing flash-bangs out of his day-pack and handing two of them to Santo.

"Like I ate my motherfucking Wheaties this morning, why?"

Inside the van, Feltrinelli argued with Monika Stern, who was raving. "Yes, Stern, I have a place we can go, but we can stay here no longer! No, we must not stay!"

"Siegfried dies before we leave!" Stern ranted, her face twisted with rage. Veins in her forehead and throat stuck out in purple cords, and the blood smears on her face mixed with the jade-green opaque of her eyes. "They killed Suzuki, our comrade!"

This quieted Feltrinelli. His cell leader was going through a breakdown because her lover was dead. It was not professional. It was a fact of life. The woman was insane with grief and nihilistic rage. Moreover, she had her submachine gun trained on him. Would she use it? Ahmet Habashi and Phillipe Marceau were posted outside, covering Hotel Dorfer's front entrance. Liam O'Brien, posted at the wheel, remained quiet as Stern and Feltrinelli argued in the back of van. Feltrinelli had no choice but to give in to Stern.

And deal with her later.

The back van door flew open. It was Habashi, and his handsome, olive-complected face was strained with worry. "Helicopters!" he told them. "Three or four of them just flew overhead!"

Then, from somewhere inside the hotel, they heard the roar of a large-bore gun firing and its impossibly loud report. Monika Stern returned her attention to Feltrinelli. "Get ready!"

"What? Even as attack helicopters assault this place? In God's name, why?"

"You are fucking crazy, Feltrinelli! Our only chance is the Microcystin, don't you see? Somehow we must get it!"

Feltrinelli knew he was dealing with a madwoman. He concluded that perhaps her rage would dominate the coming firefight with Werner-Miranda's men.

Besides, they had Microcystin to retrieve, and that was worth a fortune regardless of which side of the political fence you sat when it came to negotiation time.

"Everyone, out!" Stern shrieked. *"Out!"*

Siegfried needed seconds, no, *split* seconds. He saw the murderous glint in the squat Colombian's eyes, and the way his index finger was putting pressure on the trigger of the elephant handgun he was pointing at Simon, and then not at Simon, but himself.

Milliseconds.

Siegfried's hands flew out. Tugged on Simon's shoulders and spun him to the left.

The Casill exploded. The slug meant for Siegfried found Simon's cheek, and tore the top of his cranium off, blood and gray matter misting the lobby window behind Siegfried, whose own face had caught a bloody spray from the carnage created by the .454 round that had just killed one of the top Soviet operators of the past twenty years, someone Siegfried had finally been in a position to recruit along with the others.

But there was absolutely no time to do anything else but react.

Siegfried moved with the force and velocity of the blow,

snapping Simon back into his arms, and crashed through the window overlooking the lobby downstairs.

And bounced on the hardwood floors below, hard.

"Christ!" Santo shouted, not twenty feet away from his position behind the room door closest to the lobby. He saw two bodies, both a bloody mess. No. One was alive. A blond man, babbling incoherently in German, as he tried to crawl away from the other man, whose brains had scrambled across the lobby floor in a gray, sticky, bloody mess.

Upstairs, the command and control center's room door flew open and four men ran down the spiral staircase, submachine guns blazing at the two men who had just fallen on Hotel Dorfer's hardwood floors. Santo saw the blond man take cover underneath a lounge table.

Maslow yelled, "Hold your fire, Manny!"

Santo raised his submachine gun to fire. They had to take Werner-Miranda alive. Besides, Cortez and MacIntyre were waiting for him outside. He armed his flash-bang and got ready to throw it.

The four men dashed downstairs and sprinted through the lobby for the front entrance.

Where a hail of submachine gun fire from out in the parking lot cut the front two men down.

CHAPTER TWENTY-THREE

"Now!" MacIntyre said, and he and Cortez tossed two flash-bangs at the van and the men firing into the entrance of Hotel Dorfer. Immediately after tossing them they huddled down, squeezing their eyes shut and clamping their hands over their ears.

The flash-bangs went off with a deafening roar. Even with their eyes shut, MacIntyre and Cortez could feel the flash light up the area as if a thousand flashbulbs had gone off at once.

They looked back up. The unknown operatives were splayed out beside their van, knocked down like bowling pins. A lone, blond-haired woman was sitting upright in the snow, her submachine gun at her feet. She looked like a discarded child sitting in the middle of her tossed toys.

From inside the lobby, Humberto Werner-Miranda fired wildly at anything that moved out front. "Fire!" he screamed at his remaining bodyguard, "Goddam you, fire!" A noise to his rear. He jerked his head around. A black, palm-sized frisbee flew through the air and landed at his feet.

The little man shrieked and snapped the empty chambers of his Casill at it again and again. Then the flash-bang went off. Everything turned gray, then black.

Maslow dashed forward to grab the small Colombian with the oversized pistol, a still-weakened Manny Santo covering his rear with the MP5. Cortez and MacIntyre met them inside the doorway. The beating blades of helicopters grew louder.

MacIntyre saw what Maslow was doing and helped him sit the Colombian upright, as Maslow retrieved plastic cufflets from his utility pocket and bound Humberto Werner-Miranda's hands and feet. Then, draping him over his shoulder in a fireman's carry, he started to haul the Colombian coke broker toward the rear of the hotel, where Burchette was revving the Bell Ranger up for takeoff.

Santo noticed movement from the blond man who had crashed through the window before the melee had started. Fumbling with his back waistband, he pulled out a pistol, a Beretta .22. Gathering all his strength, Santo punt-kicked it out of his hand. *"Wintz!"* Cortez hustled over to help Santo restrain the blond man.

Maslow and MacIntyre returned. Santo knelt down beside the blond, the business end of an MP5 trained on his face. The blond man held his hands up in surrender. "My name is Horst Brandt," he said, in German-accented English. "I have been working undercover in coordination with your country's National Security Council. The helicopters you hear outside— they belong to the GSG9. You must stop what you are doing immediately."

"Right, pal," Santo said, binding the blond man's wrists behind his back with the plastic quick-ties Maslow gave him. Something was most definitely and assuredly up, but Santo knew he had no time for a question-and-answer period. The man who had introduced himself as Horst Brandt collapsed back to the floor, coughing in great pain from several ribs broken upon his fall out of the upper-level window moments earlier. Even though he hadn't been in the immediate proximity of the flash-bang that had just gone off, he was stunned from that as well. He looked longingly at a briefcase near Werner-Miranda's remaining bodyguard, where it lay at the dead man's feet. Cortez jerked him upright, and the blond man lolled his head to one side as he tried to catch Santo's attention. "You must believe me," he pleaded. "My code name is Siegfried."

Maslow and Santo exchanged glances. "The parachutes Hanlon saw earlier, Manny—"

"I know." Santo grabbed the briefcase. "What's this?" he asked the blond man.

No answer.

"We don't have time for this shit," MacIntyre shouted, above the din of rotor blades from outside, growing louder with each second. "C'mon, Manny!" He and Maslow hauled Werner-Miranda toward the rear of the hotel. Santo propelled the stranger who had called himself Horst, then Siegfried, into the lobby, his adrenaline and the tranquilizer effect finally starting to balance each other out. He felt incredibly tired.

Shuffling through the hallway, Maslow smashed his foot into the exit door and it flew open. The snatch team poured out the door, moving in groups of two.

Chaos. Utter, complete chaos. Flares from the passing helicopters lit the whole area up like it was daylight. The three-bird sortie was coming around for another pass. "C'mon," Maslow yelled, "beat feet! Rene's got the bird ready!"

Groggily, Santo followed Cortez and the self-described GSG9 agent through the door, and the group churned through the knee-deep snow toward the helipad where Burchette was waiting for them inside the Bell Ranger.

"Where's Hanlon?" Maslow yelled at her, reaching the helipad first.

A gunning engine from the tree line replied, blending with the shriek of Burchette's helo turbines. Randy Hanlon raced toward them with the snowmobile that had been cached in the tree line earlier. The skijor rope and akhio trailed the snowmobile like a whip-chain. There hadn't been a moment to lose and Hanlon was thinking on his feet.

Maslow controlled the helo entry as he and Cortez threw Werner-Miranda and the blond man into the chopper, while Rene Burchette grimly waited for the go-ahead for takeoff. The rest of the team started strapping on boots and skis.

She saw a helicopter rise suddenly from behind the hotel and climb into the sky. It was a white bird, a dove. It was pure and white and clean like the snow. Even the yellowish flares trailing their smoke trails and phosphorous glare in the sky failed to mar its ascetic beauty as the helicopter hovered over the trees for a moment, and then faded into the distance, gathering speed by the second. It was beautiful.

It was hateful.

From where she sat in the parking lot, Monika Stern stumbled to her feet and weaved toward the entrance of Hotel Dorfer, a fresh magazine in her submachine gun. The rest of her team lay in the snow in stupefied silence, waiting for the inevitable. "Pigs!" she screamed at them from the entrance steps, her eyes glittering, her face contorted with purple rage. Wheeling around, she plowed through the doors and sprayed a barrage of slugs into the empty lobby of Hotel Dorfer. She slammed another magazine into her submachine gun, ignoring the heat searing the palm of her hand where she brushed the barrel. She threw her head back, her eyes rolling white in their sockets.

"Piiiiigggs!"

A low keening began in her throat when she saw the bodies. Only the white dove kept her from enjoying true victory with the carnage. The fucking white dove got away. She hated the white thing that got away and she wanted every fucking molecule inhabiting the planet to know about it.

There was nothing inside. They had all escaped. Confusion. Explosions. Death.

No love. No friendship. Everything was hate, and only hate. No Renate. No Inge.

Only Suzuki and now she was dead too. Men had killed her.

"PIGS!"

She ran outside to the parking lot steps. The helicopters returned, huge, black, ugly. Ugly, hateful dragonflies. They hovered over their greenish clouds of mist, and the other pigs in her team of pigs were rooting in the snow, coughing, gagging, choking.

And then she coughed too.

Spots in her eyes, blood on her gunshot leg, crimson on the snow.

She coughed and watched the dragonflies hovering on their greenish clouds of mist vomit larvae suspended on spiderwebs that moored the dragonfly to the snow in an angry hover. The larvae were . . . white, with black pig snouts for faces . . . armed with black, pointed . . . sticks they would . . .

they would . . .

stick . . .

her . . . with . . .

Pigs.

A lone figure stood, legs splayed, arms akimbo, in front of the headlights of the van he had driven over the past three quarters of an hour to meet a group of people he had sworn to rendezvous with as a last pledge of allegiance to a dying man.

He had sworn this because his benefactor inside the van, who was bleeding to death, would have done the same, and had indeed insisted that he, Charlie Whitehead, meet the team at the pickup zone as promised.

Like the promise that dying man had made to another group of hired soldiers some time ago in Southeast Asia.

The snow was gentle, mellow. The reflection of the moon upon the crystal white of the night soothed Charlie Whitehead's heart, and stilled the flow of tears dammed behind his eyes. He knew he was exposed, that whoever else was involved with this operation might find his headlights and discover everything.

Would that be so bad if the Old Man wound up dying?

He returned to the van.

"Anything?" he was asked by a raspy, weedy voice.

"No, Wayne."

"They're a little late."

"Yeah. How you doin'?"

Wayne MacIntyre coughed up blood, which ran down the side of his mouth to his neckline and pooled in the depression his head made in the ambulance cot inside the van Whitehead had laid him on. An IV bottle dripped plasma into him. First-aid cravats bound the bullet holes in his arms and legs. The sucking chest wound that had penetrated his left lung was covered by a strip of plastic.

"Wayne—"

"Forget it."

The whine of a snowmobile engine gunned outside. Whitehead burst out the van's door.

Silhouetted against the setting moon, a snowmobile with a skijor chain of three skiers trailing it sped out of the tree line into the pasture and the road leading to the country intersection where Whitehead had parked the van. Seconds after spotting the inbound team, Whitehead also heard, then saw the beating rotors of the Bell Ranger bleating over the treetops, where it passed the snowmobile, circled overhead, and started to hover toward the van's front.

Two huge, black German copters were escorting the Bell Ranger, and they parked on the flanks of the Bell Ranger.

For a second Whitehead considered speeding away. Then he caught himself up short. No. That wouldn't do. Air superiority in this case ruled the situation, and he needed to get Wayne MacIntyre to a hospital *now*. The snowmobile drove on in, closer, meeting the van. Whitehead could see their faces now, the men. They were pinched and drawn. Cold. They were faces that had recently seen death. The snowmobile parked to his front at the same time Rene Burchette settled her Bell Ranger down in the pasture with the two German copters flanking her. DTM surrounded the Bell Ranger and hauled out two figures, a short squatty Colombian and another man they had snagged on the objective as well.

Soldiers poured out of the German helicopters.

Manny Santo approached Charlie Whitehead, shivering from the night and the night's events.

"The jig's up, Charlie. They intercepted us about halfway here. Where's the boss?"

"Inside the van." Whitehead reached out and grabbed Santo's arm. "He wants to see Matt, first."

Santo saw the look in Whitehead's eyes. "What's up?"

"Wilkerson's dead. Terrorists, two women, shot the suite up. We were compromised by someone. Wayne was hit in several places."

The team and a group of German soldiers escorting them approached the van, as Santo looked on in numb silence. An American voice carried through the night, ordering the Germans to let the Americans assemble. It was truly over. He thought of Matt.

"Where's Dad?"

Santo jumped. He hadn't seen MacIntyre because of the lights.

"Everyone assemble over here, if you please," the American voice called out again. The team, all of them by now, had gathered by the van, including Rene. They were enclosed by a semicircle of German soldiers, who aimed submachine guns at them. The Germans were dressed in overwhites, and their white, Aryan faces were masks as devoid of feeling as the frozen snow upon which they trod as they closed in on the team.

"Where's Dad?" Matt MacIntyre asked again, his voice gaining an edge to it.

Whitehead laid a hand on MacIntyre's shoulder. "We need to get him to a hospital, Matt. . . ."

MacIntyre's eyes widened, waiting for Whitehead to finish. Then he knew. He raced back for the van. *"Dad!"*

"Hey, you!" called out the American voice. A big blocky figure broke into the middle of the group and stared hard after MacIntyre's quick-step for the van. "Come back here!" he said, pointing his finger at MacIntyre and gaining the attention of one of the soldiers. Two men were dispatched from the German unit to intercept the young Special Forces officer. Manny Santo intercepted the American's arm. "So whose side are you on, pal?"

The big beefy man wheeled around and tried to shrug off Santo's iron grip. He found that he couldn't.

When Matt MacIntyre entered the van, he saw that his father was freezing. "Dad!"

"M-Matt. That you?"

The two German soldiers that had followed Matt MacIntyre flanked him. MacIntyre crawled inside and shut the door. He found the suspended IV, the cravats . . . the blood. His father's face was like stretched and brittle parchment. "Oh, God . . . Dad . . ."

Wayne MacIntyre raised a trembling hand and found his son's face.

"Don't cry."

"Why aren't you in a hospital?"

"We'll . . . get to one soon enough."

"Goddammit, who do you think you are, Dad, *Don fucking Quixote?*"

Wayne MacIntyre smiled. "Had to wait for the team, and I guess I had to wait for my son. I mean, what the hell. Couldn't let them . . ." He coughed, and more blood came up. Matt flew for the door handle. Somehow Wayne MacIntyre kept his hand on his son's collar. Matt turned back around.

"We've got to get you out of here!"

"No . . . son. Just listen."

"What?"

"Everything's in the vault back home in Tulsa. Will, that is. Everything's yours. Dustbowl, the ranch . . . You've been appointed David's legal guardian." Wayne MacIntyre paused for breath. He swallowed down the blood and bile that wanted to come back up.

"Don't talk like that!" He tried to shrug off his old man's hand, which was still tightly fastened on his collar. He had to get him out of here!

"No . . . listen, son. C'mere."

Matt MacIntyre bent down to give his father his ear.

And he started to cry, as his father's hand caressed his cheek and told him what he had to say.

"NSC," the American barked. "I'm with Lonnie Wilkerson from the National Security Council. Where *is* Wilkerson anyway?"

"Back at Hotel Sudtyrol," called out another voice from the group. Santo looked around. It had come from the blond man he'd picked up in the middle of the melee at Hotel Dorfer. One of the German soldiers was cutting off the plastic quick-tie he'd been secured with. Only a subdued and quiet Humberto Werner-Miranda remained bound. His posture was slumped, and his potbelly stuck out. He was a defeated man.

Horst Brandt, aka Siegfried, who really worked for the Germans, entered the circle with the broad-shouldered American. "Or perhaps he is here," he added, looking at Whitehead. "Did he live, or did Stern's gang kill him too?"

Whitehead felt a seething anger rising from deep within. "What is this?"

Santo cast black eyes on the German, regarding his thin-lipped, rose-tinted white complexion. He was a good-looking man, but had strangely lifeless, pale gray eyes. Eyes that had seen much. He would remember this man. Santo's study then found the American. Him too.

"A joint operation between your country's National Security Council and Deutschland's GSG9," Horst Brandt said, jerking his head in the direction of the Bell Ranger Burchette had flown in. One of the soldiers covering them entered the helicopter and retrieved the briefcase Santo had policed up back at the hotel along with "Siegfried." The German returned his attention to the Americans assembled before him. "The GSG9 is my country's counterterrorist organization. I think both operations succeeded, albeit somewhat awkwardly."

Santo felt the bile rise from deep within his throat. He mentally restrained the fist he wanted to plow into the German's face. Moving in closer to the group huddle, Maslow joined him. Hanlon and Burchette tightened up their own perimeter, as if ready to take on the whole group of Germans surrounding them.

"You didn't know?" the American asked with stage incredulity. "Wilkerson didn't tell you? You people are heroes. You captured a drug lord. You also, whether you knew it or not, participated in the capture of some of Europe's most elusive terrorists. As you can see, German GSG9 had a vested interest in this operation, and made sure you had a backup plan. That's all."

"What's you're name, bud?" Santo muttered.

"Bud Reasoner. What's yours, pal?"

"I'm not your pal."

"We have some questions for your unit," the NSC man said, trying not to sound deflated.

The van door opened. Matt MacIntyre stepped out. Cortez met him and walked with Matt back to the group. The two Germans who had waited for MacIntyre outside the van trailed along.

"First off," the NSC man continued, confident now of his control over the group, "we need total personnel accountability, and then we'll fly back to Germany, where we'll have us a little debriefing." Bud Reasoner's eyes fished around the group before him and found that it was parting to allow the approach of a tall, slender black-haired man with the strong, set jaw of his father and cold, china-blue eyes to match. The young man strode purposefully toward him, holding his gaze. "The first thing I wanna know," Bud Reasoner said uncertainly, "is where the fuck is Lonnie Wilkerson?"

"Why don't you ask my old man?" Matt MacIntyre said coldly, joining the group. He stood before the NSC man. "You people deal with expendable assets for deniable operations, don't you?"

And then he hit Bud Reasoner, breaking his nose.

CHAPTER TWENTY-FOUR

Flint Kaserne, Bad Toelz, Germany

The executive officer of the 1st Battalion, 10th Special Forces Group (Airborne), Major Rick Du Bois, a good-looking, muscular man in his mid-thirties, strode purposefully from his VW van to the entrance of Flint Kaserne's Officers' Club, a white stucco and dark-timbered affair with a very wet bar, and a beer cellar below which had serviced many a Green Beret who had had the very good fortune of being assigned to Toelz for over the past forty years of the organization's presence in southern Bavaria. The officers' club also had several suites that were used as guest quarters for the occasional general or Congressman visiting Alpine Europe's most agreeable assignment for soldiers serving in the American Special Operations Community.

A light drizzle, characteristic of German springs, soaked the gray skies and the air around Du Bois in forty-five-degree weather, and he gingerly stepped across the asphalt, careful to avoid spattering the mirror-gloss on his Corcoran jump boots, which matched quite nicely with his recently pressed Class A uniform. The chrome U.S. and German jump wings over both breast pockets of his forest-green uniform tunic shone. He also had a chrome SCUBA badge gleaming alongside the garish chrome, gold-and-red-painted Pathfinder badge on his left breast pocket flap. What little "fruit salad" he wore (consisting primarily of three good-boy ribbons and three "I was there" ribbons) over his left breast pocket beneath his U.S. jump wings was neatly arranged in two brightly colored rows of red, yellow, green, blue, and white. For once, he'd tied the

Windsor knot cinched over his football player's neck correctly, and the beret he wore was immaculately shaved, shrunk, and formed to his head, the gold oak leaf he wore pinned onto the Green 10th Group flash glowing smartly against the beret's forest green.

In other words, Du Bois looked pretty. He shivered too. The uniform was for show and tell only. Reaching the porch steps of the squat, heavily timbered chalet, Du Bois was glad to see and smell the wood smoke curling from the chalet's chimney. This cold, wet morning warranted a bed, heavy down German comforters, hot German coffee, bread, and cheese.

But now there was a briefing to be conducted, and Du Bois's battalion commander, one Lieutenant Colonel Jake Blane, had made it clear in no uncertain terms that Du Bois was to personally escort the group of people who had been put up in the officers' club's guest quarters overnight to the kaserne headquarters. Himself. And so Du Bois had put on his Class A's at zero-six on a groggy Sunday morning, kissed his wife back to sleep, and drove his family van up the hill to the officers' club to pick up the VIPs—four men and a woman. A damned good-looking woman at that.

Oddly enough, though, two of the battalion's own had spent the night with the VIPs. Captain Matt MacIntyre, the executive officer of Alpha Company, and Sergeant First Class Corky Cortez, Alpha Company's operations NCO. The two of them had been involved in some sort of shit the night before, which had warranted Colonel Blane driving hell-bent to the American Consulate in Munich thirty miles north to escort them back down to Bad Toelz, where, at 0300 hours, the VIPs had been put up for the remainder of the night. That had been only four hours ago, and the VIPs couldn't have gotten much sleep at all. Something was up. Something classified. Something Du Bois had every intention of finding out.

And he didn't even know who the hell they were. Blane. "Make It Happen Blane." A goddam Ranger pinhead. Du Bois snorted, as he pushed open the officers' club entrance door and walked down the red-carpeted hallway, where camouflaged battalion-officer beer steins flanked the hat shelves overhead.

He reached the guest quarters. Knocked on the door. Entered.

One man, dressed in civilian outdoor clothes, slouched in an easy chair, where he stared at the fire blazing in the porcelain-tiled stove. He was stoking coals with a fireplace poker. Du Bois pulled at his necktie and approached the well-built blond man. "You're, uh . . . ?"

"Hanlon. Randall P. Private Fuckin' Civilian."

"Where are the others I'm supposed to pick up, Mr. Hanlon?"

Hanlon glanced up at the major and read the name tag over his right breast pocket, beneath his German jump wings. Du Bois. "They'll be here in a minute, Major."

Du Bois knew he was dealing with a soldier. Taking a seat, they waited in silence. The atmosphere was hot, and thick with tension.

Moments later, three other men descended the staircase which led up to VIP suites. "And this is Charles Whitehead, Manuel Santo, and Winston Maslow," Hanlon muttered to Du Bois.

Du Bois extended his hand. Only Charlie Whitehead took it, while the others in the group found chairs to sit in so they too could contemplate the morning's fire. Another man descended the staircase. This time Du Bois found a familiar face.

"Sergeant Cortez!"

"Sir?"

Corky Cortez lumbered toward his battalion executive officer. Du Bois wasn't a bad sort. Led PT with the headquarters detachment. Didn't have a superior attitude like some officers had. He'd successfully and intelligently commanded Alpha Company the year before.

"What's up, anyway?" Du Bois asked Cortez, leading him away from the group.

"Classified, sir," Cortez replied softly. "You don't have a need to know."

"Where's Captain MacIntyre? I understand he's supposed to be with these people."

"He stepped out about ten minutes ago. Wanted to walk to the kaserne alone."

"He's supposed to be escorted!"

Du Bois caught four stares aimed his way. He'd spoken too loud. This time, Cortez took Du Bois's arm, and led him farther away. "Let him be, sir. Matt's strung pretty tight this morning. Needed a few minutes alone."

"But—"

"Just let it be, Major. His father died last night."

"Oh. Was it a protracted illness?"

Cortez rejoined the group. Du Bois followed, consulting his watch. Another fifteen minutes until the briefing. Seeing him, Hanlon climbed out of his chair. "I'll get Rene," he announced.

Moments later, after ascending the staircase and knocking on her door, only to receive no answer, Hanlon knocked again, and said, "Rene? C'mon. The others are waiting."

Silence.

"I'm coming in."

He found her sitting in a rocker and staring out the window. He approached her and, simultaneously, she stood up and faced him. She'd been crying, and now she wiped at her eyes. She was ready, dressed simply in woolen slacks, a sweater, and hiking boots. She reached for her down jacket, which lay on the bedside table. Hanlon intercepted her hand.

"Don't . . ."

"Rene, I . . ."

She tried to free her hand from his, and at first Hanlon wanted to restrain her, to crush her to his chest and tell her everything would be all right, and that he wanted to kiss her face, and feel her light brown hair silk through his fingers, and how he wanted to give her all he had of himself. . . .

She yanked her hand away.

"I'm sorry."

"Forget it." She wiped the hard lines of her face with her shirt sleeve. "I'm a mess this morning," she said softly. "Wayne and I were close."

Hanlon looked away and swallowed in embarrassment.

Then she came closer and surprised him by touching his cheek with her fingers. "It would be . . . inappropriate under the circumstances, Randy. We work together."

"Right." He attempted a smile. Mouth only.

"Your eyes look so hard."

"Hard as my heart, lady," he said, grinning emptily. "And yours too, I might add."

"But—"

"It's over, Rene." Hanlon gestured his hands about the room. "DTM, the organization, our mission, our purpose for being here in the first place. It's all fucking well over." Hanlon blinked several times, suddenly aware that salt was in his eyes.

Then he looked back at her. "And I can't help the way I feel about you. So give me a break."

She took his hands and gave them a squeeze. They exchanged looks, neither one speaking. Then, reaching for her jacket, she led him out the door.

Clean-shaven and dressed in an immaculately pressed and tailored Class A uniform, Matt MacIntyre entered the main headquarters door of Flint Kaserne, walked a few steps into the hallway, and stood before the wooden statue of a Green Beret. The "wooden man," it was informally called. The halls were quiet. After all, it was 0630 hours on a Sunday morning. A sergeant dressed in BDUs poked his head out of the staff duty office. "Sir?"

"It's just me, Smitty," MacIntyre replied to the staff duty NCO, recognizing the young sergeant as a team weapons man from Bravo company.

The staff sergeant joined MacIntyre by the statue. "There are some VIPs I escorted upstairs to the war room about half an hour ago. They look like spooks to me. Colonel Blane's waiting for you up there."

"Okay."

"I'll enter you in the staff duty log then."

"You do that."

The soldier returned to his post. MacIntyre continued to stare at the wooden man. Things could be really hard, sometimes. Like having to attend a debriefing, only hours after your own father had died in your arms, and you were about to spend the next several days checking him out of the Munich morgue and returning Stateside to bury him next to the rest of your dead family.

And that was when the full sledgehammer weight of the blow of his father's death would hit him square on the head. Even seeing his father die in his arms had yet to fully register. Later on, he'd realize that there would be no more calls and long talks through the overseas lines, and to hell with how expensive intercontinental telephone communications could get. Those few and increasingly infrequent visits back home, on the ranch, out in the deer woods would be no more.

No more. There would be plenty of time to cry later. It would come.

"This place was once an SS barracks, you know," an accented voice murmured quietly from behind.

MacIntyre wheeled around. He saw an older man in his mid to late fifties, with salt and pepper hair and a huge mustache, standing behind him, dressed simply in a Bavarian hunting jacket, tweed slacks, and Eddie Bauer field boots. The Mad Russian.

Colonel (retired) Andrei Volensky, his former battalion commander. Two years ago, Volensky had commanded MacIntyre's first unit of assignment, back at Ft. Bragg, and during one of their desert training deployments, had selected MacIntyre's team to interdict the drug smugglers south of the White Sands Missile Range.

"Sir!"

Volensky walked up to MacIntyre. "Hello, Team Leader." Volensky grinned, reached out, and clapped MacIntyre on the cheek. Then, standing back, he straightened his shoulders and cleared his throat.

"Sir," MacIntyre sputtered, "What are you—"

"Listen to me, Matt," Volensky said, fumbling with his breast pocket for a package of dark-skinned More cigarettes. "I have only a few moments. You won't be seeing me at the briefback about to commence upstairs with Jake and his 'guests' from Washington. I do, however, want to convey my condolences, in light of what's happened."

MacIntyre took a step back, blinking rapidly, shaking his head.

Volensky stepped closer, reached out, and put his hand on MacIntyre's shoulder. "You've been through much, Matt. You'll be talking to people soon who would rather see you leave the Army and dismantle the organization your father created."

Speechless, MacIntyre let the Old Man continue. They walked down the hallway, where dozens of battalion chain-of-command photographs, one taken for each year dating back to the early sixties, flanked the walls. "As I said," Volensky went on quietly, dragging deeply on a cigarette, with his hand still around the younger officer's shoulders, "Hitler once used this kaserne as a training post for Waffen SS cadets, a breeding ground for SS officers."

"Why are you telling me this? What does this have to do with—"

"Hitler himself used to swim in the very same swimming pool next to the gymnasium where your SCUBA teams in Alpha Company conduct their pre-SCUBA training for the wanna-be's," Volensky added, disregarding the question.

It was all too much for MacIntyre, too much at once, the growing realization that his father was in fact dead, and now this former commanding officer of his, his mentor and commander of his former unit prior to reporting to Bad Toelz, was strolling down the hallway with him, discussing historical minutia regarding Hitler's Waffen SS with the pictures flanking the hallway and the living and dead men inhabiting those pictures serving as their audience.

Their boot steps echoed hollowly through the hallway, like ghostly totems, beating cadence to the martial spirit inhabiting the kaserne headquarters.

And Volensky was like a ghost from the past himself. MacIntyre had to remind himself that the Mad Russian was simply retired and residing with his German wife in Deutschland.

Reading his mind, Volensky cleared his throat and announced, "I used to work with Manny Santo in the Company, Matt. Corky Cortez as well. You could say we've all been in bed with each other for a very long time. This operation to snatch Humberto Werner-Miranda was tied in with a German GSG9 desire to enact a terrorist roundup."

Matt MacIntyre stopped in his tracks and regarded the older man standing before him. "So you were in on this too?"

"I knew about the operation, yes. Those in the Soviet Union's military intelligence apparatus say it costs a ruble to get in, but two to get out." Volensky shrugged. "It is the same in any country's intelligence organization. Once you are in, Matt, you are always in. Your father wanted in in a very big way."

MacIntyre turned sharply away. "Yeah. My father's dead now because of that goddam philosophy."

"And would you dismantle what he has created because you disagree with that philosophy?" he called after him.

"*Hell, yes!*" MacIntyre screamed, spinning around and slamming his fist into one of the pictures on the wall. It crashed to the floor. The staff duty NCO poked his head out his office's door. Seeing him, Volensky waved at the young sergeant that all was under control. Reluctantly, the NCO returned to his chair.

MacIntyre angrily turned to his former commander, his face contorted with rage and hurt. "What did he gain, sir, a goddam immortal chair in Valhalla for the greater glory of the United States of America? No! Goddammit, no! He died on a worthless motherfucking deniable operation that snatched a drug lord and wound up killing some terrorists along the way! He hired a mercenary outfit, got it involved with some . . . some motherfucking Waffen SS intel spooks from the National Security Council, and died jousting at windmills! Was it worth it? *Jesus Christ, Colonel, was it worth it?*"

Volensky grabbed the sobbing young captain by the shoulders and held him for a moment. Then he cradled MacIntyre in his right arm and led him back toward the wooden man near the kaserne's main entrance.

"It was an individual choice your father made, Matt. He knew the risks. He should not have personally gone on the mission, but it was his decision to do so. He could have gone straight to a hospital, but instead he chose to meet the team he had sent in on a mission at the scheduled pickup spot. Had he not done so, then . . ." Volensky paused. "It would have been very easy for the team to have been cornered and shot down by the organization they had been working with to ensure deniability. Whether DTM knew it had been working with GSG9 or not."

MacIntyre wiped off his face with the sleeve of his sharply pressed uniform tunic, and pinched his eye sockets with the thumb and forefinger of his left hand. "I just don't understand. Why are you here now? Why will I be attending a briefing with people I don't know, and what will happen to my friends who were working with my father?"

"Then allow me to tell you. DTM will be told to cease to exist as a covert unit. Sergeant First Class Randy Hanlon will be asked to return to the Army and will be reinstated with back pay and his unit of choice. Master Sergeant Manuel Santo will be direct-commissioned to captain and assigned to a Special Forces unit of his choice. Winston Maslow will probably return to civilian life, since he is retired. That leaves Rene Burchette and Charlie Whitehead. Since you are now the legal custodian of your father's estate, their future is now your decision.

"And what you do with your father's estate and the custodianship of your brother is also totally up to you, Matt," Volensky gently added.

MacIntyre's face blackened, and everything grew numb. His mother was dead. His brother, Donny, was dead. And now his father too was dead. His youngest brother, David, now attending boarding school, and having to struggle through life with a crippled arm. All victims of drug abuse and terrorism.

And now he had to decide whether or not to stay in the Army. If he stayed, then who would run Dustbowl Enterprises? Who would take care of David?

"You have many choices to make, Team Leader. You also have many people you are now directly responsible for. Do not be taken in by those people waiting for you upstairs who profess to a higher morality when it comes to the deniable operations such as this one your father sponsored."

Volensky leaned in close to MacIntyre, as they returned back to the wooden man. "And always remember to be true to yourself and your country's constitution, young Captain. Integrity is a rare commodity these days."

MacIntyre straightened up and cleared his throat. "I've heard this line before, Colonel. Duty, honor, and country only goes so far."

Volensky nodded. *"Ein Volk, Ein Reich, Ein Führer,"* he said.

MacIntyre glanced sharply at Volensky. "Sir?"

"One People, One Reich, One Leader," Volensky translated quietly. "That slogan was inscribed on their currency half a century ago—and that philosophy turned out to be the cement binding an entire society together to promote actions they justified later on as a higher morality when the world looked upon the Germans with horror. How soon history forgets, Matt."

Volensky nodded at the entrance door, spotting a van that had pulled up inside the square-shaped compound and parked alongside the commander's parking space. Five men and a woman hopped out, escorted by a uniformed major, no doubt Jake Blane's XO. MacIntyre took note of them as well.

"These are very strange times, Matt. Germany has reunified, and the Soviet Union is no longer the organized and committed menace to the West it once was. This 'peace dividend' heralded by our naive and militarily inexperienced Congress is a utopian pipe dream. The European Economic

Community will become a mere hostage to the deutschmark. And you are only one operator now in charge of five others who can quite possibly become tools for those who, like the Germans in the thirties, proclaim a higher morality in the name of our own government. The question is, how will you deal with that?"

MacIntyre gazed at the people approaching the battalion headquarters with a thousand-yard stare. It was all simply too much, too soon. He felt Volensky's hand, which had been gripping his shoulder, now slip off. "Good luck, Matt," Volensky murmured. "And remember what your father told you."

Volensky's boot steps faded back into the hallway and MacIntyre heard a door open and close with a lonely echo far down the hallway. The parting words Volensky had left him with sunk in. MacIntyre wheeled around *"How did you know what my father—?"* But the Mad Russian was gone. A ghost from his past.

Then the headquarters door opened, and the unit operators comprising DTM congregated with Matt MacIntyre by the wooden man.

The Class-A-uniformed major, one Rick Du Bois, gestured with exasperated hands. "C'mon, people, we're running late."

Corky Cortez said, "Go on ahead, Major. We're not going anywhere." The calm purpose in Cortez's voice convinced Du Bois that they'd comply when he was out of earshot. Du Bois began the three-story ascent toward the briefing room.

The group redirected its attention on MacIntyre. Santo spoke first.

"So where do we go from here, Matt?"

MacIntyre's face hardened, and he wiped at his eyes. "Let's just get through this briefing first. And then we'll talk."

"Where, Matt?" Wintz Maslow asked. "Here?"

"No. Home."

"Where's home?" Rene Burchette said gently.

For a long moment, Matt MacIntyre looked at Charlie Whitehead, and thought of the way things used to be when everyone got together a week before Thanksgiving for the annual deer hunt, in another time, another era. "Home," Matt MacIntyre replied, his voice thick with emotion, "is in the southeast part of Oklahoma, up in the hills at a deer camp run by an old broken-down cowboy named Claudie." He swallowed, and then looked up and smiled at the group, even though twin streaks ran down his cheeks. "Home's where your family is. It sure as hell isn't here. When this debriefing's over, I'd like to meet all of you back at the ranch to help me bury my old man."

MacIntyre looked away and swallowed. "I'd really like that," he added.

Randy Hanlon stepped up to Matt MacIntyre and clapped both hands on Matt's shoulders. He held him there until eye contact was made. No words were spoken for several moments.

Then, smiling, Hanlon gestured at the rest of the group with his other hand. "Meet the new boss," he said.

First there was *INFILTRATORS!*
Then there was *PENETRATORS!*
Don't miss *OPERATORS* by Mark D. Harrell

COMING SOON FROM JOVE BOOKS!

Follow the further adventures of Special Forces
Captain Matthew D. MacIntyre.

Turn the page
for an exciting excerpt
from OPERATORS,
available from Jove
in September 1992.

Munich

Captain Matthew D. MacIntyre slurred over his glass of beer: "So this was the way it really was. There we were, at the Oktoberfest. Now this is no shit, Silvia. Randy, Rene, and David finally egg me into getting onto this . . . this Wheel of *Fortune* thing—"

"Bitte?"

Pick up the Pieces was being saxophoned quite nicely in sync with the Katmandooze's rhythm guitar section up on the stage not fifteen feet away from their table, as MacIntyre took another long pull from his beer before going on to explain the Wheel of Fortune concept to his date, Silvia. Gulping down what was left of his beer, he raised his forefinger in the air, managed to say *"Ein moment,"* between burps, twisted around in his chair, and cast a lusty look at the inner thigh of the Scottish girl sitting the next table over before flagging down one of *Der Nacht Kafe*'s fashionable but aloof waiters. This time, MacIntyre, a tall, slender and intense man in his late twenties, managed to set aside his drunkenness for a moment to bore china-blue eyes through the skull of a rather foppish young man with a Pepsodent smile and dyed brown hair moussed quite concretely against his scalp; the waiter meandered toward their table. If MacIntyre would have been more sober at the moment, he would have seen the waiter make meaningful eye contact with his date, Silvia.

The waiter, smiling magnificently, tossed down a fresh coaster and stood by to receive the order from this strange American who frequented *Der Nacht Kafe* quite often; the Ami was a playboy who liked to affect baggy German trousers, white socks, Bavarian shoes, and a German leisure jacket with its sleeves rolled up his forearms.

This Special Forces soldier from Bad Toelz.

"Wanna 'nother beer, pal."

"*Jawohl*," the waiter replied, making fastidious scribbling motions on a pad.

MacIntyre squinted in Silvia's direction. "You too, babe?"

Silvia, a local fraulein that a Warrant Officer in MacIntyre's company had "hand-receipted" to him prior to rotating home, pitched her voice up an octave, wrinkled her brow, swept her hair back in a histrionic display of concern and said, "Matthew! You are trying to make me drunk?"

MacIntyre eye-balled the curve of Silvia's shoulders, the way the hollow of her cream-colored throat led smoothly down toward the crimson blush of her chest, and how the fabric of her black minidress barely constrained her breasts. It was the best lecherous look he could muster. "Yep."

MacIntyre wheeled back around in his chair as the waiter swished away, reveling in the band, the place and the hour. He loved the way the bald-headed saxophonist from Liverpool with the red-haired pirate's beard belted out tunes from The Average White Band, the occasional one from Pink Floyd, and when he got mellow, Supertramp, and how the four-piece rhythm section backed him up through it all. He loved to watch the spiked-hair dance crowd punks suck espresso down their gullets and gyrate against the transvestites and prostitutes. It was already zero-one-thirty this early Christmas-season morning, and the sheer proliferation of weirdness bouncing off the walls of the late-night jazz club encompassed not only queers, prostitutes and punks, but jet-setters, soldiers, terrorists, rich, poor, and anybody from any class and any where within *Der Nacht Kafe*'s live fold of cosmo glitz, sound and accents.

In short, if you were weird, you were in. If you were rich, you were in. But if you showed up with a GI haircut and a T-shirt advertising the excellence of the U.S. Army Ranger School, or wore a cowboy belt with the strap dangling between your legs, forget it. Rednecks and GIs with a wardrobe labeling Fort this or that were a no-go at the *Der Nacht Kafe* on *Goethestrasse*, in downtown, low-brow, railhead Munich.

Silvia said something. MacIntyre leaned forward and cupped his hand to his left ear. "What?"

Silvia pouted. "Matthew, you completely ignored what I said."

Pick up the Pieces tuned into a Joe Cocker song, and the bald-headed sax player grabbed a mike stand and started agonizing with *"My baby . . ."* MacIntyre leaned forward, his hand cupped over his right ear. He'd blown out the eardrum years before on the demo range at the Q-course, and had had a hearing loss ever since. It only gave him an excuse to peg the volume knob of his compact disc player into the "right" mode when jamming tunes in his RX-7. MacIntyre grinned hugely and said, "What exactly was it you said, you sweet piece of she-meat?"

"Meennsch, Matthew!" Silvia pressed the fingers of her right hand against MacIntyre's forearm. She followed through with a kiss of her full lips onto his mouth. MacIntyre did not see her palm a half-gram of powder into his beer glass because her fingers slipped from his forearm to play with the inside of his thigh under the cocktail table. Leaning back in her chair, she traced a promise on her lips with the tip of her tongue.

MacIntyre grinned and slugged down half his beer. "You're a terribly, terribly naughty girl." MacIntyre flashed her his best "Let's go home and fuck" smile. Reaching forward, she dabbed at the lipstick she'd smeared on his mouth. The pre-planned act informed the waiter, who observed them from the back of the room, that she was ready. "The hour grows late," Silvia pouted.

MacIntyre's bladder informed him of another pressing matter. Squinting through increasingly bleary eyes, he announced: "I'll just be a minute. Then I'll take us back to the ranch and explain the mighty wheel concept to you there, sweetheart." He pushed away from the table, got up, and made for the men's room through the crush of weirdness bee-bopping through the punk Euro-dog madness writhing to Joe Cocker's croaky gospel booming in *Der Nacht Kafe*.

Two growl-throated Harleys prowled through the wet slush of *Goethestrasse*. Corky Cortez's helmet remained perched on his low backrest so he could get a good look at the bobbing silhouettes lined up and down the access line of people waiting to get into *Der Nacht Kafe*, as he and Brett Darby profiled their bikes down the icy-wet central Munich back street. Pulling his

1200cc Low-Rider alongside Cortez's Sportster, Brett Darby exchanged looks with his partner.

Cortez nodded. This was the place. Cortez slowed his bike in front of the collection of glass-walled buildings, hedgerowed for privacy. It was close to the Free University of Munich, and the railhead servicing Munich's old-town. It was late-night too, the time and place where hookers and the sweet smell of hash went hand-in-hand with the jazzy mood stoking from the club like coke-accelerated heartbeats. Cortez exchanged looks with Darby, whose somber, thoughtful eyes reminded Cortez of old westerns and gunslingers facing down villains at the OK corral. Darby's down-turned, regulation-defying mustache completed the picture.

"Well, Festus?"

"What's this Festus shit?" Darby snorted, sniffling in the cold December air. The fifty-k bike ride from Toelz hadn't helped, and his leathers felt like armor, rigid from ice. Darby nodded his head in the direction of the revelers lined up before *Der Nacht Kafe*'s entrance. "We going in or not?"

A navy blue Merc four-door passed them and slowed to a stop several meters to their front. Cortez regarded the four men occupying it. Darby caught his eye, and revved up his Low Rider. "Cork . . ."

"I see 'em. Those the ones at Ziggy's?"

Two men got out of the Mercedes, which was a big one with lots of power under the hood. Automatically, Cortez and Darby reached for their helmets. "Yeah," Darby replied. "See the radios?"

Before replying, Darby thought about the antennas the two men had elongated, as they purposefully assumed flanking positions at the front of the jazz club by the hedgerows. Darby coasted his Low-Rider ahead a few feet, and Cortez caught up.

"C'mon," Cortez told him, his voice tight with adrenaline. "I know a good route."

"Anything you say, Marshal Dillon," Darby answered with a hard smile. It had been a while since he'd been in a fight, and the Hitler wanna-be's back at Ziggy's had kind of put an edge on he wanted to whet.

They followed the road down to the street corner, where Cortez turned a column right into a road lined with firs, their branches laden with heavy, wet snow draping the flanks of the street in winter quiet. The din of late-night partying faded, and soon only their Harley's panther growls broke the neighborhood's sleepy silence. Cortez made another right into the portion of Goethe Park flanking *Der Nacht Kafe*'s northern approach. Darby's heart picked up a beat. They were on snow-covered grass now, their hogs illegal and suspect to the *Polizeis'* wrath if caught.

Cortez sped his Sportster up and Darby matched RPMs with a flick of his wrist on the throttle of his Low-Rider. They were doing thirty in a zero-k-per-hour zone, then forty. Glancing down, Darby saw his speedometer crawl inexorably toward forty-five. Goethe's statue loomed into view, the old philosopher pondering his park underneath a frozen crust of pigeon droppings, while the nightclub's jazz-funk bounced off his corroded bronze skin. Catching Darby's eye, Cortez made a cutting motion with his hand over his throat, and killed his engine. He started to slow down, and, doing the same, Darby silently coasted in Cortez's snow-plumed wake. Weaving through a stand of evergreens, Cortez cut his headlights and closed in toward the nightclub. When they were fifty feet away, he abruptly spun on his rear wheel in an about-face. Darby passed him and copied the move. They dismounted their bikes in tandem and advanced on the nightclub's back veranda, where in warmer weather, late-night revelers smoked hash and stole a few moments of furtive, anonymous sex in the decadent backwash of the club's primal beat.

Darby's biker boots crunched wet snow underneath his Vibram soles. Cortez pulled him in close, as they neared the nightclub. A German male in his mid-thirties was holding a radio and prowling the back gate, his attention riveted on the crowd inside the club. Cortez and Darby moved closer to the club's back entrance, automatically on patrol, their senses of sight and hearing tuned on high. Catlike, Darby led out first, shrugging off Cortez's hand that had tried to restrain him. *"Entschuldigen Sie, bitte,"* Darby called softly to the German when he was an arm's length away.

Startled, the German wheeled around, *"Was?"*

Darby cold-cocked him on the spot, the knife blade of his outer wrist slicing into the side of the German's neck. The German smashed headfirst into the snow, paralyzed from the blow.

Cortez dashed up from the treeline, his Browning Hi-Power

drawn. "What the *fuck* are you doing?" he hissed through the cold night air.

Darby pulled a brick-like object from the pocket of his jacket. Pressing the electrodes protruding from one end against the stunned German's hip, he squeezed a black button. Cortez heard the crackle of voltage as the German convulsed. "Jesus Christ, Brett. . . ." Cortez sunk to one knee, covering his partner with his Hi-Power in case Murphy came to pay a visit. But the law was only in effect when you had a well-thought-out plan for bait. Darby's action had been totally spontaneous.

Darby stuck his gun back in his jacket pocket and drug the German into the trees. "He'll come to in about thirty minutes," he affirmed.

"But you don't know that—"

"Call it an educated guess then. This was one of the guys looking for MacIntyre back in Toelz."

Cortez cast a furtive look around. No one else had seen them. If the German had a partner, he was posted on another side of the nightclub. Darby returned from the trees, wiping his nose against the sleeve of his jacket. Looking at Cortez with his mournful dark eyes, he winked. "Let's party, my man."

The two walked casually into the glass-walled veranda, welcoming the warm blast of club-heated air, even if it did stink of unwashed bodies and dance hall sex-sweat. Mixing in with the crowds wasn't difficult. They weaved past the punks and other screaming denizens hailing from the continent and the commonwealth, all merging together in an orgy of international hormones, as the live jazz-funk-rock band screamed Joe Cocker to the crowd. They approached one of the three bars flanking the dance floor. Darby raked his eyes across the crowd, Cortez doing the same. He felt alive, tuned up, vibrant with adrenaline. It was hard not to groove to the beat, get into the rhythm of pending action.

Cortez felt Darby nudge him in the ribs. "Where?"

Darby nodded toward the front center table not ten feet away from the tiny dance floor and the band. "There she is."

Cortez surveyed a leggy German woman sitting at the cocktail table, dressed in a clingy black minidress and black lace hose tracing the curve of her thighs and calves. She was talking animatedly with one of the waiters, a thin, smallish man with black moussed hair and black, thick-framed glasses.

She pointed in the direction of the men's room. "Long legs, big tits, auburn hair, just like you said," Cortez commented.

"Name's Silvia."

"Yeah," Cortez said, nodding his head. "I've seen her before. Chief Gadczik used to date her." Cortez watched the waiter she'd been talking to leave her table and head toward the men's room.

Darby spotted two Germans wearing sunglasses and leisure jackets near *Der Nacht Kafe*'s front entrance, looking as if they were doing the same thing he and Cortez were: searching for MacIntyre. Clearly the bulges in their jackets were not just tourist billfolds.

"Check out Fritz and Hans over by the front door, Cork."

"I see 'em."

"What about Mac's squeeze?"

"What about her?" Cortez glanced at her table. The waiter they'd seen talking to her earlier was now headed toward the men's room a few tables down from where they stood near the bar.

"What about *him*?" Darby said, his voice taut with impatience. "Where *is* MacIntyre?"

"Where else can he be? Cover me, Festus. I'm going to the can."

MacIntyre finished at the urinal and traded glances with a lecherous looking Italian with large dark eyes, two gold-hoop earrings, and a half-beard, who'd been staring at him. Zipping up his pants, MacIntyre said, "Sorry pal, wrong sexual persuasion."

The Italian smirked and looked down at the black and white tiled floor.

MacIntyre weaved to the sink counter to wash his hands. He felt dizzy, more so than warranted by his alcohol consumption that night. Turning on the faucet's cold tap to full blast, he bent over the sink and scrubbed his face with Munich's ice-melt, welcoming the frozen sobriety it brought. MacIntyre held his face in his hands a moment longer than intended, the roar of the tap beating back the band's noise from upstairs.

Where had he gone? he thought. What had he become? A playboy drunk? Was he really in charge of the legacy his father had left behind? The legacy of lies and hidden agendas and . . .

Covert operations. You lost your soul in deniability and in promises you didn't keep. MacIntyre remembered the kaserne on that early spring morning, the morning after his father had been killed, when Hanlon had proclaimed, "Meet the new boss." Yeah, right. That was before Hanlon found out in the classified debriefing later on that the Army would ressurrect his ruined career and access him back into Group. That was before Santo was advised a direct commission was pending his acceptance.

Bribes for being quiet and efficient. Payoffs for belonging to the vice president's personal band of illegals, and quietly burying Wayne MacIntyre next to his favorite deer stand back home in the Kiamichis with no fuss.

And so during the eight months following his father's funeral, Matt MacIntyre had simply decided to let sleeping dogs lie. There was no need for a new boss. There were only individual careers to be picked back up, dusted off, glossed over with a fresh coat of respectability. Rene was still driving Lears and Blackhawks for Dustbowl Enterprises, and he'd hired Wintz Maslow to give Charlie Whitehead a hand in realigning corporate security. Everyone was getting paid to do what they did best. Everyone was happy. Everyone was accounted for.

Who was he to lead DTM anyway? MacIntyre's eyes refocused on the mirror and he took a deep breath. What he found there he couldn't respect anymore. The haggard image he'd consulted in the mirror before glancing away conveyed red-rimmed eyes and a white-patched face bloated with too much tequila at Niagara's, scotch and soda at Ziggy's, and too damned much beer at *Der Nacht Kafe*.

Just too damned much of everything. He felt sick. The mirror seemed tilted. Was he just drunk, or . . . ?

What MacIntyre did not see was the Italian standing to his left, poised with a syrette aimed at his neck. Suddenly the latrine door banged open, and someone shoved another man down the entrance steps onto the filthy floor, where he slammed into the legs of the Italian. Wheeling around, MacIntyre saw the syrette fly out of the Italian's hands. Startled, his eyes flashed toward the entrance. A leather-suited figure blocked the door.

"Corky!"

"On your right!" Glancing back at the Italian, MacIntyre

saw him whip out a skinny rectangular handle that flashed mother of pearl against the fluorescent bathroom light. The Italian flicked his wrist, and the pearl handle he was holding snapped out a razor with an audible click. At MacIntyre's feet, the waiter who had been attending his table shoved his hand into his jacket.

Jumping down the steps, Cortez threw his motorcycle helmet across the room; it bashed into the Italian's face like a well-aimed basketball. The Italian shrieked and sank to his knees. Cortez, lunging forward with the throw, tripped against the prostrate waiter and crashed against a stall door.

The waiter yanked a small automatic from his jacket pocket. MacIntyre willed his leaden feet to punt-kick the waiter in the face. The gun clattered to the floor. The Italian's hand stretched forward to grab it, the other holding his nose where Cortez's motorcycle helmet had broken it. MacIntyre lunged forward and side-kicked the Italian in his shoulder. The force of the blow slammed the Italian against the men's room wall, snapped his head against the whitewashed concrete, and put him out. MacIntyre reeled on his feet, feeling like he wanted to pass out, and grabbed the faucet counter behind him for support.

Cortez's breathing labored in the humid, unwashed air as he grabbed the waiter's automatic, wiped it down, and stuck it in the waistband of his leather trousers. Shaking his head, MacIntyre finally rasped, "Hiya, Cork."

Cortez flashed hooded black slits in MacIntyre's direction. "The battalion commander wants to see your sorry ass," he accused, straightening up. His face contorted in concentration, while he tried to figure out how he was going to get MacIntyre out of the men's room unnoticed by the German spooks outside the door. Reaching down, he grabbed a pair of black-framed glasses, which had been knocked askew by MacIntyre's size twelve, from the unconscious waiter's face.

"Didn't want to go to his party," MacIntyre slurred drunkenly.

"And that's not all who's looking for you tonight, Captain." Cortez grabbed MacIntyre by the arm and hauled him up the stairwell leading up to the dance floor.

"What? Who? What's going on?"

"That's what I'd like to know," Cortez growled, yanking MacIntyre along with him.

"I thought you were pulling staff duty tonight."

"Yeah, no shit. Look where I've had to go to attend to official business in the name of staff fuckin' duty."

They reached the top of the stairs, and Cortez cracked open the double doors to the nightclub's main floor, his eyes searching for Darby, who was still posted by the bar. After a second, Darby deadpanned a look his way and nodded at the nightclub's front entrance. There, Cortez spotted the two goons they'd seen driving by in the Mercedes earlier. Now the Germans were posted up front, scanning the crowd. They'd be spotted if they weren't careful.

Cortez produced the waiter's black-framed glasses. "Put these on." He started to shrug off his riding jacket.

"Goddammit, what's going on? Those two down there tried to take me out!"

"No shit, Sherlock. There's a German goon squad looking for you, too. They're posted out front, checking out the crowd. Now put on these motherfucking glasses."

MacIntyre put on the glasses and Cortez's riding jacket. "I feel sick. Something in my drink . . ."

"C'mon."

The two men walked through the double doors. Gripping his elbow, Cortez guided MacIntyre through the teeming crowd on the dance floor. Seeing them, Brett Darby snake-eyed another look at the two Germans up at the front entrance, then followed Cortez's and MacIntyre's exit route across the dance floor. He stole a glance at Silvia, realizing that she'd set MacIntyre up. His blood pressure skyrocketed, and stars wheeled around his periphery of vision. That moment, that fleeting glance between them, told him everything. He saw her mouth open, mouth the word—

"Matthew!"

Cortez pushed MacIntyre along, steering him toward the back entrance. Mac's date was up and yelling, pointing, frantically searching for the Germans up front.

"Matthew!" Silvia shouted again, her voice a clarion. Suddenly a squat, heavily-muscled young man stood poised before her with a martial artist's grace. Surprised, she tried to move around him. "Out of my way!"

"You got a big mouth, lady." Darby zapped Silvia on the butt with his stun gun, and then eased her down on her seat, leaving her to stare fried-eyed at the Katmandooze's rhythm section. Pocketing his stun gun, he snatched her handbag and followed Cortez and MacIntyre through the rear entrance toward their bikes.

The two goons up front had seen what he'd done to Silvia. Heading for the back door, Darby realized he'd have to be ready for them, too.